RIVER OF PERIL

SPIES OF THE CIVIL WAR
BOOK FIVE

SANDRA MERVILLE HART

WILD HEART
BOOKS

Only be careful, and watch yourselves closely so that you do not forget the things your eyes have seen or let them slip from your heart as long as you live. Teach them to your children and to their children after them.

— DEUTERONOMY 4:9 (NIV)

Dedicated to

Morgan,
Who can't wait for each book's release and stays up all night to read
them when they arrive,
even with high school looming in the morning.
What a thrill it is to hear her honest reactions to each story.

And to Fran,
One of my most enthusiastic cheerleaders.

CHAPTER 1

elicity Danielson hurried through the city streets of Vicksburg in the early-morning fog toward her volunteer job at the City Hospital. Some shops she passed were unlocking their doors for the day's business, while others had been closed since the Union navy's two-month attack on the city. Ultimately, the Confederates had won the battle, more's the pity—and not only because Felicity supported the Union. Northern military leaders were too interested in her city located on a bluff by the mighty Mississippi River to leave them alone. They'd be back.

Her pace slowed as she approached an intersection. Five Confederate soldiers headed down the steep sidewalk toward the center of town, another common occurrence in occupied Vicksburg. Some soldiers had left after running the Union ships from the river, and others had replaced them. She lowered her eyes as their booted steps passed her on the other side of the cobblestone street. If the Twenty-first Mississippi Infantry—her beau Luke Shea's Confederate regiment—were assigned to guard the city, she'd sleep in peace. Not because his regiment was better but because Luke and many of his comrades were from the area. They loved the city and its citizens.

If that happened, he'd be close again, where she could speak to him, look into his beloved face, and know he was safe and unharmed, something she prayed for every night. His only furlough had passed in a whirlwind of activity, what with him standing as best man in Ash Mitchell's wedding that fall. Luke's furlough had caused him to miss a terrible battle at Sharpsburg along Antietam Creek in Maryland, for which she thanked the Lord most fervently.

Yet other battles followed relentlessly. She scoured the daily newspapers, praying *not* to find Luke's name among the wounded or killed lists. He'd often teased her that he had the luck of the Irish on his side, and it seemed to be so. He'd escaped injury so far. His worst malady was a mild case of typhoid fever last year that had landed him in a Richmond hospital, all the more terrifying because the same illness had taken the life of Willie Sanderson, one of his dearest friends, a month before.

Felicity shuddered. The war had changed everything for the six friends who had enjoyed so many picnics and parties together, especially Willie's girl, Savannah Adair, whom everyone expected to wed after the war's end.

The hospital loomed ahead with more activity than normal at six in the morning. A wave of foreboding swept over her. Had more wounded soldiers arrived overnight? She hurried to the nurse's room on the first floor.

Katie Ellis, one of the nurses on the ward next to hers, set a bottle of pills back onto a shelf with other medications as Felicity stepped inside the room. Leaves and roots arranged in marked dishes lined a long table along with a mortar and pestle for preparing medicines mixed by the surgeons. Next to the table was a four-shelved open cupboard on the back wall. An enticing aroma wafted over from a coffeepot on the cookstove. A ladle nestled inside a bucket of water. Another table with wooden chairs served as a place for nurses to grab a bite to eat.

Katie turned to her. "Felicity, I'm glad to see you. Eleven soldiers arrived from Virginia last night, all injured in a battle at Fredericksburg."

"Do I have time to warm up with a cup of coffee?" Shivering, Felicity hung her blue wool shawl on a wall hook next to other cloaks and coats.

"Better take a break later." Katie shook her head. "Two of the new patients are in your ward. You'll need to feed them beef broth—if they'll take it from you—and then give them their medicine before seeing to the rest of your patients."

"Where are these soldiers from?"

"These men are local." Katie pushed a wisp of blond hair behind her ears as she studied a page. "The Twenty-first Mississippi."

Luke's regiment. Felicity's skin tingled. "What are their names?" Crossing the room, she peered over Katie's shoulder.

"Let's see—your patients are Oscar Miller and Luke Shea."

Luke! "What happened to Luke?" Her whole body shook.

"Head injury caused by shrapnel. Oscar lost his right hand—"

Felicity didn't hear anything else as, lifting her black skirt, she fairly flew up the stairs to the second floor. *Please, God, not Luke. Don't take the man I love from me too.* Opening the door to her ward, she hurried toward the two beds that had been empty yesterday.

Her steps faltered at the sight of her battered beau lying on the cot, a bloody bandage covering his thick auburn hair as he talked to Dr. Watkins. He was conscious. Relief flooded her to hear his beloved Irish lilt that filled her dreams every night.

She wanted to run to him, press her cheek against the unaccustomed whiskers lining his face. Clasp his callused hand and never let him go again. The doctor's presence halted her even as the wall lantern's shadow covered her.

"Are ye certain all the metal be gone from me wounds?" Luke's brown eyes stared anxiously up at the doctor.

"You've only one wound. The battlefield doctors must have done a good job removing any shrapnel. All I found left in the wound was a bit of cloth from your hat." The family man in his forties put his hand on Luke's shoulder. "That's gone now and you're bandaged up. You should recover."

"Me head pains me something fierce." He touched his forehead.

"I'll ask Miss Danielson to bring laudanum for you." Dr. Watkins looked at Felicity, who couldn't stop drinking in the sight of Luke, standing at the foot of the bed. "Ah, there you are, Nurse. Feed him some broth before giving him medicine. Then we'll need to contact his family. He's local."

"His family passed in 1857, Dr. Watkins." Falling to her knees beside Luke, Felicity clasped his hand. "Luke, I'm here now. We'll have you healed in no time."

"Ye knew me parents?" Luke stared up at her as if he'd never seen her before.

Her breath caught in her throat. He knew this. Why didn't he clasp her hand in return? Caress her cheek as he'd often done to comfort her? But head wounds could discombobulate patients. "I regret I never had the pleasure. I didn't meet you until 1859, when I moved to Vicksburg."

"Miss, ye be speaking in riddles." He removed his hand from hers. "Is this not 1857 still? The last thing I remember with any clarity is me parents drowning in the Mississippi." His gaze shifted to the surgeon without moving his head. "Dr. Watkins, tell me true. What is the date?"

The doctor's brow furrowed. "It's 1862. The nineteenth of December."

Luke slumped against his pillow. "Five years have passed? How can this be?"

He didn't remember her? Felicity fought off waves of dizziness. Then everything went black.

~

$\mathscr{L}$uke reached for the nurse as she slumped onto the floor. Pain shot through his head, and he fell back against his pillow. Five years had passed since his parents drowned? How could that be? Raw longing tore at his heart for his pa's wisdom, his ma's sunny laughter that had chased away the hard times. Five years? It couldn't be. He touched his whiskered jaw. That was new. Maybe more time had passed than he realized...

Everything that had happened in the intervening days was shrouded in a hazy mist. In truth, his pretty nurse had seemed no less shocked than him to receive the news. Gingerly, he turned his head toward her prostrate body.

Gasps and a few shouts followed her fainting spell. The doctor rushed around the bed. "Miss Danielson?" He massaged her hand as another nurse rushed over.

"What's the matter with Felicity?" A plump, red-haired nurse in her mid-twenties leaned over her.

"She's fainted, Miss Guthrie. Help me raise her head and shoulders." Dr. Watkins squatted on one side of Felicity with the nurse on the other.

Once propped against the doctor in a seated position, Miss Danielson groaned.

"She's coming to." Miss Guthrie shifted her away from the doctor.

"Gently, now. She's had a shock of some kind." Dr. Watkins

frowned at his semi-conscious employee as yet another nurse approached.

Miss Danielson's startlingly blue eyes fluttered open and fastened on Luke's face. The stark pain clouding her gaze made him wonder if her fainting spell had been caused by compassion for him. She claimed to know him. He studied her shoulder-length blond curls and heart-shaped face with its pink lips slightly parted. No memories stirred.

"Luke?" Miss Danielson braced herself against the bed and leaned closer. "Don't you remember me? I'm Felicity."

"Nay, miss." His chest tightened at the sorrow in those eyes the color of a summer sky. Had he seen eyes such a startling blue as hers, he'd surely remember. "'Tis a sorry state of affairs to admit."

"Felicity, let's get you that cup of coffee." A blond nurse put her arm around Miss Danielson's waist.

"No, Katie. I must help my patients." The petite woman's frantic gaze clung to his.

"In a few minutes." Katie led her away from Luke's bed. She looked over her shoulder at the other nurse. "Bessie, see to your patients. One of us will be up shortly to feed Felicity's patients and administer their medicine."

Miss Danielson continued to protest as they left the ward.

"My apologies for my nurse. Miss Danielson seems to know you. You don't remember her?"

"Nay." Hopefully, she'd soon recover, but her fainting spell had interrupted his conversation with Dr. Watkins. "Doctor, ye didn't explain how the metal came to be in me head."

"You were in a battle—a brutal one, by all accounts." Dr. Watkins sat on the edge of the cot. "Musketry. Cannonballs bursting all around you. Shrapnel flying in every direction. Does that sound familiar?"

"None of it." A shrapnel wound? How could he forget such

a terrible battle? "But why was I there? What's this battle that happened?"

"There's a war between the states. The North has been fighting against the South almost two years."

Luke shrank from him. "Our country be fighting a war against itself?" Bitter disagreements between the North and South had escalated his whole life. That had led to actual battles?

He nodded. "But you're fighting for the Confederacy, the winning side. The Union will lose this thing, don't you worry none about that. You've done your duty for the South. The Yankees will be sorry they raised a musket against us."

A few men cheered at the doctor's proclamation.

How could this be? Surely, this whole thing was a nightmare. He pinched his arm, and the sharp sensation verified that this was no dream. Something didn't seem right about this whole thing, but Luke couldn't figure it out. Not with this pain blasting in his head. "Can I trouble ye for that medicine now, Dr. Watkins?"

The doctor spoke in low tones to the nurse hovering nearby. Luke closed his eyes, not wanting to hear anything else. A few moments later, someone who smelled of lilacs lifted him from the pillow. Cradled his battered head against her shoulder.

"There, just take this pill with a sip of water." A gentle, familiar voice.

He took the pill. As the dipper pressed against his lips, he looked up. Miss Danielson was back. His own nurse. The compassion in those blue eyes grounded him as nothing else had done. Strange. Something deep inside, so deep he couldn't reach it, responded to her loving care.

"Rest now." She laid him back against his pillow. "I'll be here when you awaken."

That comforted him. Closing his eyes, he slept.

~

elicity stared at Luke's beloved face that had several days' growth of auburn whiskers, a foreign sight because he'd always been clean-shaven, even when he came home on his furlough three months ago. How that month had flown, each hour filled with joy for her.

Neither of them had dreamed they'd see one another again so soon, or that he'd return wounded and without his memory. A thousand memories flooded her mind...long strolls to the riverbank, church picnics, meals in her aunt's cozy dining room, wishing on a shooting star together, and sealing their dreams with a kiss.

Before he climbed onto the train that fall, he'd caressed her cheek with his fingertips. Looking into her eyes, he whispered that he loved her. He promised to return to her if it was within his power to do so.

He'd come back, but this was not the homecoming either of them wanted.

She wasn't the only one who loved Luke. Gracious, she hadn't thought to send the news of Luke's wounds to his childhood friend and her part-time employer. Perhaps seeing Ash again would nudge those remembrances to life.

"He'll sleep for a few hours." Katie bent to adjust the blanket over Luke's shoulders.

Felicity gave a start. She'd forgotten Katie had accompanied her back to the floor after insisting Felicity eat a boiled egg and drink some coffee, neither of which she had wanted. "I hope he will awaken to eat his lunch."

"If he doesn't, feed him whenever he does. He'll likely have a headache for weeks." Katie straightened. "If you've recovered, your patients are waiting for their breakfast. I'll take care of Oscar Miller, your other new soldier, to catch you up."

"I'm fine." Felicity stood, lifting her chin. She must carry on.

No more fainting or moments of weakness. Luke was alive. Sleep was the best thing for him for now. Other folks needed her. She'd seek out the doctor for more information after seeing to her other patients. Then when Luke woke up, she'd be ready.

Felicity held herself together through feeding her patients and administering medications. She did her best to smile. The Lord knew these men needed it. Finally, she had a few moments to talk to Dr. Watkins. She found him just stepping away from the last bed in another ward. "Doctor, may I speak with you?" She held up her hand to capture the busy man's attention.

"Of course, Miss Danielson. One moment." He scratched a note on a pad and then followed her into the hall leading to the stairs on one end and the two wards opposite one another. "Is there a problem with one of your patients?"

"Yes, sir. I'd like to ask you about Luke Shea's memory loss."

"Yes, that is troubling. He was unconscious following his injury. Slept through his surgery at the field hospital. He woke up on the train here where the attendants gave him water and laudanum."

Luke had been unconscious for three or four days, then. She gripped the table's edge to steady her trembling legs. A serious injury but he was awake and talking. How frightening to wake up on a train amongst strangers. "He'll need water and nourishing broths."

"Exactly. Water, certainly, and broths as he can tolerate them." Tucking his stack of notes against his side, he folded his arms. "You knew Shea before the war?"

"Yes." Courted for two years. They'd expressed their love for one another before the war began. He'd plainly stated he was saving for their future, plans now set aside. But something held her from speaking of their courtship to the doctor. Her pain of being forgotten was too raw. It seemed wiser to keep her relationship a secret. "We have friends in common. We've attended many of the same functions." That seemed harmless enough to admit.

"And he doesn't remember you. My dear, I'm very sorry. That must cause you considerable pain."

If he only realized. Felicity drew a shuddering breath. Released it slowly. She must be strong. She must.

The fatherly man with gray at the temples mixing in with his black hair studied her. "I can ask Miss Guthrie to take over—"

"No, please, I want to nurse him." Male attendants bathed the soldiers and saw to their personal needs. Nurses did everything else. "Shall I remind him of our friendship?" Surely, she could give him a certain look that gave away their prior relationship. Or throw caution to the wind and kiss him to remind his heart of their love.

"Best not to speak of it unless he asks you. If you notice him growing agitated during your conversation, change the subject entirely. He needs calm...rest to heal."

Her heart plummeted. How was she to mind every word, every look, every touch when in Luke's presence? Did the doctor know what he demanded of her? Of course, he didn't. She'd kept their courtship to herself so she could remain his nurse. "Should everyone avoid reminders of the past?"

"Certainly, everyone he doesn't remember should avoid such references. It's best not to agitate him." He shook his head. "Amnesia is troubling after a traumatic event. No telling how long it will take him to remember what's happened the past five years." He raised his hands, palms up, with a shrug. "His mind may remain hazy for many weeks. Perhaps his heart will be the first to remember. Who can say?"

Months? "But he will remember?" Felicity waved her hand over her hot face to try and breathe past the knot in her throat and the returning dizziness. She knew little about amnesia...

only that it was *Luke* lying on that bed, in need of assistance and unable to remember her.

"I expect so, though you must prepare yourself for the possibility he won't. Best not to push him before he's ready. He needs you to be calm, supportive."

"I will." She'd do anything and everything to help him get his memory back...except she mustn't allude to their courtship.

How different she'd expected his next homecoming to be. Why, three months before, he'd hinted at a proposal once he established himself in a position after the war. She must set those dreams aside and focus on getting him well.

CHAPTER 2

"We'll come to the hospital with you immediately." Ash Mitchell's hazel eyes had filled with horror as Felicity recounted her morning with Luke. He reached for his wife's hand as Julia stared at Felicity.

"Be prepared for him not to remember you either." A biting wind blew Felicity's shawl open. She hadn't waited for Luke's best buddy to close his front door before delivering the news.

"Dearest Felicity." Julia rushed to give her a one-armed hug without releasing Ash's hand. "As devastated as we feel, this is far worse for you."

Felicity braced herself. She mustn't give in to her grief. "I must get back. Want me to go on ahead?" She strove for a calm tone. Ash's long-standing friendship with Luke might stir dormant memories. She clung to the possibility. The sooner he remembered, the better.

"We'll come with you." The tall man's face turned grim. He shrugged into his coat while Julia donned her cloak on the walk in front of their two-story home beside Ash's saddle shop.

In a hurry to reach Luke before he awakened, Felicity sped

along under the hazy sky. The couple fell behind. She looked back at them. Ash's limping gait from a childhood injury prevented the quick pace. Biting back her frustration, she slowed her steps.

"To think that the last thing he clearly remembers is his parents' deaths." The petite Julia, her blond curls swept back with combs underneath the hood of her blue cloak, clucked her tongue. "I wonder if he thinks he still works at the book bindery."

Luke had quit school to work there shortly after becoming an orphan. That happened before Felicity knew him. It broke her heart that his grief felt fresh again, a sorrow she knew all too well. "He's thinner than he was just two months ago. I gave him beef broth as soon as he woke up. He fell asleep before finishing."

"We shall all see that he has nourishing meals once he gets out of the hospital." Julia's brow puckered. "How will you cope until he remembers you?"

"The best I can. Please don't tell him about me unless he asks. Dr. Watkins says not to agitate him." Felicity fought a surge of longing for the faithful, steady man she'd fallen in love with during their courtship. Luke loved her too. His affection had been an unchanging rock she'd leaned upon in the uncertain war days. Now he knew nothing about her beyond her name.

～

*L*uke had been stirring restlessly for what seemed like an hour. His head ached abominably. Wasn't it time for another pill? When the air stirred beside his bed, he opened his eyes to the welcome sight of his childhood buddy. "Ash, is that you?" Relief mixed with gratitude to recognize his friend. His sanity hadn't completely deserted him. He extended his hand. It was firmly grasped. "And you brought Julia along with you."

"It's good to see you, my friend." Ash's grin held a hint of tension. "Yes, Julia is here with me." Holding her hand, he brought her closer.

"Hello, Luke." Julia released Ash's hand and hugged Luke. "I'm glad to see you're awake. Felicity brought us the news that you were here and you'd been wounded."

Felicity? Luke's eyes darted to the pretty nurse standing on the opposite side of the bed. Once again, pain twisted her face. "Miss Danielson? Are those tears in your eyes?"

"No." Fishing a handkerchief from her pocket, she turned away. "The effects of a blustery wind on my way back. I'm fine now." But she appeared to be swiping at her cheeks.

Julia moved quickly around the bed and whispered something to the nurse.

The nurse's back straightened. She turned to Luke. "It's time for your next dose of medicine. Shall I fetch it while you speak with ou—your friends?"

"Aye. Me head aches a wee bit." An understatement, for it felt as if someone had taken one of Ash's saddle shop mallets to his head.

"Then I'll return shortly." Her swift glance at Julia seemed to hold an unspoken message. Then she was gone with a rustle of her black skirt.

"So you had a piece of shrapnel in your head." Ash peered at the bandages wrapped around Luke's wound.

"Aye. It appears that I've been off at war." Luke strove for a hearty tone. It fell short. "I know nothing of it. Can you tell me what's happening?"

Julia's hand slipped into Ash's as she looked up at him.

"I'll be happy to explain. Why don't we hold off on that until you feel stronger?"

"As long as you don't forget."

"I give you my word."

Luke didn't feel up to forcing an explanation. Perhaps that was best. He could barely think at the moment, but there seemed to be some special feelings between Ash and Julia. "Pardon me for asking, but did the pair of you begin courting while I was away?"

A flicker of sadness crossed Ash's face. It was quickly smothered. "Actually, Julia and I were married this fall."

"Ye don't say." Joy sputtered through him, the first he'd felt since his injury. "I always did think the two of you should court. Me heartiest of good wishes to both of you." Ash married Julia while he was away? How much else of his life had he lost?

Miss Danielson returned with a cup and a pill.

"I wish I could have stood up with you. Willie and Savannah were there, of course."

His nurse gasped, her eyes on Ash. "Forgive me. Luke needs to take his medicine. Will you lift his head off the pillow so he can drink?"

"Of course." Ash's hands shook as he propped him up. Must not be used to the sick room.

"Here's your water. Drink all of it." She put a pill in his hand. "With this."

The cold water slid down his parched throat with the medicine. He looked at Ash. "This will make me sleep. Will ye return?"

"Sure thing." Ash lowered him onto the pillow.

"Next time, bring Willie. Me has a hankering to see our old pal."

"Just rest. I'll be back."

Luke's eyes closed. Why didn't Ash say he'd bring Willie?

❧

*A*s she stared at Luke's still face, Felicity's heart was in turmoil. He remembered Ash, Julia, Willie, and Savannah but not her, his girl.

The one he'd professed to love.

"Let's speak with Dr. Watkins." Ash crossed around the bed to where Felicity still stood beside her sleeping beau. "He'll no doubt wish to know that Luke recognized us."

"True. The doctor will watch him closely these first days." Felicity met Ash's concerned gaze. Ash, who'd been friends with Luke for years, might have other insights for the doctor. "He's likely mixing medicines in the nurses' room, as he does most afternoons." She led them down the center aisle that divided two rows of twelve beds, trying to avoid Bessie's gaze as the women carried around the water bucket. Her coworker could be quite bossy, even without the authority to do so.

"Felicity, Joe's asking for you to pen a letter to his family for him." Bessie took care of patients on one side and Felicity on the opposite side. "You're not leaving, are you?"

"No." She bit back a sigh. Joe, a married father of three, was expected to be released before the new year. He'd learn to farm without his left hand eventually, for the war was over for him. She had responsibilities to her other patients, not just Luke— even though Luke held claim to her heart. She'd keep her prior relationship to Luke a secret for the moment, even from the other workers. Besides, Bessie had been fractious since her fiancé died in battle, so Felicity had never mentioned her beau. "I'll fetch paper and pen after showing my friends to the nurses' room." She made quick introductions.

"I'll take them." Bessie's glance slid to the married couple. "I'm parched for a cup of coffee, anyway."

"All right." Felicity would have preferred to hear their first impressions *and* Dr. Watkins's instructions herself. But best not to make a fuss with Bessie.

"We'll wait for you downstairs." Julia patted her arm. "You'll no doubt need some refreshment yourself after writing your patient's correspondence."

"Yes." It was torturous to wait for news, yet she must. "I'll come when Bessie returns."

After they left, Felicity glanced over at Luke. He'd likely sleep for hours.

As she settled onto a wooden chair at Joe's bedside, she ached to know what Dr. Watkins would say about Luke's partial memories.

~

*T*hirty minutes later, Felicity lifted her skirt to run down the stairs, praying her friends had waited for her as they promised. "There you are." Relief flooded through as Julia and Ash exited the nurses' room. "I apologize for taking so long—"

"We didn't mind waiting." Julia drew a deep breath. "We talked to Dr. Watkins."

More bad news? Felicity would shoulder it for both her and Luke. "Tell me quickly. I can't be gone from the floor above ten minutes."

"Come inside." Taking her arm, Julia led her to the room's round table. "I'll pour the coffee. Ash, you tell her."

"It's actually good news that he remembers us." Ash straddled a chair opposite Felicity's. "Dr. Watkins believes that Luke will recognize people he knew before his parents died. He's known me a dozen years and Julia nearly that long."

"I didn't move to Vicksburg until two years after they drowned. Makes sense, I suppose." It was some comfort to cling to...that Luke hadn't forgotten her because she didn't matter to him. His trauma was connected to the loss of his parents. Luke had spoken so often of his parents' shared sense of humor, his mother's cooking, and his father's teasing that she felt she knew them. "Anything else?"

"Yes, about Willie." Wisps of steam arose from the two cups Julia set in front of them before she went back to the long table lining the wall for her own. "The doctor advises us not to discuss difficult topics with Luke until he's stronger. They just removed the last of the debris from his wound yesterday evening upon his arrival. It's a wonder he's awake." She sat beside her husband.

"Likely a testament to his physical strength." Ash wrapped his hands around his tin cup. "Though he's lost too much weight."

"I intend to remedy that at my earliest opportunity." She looked at Julia. "Bread and preserves are appropriate to bring to patients. Or apple butter, his favorite."

"It will be our pleasure." Julia sipped her coffee, frowning. "Perhaps we should arrange our visits when Luke is napping for the first few days so we don't have to speak of Willie's death."

"I'll have to talk to him about the war. He'll hear enough by sharing a ward with soldiers." Ash sighed. "Can't put it off so long that *not* knowing increases his agitation."

"Agreed." Felicity leaned on the couple's strength. Ash's understanding of his friend's personality was a tremendous help.

"Do you want a few days off from the cleaning job to devote your time to Luke at the hospital?" Julia gave her a compassionate look.

Felicity released a long breath, relieved that Julia understood her need to be with Luke. "I didn't like to ask, but yes. Can I see how he's doing after Christmas and decide when I'll return to work?" Three days a week was all the Mitchells needed her to work as a maid, though she was grateful now that the volunteer hours she put in at the hospital allowed her to nurse Luke. Yet these days, many men had been laid off from their jobs. Felicity had hoarded every penny she could toward her future with Luke, one pushed off indefinitely by his amnesia.

"Of course." Julia covered Felicity's hand with her own. "We still hope you'll attend Savannah's annual Christmas ball with us. Your aunt and uncle are welcome to join us, as well."

"Thank you. It depends on how Luke is doing." Felicity couldn't even consider the Christmas Eve supper and dance that she had formerly enjoyed. "Aunt Mae doesn't even know he's been wounded."

"I'll come every day and seek you out before coming into the ward." Ash drained his cup and then stared at the grounds.

"It's for the best." Felicity stood. "Pardon me, but I must return to the ward."

"We understand." Standing, Julia gave her a long hug. "I'd be trembling, too, were Ash in that ward."

"I know." Felicity stepped away, fighting back the tears.

Ash hugged her. "Luke will recover. I feel it in my bones."

"Thanks, Ash." Tears shrouded her dear friends' faces at that. "I'll hang on to that assurance. See you tomorrow." She exited the room with a wave and hurried up the stairs.

Outside the door to her ward, she paused to swipe a handkerchief over her wet cheeks. Luke probably wasn't awake, but none of her soldiers needed her tears. They'd endured enough already.

Luke had always been a tower of strength for her. They'd met within months of her parents' deaths, and he'd comforted her. She'd already lost her parents. Her siblings lived in other states and rarely wrote. She couldn't lose Luke too.

*T*he scent of lilacs stirred Luke's senses. Miss Danielson had returned. He opened his eyes, trying not to shift his aching head. "'Tis good to see ye return." He glanced at the windows lining the wall opposite his bed. "But it's dark. Surely, you'll not walk home in the darkness."

"No matter. It's but a ten-minute walk from the hospital."

"Where do you live?"

"I live with my Aunt Mae and Uncle Charles Beltzer. They live on Locust Street, near the corner of First East Street." She watched his face as she said their names—as if he should know them. Alas, he didn't.

"I know of that location."

"That's encouraging." She clutched her throat. "I waited until you awoke so I could feed you more beef broth."

"'Tis sorry I am to make ye wait." The curtainless windows on the opposite wall showed a few stars shining in the sky. "Let me eat with haste so ye can get to your aunt's home."

"I'm in no hurry. You need nourishment." Miss Danielson set a large tin cup on a rectangular table between the beds. "Let me lift you so you can eat." Her arm slid underneath his pillow, and she raised him slowly.

He bit his lip to keep from crying out as his head jarred. She rested his pillow against her shoulder, cradling him in a cocoon of warmth.

"Sip slowly, as you did this afternoon." She raised the steaming cup to his lips.

Relaxing against her, he complied. "Tasty."

After two minutes, he sagged against his pillow, exhausted from the effort.

"Good." The broth was nearly gone. "That's about as much as your system can handle today." She laid him back. "It's not time for your medicine yet. The night nurse will administer the next dose in about two hours." She arranged the blankets over his shoulders. "Rest until then."

Her touch was gentle, almost loving. "Will ye return tomorrow?"

"Yes, I'll give you breakfast." She laid her palm across his forehead. "You have a bit of fever. I'll mention it to the doctor before I go. Rest now."

His eyelids drooped. "Goodnight." He closed his eyes.

"Goodnight." Warm fingertips brushed against his beard in almost a caress.

He was ready for this horrifying and confusing day to end. He'd think about the war, his wound, and his nurse tomorrow.

CHAPTER 3

elicity halted beside a notions shop ten minutes later. A shadow moved on the sidewalk ahead. She drew a relieved sigh when a thin, balding man of medium height stepped under a street lamp. "Uncle Charles?"

"Felicity, what's kept you? We held supper for an hour before eating. Your aunt is worried sick about you." Uncle Charles put an arm around her. "You look exhausted. Did new wounded arrive today?"

"Yes, from the Twenty-first Mississippi."

Stepping back, he studied her face. "Not...Luke?"

"He's here." Felicity explained his injury as they hurried toward the Beltzers' two-story brick home.

"You mean he doesn't even remember there's a war going on?" Uncle Charles climbed the dozen stone steps leading to the porch. "But he knows you, right?"

Felicity shook her head as Aunt Mae opened the arched oak door.

"My dear, you work too hard for no pay at that hospital." The petite red-haired woman in her early forties who looked so much like the mother Felicity desperately needed right now ushered her inside the home's warmth.

She hung her cloak on a hall hook and scurried inside the small parlor decorated in shades of blue. "Aunt Mae, Luke's been wounded. He's in my ward." Speaking over her shoulder, Felicity held icy fingers toward the fire crackling in the parlor's hearth.

"My dear, you should have sent word." Aunt Mae's brown eyes widened. "We'd have come straight away."

"It's not that simple, my dear." Uncle Charles explained about his injury. "Felicity was just telling me about his amnesia."

"He doesn't remember me or either of you." Felicity sank onto a cushioned armchair. She explained that his last clear memory was after his parents' drowning and that he seemed to recognize only those people he'd known before that occurrence.

"Well, I declare." Aunt Mae sat on the sofa beside her husband, hands covering her mouth. "I've never heard of such a thing. Does he recall getting injured?"

"Nothing. Dr. Watkins warned us not to speak of anything that might upset him until he's stronger." Felicity stared into the flames. "I think it's best you postpone any visit for at least a week."

Uncle Charles exchanged a look with his wife. "We'll follow the doctor's advice, but what about you?"

"I'll go in every day." His bandages would require changing daily, and she was determined to see to it herself—unless the doctor needed to examine the wound. "His head must ache something fierce. Otherwise, he'd not speak of it at all." His mild complaints didn't fool Felicity.

"There's no chance that he'll be well enough to attend the Christmas ball with us?" Aunt Mae frowned.

"None at all." Not when merely eating broth had exhausted

him. And the ball was the least of her worries. "I will go if I'm able."

"My dear, we can't disappoint Savannah. She's suffered so much from this war with the Yankees." Uncle Charles patted his wife's hand. "And your aunt is quite looking forward to the ball."

Felicity's friendships with Julia and Savannah had opened a door for them to socialize with wealthier folks above their station. Such entertainments didn't come often. "I will come unless Luke needs me, and certainly, you must go."

"Supper is warming in the oven." Aunt Mae rose. "Let's get you something to eat."

Indeed, her only meal had been a boiled egg that morning, something Katie had forced her to eat after she fainted. Probably best not to mention her fainting spell. Her aunt had worries of her own. Her daughter, Petunia Farmer, hadn't been in the best of moods lately. She'd recently moved her two young children back to a rented home in Vicksburg. Felicity guessed there were financial concerns with her husband off fighting for the Confederates.

She couldn't expect Aunt Mae to carry her burdens. She'd have to rely on God's help for that.

~

*L*uke spent a restless night, trying to recall any part of the missing five years. The war caused his greatest confusion. Why had he been on a battlefield in the first place? All he knew of weapons was shooting cornhusks off a fencepost with his pa before hunting deer—or really anything his ma could cook. But he reckoned he had been mighty good at it, to hear his pa brag.

He didn't have siblings. He'd crossed the Atlantic Ocean from Ireland when still a tot. His pa holding him up to peer over the bow was all he remembered of the crossing. As normal as it might be to forget events that happened when one was two... at twenty? Not one birthday after the age of fifteen did he recall. He'd lost part of himself, and he didn't know how to patch himself together.

Concentrating on piercing that haze only made his head ache worse than the fellow's snores across the aisle did. At last, Miss Danielson arrived with the brightening of dawn on the horizon.

She came directly to his side. "You're awake already?" She touched his forehead.

"Still awake. Trying to remember things."

"Don't force those memories." Her blue eyes met his sternly. "You're to rest and heal. Doctors' orders."

"Nurse Danielson's orders too." He gave her a lopsided grin, trying not to wince.

"Exactly." She smiled at him. "Are you thirsty?"

"Near parched." He touched his throat. "The night nurse didn't bring my medicine last night."

"We'll rectify that omission." Her eyes narrowed. "I'll bring a dipper of cold water first."

Rubbing his forehead, Luke rested his eyes after she left.

"I brought the bucket in case you want more." She lifted his shoulders gently and put the dipper to his lips.

He sipped gratefully. She possessed a gentler touch than last night's nurse. Hopefully, she'd be his nurse every day. "A little more?"

"Of course."

The sound of the dipper plunging into the bucket was a familiar one. Recognizing sounds somehow grounded him as he sipped again. He held up his hand when he'd had enough.

"It's best we save room for broth. I'll find Dr. Watkins. Your wound has been bleeding. We'll change the bandage."

The scent of lilacs lingered after she left the ward. He

touched the spot near his ear that throbbed the most. Moisture. He examined the pink stain on his fingers. Aye, his bandage did indeed need to be changed. He rested his eyes while he waited.

"So...how are we this morning?" The mattress sagged when Dr. Watkins sat on the edge of his bed.

"Me head aches a wee bit." He looked beyond the doctor's shoulder into his nurse's anxious eyes.

"I'll wager that's an understatement. Let's see what's going on under that bandage. Close your eyes, son. We'll be as quick as we can."

Bracing himself, Luke followed the doctor's advice. Mattresses creaked across the aisle as the cold metal of scissors eased under his bandage.

"It's stopped oozing. That's a blessing." The doctor spoke softly, as if Luke wasn't meant to hear. Something soft went on top of the wound.

All Luke heard for a few moments was the sounds of men getting up or speaking with one another. Someone said that President Jefferson Davis was in the city. James Buchanan had been president when Luke's parents died—and it felt as if two or three months had passed since then.

"I'll raise his head while you wrap it."

Luke just barely managed not to wince at what felt like a vice going about his head. Then, thank goodness, he rested against the pillow once more. "Much obliged."

Miss Danielson covered some rags in a bowl with her hand. "Do you want buttermilk stew or your medicine first?"

"Medicine." The mallet going off in his temples felt as though it had been exchanged for a sledgehammer.

"Feed him when he awakens." A compassionate expression crossed Dr. Watkins's features.

"Very well. I'll fetch the medicine." She scurried away.

The bed shifted when the doctor stood. "Sorry about that. Next time, I'll bring a chair."

"Thanks."

Miss Danielson was back. The doctor raised his head this time while Luke took the pill. "Much obliged. To both of ye."

His nearly sleepless night coupled with the ordeal of having his bandage changed caught up with him. With one last look into the nurse's caring blue eyes, he fell asleep.

~

For the next few days, Felicity devoted herself as much as possible to Luke's care. She could hardly bear to leave his side when he was awake lest Bessie swoop in and tend him. Since dispensing a dipper of water, medicine, and nourishing soups was all that could be done for him regularly, Felicity wanted to be the one to do it. Dr. Watkins had switched his medication to quinine, normally given to treat malaria and fevers but also taken by patients with headaches. Quinine had been in short supply for some time so the doctors mixed a substitute made of dried poplar, dogwood, and willow bark. The soldiers referred to it as "old indigenous." Taking it seemed to ease Luke's headaches somewhat, and he stayed awake longer, a hopeful sign.

So far, Ash and Felicity had managed to arrange Ash's daily visits to coincide with Luke's naps. No one wanted to tell Luke of Willie's death until he was stronger.

On Christmas Eve morning, Felicity finished giving every patient in the ward a dipper of water and then peered down the row of beds. Ash was due in about in an hour, and Luke was still awake after eating egg gruel for breakfast.

Bessie entered the ward with a pile of bedding. "Will you help me change some sheets?"

"If you'll help me with mine." The task itself wasn't difficult, but assisting patients out of bed who outweighed her was challenging—and Felicity had learned to negotiate up front with the self-absorbed nurse.

"Will do. Fred's taking a walk. Let's do his bed first."

Felicity stripped the bed and deposited the soiled sheets near the door.

"Are you working tomorrow?" Bessie plumped a pillow inside its clean pillowcase.

"Just the morning." Today was Christmas Eve. It had never felt less like Christmas. The best gift she could receive was recognition and love once again in Luke's eyes. Seeing him in such depressed spirits and in pain robbed all the joy from the season. Felicity would rather spend all of Christmas Day with Luke, but Aunt Mae had persuaded her to leave after lunch. Aunt Mae wanted to take her daughter and Petunia's two children to Julia's mother's open house Christmas afternoon and felt she shouldn't go without Felicity, who had a stronger friendship with them—the same reason she was attending the Adairs' Christmas Eve ball in a few hours. "How about you?"

"I'll work all day. Got no family in Vicksburg. The Yankees killed my fiancé." Bessie's bitter tone rose with each word. "Why shouldn't I work?"

Felicity might have lost Luke for the time being, yet he was alive. Bessie's greater loss stirred her compassion. "You do a good job. Our patients will be glad to see you." Felicity retrieved a chair from the corner. "Who's next?"

"Eli." Bessie crossed to the next cot. "You ready for clean sheets, Eli?"

"Sure thing." The man missing a foot pushed himself to a seated position.

Felicity set the chair near the foot of the bed and then helped support Eli into the seat.

"Learning anything interesting from that new amnesia patient?" Bessie's eyes narrowed as she folded a blanket.

"He still doesn't recall the past five years." Felicity didn't want to discuss Luke with her unsympathetic coworker.

"You spend too much time with him, neglecting your other patients." Bessie dropped the dirty sheets into a pile.

Felicity tensed. "I beg your pardon? There's no neglect."

"Oscar Miller lost his hand, and you've spent half as much time with him."

"I feed him all his meals and change his bandages daily. He sleeps a good bit." Felicity put her hands on her hips. No one had ever accused her of neglect.

"I'm just saying you seem mighty interested in Luke Shea. Don't get any ideas about him." Bessie tucked the sheets on her side and frowned at Felicity's untucked side.

"You needn't concern yourself." She finished with the sheets and reached for the blankets.

After they helped Eli back into bed, Bessie turned to her. "If I believe you're neglecting our brave soldiers to indulge in flirtation, I'll speak with Dr. Watkins myself."

"Nothing like that is happening." Felicity reeled from the threat. Bessie was a difficult woman but a good nurse. She'd never treated Felicity with such disrespect. "I won't require your help changing sheets, after all."

"Suits me." Her lips tightened.

Felicity ran downstairs to fetch clean bedding. She must guard herself around Luke when on duty, especially under Bessie's watchful eye.

~

*L*uke pushed himself up toward the wall. Felicity worked her way down the row to change sheets, and he wanted to sit in the wooden chair she toted with her for other fellows like himself.

Looking down the aisle, he glimpsed Ash peeking into the

ward. He raised his hand. He'd been asleep for all his visits, more's the pity, especially when he had so many questions.

Ash waved. He spoke to Felicity briefly and then strode down the aisle. That limp of his had grown more pronounced during the past five years that he'd lost. Frustrating. He ought to know what happened to worsen his best friend's childhood injury.

"Luke, you're awake. How's the headache?" Ash clasped his hand in a hearty shake.

Luke managed to control a wince. "A bit of improvement with the new medicine. Fever's gone." The missing events of his life concerned him the most.

"Glad to hear it." The tension in Ash's face eased.

"Can ye do me a favor?"

"Anything." Ash sat on the end of the bed.

"Help me sit. Lying prone for days has left me weak, and Felicity's heading this way with clean sheets. It'd be a kindness if ye were the one to assist me to the chair."

"Not a problem." Ash reached for his hands.

"Could ye ease me upward by me shoulders? That's the way Felicity does it."

"Sure thing." Sliding an arm under his shoulders, Ash hefted him to a seated position.

"Hold up." A wave of dizziness caused a nauseous feeling.

"Dizzy?" Sympathy colored Ash's voice.

"Aye."

"I was in bed a week when that horse kicked me as a child. When I first sat up, I retched."

"Aye." Luke put his hands on either side of his face. "I hope to spare ye that indignity."

Ash chuckled. "Rest as long as necessary."

His friend's laughter was strangely comforting. "It may help if me feet were on the floor. Slow-like." The dizziness had faded somewhat.

Ash turned him slowly.

Luke kept his eyes closed until his bare feet touched the cold wood floor.

"Stay still a minute." Miss Danielson's voice.

"Aye." As much as he preferred she not witness his weakness, he was glad for her presence.

"Dr. Watkins planned to give you two more days before getting you up. How do you feel?"

"As though I'm getting me land legs back on solid ground." He looked up into her tense face.

"Good. I wasn't going to change your bedding—"

"Ash will support me to my chair." And her pleased smile made it worth the effort.

"Then you'll be next." She looked up at Ash. "Thank you."

Ash fetched a chair. Set it in the aisle.

Luke eyed it. The distance seemed like a mile. "Let's go."

With Ash's support, hesitant steps took him to the chair. He looked down. His night shirt reached his knees. "Can I trouble you for a blanket?"

Ash handed it to him, and Luke spread it over his legs with a sense of accomplishment. "Now, tell me about the war."

~

Luke pretended to sleep after Ash left to give himself a moment to absorb the troubles between the North and South. The major battles with loss of life in the thousands. Apparently, Luke had been on furlough while his regiment participated in a terrible battle that fall in Sharpsburg, Maryland.

There'd been hostility between the North and South for several years over slavery, something Luke had despised since first encountering it as a child. Most folks in Mississippi accepted slavery as part of life, while others, like him and Ash, wanted to do away with it. The terrible conflict of a country at war with itself compounded his blinding headache. It was inconceivable that the leaders had allowed the bitterness between the two sides to reach this point. It would be nearly impossible to believe if not for the Southern soldiers recuperating in the ward with him, irrefutable truth.

He hadn't missed Ash's furtive glances at soldiers writing letters or speaking with other patients. Luke understood without being told that Confederate soldiers recovering with him didn't want to hear any defense of the Union.

Which was exactly what he wanted to do.

Yet, unbelievably, he'd fought for the South. His frustration at his inability to recall any of it mounted to a fever pitch. Pretending to sleep was his only way to hide in the crowded ward.

"How long has he been sleeping?" Dr. Watkins spoke close to his ear.

"Three hours. He missed lunch." The concern in Miss Danielson's voice persuaded him to open his eyes.

"He's awake." Dr. Watkins rested his elbow in his hand. "Luke, I understand you sat for some thirty minutes. How do you feel?"

"A wee bit tired." And horrified about the country's turmoil. Terrified of what might come—what had already happened, for all he knew. None of this could he admit to the doctor who'd already demonstrated loyalty to the South. "But glad to arise from this bed for a while."

"We'll try again tomorrow. That's quite a Christmas gift you gave to yourself—and a hopeful sign after all you've been through."

Aye. More than the man knew.

"Miss Danielson, it's time for his next dose of quinine. Then some lunch if he'll take it."

"I'm leaving in an hour." Was that regret in her eyes? "Luke, are you hungry?"

"Not now." He was too upset over the country's division to eat.

"No matter. Miss Thomas is here this evening. She'll feed him."

"Very well." She hurried away.

The doctor began talking about his family's plans for Christmas, which only heightened Luke's grief on this first holiday without his parents. He was still talking after Luke propped himself up to take his medicine. When he closed his eyes again, the doctor finally took his leave.

"Hey, Luke."

Luke turned his head gingerly. From the next bed, a blond man missing a hand stared at him. The stranger had been sleeping hours a day, evidently despondent as well as injured. "Aye. Who are you?"

"Oscar Miller, from the Twenty-First Mississippi. Don't you remember me?"

"Nay. I have amnesia."

"Heard about that. Thought you'd remember me since we were injured at the same battle." He searched Luke's face for signs of recognition. "At Fredericksburg, Virginia. We had a time of it."

Luke tried to imagine it. Failed. "Sorry. Who won?"

"We did. We whopped up on them Yankees. I saw most of it." Oscar started to prop himself up on his elbow, then stared at his bandaged arm. "I heard your friend explaining the war to you. Must be tough...not remembering. Anything you want to ask me about what happened with us, just let me know."

"Obliged to you." Luke closed his eyes.

What he most needed to know Oscar couldn't tell him.

How had he ended up fighting for the Confederacy when he supported the Union?

CHAPTER 4

*I*t was well past midnight, and officially Christmas morning. Felicity had danced with a dozen soldiers when all she wanted was to sit beside *her* soldier...perhaps eat roast turkey with oyster dressing together or sing Christmas carols as they had before the world had gone mad.

Aunt Mae was talking with Mrs. Dodd, Julia's mother. Felicity tried to catch her aunt's attention to signal that she was ready to leave. In vain. Felicity's cousin Petunia hadn't been invited to the party, though she couldn't have come, anyway, with four-year-old Wilma and two-year-old Miles Junior spending a few days at Mae and Charles's home for the holidays. Undoubtedly, the children would awaken their grandparents, mama, and cousin Felicity before anyone was ready to meet the day, so great had been their excitement earlier the prior evening. It was a shame that Petunia's husband, Miles, couldn't get a furlough. His family missed him desperately.

"May I have the pleasure of this dance?" A bearded soldier not much taller than Felicity reminded her of her surroundings.

She agreed with a curtsy. But did she have the energy to dance a polka?

As she walked beside him to the dance floor, a disheveled man pushed her partner aside as he skirted his way toward a lieutenant in the troops guarding Vicksburg. The music continued, but Felicity and her partner stared as the officer listened to the messenger. His face paled.

"This ball is over." The Confederate officer waved toward the band.

The music stopped. Everyone immediately began asking questions. Felicity clutched the sides of her green dress. A moment before, she'd longed for an excuse to leave. And now she had one. But what had happened?

The messenger made his way through the crowd. Felicity's partner stopped him. "Pardon me, sir. What is the news?"

Others turned toward the man.

"Seven Yankee ironclads with about fifty transport steamers were spotted upriver. General Sherman is landing at Milliken's Bend."

Several women gasped.

The Union army was up the Mississippi, a bit north of the city.

Felicity's heartbeat quickened. She'd learned the names of Union generals, and not only from the city's six newspapers. Her wounded soldiers often spoke of the war.

"All noncombatants should leave Vicksburg." Then he left, presumably to spread the news.

"Pardon me, but I must return to my regiment for orders." Felicity's dance partner bowed to her. "I regret that we'll not have our dance."

She inclined her head. "Thank you for keeping our city safe." As he joined other soldiers leaving the room, Felicity's breaths came in gasps. Fifty ships must carry thousands of Union soldiers. Were there enough Confederate soldiers in the city to protect them? Strangely, she supported the Union yet craved the protection of Southern soldiers.

Like Luke...who couldn't defend anyone right now. How grateful she was for his presence in the city...even if he didn't know her.

Aunt Mae hurried over. "Such goings on. That Yankee army closes in on us." She wrung her gloved hands. "We must go. Charles is fetching our cloaks."

"Let's give our thanks to Savannah and her parents for the party." Felicity spoke as calmly as she could manage with her insides quaking. She scanned the thinning crowd for her hostess. Mr. Adair was speaking to the lieutenant, but Savannah and her mother were not in the parlor.

"Charles and I spoke with Mrs. Adair." Aunt Mae flapped her hand to the side of her face as she often did when agitated. "Will these Yankees give us no rest? Must they attack us at Christmas?"

A shiver ran through Felicity. The Northerners were close enough to arrive in Vicksburg within hours by boat.

Ash ushered Julia and her mother, Martha Dodd, over to them.

"We'll stay with Mama and my little brother, Eddie, tonight." Julia looked at her mother, who nodded. "If we're not under attack, we'll open Mama's home for guests tomorrow afternoon as usual."

"Eddie's been asking to visit Luke." Ash seemed to have difficulty refusing any request from his ten-year-old brother-in-law. "We'll all come after breakfast—if all is well in the city."

"Visitors will be a tonic for Luke." Felicity couldn't give Luke the new shirt she'd sewn for him because she had nothing for her other patients. Visits from loved ones Luke remembered were the best medicine. How she longed for his memories to return so she could be among his loved ones again. "I'm working so I'll see you there."

"Your uncle will escort you to the hospital, my dear." Aunt Mae patted her arm.

Since she'd arrive about an hour before dawn, Felicity didn't argue. She was glad she'd be able to warn Luke about the Union army's presence. Would that stir any memories?

⁓

*T*he sound of drums woke Luke from a fitful sleep in the middle of the night. A single lantern was lit in the hall, leaving the room in darkness. For some reason, the drumbeat caused sweat to bead on his forehead.

In the next bed, Oscar's mattress creaked. "The enemy must be near."

"Aye," another soldier answered from across the room. "Those drums beat out orders for our comrades. They'll defend the city."

Luke didn't recognize the soldier's voice, though the words quickened his heart rate. Even if he could remember his training, he was in no shape to fight.

"Let me have my musket. I got a few rounds in me."

"I'm game for another battle."

"Count me in. I'm plum tired of this bed."

A couple of cheers rang out.

Luke understood the desire to defend Vicksburg, the place his heart called home. A rush of love for his city welled up, filling a bit of the void left by his amnesia...as if a piece of himself returned and he had the threat of an approaching army to thank for it.

Someone carried a lantern into the ward. "I see the drums woke you." Wyatt, the night attendant, raised his voice over the din. "Those drum rolls are calling soldiers to defenses north of the city. Yankee steamers were at Milliken's Bend a couple of hours ago."

In Louisiana. Less than twenty miles as the birds flew but longer on the winding Mississippi River. Too close for comfort.

"Don't you worry none. Our brave troops are defending us." Someone across the aisle raised a fist.

Men who felt strong enough to cheer did so.

Luke tried to remember how it felt to fight, to point a rifle at a Union soldier. Had he shot, maybe killed, one of them? Many more? What could have led him to raise a weapon against them? Union loyalties ran deeply, as if his own parents had ingrained them into him. Surely, he couldn't have so forgotten himself that he did something he would regret. He tried to calm his troubled spirits, yet the truth was, he didn't know *what* he'd done...and that scared him.

His head throbbed. He fingered the ever-present bandages. How long would these headaches continue?

Turning on his side, he pulled the blankets tightly to his chin. Suddenly, he felt like that fifteen-year-old boy again who'd witnessed his parents' deaths. Grief for them stirred a deeper ache, one more penetrating than pain in his body. Regret bore down on him on this first Christmas without them —at least, the only one he knew about.

It had been a sunny, warm May day when he arrived home from school to find a note from his mother. Mr. Tomlinson, the owner of the bookbindery where Papa worked, had taken a train trip to Jackson and closed the shop, so his parents were taking their rowboat out on the river. Luke had been happy for them because a day of freedom was a rare treat for his father.

Dropping his books, he ran to the river to await their return. When he spotted them coming south toward town, Luke ran along the shore, calling to his pretty auburn-haired mother. Smiling, she waved. Facing her, Papa shifted his body to call out to Luke. Too quickly.

The boat rocked in the current and overturned.

Mama screamed as they both tumbled into the muddy water.

Luke's heart nearly hammered out of his chest. Papa was a strong swimmer, but Mama had never learned. Her heavy skirts would weigh her down.

Shouting behind him jolted Luke from the immobility of shock. Tossing off his boots, he plunged into the cold river. Papa bobbed out of the water but not Mama.

"Stop, boy!" A stranger's voice from the shore. "The current's too strong."

Luke ignored the command. Fear lent strength to his arms as he propelled himself toward the boat.

"Stay back, Luke! I'll get her." Papa dove under water.

For once, Luke disobeyed his father, figuring he'd need help to get his mother to shore. The overturned boat teetered on the water as though it weighed no more than a sack of potatoes.

Luke swam toward the spot his father went down and heard splashes behind him. Where was Papa?

Fear gripped him as he neared the spot where his parents had disappeared. Mama had been under too long. Taking a breath, he dove under the surface. He couldn't see anything. The current was stronger here. He went up for air.

"Boy, save yourself! Swim back to me." A stranger took brisk strokes toward him.

Luke made a frantic circle in the water. Where were Mama and Papa? He dove again, making wide sweeps with his arms and legs. He felt nothing. Then muscular arms pulled him to the surface. He opened his eyes. The bearded stranger wasn't Papa.

"The current's too strong." The man kept a grip on him as Luke sagged. "Don't give up on me. Let's get back to shore."

Knowing in his soul it was too late, Luke forced his tired arms to swim toward the bank. His mind went numb.

When he got to shore, all he could hear was heart-wrenching sobs. A woman he didn't know wrapped a blanket around him. "Don't cry, lad. We'll take care of you."

But she hadn't. Ash's family had given him a home. He'd lived with them for a few weeks and then taken on his father's job at the bookbindery. Mr. Tomlinson let him stay in the apartment above the business as part of his pay.

Luke swiped at his wet cheeks and then looked around the dark hospital ward, now silent.

He hadn't been strong enough to save his parents.

He'd always tried to emulate his father's considerable moral strength, a Herculean task for a boy engulfed in grief. His service to the Confederacy, in spite of his Unionist views, proved he still wasn't strong enough.

~

When Felicity arrived at six o'clock, the ward was still dark. Uncle Charles had indeed escorted her to the hospital with many reminders he'd return at one unless it was unsafe for her to stay that long. Little Miles and Wilma had already risen and were staring at gifts under the Christmas tree when Felicity left. She had encouraged Aunt Mae not to make them wait, but her aunt wanted a family celebration together. The children each had several gifts. Uncle Charles and Aunt Mae, along with Petunia, were hoping to keep the festivities as normal as possible for the little ones.

After lighting a lantern, Felicity walked past each bed. No one was awake, which didn't surprise her. Wyatt, the burly night attendant, had told her the drums had awakened them during the night, stimulating much conjecture about an upcoming battle.

She whispered a prayer that the fighting would stay well north of the city this time. She'd been in town for part of the summer's attacks from a Union fleet and never wanted to endure another. The Union ships had lobbed mortar shells on innocent citizens that sometimes exploded overhead and sometimes on impact. The bombardment still reverberated in Felicity's memories. Screams of terrified children and cries of their mothers desperately longing to protect them lived on in her nightmares. Must they face that barrage again?

She turned to make one more sweep of the room. Might as well drink a cup of coffee and then return. Bessie wasn't here yet.

"Happy Christmas, Miss Danielson." Luke's voice.

She held the lantern toward his dear face. "Happy Christmas, Luke." The joy of being able to say it directly to him this year bubbled up inside her. "I'd welcome it if you'd address me by my given name, Felicity."

"Happy Christmas, Felicity."

That Irish lilt played havoc on her heart as much as hearing her name on his lips. "How are you?"

"Thirsty. A dipper of water would be most welcome, if it's not too much trouble." There was sadness in his eyes.

"Let me fetch the bucket." Perhaps grief for his parents struck him a hard blow this Christmas. As far as Luke recalled, this was his first one without them.

When she returned, he was propped up with his back against the wall. "How good it is to see you sitting again today."

He accepted the dripping dipper from her and drained it. "The dizziness passes quicker if I don't move quickly."

"Makes sense, what with your head wound and lying prone for nearly two weeks." She accepted the empty dipper from him. "Wyatt tells me the drums awoke you last night. Did that stir any memories?"

He looked away. "Nay."

She was determined to find the key that would unlock those dormant memories. "There are no cannon blasts in the distance. Perhaps peace will reign this Christmas." Though there was precious little peace in her heart.

"Miss Danielson, could I trouble you for some of that water?"

"No trouble, Jim." Others stirred. Best offer water to everyone and then serve breakfast. She turned back. "Luke, I'll bring your breakfast soon."

"I can manage to feed meself." A smile crossed his lips. "Not that I don't like the company of a pretty girl at me meals, but ye be busy."

A pang of regret was quickly squashed. This was a positive sign, one he needed. How could she be sorry when he'd just called her pretty? "If I can sit with you while you eat, I will." She picked up the bucket. "Ash and Julia are bringing Eddie and Mrs. Dodd to see you today."

"Welcome news." His grin widened. "Me heart has a soft spot for young Eddie."

Of course. He remembered Julia's brother, not Felicity. Water sloshed on her brown wool dress as she hurried away. Drumbeats didn't jog his recollections. Maybe seeing Eddie again would accomplish it.

~

"'Tis good to see you all." Joy flickered in Luke's heart for the second time this Christmas morning. It first happened when Felicity invited him to call her by her given name, a beautiful name for such a beautiful, compassionate woman. The second was in recognizing two more people, Eddie and Mrs. Dodd, for Julia's mother had accompanied her and Ash on this visit. It was a shock to see Eddie looking so much older. Why, the last time he'd seen the boy, the top of Eddie's head reached Luke's waist—the greatest proof so far that five years had passed. While Luke's head swirled from the changes in the boy, Ash had rustled up two chairs for the ladies, who had sat after exchanging greetings of the season with him.

"We brought you some plum pudding and mince pie." Eddie, a lad of ten dressed in a brown coat with a red-checked, collared shirt similar to Ash's, set a napkin-covered plate next to Luke on the bed. He turned eleven next month, according to Ash.

"A treat, indeed." Though Eddie's voice had even matured a little, it was still recognizable. Anything familiar was a comfort. Luke lifted the napkin. Generous portions he'd share with Oscar, who'd had no visitors yet. Luke's appetite had been slow to return, but this food tempted him. "Thank ye all for this fine Christmas present."

"Our pleasure." Ash leaned his shoulder against the wall. "It's good to see you sitting up."

"Sitting eases the throbbing in me head." He returned Mrs. Dodd's smile. It was plain to see where Julia inherited her blond hair and her beauty.

He met Felicity's glance as she carried a bowl of broth to another patient. He couldn't help noticing his nurse's beauty surpassed them all. He gave his head a shake. Best keep his mind on his guests.

He'd attended some picnics where Julia's whole family attended. Ash had told him that both Julia's father and his own father had passed during those lost five years, making the formerly vivacious Mrs. Dodd a widow. "Will your doors be open to guests today?" he asked her. His family had attended the Dodds' event last Christmas—that was, in 1856—eating delicacies and singing carols together. It had been a happy celebration. Grief jabbed at his heart that he'd never share such a day with his loved ones again this side of heaven.

"I hope that many brave the threats from upriver." Mrs. Dodd's lips tightened. "I find I'm not as afraid of battle as I once was because we endured an attack that lasted over two months in the summer."

"Me beloved Vicksburg was attacked?" The scrambled eggs and biscuit he'd devoured for breakfast suddenly felt like a cannonball in his stomach.

"Yes, but it's been quiet since then." Ash spoke calmly. "When you get out of here, Julia and I want you to make your home with us."

"Me thoughts are to return to me job at the book bindery." Luke's head still reeled from news of the extended attack. "Me apartment is above Mr. Tomlinson's business."

"He closed it and left town months ago." Ash's brow furrowed.

Luke flinched. Reliance on the job waiting for him had sustained him. Now what? Where was he to live? How was he to provide for himself?

"I believe the army will discharge you," Ash said quickly. "If so, I'll train you to make saddles. How does that sound?"

"There does seem to be some recollection of spending some time there tucked away in me head. Yer shop always smells of leather."

Ash gave a nod. "You lived with my family about a month before taking the bookbindery job. I showed you some things then."

"Aye." A hazy memory of sleeping in their guest room and dining with the family surfaced. "The time immediately following...some things I recall."

"So it's decided, then." Ash gave him a direct look.

"We'd love to have you live with us." Julia leaned forward. "We know how hard this must all be for you."

"Sorry, old friend. Didn't mean to push our plans on you." Ash cleared his throat. "It just seemed the perfect solution to us."

"Aye, so it is." Grateful that Julia also endorsed the offer, he extended his hand, which Ash clasped.

"Yippee." Eddie danced a little jig. "I'll see you more."

He grinned at the lad's happiness. He, Ash, and Willie had taken the boy fishing a time or two. "I hope Willie will stop in soon."

Eddie stilled. He looked up at Ash.

Luke's heart skipped a beat. "What is it?" Was Willie ill?

"Ash said there's some things I can't talk about." Halting steps took Eddie to his mama's side, who put her arm around him.

Luke looked up at Ash, who avoided his gaze. "Ash?"

"We must get back to prepare for our guests." Ash tugged at his ear. "I'll return tomorrow. We'll talk then."

They left moments later. Strong foreboding swept over Luke.

Neither Savannah nor Willie had visited. Why not?

Did some serious illness prevent him from coming? He dared not consider a worse fate.

CHAPTER 5

There'd been no signs of battle, but as promised, Uncle Charles was waiting outside the nurse's room at one to escort Felicity on a brisk walk home under overcast, gloomy skies, a reflection of her mood. She needed to push her hurt aside for the sake of Wilma and Little Miles.

After a quick wash and change, Felicity emerged from her cozy second-floor bedroom in her aunt's brick house. The family had already eaten lunch but had waited on opening gifts for Felicity. Petunia had moved to a rented home in Vicksburg two months before, having tired of living in Yazoo City with her husband's parents, and there had also been hints of financial burdens. This was the first Christmas Felicity would spend with her cousin's family, and spending it with children was a blessing.

"Felicity?" From the main first-floor hall, four-year-old Wilma tilted her head with its blond braid toward the top of the stairs. "You're taking forever. We want to open our gifts."

"And you've been so patient." Lifting her skirts, Felicity ran down the stairs to the feisty girl. She held out her hand, and they entered the parlor with a five-foot pine tree in the corner, decorated with ribbons, pine cones, and strings of popcorn. Foot tapping in her rocking chair, Petunia held little Miles on her lap. Aunt Mae and Uncle Charles sat on a loveseat adjacent to their daughter. Her aunt looked relieved to see her. "Sorry to hold up the gift exchange."

"It couldn't be helped. At least you're here now." Petunia brushed back auburn tendrils escaping from her bun.

Stung by her ungracious tone, Felicity selected a chair a little apart from the family, leaving a chair in between her and the loveseat for Wilma.

"I'll pass out the gifts, shall I?" Uncle Charles's eyes twinkled at Wilma.

"I want to help." Wilma dashed to the tree.

"I needed a helper, thank you." He grinned at his granddaughter.

The next few minutes passed quickly. The children tore the wrappings from a peg top with string, Spilikins, Jackstones, and clothing. Fortunately, they both liked the ball and book of fairy tales that Felicity gave them. She'd sewn cotton dresses for the ladies and a shirt for her uncle. She thanked everyone for her scarf and embroidered handkerchiefs, refusing to dwell on the disparity in the value of the gifts. After all, she was indebted to her aunt for giving her a home, something her married siblings had been unable to offer. It was a debt she couldn't repay.

Amid the festive atmosphere brought about by the children's joy, she longed to be with Luke, who'd been in a pensive mood after Ash's family left.

Petunia stood after all the gifts had been opened. "We should get to the Dodds' home." She shifted her dress around her plump curves as she glanced at the clock. "It's already quite late since we had to wait so long. The children are excited to sing with the piano and taste the delicacies."

It was half past two. Neighbors came and went all afternoon

to the festivities. Felicity's face heated. "A mere ten-minute walk will take us there in plenty of time."

"Quite so, my dear. Let's fetch our cloaks." Aunt Mae's smile at Felicity removed some of the sting. "I'm looking forward to the gathering."

Felicity carried her gifts to her room, wondering at Petunia's barely veiled sharp tongue. What had she done to cause it? Perhaps it was only that her cousin missed her husband. Miles was fighting in Virginia.

Felicity was all too familiar with missing a loved one. She'd waited for Luke to come home to stay for nineteen months. Now that he was here, pain sliced deeply that he didn't remember courting her, or even meeting her. He'd recognized Ash, Julia, Eddie, and even Mrs. Dodd. As much as she tried to push her resentment away, it remained to eat at her, souring the joy of what should be a celebratory day.

∼

The next day, Luke waited tensely for Ash. Between him and Oscar, they had finished off the pudding and mince pie. For Luke, it was a way to pass the time. Felicity had stayed busy with other patients today, writing two letters already, and had just sat beside a young soldier of perhaps sixteen to start another one. She displayed an admirable compassionate manner to all of them.

He had been tempted to ask Felicity if she knew Willie. It was possible, since she was good friends with Julia and Ash... but not likely. Luke would remember her from gatherings if she'd been invited. There was no possibility he hadn't noticed the beautiful nurse that he imagined to be around his age.

Twenty, that was. How could it be that only the first fifteen years were all his memory could recall? His head ached even more when he tried to concentrate on that missing time, especially to know what happened with Willie, whose wit had passed many an occasion with infectious laughter.

Lunch had been over an hour ago. Surely, Ash should be here soon. Luke sat up in his bed. When the dizziness eased, he scooted toward the wall until his back rested against it. He'd ask the night attendant to walk with him in the ward this evening, for he'd not fall on Felicity like a sack of potatoes. His body was weak from lying abed, but he'd change that. His wound had stopped bleeding early in the week—a blessing, to be sure. She was now changing his bandage every other day. She had explained the hospital was low on bandages and several medicines like morphine. They had plenty of quinine because the doctors here made it themselves.

Quinine took the edge off his headaches. Nothing relieved them.

Closing his eyes, he raked his fingers across his forehead. How long would the pain last? More importantly, when would he recover from the amnesia? His father had taught him that the way a person lived and the choices made determined character. Had he done anything in those missing years to let down himself, his parents, his God?

"Got a headache today?"

Ash's voice. "Aye. All day, every day." Luke opened his eyes. "'Tis glad I am to see you."

"I know." Ash positioned a chair beside the bed and then slumped onto it. "I wanted you to be stronger before telling you about Willie."

"No need to wait." Luke steeled himself. "It can't be any worse than me imaginings."

Ash's gaze dropped to the floor, then raised again. "It's as you fear. Our buddy sleeps in heaven now."

Not Willie. Not the man who'd been one who lightened every mood with a timely joke. No one had ever made Luke laugh so easily. He clutched the sheets. He'd known, deep inside. Had Willie been ill, they would have told him. "What happened?"

"You both mustered into the Jeff Davis Guards in May of 1861." Ash paused. No doubt, his limp had prevented him from fighting as well. "Your company camped in various locations in Virginia. That September, typhoid fever took Willie's life. You got it later, but yours was a milder case."

This on top of his grief for his parents was too much to bear. "Savannah took the news hard, for certain." Willie had known he'd marry her when they were all but lads. The sorrow for her had to be unbearable.

"She did. Broke our hearts to see it."

Luke's heart ached for the poor girl. For himself and Ash. Best change the subject, or he'd be weeping like a child. "Is the Union army still about?"

"Undoubtedly." Ash glanced toward the window. "Soldiers guarding Vicksburg are still up north. Some folks are scared. I'll wait and see what happens and try to live as normally as possible."

"Keep me informed, will you?" Luke put his hand on his throbbing forehead. "Methinks it's time for me medicine."

"I'll fetch Felicity."

Aye, there was something about Felicity. Her mere presence soothed him.

~

*T*hree days later, on December twenty-ninth, Felicity was gathering the last of the breakfast dishes when a stillness settled over the ward and every soldier's gaze riveted on the windows. Then she heard what had captured the fighting men's attention—the roar of cannon at the bluffs north of Vicksburg, a familiar sound she'd prayed never to hear again.

The dishes rattled in her hands. She set them on a table with shaking hands to avoid chipping them.

The tense postures in sitting and standing soldiers showed that, in their imaginations, they were on the bluffs with some twelve thousand soldiers—a number she'd learned from her patients—and engaged in battle.

Surely, the barrage with barely a pause in between foretold an intense fight.

And casualties.

Bessie touched her arm and she jumped.

"Sorry to frighten you." Bessie's gaze wasn't on the fog-shrouded windows but on her patients. "Our men are more frightened than us. They know better than we what's happening. Go. Try to calm them."

"I will." The dishes could wait. One thing about Bessie—her focus had always been her patients' comfort during crisis situations, a quality Felicity admired.

"Another thing." Bessie's brow furrowed. "Wounded will begin arriving. Our ward is full. Look for some of these men to be discharged today to make room."

She gasped. "But they're not ready."

"It will happen, all the same. Those who are walking about, dressing for the day, are all nearly ready. They'll be sent back to their regiments or discharged. Be prepared. You're about to lose your favorite patient."

Felicity's gaze flew to a fully dressed Luke, who sat on the edge of his bed looking at her. He'd been walking for three days. Other than changing his bandages and administering his medicine, he didn't require medical services.

Every bed in their ward was occupied. Bessie had worked in the ward through the summer's siege. Felicity had no doubt she was right.

There had to be a way to put an end to this war that

continued to bring so much suffering to brave men on both sides...or at least speed the ending. What could she do?

A new fear caused her whole body to shake. Continuing fighting north of the city didn't threaten citizens' safety—for the moment—but it could rob Luke of his future. If the doctor released him, would the army send him back to his regiment with amnesia? He didn't remember soldier skills, commands delivered by bugles and drums. Sending him back to battle under those circumstance was akin to a suicidal mission.

Not while she had breath in her body. She'd speak to Dr. Watkins at her first opportunity.

CHAPTER 6

$\mathcal{F}$elicity's initial search for Dr. Watkins caught him in the middle of a patient examination in another ward. When two of her patients were discharged, her alarm escalated to a fever pitch. She caught up with the doctor an hour later in the nurses' room. He sat at the table with lists in front of him. "Dr. Watkins, are you discharging some patients too soon?"

"I must. Wounded are surely on their way as we speak. Several of our patients are nearly ready, anyway." He studied a page of names. "Those who have family will continue their recuperation at home before heading back to war."

"But not Luke Shea."

He sat back. "Ash Mitchell has offered his home to Luke. I've already sent a message to him. I expect him shortly."

Felicity crept closer, her heart racing in her panic to save her beau. "You won't send him back to fight."

"The South needs every soldier they can get." He sighed. "I'll recommend a month's respite at home before he goes back to battle."

Her heart skipped a beat and then thrashed out a staccato

rhythm. "Thank you, but that might not be enough if he can't remember his military training."

His brows lowered. "Or perhaps he doesn't wish to return to the battlefield. Amnesia can be a ruse to fool us all."

"No." She sank into the chair beside him. "He's not pretending."

"How can you be certain?" His eyes narrowed.

"Because he's been my beau for nearly three years"—how it broke her to admit it—"and he doesn't remember me."

"Your beau?" Dr. Watkins studied her. "He certainly doesn't appear to know you."

"Exactly." A tear rolled down her cheek. She dashed it away. Now wasn't the time for weakness.

"How do I know you're not simply trying to keep him from battle?"

Her heartbeat accelerated. "Many people know we're courting. Beyond my aunt and uncle, Ash and Julia Mitchell will vouch for the relationship. Also, Mrs. Martha Dodd, Mrs. Lila Adair, and Savannah Adair, to name a few."

"An impressive list of witnesses." He rubbed his chin. "I will speak with Ash Mitchell when he arrives. You stay on the ward. If he confirms the courtship, I'll recommend Luke be monitored for a month. I'll examine him then. If his memory doesn't return within that time, I'll recommend an honorable discharge. But you're not to tell him, or he'll simply pretend. In fact, don't tell anyone that he'll be discharged if his memories don't return. If I believe you've betrayed my confidence, I'll doubt Luke's story as well, and he'll be on a train to Virginia."

"I'll not speak of it until you've made your decision." New Year's Day was two days away, so she should know by early February. She rose and gave a somber nod. "You have my word. Thank you, Doctor."

After leaving the break room, Felicity hurried up the stairs, stopping outside the ward. She thanked God for Luke's amnesia, something she'd never dreamed she could do. Whereas before she'd tried to spark old memories, she'd now work to shield him from people who would try to remind him of his past.

Please, God, keep those memories at bay until February.

⌒

"Those cannons sure do sound familiar, don't they, Luke?" Oscar sat opposite Luke on their adjacent cots. Oscar had been sitting up the past couple of days. His wife and two sons had come up from nearby Warrenton on Christmas.

"Nay. Just from this morning." Luke searched his memories. The sound evoked fear. Caution. Nothing else.

"Still nothing?"

Luke shook his head.

"You're likely the lucky one, not remembering seeing a buddy killed before your eyes." Oscar studied his own bandage. "Reckon a missing hand will keep me out of the war. Never did like shooting at Yankees. They've got families...wives, children, maybe a girl." He looked up. "But I did it. I'd do it again for my country."

Had Luke shot someone? Likely, many someones. Something inside him shriveled at the thought. A bullet of his just couldn't have left some poor woman a widow, some child an orphan.

"Pardon me, Oscar." Felicity touched Luke's shoulder. "May I talk with you, Luke?"

"Aye." Luke followed her into the hall.

"You're being discharged today." Those beautiful blue eyes held compassion. "Ash will be here in a few minutes to take you to his house."

His dizziness returned. "What of the army? Do they have claim on me?"

"No discharge from the army at this time." Her lips clamped shut.

Sweat beaded on his forehead despite the chill on the landing. "So I may head back to a war I've no memory of?" Dr. Watkins would return him to battle in this condition. Why, he knew no more of battles than young Eddie. Distant drums beating out orders meant nothing to him. The battle's chaos would be even worse for a man in his condition. How could he cope?

Footsteps on the stairs snatched Felicity's gaze. What did she fear? When Ash limped to the landin, her body relaxed.

"Luke, I've just received the good news." Ash grinned. "You're to come home today. Pack your knapsack. Julia's got your room ready for you."

Home. That sounded good, except he likely wouldn't stay there long if the army had its way. And he'd never see Felicity again. She'd never know that she'd become his anchor. He turned to her. "'Tis grateful I am that God put you in me path."

Her expression softened into...was it tenderness?

"Oh, you'll see Felicity at our home." Ash placed a hand on his shoulder. "She's not only our friend—she also works as a maid three days a week for Julia."

Her face turned scarlet.

Did she object to the description? No shame in working as a maid. "Then I'm grateful this isn't a true parting."

"As I am."

They stared at one another. "You are a good nurse. Me thanks don't seem to be enough."

"I'm happy for your improvement. That will continue—if my prayers are answered. I'll be nearby to change your bandages, which you'll need for another week or two." She smiled. "Now I'll gather medicine for you to take with you. Shall I help you pack?"

He started to shake his head, setting off a wave of dizziness. "Nay."

"Well, goodbye, then." Her gaze clung to his. "I must fetch some medicine. The other patients need me."

"They do, indeed." As he did. "Goodbye."

She gave a nod. Lifting her skirts a few inches, she ran down the stairs.

"Let's gather your possessions." Ash gestured to the ward's door. "Julia and I can't wait to welcome you to our home...your home now."

As good as that sounded, Luke couldn't squash the disappointment that he'd not see Felicity daily. She'd make some fortunate fellow a fine wife. Strange that such a fine woman wasn't already married. But his head ached too much for him to think about anything.

~

*W*ounded began arriving before Felicity got the chance to change Luke's bedding. The first man's leg had been blown off from the knee down. Dr. Watkins gave Felicity and Bessie a list of patients to ready for discharge. As soon as those men vacated, their beds were filled. Chaos reigned for several hours. Then a male nurse arrived to help. Two male attendants responsible for bathing patients rotated among several wards.

Distant rumbles continued all day. Smoke from cannon reports drifted toward the city. The floor shook with the blasts, or was Felicity's swaying caused from exhaustion? A couple of wounded soldiers from the continuing battle bragged that they were winning this one.

Felicity, now that Luke was safely away from the fighting,

regretted hearing the Confederates were winning. However, she was ready for her city to get some relief from attacks. Who could have guessed a prewar city of some forty-five hundred citizens would generate such interest from the Union?

Uncle Charles came at three o'clock and ended up carrying men on stretchers to various wards. They both worked late into the evening, when her uncle finally convinced her to go home.

She was almost too tired to eat the supper her aunt quickly warmed for them. It was nearly nine, so the children were already in bed. Felicity was grateful, for Wilma loved for her to play with her or read to her. As much as Felicity adored the girl, she just didn't have the energy to oblige tonight.

Felicity told Aunt Mae and Petunia that Luke had gone to Ash's that day. Petunia knew of him but hadn't met him. The two women asked many questions about Luke, the soldiers that arrived that day, and the battle. Felicity was nearly too exhausted to speak. She allowed Uncle Charles to answer.

"I've heated water for your bath. It's all ready in the bath room." Aunt Mae stood. "Do you want me to fetch your robe and nightgown?"

"Mama, she's a grown woman. No need to coddle her." Petunia frowned at her mother.

"Quite right." Felicity tried not to mind the petulant tone. "I'll fetch them after I wash these dishes."

"No, my dear." As she answered Felicity, Aunt Mae gave her daughter a stern look. "I will do them. You've earned that bath."

"Thank you." Felicity trudged from the dining room before her cousin could speak. No doubt, the young mother had endured a challenging day with her children. That would account for the ungracious attitude.

As she climbed the stairs to her room, she pictured Luke in his new home. Staying with Ash and Julia was the best outcome for Luke, but she didn't get to be with him, see his dear face daily anymore.

Felicity must guard her words carefully with Ash and Julia so as not to betray her confidence with the doctor. However, now that he was abroad in the city, she must try to steer Luke away from folks who might remind Luke of events they'd all experienced together to nudge his memory, with the noblest of intentions.

His amnesia must remain for another month.

~

"*D*o you remember being here?" Ash rubbed his arms and looked around the parlor of his home—Luke's new home—after supper that night.

"Aye." Luke sat near the warmth emanating from a cozy fireplace. "We've played chess on the square table in the back of the room with your younger sisters doing their needlepoint on these cushioned chairs near the lantern's light. Your ma often bustled about here and there. Your pa would play the winner of our games."

"That was when you stayed here right after your parents..." Ash's voice trailed off.

"That's why it feels recent." Luke didn't want to talk about his parents. "It's dark outside. Sounds of battle aren't as fierce. Perhaps it's nearly at an end."

Julia entered with a tray. "I'm praying that's so—and that the battle comes no closer. Last summer's continued attacks on our city were as close as I ever want to be to the fighting. Never again will I willingly experience it. Now, I've brought you both a cup of tea. You can take your medicine with it and retire for the night."

"Obliged to you." Luke accepted a dainty cup with a pink floral design and downed the drink.

"There's more." Julia laughed. "Next time I won't serve your drinks in our 'company' cups." She refreshed both men's tea and then sat on the sofa beside her husband. "Eddie has learned you're here. Don't be surprised to see him and my mother tomorrow—as long as it is safe to move about the streets."

"A customer picked up a saddle this afternoon." Ash set his empty cup on a side table between him and Luke. "He said that the battle was going in the South's favor."

Luke studied him. "That's not to your liking."

Ash got up and closed the parlor door. So the cook and her husband wouldn't overhear?

"Tell me, man. There's so much I don't recall." His head began to throb.

"No, Luke, it isn't to my liking." Ash's hazel eyes darkened. "I'm a Unionist. So is Julia. We never wanted this conflict."

"Me gut says the same about meself. Is that possible?" His voice shook because what if he didn't like the answer? He needed to know if he was the man he hoped he was.

"Very possible." Ash leaned forward. "Before you left, we had a conversation. You told me you supported the Union. It was something important that we had in common."

So he had been right about his loyalties. That was *some* comfort. "Did Willie know my sentiments?"

Ash shook his head. "He had already left us. Your company departed Vicksburg a few hours later."

"Something plagues me spirit. *Why* did I fight for the Confederacy?"

Ash looked at Julia, who stood. "I'll bid you gentlemen goodnight. Don't talk late. Luke has been too long from his bed. Take your quinine before I go."

Once Luke had complied, Julia murmured goodnight again and left them, closing the door behind her.

"You went for Willie's sake." Ash's face was a still mask, mute testimony of his own grief. "He started having nightmares as soon as he mustered in. He feared he'd die."

"And so it happened just that way." Luke rubbed his aching head.

"It did. But you were watching over him. You showed true friendship."

Yet Willie had died under Luke's watch. "Will you mind if I bid you a good night?"

"Not at all." Ash stood. "Sleep in as long as you like in the morning."

Luke climbed the stairs to his room with a sinking heart. Had he been a comfort through Willie's illness? And after he died...what kind of person had Luke become?

CHAPTER 7

elicity arrived at the hospital the next morning to discover more wounded had come in overnight, but the best news was that the battle appeared to be over. Soldiers with minor injuries bragged to her about their part in the fighting on Chickasaw Bayou. One fellow in particular was in high spirits as Felicity cleaned his wounds.

"You ought to have seen them Yankees trudging through the swampland." The tow-headed soldier scarcely blinked as Felicity pulled splinters from his bleeding hands and arms. "Those who made it past that, the thick expanse of trees, and the Chickasaw Bayou, had to tend with our abatis."

"What's that?" She didn't look up from her task that the doctor was too busy to attend. Some fellows liked to talk as a release from adrenaline caused by battle. She didn't mind. Hopefully, she'd have his arm cleaned and bandaged before his story ran out.

"As part of building up our defenses about the city, we felled trees and arranged them in rows with the branches facing out—that is, toward anyone trying to climb the bluffs where we waited, muskets in hand. 'Course, we bent some branches and sharpened others to welcome the enemy to our fortifications."

Hardly a welcome. Felicity grimaced. War was cruel. When would the madness end?

"It slowed them considerably. We shot at them while they climbed."

This fellow must have stumbled into them himself, so many cuts did have on his hands. "Did the Union know about your fortifications?"

He shrugged. "They likely did reconnaissance ahead of the fighting. Union spies could have given them advance warning." His dark eyes narrowed. "I'd best not catch a spy, or he'll rue the day."

Were there Union spies in Vicksburg? "Sounds as though you all did a good job, advance notice or not," she pointed out in a soothing tone. "You are all to be commended. Our citizens are grateful." Though she regretted the Confederate victory on the one hand, she was grateful her city could breathe easier today.

"It ain't nothing any self-respecting Southerner wouldn't do." Despite his offhand words, his beard wasn't thick enough to mask his blush.

"You have our city's thanks, all the same." Felicity forced a smile. "I'm finished. The doctor says you may return to your regiment."

"Obliged to you, miss."

After he left, Felicity considered what she'd learned, certain that advance warnings of preparations like defense fortifications would help the Union. It wasn't the first time she'd heard such details.

It must require lots of courage to be a Union spy in Mississippi. Unionists were scorned—or worse—in this Southern state, so no one spouted Union loyalties publicly. Her own aunt and uncle supported the Confederacy. Felicity had learned to be close-lipped about her loyalties, but she admired those who possessed the courage to act on their convictions.

⁓

*T*he day after his discharge from the hospital, Luke wandered outside after lunch. He still wore his soldier's uniform because he had nothing else. The gray wool trousers and jacket seemed almost new, the blouse underneath the same.

Ash was obtaining supplies for the saddle shop out of the city today. Luke had wanted to go with him, even with the continuing headache, but he couldn't be away from his bed for so many hours. Not yet. He would continue to push himself daily. No doubt his body would soon recover.

The amnesia was another matter.

A short walk took him to a one-story building made of wood, the saddle shop. One bright spot of his injury was the opportunity to learn a new trade. Curiosity drove him to turn the doorknob.

Locked. Odd. The door had never been locked during the day. In fact, Ash had always worked with the door open except on the coldest winter days. Like today.

Perhaps all the soldiers about the city—virtually strangers —prompted such caution. So much had changed now, including himself. He felt half a man without his memories.

Maybe a short walk in the brisk breeze would ease the ache in his head.

That the brick homes were familiar comforted him. Every familiar face or location gave him hope that someday the amnesia would leave him.

Without really planning it, he ended up outside the City Hospital. Was Felicity working today? He sat on a bench in view of the place where he'd learned terrible truths about himself. He, who valued loyalty and trust above everything except his faith, had lived a lie by serving one side while supporting the other.

And that's just what he knew. What did his amnesia hide? What had he done?

He wanted to trust that others like Felicity, Ash, and Julia would be there for him, but he wasn't worthy of such trust. Evidently, he had been taking care of himself during those lost years. He'd been on his own. Independent. That was best now too.

But maybe he could become worthy of their trust. First, he must discover his past.

Closing his eyes, he rubbed his throbbing temples.

Felicity always soothed him. What could he use as an excuse to go inside the ward?

His bandages hadn't been changed. That was a good reason to drop by.

~

"What's he doing back here?" Bessie tugged on Felicity's sleeve on Tuesday morning as they bandaged a sleeping soldier's stump after surgery to remove his arm.

Felicity followed her gaze toward the open ward door. Her heart lurched at the lost little boy look on Luke's face as he stared at new patients lounging or sitting in the aisle. What brought him here?

"Wasn't your beau discharged yesterday?"

Felicity flinched. Bessie didn't know how close to the truth she was—her coworker meant the remark derisively. Only Dr. Watkins knew their true relationship. "Yes." Did Luke feel worse? He didn't look well. "I'll check on him if you can finish bandaging this man's arm."

"All right. But I get to take a break next time."

Turning away, Felicity rolled her eyes. "Agreed."

Luke scanned the hectic ward until his eyes met hers.

She skirted men sitting in the main aisle without breaking eye contact. "Luke, how are you feeling?"

"Me only complaint is a bit of a headache. 'Tis sorry I am to bother you when you're so busy, Felicity." He laid a hand over his chest.

The pain must be bad for him to mention it. "Did you take your quinine?"

He nodded. "Julia sees to that."

Felicity's throat constricted. *She* wanted to be the one to care for him.

"I almost expect her to chase me with a wooden spoon like me mama did if I don't quickly swallow it." He grinned.

She laughed. That sounded more like the old Luke. "I believe you're on the mend. Shall I change your bandage?"

"If you have a moment." He glanced around the noisy room. "New faces—and not enough beds."

"Some simply require bandages for minor injuries." She tilted her head, sensing a restlessness in him. "Come to the nurses' room with me. I'll take care of you there."

Five soldiers sat in the hall, their backs against the wall. Felicity wove around them to lead Luke downstairs and into the nurses' room.

"Please, take a seat at the table." Lifting the coffeepot from the stove, she swirled it. Good. Several cups left. "Want some coffee?"

"I will pour us a cup while you gather supplies." Rising, he gripped the table.

"Did you get up too quickly?" She took a step toward him, managing to stop short of bracing his elbow. His independent spirit wouldn't appreciate the help.

"Aye." He didn't meet her gaze.

Compassion filled her. "Please sit. It will take but a moment to pour."

"Aye." He sat abruptly.

She set a cup of the hot beverage in front of him, all too aware of how many men upstairs required her attention. "Let's change that bandage." She cut the old one off. No bloodstains. "Your wound is healing."

"Due to your good care."

A warm feeling spread across her chest. She stood so close to him that her leg rested against his. No, she mustn't notice such things. Not until he recovered his memories of her, though that would wait at least a month if her fervent prayers were answered. "H-how do you like staying with the Mitchells?"

"They've made an old friend most welcome." He stared at her as she worked. "Did you know Ash has offered to train me as a saddler?"

"I heard that." She'd been thrilled when Julia told her. "I'm happy for you."

"'Tis a great opportunity."

"Indeed. I believe Ash will be a patient teacher." She stepped away reluctantly. "There. All finished. Did that bring some relief?"

"Aye." He stood.

She looked up into his beloved brown eyes, longing for recognition of their prior courtship and found none of it. Her head must constantly remind her heart that his continued amnesia was an answered prayer...yet, oh, how her heart ached in response. She stepped back. "I'll stop in at Julia's on Thursday to change it again."

"That day marks the beginning of 1863." He spoke softly.

"That's right. It's been so hectic, I'd forgotten that tomorrow is New Year's Eve." She had spent the last one without him.

"Ye have patients. I will go." He stepped to the doorway. "Much obliged for all you've done, Felicity. Thank you."

"It's my pleasure, Luke." As he left, a piece of her heart went with him.

Each day he didn't remember her grew more painful. Yet she prayed he'd not remember her until after the army discharged him so he could remain in Vicksburg. She'd talk to Julia again about not agitating Luke by trying to spark old memories. That should protect him without betraying her conversation with Dr. Watkins.

However, Luke must remember her at some point...or her heart would shrivel like a grape on the vine.

~

"Felicity, did the City Hospital receive many wounded from the recent battle?" Mrs. Martha Dodd, Julia's mother, spoke from the head of the linen-covered dining table. It was large enough to seat twenty, but on this New Year's Day, it held only eleven with the addition of Ash, Julia, Eddie, Luke, Aunt Mae, Uncle Charles, Petunia, and her children. Extra chairs had been removed, and everyone had an arm's length of room on each side. A gleaming cherry wood sideboard held a silver tea urn and a bowl of sugar cubes. A five-year-old painting of Mrs. Dodd with her late husband, Julia, and Eddie adorned the wall.

"It was quite busy the past three days." Felicity looked up from her slice of chess pie, nearly too tired to eat the delicious dessert. "I don't know how many patients we received compared to the other hospital, but there were about one hundred soldiers injured in the fighting. Minor injuries were bandaged, and the soldiers were sent back to their regiments."

"It could have been far worse." Uncle Charles, having finished his dessert, sat back against his chair with a satisfied gleam. "A clear victory for our brave Southern men. I'm quite proud of them."

Felicity had discovered Julia's Unionist loyalties months ago, support she suspected Ash shared. Perhaps Mrs. Dodd as well. This was the day Lincoln's Emancipation Proclamation freeing slaves in the Confederate states became law, something Uncle Charles and many Southerners believed he had no authority to do. Though he didn't employ enslaved staff, his anger had burned to learn of the proclamation months before. Hopefully, no one would bring up the controversial topic and ruin the comradery of the gathering.

"It requires great courage to face an enemy army." Aunt Mae smiled at Luke, who sat opposite Felicity. "Luke has displayed such bravery over and over."

She tensed. Her aunt had been warned not to refer to their prior relationship. Felicity had half expected Luke to remember her aunt and uncle, since he had for everyone *except* Felicity so far, but he hadn't. It was some comfort not to be the only one he'd forgotten.

"Oh? Do tell us about it." Petunia looked up from slicing bite-sized pieces of ham for Little Miles, whose chair held two additional cushions to help him reach the table.

"Sad to say that's part of the haze in me memory." Luke gave Petunia and Aunt Mae a sad smile. "It makes me head ache so, trying to remember."

"No need to force it." Felicity wiggled her eyebrows at Aunt Mae. "Dr. Watkins no doubt warned that pain may continue for a while."

"Aye. I cannot claim to be unwarned." Luke toyed with his half-eaten pie. "One thing I do recall is me ma's chess pie. A treat, indeed, as this is. Please extend me compliments to Hester."

The others added their thanks.

Mrs. Dodd suggested they move to the parlor.

"Luke, let's play draughts." Eddie walked in between Luke and Ash.

"And I'll play the winner." Ash ruffled Eddie's blond hair, making it stick up at the crown.

Felicity stopped Julia in the hall as the others entered the parlor. "Please try to steer the conversation from Luke's past whenever possible. Recall that the doctor said we must not agitate him."

"Of course. Thanks for the reminder. Certainly no one wants him to remember more than you." Julia squeezed her arm. "By the way, you are handling this difficult situation with grace and dignity. I'm proud of you."

Tears scratched at the back of her throat. "I don't know how strong I feel on the inside, but it's good to know my hurt doesn't show," she whispered.

"You may talk to me anytime."

"Thanks. By the way, I should be able to return to work on January fifth." Her job as a maid usually required her services Mondays, Wednesdays, and Thursdays. By the fifth, it would be three weeks without pay, and she needed it.

"That will be lovely." She glanced inside the room, where her mama was looking at them with raised brows. "For now, we must join the others."

Straightening her shoulders, Felicity followed. It was getting harder rather than easier to pretend when she was in Luke's company.

CHAPTER 8

"*'T*is a need I have to work." Luke stepped into Ash's shop following breakfast the day after New Year's, determined to begin his training. Seeing Felicity's exhaustion after working daily for at least two weeks had spurred him to action.

Ash stopped cutting a strip of leather. "No rush. Give yourself time to heal."

"Nay. I must pay me way." Luke folded his arms. A man needed to earn his keep, as his pa had taught him.

Ash studied his determined face. "I should have figured you'd be stubborn about your independence. You were like this after your parents died."

That was a relief. His pa had ingrained hard work along with Bible reading in his upbringing. Maybe he hadn't lost everything about himself. "All I have to do is study on me past. Trying to penetrate that shrouded mist makes me head ache even worse. Please, Ash. It'd be a kindness."

He rubbed his chin. "I'll agree with some conditions."

Luke rocked back on his heels, waiting.

"You work in one-hour shifts and then rest. If that makes

you worse, you're done for the day. Maybe two. You'll return to the shop when the pain eases." Eyebrows raised, Ash tilted his head. "Agreed?"

"Reluctantly." Honestly, he probably wasn't worth more than two hours today. It was a start. "What else?"

"I will pay you as you apprentice here."

"You're giving me room and board for free already."

"All right. I'll factor that into your pay."

It was fair. "Agreed." Luke shook his hand.

"You've always been great with your hands, so the basics should come quickly. Making saddles is a skill that takes months to learn well. The passing years will only hone those skills." Ash held up a strip of leather. "This will be a billet strap. Let's begin with that."

"Obliged to you, Ash. For everything." Luke's throat tightened. A chance to learn a new skill in a city where soldiers outnumbered the citizens was a blessing, for sure.

"Then understand it's my privilege, my friend." Ash laid a warm hand on his shoulder.

As Luke listened to Ash's explanations, he wondered what Felicity would think if she could see him. Would she be proud?

~

*F*elicity washed and changed into a blue wool dress after her shift on Saturday. It had been difficult not to see Luke yesterday, but she'd had no good excuse to visit the Mitchell home. Not that she needed one, really, since she and Julia were friends.

Yet everything was different now, with Luke living there and not realizing she was his girl. She hurried downstairs and into the parlor where Aunt Mae knitted by the fire. "I'm going to Julia's. Luke needs his bandage changed."

Aunt Mae's brow puckered. "Charles won't be home from

the foundry for two more hours, when I'll serve chicken stew for supper. I should probably go with you and thank Julia once again for supper the other night, but Petunia was over earlier for the first time since she moved back home. I'm quite happy relaxing before the fire after running after Little Miles and Wilma while Petunia went to the market."

"Please, stay in your comfortable chair." Relieved to go on her own, Felicity spoke quickly. She sympathized, for as much as she loved her little cousins, they sometimes wore her out too. "Julia may invite me to supper."

"If so, have Luke and Ash escort you home. We ran the Yankees off, so we're not in danger right now." Aunt Mae frowned. "Still, there are many soldiers on our streets, strangers to us. I can't feel easy about you traipsing home after dark."

"I'll do that." Hurrying away before her aunt could change her mind and accompany her, anyway, Felicity lifted her warm cloak from a hall hook.

She carried her basket containing bandages, scissors, and lint through sunny streets. Mothers with their children scampering after them headed to the heart of town where many of the shops were located. A group of soldiers smoked cigars outside a grocery store. She crossed the street, avoiding even a glance at the dozen or so men who looked her way.

Felicity quite liked the idea of Luke escorting her home on lamplit streets, as he had done so often in the past. Would those days return?

"I've a mind to accompany you and Julia to church in the morning, Ash." Luke set down a forkful of chicken pie. Felicity had stayed for supper after changing his bandage, a hearty meal they consumed in the cozy dining room opposite the main parlor. "It doesn't seem as though I've missed more than a couple of weeks at that beloved Baptist church, but I'd be obliged for the company." His amnesia made him skittish about greeting folks he should know.

"I don't know if that's a good idea." Felicity raised her brows at Julia.

"Is there a medical reason for me to stay away?" Didn't his faith need to be grounded again back at the church he'd attended with his family? "If I rise slowly, the dizziness isn't as bad."

"Not really. It's just...the doctor doesn't want you agitated." She glanced at Julia.

"Then he can be at ease. Attending services can only calm my spirits." It was good of Felicity to care so much.

"I started attending the Methodist church with Julia's family when we began courting." Ash sipped his coffee and then looked over at his wife. "I've no objection to attending with you a month or two. Julia?"

"I'd enjoy it. Mama and Eddie might even join us on a few occasions. We're all invited to dine at her home tomorrow after the service. Felicity, please pass the invitation on to your aunt and uncle. It will be a casual family lunch."

"Thank you. I'm certain they'll be happy to attend." Felicity gripped her fork. Her brow puckered.

"Luke..." Julia turned to him. "Felicity also attends your church."

His gaze flew to her wide blue eyes. Held her gaze in panic. He'd still need Ash and Julia because Luke couldn't attend church with Felicity and her aunt and uncle. Why, some would see that as his intention to court her. That he could not do. A man with amnesia couldn't be certain what—or who—was in his past. Why, he might have a sweetheart back in Virginia. Until he knew, there'd be no thoughts of courtship. Besides, he'd best concentrate on learning the saddle-making business before considering taking a wife. "Ye implied I wasn't a stranger to you at the hospital. Did we meet at church?"

"We did." Her eyes darkened as she stared at him.

"Aye. That explains our prior meeting." He was satisfied, though it still was a wonder that he'd forgotten such a fetching, compassionate woman. It must have been a passing acquaintance.

~

*L*uke ended up between Felicity and Julia at church the next morning, exactly where he'd resolved *not* to sit.

But the feeling of homecoming when he stepped into the building had been so welcome that he'd paid no attention to anything beyond the familiar sights of the stained glass windows, the cross hanging behind the lectern.

He could only pray no one misread the situation. After all, Felicity's aunt sat beside her with her uncle at the end. Ash, Eddie, and Mrs. Dodd were on Julia's other side, so it made sense.

A few folks turned around to wave or smile at him. Some faces he recognized. Others he didn't. He prayed they'd understand.

After the service, folks scarcely waited for Luke to reach the aisle hastening to greet him, a warm welcome in their eyes.

"It's good to see you back from war." A middle-aged man wearing an expensive coat shook Luke's hand.

"Thank you, sir. 'Tis good to be home." Best keep his comments general because he didn't recall this man. Sweat beaded on his brow.

"I see you have a head injury." The brown-haired man with a mustache glanced at Luke's bandage. "What happened?"

"Shrapnel. Battlefield surgeons got most of that out and

then the surgeon here cleaned it further." It was easier to spout what he'd been told than admit his forgetfulness.

"Ah, I see." The man glanced at Felicity. "It's good that your girl works at the hospital."

"Me pardon, sir?" Luke's face tingled, and then the shock waves raced to his heart. Did the man mean to say...

"I'm certain it was a blessing to see Miss Danielson there." His gaze traveled past Luke's shoulder. "Ash, it's good to see you. How are your dear mama and sisters?"

Luke scarcely heard his friend's response. She had known him. She'd fainted when he didn't remember her. Could it be... He turned to Felicity, whose ashen face and tormented eyes confirmed the stranger's claim. "Pardon me, I won't be joining ye for lunch, after all. Me head aches abominably."

He stalked away from folks gaping at him, wanting a word with him. He had none to give them.

He put on his kepi when reaching the frigid streets. Long strides took him away with no idea of where to go, for where did his memories lodge?

What pain he must have caused Felicity the past three weeks, all unknowingly. How could he have forgotten the woman he courted?

"Luke, wait!" Ash's voice.

He didn't feel too kindly toward his best friend right now. He kept going.

"Luke, you know my limp slows me on these hills. Please, slow down."

Aye, he knew Ash's long-ago injury hindered his pace. Why did he remember the details of the horse kicking Ash and forget Felicity? He stopped without turning around.

Ash reached his side, breathing hard. "I'm sorry, my friend. We didn't mean for you to find out that way."

"Aye, ye are me friend. Why keep such an important aspect

of me life from me?" Churchgoers, staring curiously, milled around them.

"The doctor's advice was to allow you to remember things at your own pace, as you could handle it." Ash's eyes were nearly as tormented as Felicity's had been. "Please, let's you and me go back to the house and talk." He frowned at a family who'd stopped on the sidewalk and unashamedly listened. "Everyone else will attend the luncheon."

"Nay, I need to clear me head first." Luke shoved his hands into his pockets. "I'd be obliged if you'd wait on me there." He had questions.

"Agreed." Ash hung his head. "I'll be waiting."

Luke strode away, unable to forgive himself for the pain he'd unwittingly caused such a compassionate woman. How was he ever to face her again?

~

Felicity was grateful Julia stuck by her side during the tormentingly long meal, for she could barely think, much less eat the roasted beef that tasted like sawdust on her tongue.

Eddie was subdued since Ash and Luke hadn't come. He asked to go to Julia's house, a request firmly squelched until after school the next day.

Felicity was glad her friends respected Luke's privacy. He hadn't been ready for the news. The doctor's counsel to keep quiet about the topic had been wise. They'd heeded it, but there had been no way to protect him once he'd insisted on going about in public. She'd tried to prevent it but couldn't without giving away the doctor's secret decision.

How happy she'd been to sit at his side at church, a safe haven. She'd planned to stay by Luke's side and prevent personal conversations, but he'd exited the pew away from her. Mr. Maxwell couldn't be blamed for his innocent question. Some folks knew of Luke's amnesia, but it hadn't been mentioned in the newspapers—only that he was recovering from a head wound. If it hadn't been Mr. Maxwell, it would have been someone else.

No, her anger was directed at herself. She should have done a better job of forcing herself between Luke and other church-goers, perhaps dragged him out immediately following the closing prayer. Luke's shattered look at finding out he'd been courting her hadn't been the emotion she'd hoped to see when he learned the truth of their relationship. It splintered her heart.

"Felicity?" Julia's voice penetrated her sorrow. "Do you want a slice of apple pie? Hester made it with dried apples."

"None for me." She'd barely touched her lunch. Mrs. Dodd shouldn't have to waste food on her account. "Everything was delicious," she lied. It had tasted of ashes.

"I'll have some later, Mama." Julia stood. "I'm certain you all won't mind if I whisk Felicity away for a few minutes."

"Not at all." Mrs. Dodd gave Felicity a sympathetic look. "We'll retire to the parlor after our dessert."

"Go ahead, dear." Aunt Mae's hand trembled as she patted her mouth with a white linen napkin. "No hurry on our account."

"We'll return shortly." Felicity followed Julia into the hall. "Thank you."

"Of course." Julia squeezed her hand. "Come upstairs to our family parlor."

Felicity climbed the stairs and entered the chilly room, grateful beyond words to be away from curious eyes.

Julia built up the fire in the fireplace before sitting in the cushioned chair adjacent to Felicity's. "I can't tell you how sorry I am. I secretly hoped someone would mention your courtship. I truly thought it would be a blessing all around."

"Oh, Julia, did you notice how shattered he looked?" Felicity fished a handkerchief from her pocket and swiped at a single tear.

"Ash fears Luke will feel betrayed. Ash has had much practice keeping secrets." Her cheeks flushed scarlet. "As we all have, I'm certain."

War secrets, possibly? "No doubt, he's right. Luke prizes loyalty in a friend." Felicity rubbed a trembling hand across her clammy forehead. "What am I to do?"

"You know him best." Julia folded her hands in her lap. "What do you think?"

Felicity stared into the fire beginning to sweep over the logs and knew the answer. "He'll want time to think. In Luke's mind, I was his nurse and your friend. Though there were times when I dared to believe..."

"Yes?" Julia leaned closer.

"Well, just before his discharge at the hospital, he stared into my eyes as if sorry he'd never see me again. I saw what I wanted to see, not what was really happening." Heat rushed up her face at her admission. "His shock today proves how wrong I was. He thinks of me as his nurse."

"Give him time." Julia's tone was urgent. "Don't give up on him."

What if finding out she was his girl led to other memories returning? A chill spread over her heart. Dr. Watkins would send him back to Virginia.

That must not happen.

CHAPTER 9

*L*uke walked in the winter's chill until his feet turned numb, reeling with shock. How could he have forgotten such a wonderful, compassionate woman? The soft curve of her cheeks, eyes the color of a brilliant summer sky, and blond curls that bounced off her shoulders when she quickly turned her head...why didn't he remember? Worse that that was the pain he'd undoubtedly caused by forgetting her.

The best question of all was, why hadn't Ash told him? He stalked to his temporary home and asked him.

"The doctor instructed us not to agitate you." Ash gestured to a chair in front of the parlor fireplace.

"Good job on that, buddy." Luke's temper was no cooler than the crackling fire that prompted him to remove his coat before sitting. Not that he wanted to sit, but it wasn't worth an argument.

"I know. I'm sorry." Resting his elbows on the armrests, Ash put his fingertips together in a prayerful pose. "I talked to him for a long time. Since you still suffer from memory loss, Dr.

Watkins suspects you suffered some trauma beyond your head wound."

Luke slumped against the cushioned chair. "Like what?" He'd feared something prevented his memories, that he had done some terrible thing. He wasn't worthy of Felicity.

"It's anyone's guess, until you remember." Ash stood. "You must be frozen. Jolene left us a pot of coffee and a sandwich—"

"Nothing for me." Luke rubbed his throbbing temples. "Did ye even consider poor Felicity's feelings in all this? How she must despise me."

"Far from it. She understands more than you realize." He hesitated. "She'd do anything to help you."

"Tell me about her." Luke steeled himself.

"You met at church about three years ago, about the time she became friends with Julia." Ash stared into the fire. "I wasn't calling on Julia at that point, though I wanted to. Our time wasn't right yet."

That's why he didn't remember Ash courting Julia.

"You were courting Felicity when you mustered into the Confederate army. The two of you wrote to one another while you were gone." He looked across at Luke with a sad smile. "You both attended our September wedding."

Frustration escalated. "None of this do I remember. Do you know if Felicity expected a proposal?"

"Those are private matters between you." Ash frowned. "I don't wish to overwhelm you. There's no need to shove the whole pie in your mouth at once. Take it in small pieces, as it comes. God may be protecting you from something."

"Not what I want to hear." Yet whatever was hidden in his past tormented him. "I'd appreciate some solitude. I'll take a plate and my coffee to my room"

"Best take your next dose of medicine if you don't want to be disturbed."

Luke took it, knowing Julia would bring it to him if he didn't.

That night, he was awakened by a nightmare. He dreamed he was in the river again, swimming with all his might to save his parents...and never reaching them.

He awoke with a blistering headache that medicine didn't ease. Maybe he'd be better off not taking it. He'd go a day without it. If he felt the same tomorrow, he'd dispense with the medicine.

His solace would have to come from working, as it had after his parents' deaths.

First, he reached for the scissors he'd found in Julia's sewing basket to cut strips of cloth from his head. Felicity wasn't going to be subjected to changing his bandages anymore. Had she kept up the practice as an excuse to see him, be close to him?

He shuddered, not in revulsion but from shame. A beautiful girl like her deserved a better man than himself, one who understood his past so that he might learn from his mistakes.

This morning, he'd work with Ash as long as his aching head allowed. Felicity was coming to clean today. He'd seek her out and apologize as soon as he felt strong enough, though what one said to mend such an offense was beyond his ken.

~

"Where's Luke?" Felicity stepped inside the Mitchell residence the next morning when Julia opened wide the front door.

"In the shop with Ash." After closing the door, Julia guided her into the parlor. "The two men had a long talk yesterday. Ash didn't answer all of his questions about you."

"Such as?" Felicity leaned closer.

"He wanted to know how long you'd courted, whether the two of you had discussed marriage."

"We did," Felicity whispered. "He planned to propose after the war ended *and* he had a steady job." They'd both been saving money for their future. Luke had even given her fifty dollars of his pay in the fall to add to her savings for their wedding. The bookbindery had closed by then. The money had given her confidence they'd actually marry. His face yesterday had stripped her of that confidence. "How is he?"

"I doubt he slept." She started to speak and then stopped.

"What is it?" Felicity braced herself.

"Well, he cut off his bandages. Said to tell you he doesn't need them."

Stung, she closed her eyes. How she'd enjoyed the excuse to get close to him, to touch him. "He's right. Should I avoid him?"

"He may come to you, but if you're expecting him to start courting you..." Julia shook her head. "Ash says that's unlikely until he actually recovers his memories."

Felicity gasped. What if that never happened? "Did Luke say that?"

"No, just Ash's impressions from their conversation."

Feeling the warmth from the fire, Felicity removed her cloak. "It's the amnesia. It weighs on him." It was impossible to admit that she prayed for his memories to remain lost for a few more weeks.

"Agreed. Now, do you want a muffin before you start cleaning?"

"No." She couldn't eat with her stomach in tangles. "Shall I start in here?" There was a layer of dust on the mantel.

"Yes, please. I kept up with it as well as I could with all that's been happening."

"Say no more. That's why I'm here." And grateful for the job, because her future with Luke was in limbo.

*L*uke cut a piece of leather to Ash's specifications later that morning. It was difficult to concentrate with cold wind sweeping through the shop. "Do ye mind if I close the door?"

Ash, standing near to observe his cuts, tensed. "I find I can't abide being shut inside the shop any longer."

"'Tis nothing new." Ash had shunned being closed up in small places for years. The stove in the corner barely heated to a radius of two feet in this frigid weather. Luke set down the knife to rub his hands together. "But don't you shut the door on cold days?"

"Not this winter." Ash stared at the open door. "I'm sorry. I'll explain it someday. Warm yourself inside the house. You've been hard at it all morning. Besides, lunch is in thirty minutes."

"Time enough for me to apologize to Felicity." It wasn't a conversation he wanted to have. How he hated disappointing her.

"Yes, talk to her." Ash blew on his hands. "But Luke..."

He stopped at the threshold.

"Your amnesia isn't your fault. She understands."

"Then she understands more than me." Luke walked the stone path to the house. He paused at the door to whisper a quick prayer for the right words and then pushed it open. There she was in the dining room, dressed in a brown dress adorned with a white apron. How blessed he had been to court such a beautiful, kind woman. Perhaps when he recovered...no, he mustn't allow himself to think of something that might never happen. He didn't even know himself anymore.

He stepped inside the dining room where she dusted the sideboard. "Felicity, have ye a minute to spare?"

"Always." Drawing a ragged breath, she laid her duster on the long serving table that bordered the sideboard. "Shall we talk in the parlor?"

"Aye." He stepped back to allow her room to pass with the scent of lilacs—one he'd forevermore associate with her. He followed it across the hall. "Shall we sit?"

She chose the sofa. "I've wanted to apologize to you."

"And I you." He sat beside her. "Though you have no reason to express regret for your actions. You've been nothing but kind to me."

"I wanted to tell you immediately." She bunched her crisp apron into knots. "Dr. Watkins advised otherwise."

"As much as it pains me, the dear doctor was right. This shock has stymied me." He rubbed his hand over his knees. "I can only imagine the hurt it caused when I referred to you as Miss Danielson. 'Tis sorry I am...sorrier than I can say."

"I understand." She spread her crumpled apron across her lap. "Truly, I do."

How easy it would be to accept the caring concern she offered. He must be strong. "One might expect our courtship to continue." His gaze dropped to the rug. "But that would be wrong."

A tiny gasp.

He darted a glance in her direction. Her face had paled. The hair stiffened on the back of his neck. He'd wounded her again. He stood. Began to pace. "Five years are lost to me, including the part of me that knew you. It cannot be as it was." He stopped before the fireplace and turned to her. He must not bind her to himself until he learned what those years held.

"I hope we can be friends..." Her voice trailed off. She looked away.

"Aye, one hopes for that much." He'd run out of words to comfort her. "Though I don't remember it, I served as a soldier. This struggle to recall those missing years feels like the battle of me life."

She stood. Those magnificent blue eyes latched onto his.

"Then know I will help in whatever way I can." With that, she left the room.

Leaving him with the broken heart he'd thought he'd leave her.

~

 $\mathcal{J}$ t was easy for Felicity to avoid Luke, for he went to his room following their conversation. Ash took a sandwich up to his room with his medicine. Within minutes, he was back to say that Luke would try to ease his headache by napping.

After she swept the rugs on the main floor, Felicity sought out Julia, who tatted lace in her cozy parlor on the second floor. "I'm leaving now. I'll be at the hospital tomorrow and be back on Wednesday."

Julia set her tatting aside and rose to shut the door. "Won't you tell me about it?"

Felicity didn't know if she could squeeze the words from her tear-clogged throat.

"Let's sit."

She sat before the fire in the small hearth and told Julia about her conversation with Luke.

"Hope isn't lost." Julia spoke softly. "Ash said that, according to Dr. Watkins, most amnesia patients he or the other doctors have treated recalled most things within a few hours or days. He's not personally seen a case where it lasted beyond three weeks."

That must be why he'd stipulated waiting an additional month. Despite her friend's reassurance, there were no guarantees. "Please don't worry about me. I'm fine." *Liar*. Her heart felt as if it were cracking. "Luke is the most important one."

"I've been sitting up here with the door open to hear when

he emerges from his room. Do you mind checking if his door is adjar?"

"Of course not." Felicity opened the door with a peek into the hall. No Luke. She returned to the fire but didn't sit. "He's not there."

"I'll have Ash check on him later." Julia hugged her. "You're in my prayers."

She needed them. "Please, pray for Luke."

"I am. So are Ash, Mama, and Eddie." She put a hand over her mouth. "Why, he's supposed to come after school. That will be a great reason to get Luke out of bed."

"Agreed. Enjoy your visit."

Felicity said her goodbyes and left as soon as she fetched her cloak. Seeing Eddie would do them all a world of good... while Felicity was a reminder of what Luke had forgotten.

CHAPTER 10

$\mathcal{F}$elicity reached her ward the next morning before dawn. Bessie hadn't arrived yet, and only one lantern near the door was lit. Most patients in the nearly full ward were sleeping, proven by an overabundance of snores. A new patient, Seth Albers, shifted restlessly in the bed Luke had vacated. In the past week, two patients had occupied that same cot.

The war went on even if she felt a part of her had died along with her dreams of a happy marriage with Luke. How she missed him needing her, if only to deliver medicines and meals.

She shook her head to clear such thoughts. Her patients needed her. Such as the new one. She hurried to his side. "Mr. Albers?"

Above a bushy beard, brown eyes squinted up at her. "Yes?"

"I'm Miss Felicity Danielson, your nurse," she whispered. "You seem to be in some discomfort." The man suffered from dysentery, an illness that had claimed a few lives at the City Hospital since she began volunteering.

"I am. Can I trouble you to bring my medicine? The night

attendant helped me to the privy but didn't bring more Dover's powder."

"I'll fetch it." She'd read the doctor's notes about him before coming to the ward, and the medicine could have been given at three. Wyatt might have fallen asleep in the chair he kept near the door at night so he'd know when one of the patients got up. She'd speak to him. She was back with the medication and a dipper of water within five minutes.

Mr. Albers slurped the water with the powders. "Thirsty too. My thanks."

"You weren't sent to us due to battle, right?" She dropped the dipper back into the water bucket.

"Nah, the Army of Tennessee sent me home to recuperate as they were leaving a battle at Murfreesboro and heading toward Tullahoma. That's in Tennessee too. Some of the fellows said we were winning when we pulled out and couldn't figure why General Bragg had us up and run." The man, who appeared to be in his mid-twenties, slumped against the pillow. "I was too sick to fight. My wife brought me in yesterday. Said I was getting worse, not better."

"She did the right thing." Felicity touched his forehead. A fever but not alarmingly high. "Try to sleep. I'll bring you broth when you awaken."

"Thanks, but my wife might be here by then. She's coming after my boy goes to school." He closed his eyes.

Glad for both bits of information, Felicity hurried to the nurse's room to make a note on Seth's chart about receiving his medication. First, it relieved her load when wives, mothers, and sisters took over the main care of their loved ones, such as feeding them. Second, he'd said that the Army of Tennessee was headed to Tullahoma. Did the Union army know it? Such information would help plan upcoming attacks, no doubt.

This was the second time she'd discovered useful information recently. There had to be reason. Here was something she

89

could do, a way to serve the Union. Whom could she tell? Julia was a Unionist, and she'd hinted that Ash knew how to keep a secret. She'd seek out Julia and Ash while working tomorrow to ask if they knew whom to share such information with—and if it was important.

She hurried back to the ward, equally afraid and excited with her decision. Bessie was late, a common occurrence. Felicity offered water to the half-dozen patients already awake. A few minutes later, Bessie passed her with the briefest of greetings as Felicity left the ward to fetch breakfast. The embittered woman only cared about healing her patients to send them back to their regiments. To her, the South must win at all costs to punish the Yankees who killed her fiancé.

Such an attitude gave Felicity pause. Spying was a betrayal to her patients, to Aunt Mae, and to Uncle Charles. Sharing information she learned in the course of her job with the Union could place these soldiers in danger. It was a betrayal she didn't take lightly, but she had been hoping for a way to stop the endless parade of wounded soldiers for months.

Doing *anything* that would hurt Luke while he was fighting for the Confederacy had been out of the question. He wasn't facing the Northern army toting a loaded musket now. If God answered her prayers, he'd be honorably discharged because of his amnesia.

Even so, her dreams to marry Luke lay in ashes for the foreseeable future. She was a plain, simple woman. Certainly not significant enough that Luke remembered her. Nor was she able to give him what he most wanted—his memory.

A sigh escaped her. If she dwelt on that sorrow, she'd lose her courage.

The money she'd saved for their marriage could be put toward purchasing a seamstress shop—like the one she'd worked in last year with the main residence above the shop. Unfortunately, Mrs. Cummings, her boss, had closed her shop when folks stopped placing orders. Money had grown scarcer. So had fabric because few ships came into the harbor.

No, the shop must wait until after the hostilities ended.

In the meantime, serving her country in this small way was something important she might be able to accomplish to end the hostilities and help everyone get back to normal life. But how did one go about this spying business?

~

"The tasks left for me have been done long hence." On Tuesday afternoon, Luke put his hands on his hips as Ash limped into the shop and added a single skin to the stack used to make saddles. "Ye've been gone all day. Why didn't ye take me along?" Felicity had been so hurt yesterday by his decision not to court. Since then, the sorrow in her eyes had been his constant companion. He needed work to occupy him.

"You must have a pass to leave the city. We'll get you one." Ash eyed his soldier's garb. "And some everyday clothes more befitting a saddler than a soldier."

Luke rubbed his hand across his gray wool jacket, none too warm. "I've not been discharged from the army."

"No, and my hope is, the doctor won't send you back when you can't remember your training."

"Aye." The possibility of returning to the war made his blood run cold. "I'll ask Dr. Watkins about a discharge. Then a visit to the tailor is in order once I receive my pay this week."

"I can give you what you've earned so far, but the tailor left town in December when General Sherman's army threatened our city." Ash rubbed his jaw. "I know a good seamstress—two of them, in fact—who had plenty of experience sewing men's clothing last year."

"Be they reasonable?" Luke was ready to rid himself of these clothes.

"Very. Felicity used to make her living in a seamstress shop. Julia volunteered there for months to help clothe Southern soldiers."

The ever-present ache in Luke's head began to pound. "I can't ask the very woman whom I cannot recall *courting* to make me trousers and blouses."

"Why not?" Ash sat on a bench, stretching out his legs. "It wouldn't be the first time."

"Ye mean..." Luke surveyed his nearly new gray trousers.

"Yep. When you left in the fall, you wore a uniform Felicity finished while you were here."

"Will me debts to the woman never cease?" Felicity had made the very clothes he was wearing. Luke raked his fingers across a wrinkled brow. "I can't ask her to do more."

"It's not a debt. You'll pay her, just as Julia does for her to serve as our maid." Ash folded his arms. "If you ask me, Felicity will appreciate the extra income. She lost her home when her parents died three years ago and now lives with her aunt and uncle. From what I've gleaned from Julia, they don't charge Felicity room and board, but she's too proud to accept anything beyond that. She's independent—and a hard worker."

Admirable. No wonder he'd fallen in love with such an amazing woman.

"Julia and I hire her whenever we need seamstress work. In fact, Felicity altered Julia's wedding dress and made you a coat and trousers. It wasn't completed for the occasion, but you wore it to some celebrations afterward." Ash massaged his leg.

Where were the clothes? He could wear them to church or occasions like supper at the Dodds. "Did Julia store them?"

"I'll ask her, but my best bet is Felicity."

Luke's was too. "Just how long did I court Felicity?"

"I told you...no details." Ash's face shuttered. "Not from me or Julia—especially after how upset you were after learning about your relationship with Felicity."

"From a total stranger, not me friend." Luke's stomach hardened to recall it. "Ye'd not put me in the same position again, would you?"

"Mr. Maxwell isn't a stranger. He's just another person—"

"I don't remember." Luke drummed his fingers on a work table. "How many more surprises await me?"

Ash hung his head. "Let's give you time to heal. There's a lot to tell."

Aye, five years of living. His frustration mounted.

∼

*A*n hour later, Luke strode to the hospital in the blustery breeze that eased his headache a bit. Gray skies fit his mood. Felicity worked at the hospital on Tuesdays. Luke hoped to avoid her, for both of their sakes. This visit was for Dr. Watkins.

Once inside the familiar hospital, Luke peeked into the nurses' room. His heart sank.

"Luke?" Felicity, standing in front of a cupboard, held a medicine bottle. "Are you feeling worse?"

His jaw clenched. He was tired of questions about his health. "Nay. Is Dr. Watkins about?"

"He's in my ward. I'm taking him this medicine." She studied him. "Shall I ask him to come down when he's finished?"

"Aye. Thank you." Gratitude welled up that she didn't probe the reason for his visit.

She poured coffee from a pot on the stove. "Have a cup of coffee while you wait."

"Obliged to you." Those blue eyes saw too much. He looked away. A slight breeze let him know she was gone. He slumped into a hard wooden chair to wait. His coffee was half gone when he heard footsteps. A man appeared in the doorway. "Dr. Watkins, I regret bothering you."

"No bother, Luke." The doctor sank onto the chair beside him. "What brings you here?"

"When will I be discharged from the army?'

He frowned. "Who have you been talking to?"

"Ash asked me about wearing clothes other than my uniform." Luke looked at him directly. "Is that allowed before my discharge?"

"There's a shortage of fabric. Our women stopped stitching uniforms months ago. Quite a number of my patients wear farm clothes or whatever they have these days, so wearing other clothes isn't of great concern." Dr. Watkins eyed him. "I've not decided to request your discharge."

Luke gulped. He couldn't go back to...what? He touched his wound. He didn't know what a battle looked like...just how a man came out scarred.

"You were wounded on December thirteenth. Today is January sixth—not even a month of recuperation." He titled his head, studying him. "Let's wait a while on that decision, shall we?" He stood.

Luke rose also, slowly. This wasn't the news he wanted or expected.

"We'll talk again in two weeks." The doctor gave a crisp nod and hurried from the room.

Two weeks. How long would this go on?

Luke trudged home, regretful that the Confederate army still laid claim to him.

~

The next day, Felicity fidgeted with her apron, trying to delay leaving the Mitchells' kitchen with the lunch tray. When Dr. Watkins had returned to the ward yesterday, he'd only said he'd talk to Luke again in a couple of weeks. No discharge yet. Luke's curiosity was understandable, but the less she said about it the better, for she was scared someone would say or do something that unlocked those memories far too soon. Her nerves were stretched as tight as a guitar string.

"What are you waiting for?" Jolene Hutchins, the Mitchells' cook, furrowed her brow. A white apron covered her high-collared blue dress, and a snood covered her brown hair, arranged in a bun. "Joseph will be home before we serve these sandwiches and soup." Her husband worked at Paxton Foundry, a business that made artillery for the Confederate army.

"Sorry. I'm a little nervous."

"About seeing your beau?" The plain-spoken cook eyed her sympathetically. "I heard him say he wants to focus on getting over his amnesia."

"You heard that?" Felicity blinked.

"Don't look at me like that. I wasn't *trying* to listen. You were in the parlor with the door open. Voices carry down the hall unless you whisper or the door is closed." She shrugged. "'Course, if you was to whisper, I'd wonder what you was saying."

Good to know. She was especially glad to learn it before her conversation about spying with Julia. She'd include a warning for them to always close their doors. "Let's carry these trays in, shall we?" Felicity ate with the family. Jolene liked her own privacy in the kitchen.

"It's for the best, since the soup's getting cold."

Felicity liked her. Her blunt speech ensured one always knew where one stood with her, and Jolene liked Felicity because she did her job.

Julia was already seated in the dining room with Ash and Luke, who seemed frustrated about something. Conversation halted when they entered.

Felicity kept her eyes lowered as she set a plate with a ham sandwich before each person and then took her place at the table opposite Luke.

Ash asked the blessing.

When Luke cleared his throat, she looked up.

"Felicity, Ash says you're a seamstress, and I am a paying customer. Can you make me two sets of clothes, that is, trousers and blouses, and a warm woolen coat?"

She gaped at him. Why hadn't she considered this already? "It would be my privilege. I have fabric that Mrs. Cummings, my former employer, gave me upon leaving the city. I'll start on them tonight." What a comfort to do something that mattered for him.

Putting down her spoon, Julia turned to her. "Luke was just asking me about the suit he wore to parties after my wedding. I don't have it. Do you know what became of it?"

Felicity's gaze captured Luke's. *Please don't remember.* "You remembered something?"

"Nay." With a sigh, he ate a bite of vegetable soup. "Me information comes from Ash."

Her mind traveled back to those happier days. "I have it. You left it with me." Along with nearly all the money he had with him. It didn't seem appropriate to mention it in front of the others, necessitating a private conversation. "You also stored a box of your possessions from your apartment over the book-bindery shop in my aunt's attic. It has a blouse, handkerchiefs, and such, from what Mr. Tomlinson said when he dropped it off to me." Mr. Tomlinson had closed the shop after Union navy boats shelled the city for two months that summer and brought Luke's things to Felicity before leaving town.

Julia gasped. "That's wonderful. Handling those items may spark memories."

Precisely the reason Felicity hadn't yet mentioned it, as Julia should recall. *Not too soon, Lord. Keep those memories at bay a while longer.* Today was only January seventh. They had over three weeks to go, according to Dr. Watkins's original plan.

"Aye. 'Tis possible." Luke gave Felicity a questioning look. "When can I pick up the box?"

"I'll have to locate it." Perhaps she could stall its delivery a bit. "I will bring your suit tomorrow." And his money. No doubt, he needed it.

"Ladies, we'd best get back to work." Ash stood. "A customer is coming for a saddle on Monday."

This was her opportunity. "Might I delay you a moment, Ash? I wanted to speak to you and Julia after clearing the table."

"Of course." Ash glanced at Julia, who shrugged. "Let me get Luke started on his next task. I'll be right in."

Luke studied Felicity's face. "Me thanks for the meal."

She watched him leave, wishing she could tell him her hopes of spying on her patients. Yet Luke was a Confederate soldier, much changed from the fellow she'd known before the war. He'd been quiet about battles and skirmishes in the fall, too, making her wonder which side claimed his loyalty.

All she knew was that she no longer claimed his heart.

~

*F*elicity hurried to the parlor after gathering all the dishes for Jolene. It wasn't part of her job, but these small gestures had early on thawed the cook's reserve toward her.

Was trusting Ash and Julia to advise her a good idea?

Too late now. She'd set everything in motion.

They were already there when she arrived. Ash added another log to the fire and then straightened as Felicity closed the door behind her.

Julia tilted her head. "Is this about Luke?"

"No." Felicity sat in a chair facing the sofa while Ash chose a spot beside his wife. "I shut the door because Jolene mentioned she can hear conversations in the parlor."

Ash and Julia exchanged a wide-eyed glance.

"I know you're a Unionist, Julia." Felicity studied Ash's wary expression. "I am as well. Dare I ask your loyalties, Ash?"

"They are the same as yours." He gave a shaky laugh. "Why broach the topic now, when the war is nearly two years old?"

"Because I sometimes hear things at the hospital," she whispered, "information that might be helpful to the Union."

Ash straightened, all traces of laughter gone. "What did you learn?"

Taking a deep breath, she explained her conversation with Seth Albers, the Confederate patient who'd been sent home from Murfreesboro.

"Troop information is quite valuable to the Union." Ash exchanged a look with Julia, who nodded. "Felicity, you were right to come to me. I'm a Union spy."

"Wh-what did you say?" Her skin tingled. Ash, a spy? Julia had mentioned he knew how to keep a secret. Felicity had hoped for some direction from him, prayed for God's leading. This seemed to solidify that she was right to pass on the information.

"I gather information and then deliver coded messages on up the line." Speaking softly, Ash held Felicity's gaze. "Do you want to help us?"

"Us?" Her gaze flew to Julia, who shook her head.

"Not Julia. There are others." He clasped his hands together. "There's risk involved. Danger of imprisonment, even death, if you're caught."

Her heart skipped a beat. Of course, she'd heard of spies being hanged. Did she really want to take that risk?

"If all you do is tell me your information, you may never be caught." Ash spoke in hushed tones. "It's when you tell others that you're at greater risk. Delivering messages would also place you in danger, but that won't happen."

"Because I'm a woman? Or because I can't handle doing anything important?" Felicity didn't know whether to feel indignant or happy to be spared the peril.

"Because that job's already covered right now, though I'm uncertain what will happen when we move to Texas in the spring. One of my spies will certainly accept my responsibilities." Ash looked at Julia. "How much should I tell her?"

"I'll do it." She patted his hand. "It *is* dangerous, Felicity. We can vouch for it. Last summer, Ash was captured and imprisoned for five days."

Shocked to her core, Felicity covered her mouth with her hands to keep from crying out. "Ash, you're so brave. Both of you."

"He is courageous, though it took a toll on him." Julia glanced at his leg. "Obviously, he escaped, but it's not safe for him to return to that location because he might be recognized."

"Absolutely not." This was more than Felicity imagined. Could she be brave enough?

"I will protect you at all costs. It's imperative you keep my secret. My life isn't worth much if you whisper it to *anyone*." Ash pressed his fingertips together. "Luke won't like it if he ever learns you're spying."

True. If Luke was still her beau, Ash wouldn't have to protect her. Luke would take a bullet for her...at least, the old Luke would have done so, because he'd loved her. "We'll keep one another's secrets." She hesitated. "Luke's too smart for you to fool him long. You should take him into your confidence, and if you must, tell him about my involvement."

"I'm praying about it. He's still not himself." Ash studied the rug and then raised his gaze without raising his head. "Do you know if he's still a Unionist?"

"I only know that he was when he enlisted. He was careful what he said in the fall."

"Luke's the wisest of my friends." Ash gave a slight shake of his head. "Perhaps that caution he lived with so long lingers still, even with amnesia."

Felicity gripped the arms of her chair. "I believe you're right."

"You have a prime opportunity to overhear soldiers talk." Ash leaned toward her. "And whatever you learn from new arrivals is the most important. Once the soldiers have been there several days, it's likely spies and scouts in other areas have already reported any news they had."

"I don't hear it often." Her fingers were icy cold, despite the fire's warmth. They'd explained the risks, and it was more than she'd anticipated. Was it worth it to help the North win the war?

"Doesn't matter. Others report to me." Ash gave her a reassuring smile. "With all the activity in our area, plenty happens every week."

"Thank you for all you're doing, Ash." Gratitude swelled inside her at his sacrifices on the North's behalf. "History will never know how indebted it is to folks like you in ending the war."

"There are many of us longing to remain in oblivion." Ash stood. "Did we just get one more?"

"You did." Excitement kindled in her soul. She'd help the Union. Her greatest desire was to protect Luke from getting sent back to the army. Yet his memories might return despite her best efforts, and how could she hold back that tide if it came?

CHAPTER 11

*L*uke was frustrated with Ash by noon the next day. Not only because the man was on a trip for supplies for the second time in two days, but also because he, Julia, and Felicity had been in a private conversation yesterday. With the door closed, for Luke had gone to fetch his boss after three-quarters of an hour had elapsed. What had they discussed? That Dr. Watkins didn't give Luke hope that he'd be discharged? That the physician simply waited for Luke's memories to return before sending him back to the Twenty-first Mississippi? Or one of the myriad past events Luke couldn't know about until he healed?

Well, he wasn't a wee babe to be coddled but a grown man. One who'd been battle-trained, apparently. Someone who'd lived off his wits.

And something was afoot.

Worse, as he tried to complete the tasks Ash had left for him, he couldn't figure out how to fit the pigskin over the iron shape, and he feared ruining the leather. He'd have to wait for Ash's return to resume. He hadn't returned on Tuesday until about four o'clock. It seemed today would be the same.

Frustrating, indeed, for a man who needed to earn a living.

It was time for lunch. He locked the shop and stalked to the house, willing himself to relax. He might not have his memories, but he knew himself. Or thought he did. He was generally even-keeled, someone who enjoyed a good joke, a hearty laugh.

Wasn't he?

No one would describe him that way now.

When he stepped in the hall, Felicity had her hand on the wall hook containing her cloak.

"Going out?" He didn't want her to leave, even if he did avoid conversations with her out of guilt.

"I was coming to remind you of lunch." She scrutinized his wound and then looked into his eyes. "You've a headache, don't you?"

Those compassionate blue eyes steadied him. "Aye. A constant companion."

"Are you taking your medicine?"

"Quinine eased the pain for a few days. Can't tell much difference lately." What was the point of taking it? His head ached either way.

She looked as if she wanted to protest and then changed her mind. "Julia's packing a trunk and will be down shortly, so we have a minute. May I give you something?"

"My parents' box?" His spirits lifted.

"I'm sorry. I'll—er—locate it soon." She blushed. "But what I did bring is in the parlor."

He followed her into the room where she stopped at the table with crisply folded clothing. "Ah, me suit." He fingered the wool coat. "'Twill be a welcome change to me uniform. And a blouse, handkerchiefs, and..." Underclothes. His face heated. "Thank you."

"My pleasure." Her eyes sparkled. "There's something in the coat pocket."

He fished out a thick wad. Money? Why, it was fifty dollars. "I can't accept this." He pressed it into her soft hands.

"It's not mine." She put it into his right hand and pushed his fingers over it. "It's yours. You gave it to me for safekeeping in October."

Safekeeping? "If I feared being robbed, why didn't Ash hold onto this money for me?"

"We were courting at the time, and..." She released his hand with seeming reluctance. "Well, it doesn't matter now why I held it for you. It's yours."

He stared at the bills. Only five dollars had been in his knapsack. This additional money felt like a fortune. "'Tis a welcome sight, indeed. Why did you tarry to give it to me?"

Flinching, she took a step back. "I waited for you to remember me or at least learn of our courtship. That was wrong of me. Forgive me."

He looked up at the sound of footsteps in the hall.

"There you are." Julia entered the parlor, a concerned glance darting between them. "Jolene is ready to serve lunch."

"I'll help her." Felicity scurried away without looking at Luke.

A scent of lilacs lingered in the hall as he and Julia exchanged pleasantries on the way to the dining room. All the while, he couldn't help wondering if Felicity would have kept the money if Mr. Maxwell hadn't spoken up.

Nay, he didn't really think so. Yet he only knew her as his nurse. Was she the type of woman to betray a trust?

There were too many secrets in Vicksburg. His pa, the wisest man he'd ever known, could help him ferret out the truth. Fresh waves of grief nearly choked him as Jolene set a steaming bowl of beef stew in front of him. The aroma brought him back to the present, back to his current dilemma.

He'd confront Ash tonight about all that had been hidden

from him—beginning with the secret parlor conversation yesterday from which they'd shut him out.

~

*D*ejected about Luke's mistrust because she didn't give his money to him immediately after his hospital release, Felicity pushed open the door to her aunt's home later that afternoon.

"Felicity's here!" Wilma ran down the hall from the kitchen. "We're making ginger cookies with Grandma while Mama shops."

She bent to hug the four-year-old. "They smell delicious." The gingery aroma tempted Felicity's appetite. "May I have one?"

"Grandma says after supper." Wilma wagged her finger.

"All right. I'll be patient." So they were staying for the meal. Petunia usually left for home before nightfall. Her cousin, who'd been married and living in Yazoo City when Felicity moved to Vicksburg, hadn't been as friendly lately. She was at a loss to figure out what she'd done to cause it.

Petunia arrived as the last cookies came out of the oven. "Some foods are getting scarce, including eggs. Good thing Mr. Farmer gave us some chickens." She set a sack of flour next to a filled basket.

"Miles's parents have been quite generous to all of you." Aunt Mae kissed her cheek. "I may need to get some eggs from you."

"That's fine." Petunia eyed the cookies. "Those look delicious. Wilma, did you and Little Miles make those to surprise me?" She hugged her children.

"Yes, but they're for everyone." Wilma smiled up at her.

"Thank you." Sitting down at the kitchen's round table,

Petunia settled with her son on her lap. "I didn't expect you to be home from the hospital yet, Felicity."

"I worked at the Mitchells' today." Felicity flipped a sizzling potato cake in the skillet, glad to be acknowledged.

"Do they need another maid?" Petunia tilted her head.

"Doubtful." Felicity blinked. Petunia was looking for a job after bragging many times that Miles sent nearly his whole monthly pay to her? Yet Aunt Mae had hinted of money concerns. Perhaps it was because prices of most goods had escalated. Petunia had been so sensitive of late that Felicity didn't like to ask the reason. "I only work three days weekly."

Her cousin seemed lost in thought. "That would be enough. Mama could watch the children. Will you ask them for me?"

Her cousin didn't consult Aunt Mae. Felicity looked at her inquiringly. Aunt Mae gave a half-hearted shrug.

"I'll ask Monday." She'd be at the hospital Friday and Saturday. If there were new patients, she might discover something worth passing along.

Spying on her patients wouldn't put her in her cousin's good graces. In fact, having her at the Mitchells was a bad idea, what with Ash's spy activities—so clear to her now that she knew what to watch for.

She'd advise Julia not to hire the wife of a Confederate soldier.

~

*L*uke was determined to discover why Ash traveled by train twice this week and came back with one pigskin each time. Why not purchase more in one visit? Something didn't feel right. He waited until supper was finished. Then he looked at Ash. "May I have a word with you?"

Ash raised his eyebrows. "Of course." He followed Luke into the parlor, his limp more pronounced this evening.

Luke sat on the edge of his seat. "We've been friends since boyhood. You're protecting me from something because of my amnesia. I'd take it as an act of friendship if ye stopped coddling me."

Ash closed the parlor door. "Are you certain you're ready?"

"The not knowing hurts worse than the headaches. What did you and Julia talk about with Felicity yesterday?"

Something flickered on Ash's face as he sat on a chair opposite. "The Luke I knew could keep a secret."

He lifted his chin. "I'm the same man." At least, he hoped so.

"First, I already told you that you were a Union man when you mustered in. Is that still the case?"

"Aye." Shouldn't Ash have known without asking? "What of your conversation with Felicity?" He wouldn't allow Ash to skirt the original question.

Ash quirked an eyebrow. "You feeling the protectiveness of a beau?"

"Nay." Was he? "The kindred spirit of another orphan." That sounded plausible, but it was more than that...feelings he didn't want to probe.

Ash looked at the door. "Felicity heard something of value to the Union army this week." He spoke softly. "She wondered if I knew how to pass it on."

Luke's body tensed. Felicity was spying? "And?"

"I do." His eyes darkened. "Luke, I'm a Union spy."

Ash? His heart fairly galloped, so fast did it beat. "Did I already know?"

"I'm not certain. I hinted at it when you were on your furlough."

"You mean to tell me, I might have spied for the Union had I remained in Vicksburg?" To do good for his country would have fed his very soul.

"It didn't happen that way." Ash held out his hands, palms up. "You're still in the Confederate army for now."

"Aye. That I am." Blood rushed through his veins. This opportunity made him long all the more for that honorable discharge. Perhaps he could right the wrong he'd done—whatever that might be, no one knew—by becoming a Union spy. *If* the doctor saw fit to discharge him. If his headaches continued after his memories returned, perhaps Dr. Watkins would keep him out of the army for that reason.

"If you get that discharge, consider the danger before you decide to spy. Getting caught can cost your life. Imprisonment. Spies have been shot. Some have gone missing, and to this day, no one has heard from them. Are they in prison? Dead and buried where no one will find them?" Ash's brow lowered. "Until they're found, we won't know. Sad to say, we may never know."

Such a fate wasn't to be taken lightly.

"I was captured last summer."

"You?" Luke gripped the arms of his chair.

"It was while Union gunboats shot mortar into our city."

Luke swiped at his clammy forehead. Maybe he wasn't up for learning so much at one sitting.

Ash stared toward the glowing fire as if not seeing it. He went on to explain that he'd been delivering coded messages— an activity he was still involved in—in Yazoo City when captured. Though he'd managed to get rid of an incriminating message before the Confederates found it, they kept him locked up for five days. He'd been rescued after the soldiers left on an ironclad, but Ash still had to make a long journey back to his Union contact. "I paid for my loyalties with that imprisonment. My leg is only now recovering its strength."

Luke whistled. "And prison heightened your childhood fear of tight places. Is that why you never close the shop door?"

Ash nodded. "There's something else."

There was more? What had been happening in his city these past five years? "Might as well hear it all."

"Of course, we told you immediately that my mother and sisters live on my uncle's ranch in Texas now."

"Aye. I miss them." They'd given him a family to love after his own died. He'd be forever grateful to them.

"What I didn't say is that I'm to inherit my uncle's ranch."

Luke's jaw slackened. "Congratulations. I'm happy for you." He himself had inherited a legacy of faith and hard work, and he had no regrets.

"Uncle Clark's condition is that Julia and I live on the ranch so I'll learn to run it. They need a saddler out there. My uncle is building a shop to my specifications."

"Bigger, one hopes, so you can close the door in bad weather."

Ash chuckled. "It will be. Uncle Clark sent money for me to order new tools. A blacksmith friend has already completed that order, and I sent them on the train before Christmas, along with a load of trunks and boxes from Mrs. Dodd. She and Eddie are moving to Texas with us."

He wasn't ready to lose Ash—who'd been a rock to lean on since he left the hospital—and his temporary home. Where would Luke go, a man with no memory? "When will you leave?"

"Plans are for early March, depending on the war. I'm keeping a close eye on what's happening with the Union army being so close. Mama took most of our valuables on to Texas so Julia doesn't have an inordinate amount to pack. Mrs. Dodd has more to do than us."

Two months. Would Luke be back in Virginia by then? He'd pray for an honorable discharge. But what then, if Ash was gone?

Ash rose slowly. Facing Luke, he rested an elbow on the mantel. "There's a reason I'm pushing you to learn every aspect of the business. If the army releases you, I want you to live here. Watch over the place for me. The shop is yours, at least until the end of the war."

"I'll double efforts to learn the saddling trade." Luke had a home again? What an amazing gift...unless the Southern army refused to let him go. His eyes misted. "I accept on one condition."

"What's that?" Ash tensed.

Luke stood. "That you'll teach me how to be the spy you've become."

"Agreed." Ash shook his hand.

Something akin to peace crept into his heart. He needed to get back to the man inside him who would never fight against the Union army. The opportunity to be of service to the North was a balm to his spirit.

CHAPTER 12

elicity had accompanied her aunt and uncle to church yesterday but didn't sit with Luke, Ash, and Julia. She'd caught Luke looking at her during the singing but had tried to ignore him. The last time they'd talked alone, he'd practically accused her of withholding his money from him. It had been good to be away from him for three days. When Julia invited them to lunch, Felicity declined.

That afternoon, she took a break from sewing Luke a new coat and fetched his large box from the attic. She didn't wish him to worry about his possessions, and she certainly didn't want to hear accusations that it should have been there sooner. Delaying its delivery might protect him from memories it held, but it would also decrease his waning trust in her.

However, she walked to Julia's house the next morning without it. The box was too heavy to carry so far. It was a foggy morning and slightly warmer than in recent days. The men were already in the saddle shop when she arrived, and she passed the open door with only a wave. She'd deliver his box before speaking with him again.

Julia was descending the steps when Felicity stepped inside.

"There you are. I'm glad you came before I had to leave. Mama wants my help packing." She looked down the empty hall toward the kitchen. "Actually, I have to dig up valuables I hid in the cellar before the gunboats came," she whispered. "Mama's got a bad feeling she waited too long, so we'll send them today if at all possible. Ash has a saddle to finish, or he'd come with me."

"I'll help." Felicity grinned. "That is, if my boss agrees my chores can wait."

"She most definitely does." Julia took her blue cloak from a wall hook. "It's bound to be a messy job. I hated to ask you."

"Think nothing of it. Will we take the buggy?"

"Good idea. We'll get there quicker." Julia opened the door. "My, but it's foggy today."

"I have a little favor to ask." Felicity smiled inwardly. This was the way she negotiated for help from Bessie. "Can we stop by Aunt Mae's for Luke's box on the way back?"

"Of course. He'll be pleased to receive it." She swept into the shop in front of Felicity. "Ash, will you hitch up the buggy? We're going to Mama's."

"Good morning. I'll be happy to oblige you." Luke left with a glance at Felicity. The stable where the horse, buggy, and wagon were kept was several yards behind the shop.

"Thanks for your help, Felicity." Ash peered out the door and then stepped closer. "Did you learn anything?"

"No new patients on my ward. Sorry." She'd been both excited and scared but had learned nothing. Perhaps that was a good thing. She'd be more ready when news came.

"Not to worry. The one who gives me my marching orders is pleased to have a spy at the hospital."

"What do you mean?" Felicity knew other spies were reporting to Ash. That *he* reported to someone was news.

"It's a new source of information. He's as glad as I am." Ash grinned at her.

"Thank you." That affirmation fed her spirit. She was doing the right thing.

The sound of wheels stopped outside the door.

They all went outside. Luke helped Julia into the buggy and then gave Felicity his hand. She accepted his help, reveling in his strength. He'd held her hand on hundreds of strolls.

She mustn't think about it. Still, releasing his hand gave her a pang.

With a wave, Julia drove away.

Felicity resisted the urge to look back at Luke. He might never remember her.

She must begin to build a life without him. Spying for the Union was an excellent start. She'd already passed on information gleaned from Seth. There'd be more opportunities—not daily and probably not weekly. Ash understood. Come to think of it, didn't all his spies face the same dilemma? Sometimes there must be a flood of information and other times...nothing.

She'd listen and be ready.

⁓

*L*uke watched the buggy leave, wishing Felicity had spoken to him. He regretted the mistrust she must have detected in his tone when he asked what took her so long to return his money. Of course, she understood his underlying thought had been that she wouldn't have given it to him had he not learned of their courtship. She *knew* him.

The not knowing was on his side.

"Did you remember something?" Ash leaned his hands on the divider wall where the nearly completed saddle rested.

"It's likely nothing."

"What is it?"

"It happened in the barn. When I hitched Rosebud to the

buggy, it seemed as though I'd done it before. We rented one when we needed it."

Ash sighed. "You helped me hitch the buggy nearly daily when you lived with us before. Doubt that's a new memory." He began to add stitches to the saddle.

Now that he thought of it, Mrs. Mitchell had gone to the shops often during his stay. "True. I recall it now. Ash?"

"Hmm?"

"You'll protect Felicity from danger, right?" Luke leaned a hand on the post, his gaze fixed on his friend's face.

"Careful. We mustn't be overheard." Ash peered beyond his shoulder and then darted his gaze back to Luke. "I will, but there are no guarantees of safety. For any of us," he whispered. "My task is the riskiest."

"Then let me help absorb the risk." He had no family to mourn him should something go awry.

"You mean..."

"Let me deliver with you next time. The doctor may send me back to Virginia in two weeks." He sighed. "It'll be something I can do for the Union in the meantime."

"You can't deliver messages dressed as a Confederate soldier, and your chest is too broad to fit into any clothing of mine." He shook his head. "Let's wait for your new clothes. After that, we'll get you a pass to leave the city as an employee of the shop. Now, help me stitch up this saddle."

Luke chafed at the delay yet understood its wisdom. If he was able to stay, he needed to know all aspects of saddle making too. Both built toward a future.

If Ash wouldn't guarantee Felicity's safety, Luke would do it.

*A*t the end of a long day of digging, Felicity ended up giving the box to Julia when she dropped Felicity off at her aunt's home. She would have loved witnessing Luke's pleasure to have the items in his possession again. But those things were Luke's, anyway, and had nothing to do with her.

Bessie was in a foul mood the next day, and Felicity avoided her in the ward as much as possible.

Dr. Watkins was on the ward after lunch examining Oscar's wrist where the hand used to be. Felicity hovered near in case he needed her to fetch something.

"It'll come as no surprise that the war's over for you." Dr. Watkins wound a fresh bandage over Oscar's wrist. "You'll soon receive your discharge."

"I expected as much. I've had weeks to come to terms with it." The family man stared at his arm. "Funny thing is...I can still feel my missing hand. Strange."

"Not so strange. I've heard that from others." Compassion crossed the doctor's face. "I've got good news. You'll be going home by the end of the week."

"My wife and son will be happy." Oscar started to reach for the doctor's hand to shake it. Realization that he couldn't perform the simple gesture must have struck him deeply. He slumped back on his pillow. "I'm obliged for all you've done for me, Dr. Watkins. You, too, Miss Danielson."

"It was my pleasure." Felicity clasped her hands together. "It will do you good to be home."

"It will." Rubbing his arm rather absently, he looked up. "Say, have you seen Luke Shea? Been wondering about him."

The doctor turned to her.

"Actually, I have." Felicity flushed at the mention of her beau—her former beau. "He's staying with a friend of mine while he recovers."

"I saw him last week and will examine him again next week. How's the amnesia?" Dr. Watkins studied her.

"No change." She sighed. As much as she'd prayed those memories remained at bay until Luke's discharge, his lack of remembrance tortured her. He'd said he loved her. How did one forget that?

"Hmm. It's January thirteenth." Dr. Watkins tapped a pencil against his fingers. "Perhaps I should speak with him sooner. Will you tell him to stop in on Thursday, two days from now? I gather he's anxious to recover those memories?"

"Very much so."

"Good to know. He'll want to return to his duties—if he's fit." The doctor eyed her. "Which he certainly isn't at the moment." He moved on to the next patient.

"Reckon the war's over for both of us." Oscar's tone was mournful.

Felicity glanced at him. She'd forgotten they stood at his bedside. "I'm sorry, Mr. Miller. You're a brave man. I'm certain you'll be missed."

"Thank you. I've a hankering to see the old fellows from my regiment. Will you ask Luke to stop by after he's done with the doctor here?" Oscar looked at her with a pleading expression.

The request filled her with trepidation for some reason. She patted his arm but promised nothing. She'd pray about it first, but what harm could there be in two friends commiserating with one another?

~

*L*uke excused himself for the night immediately following supper with Julia and Ash that evening. Ash had told them that the ferry boat was to stop crossing the Mississippi River to Louisiana. They could rent a skiff or hire a boat to take further loads bound for Texas across for them, but Julia worried they should push up their departure, something Ash was loathe to do.

Hopefully, Luke's memories returned before they left. He felt like a rudderless boat as it was, even with them here.

Luke trudged up the stairs to his room. His head had ached too much last night to unpack. There had been no time today. Ash had left him a slew of tasks in the shop while he headed out to deliver messages. He'd finished but it tuckered him out. Exhaustion warred with his throbbing head for attention.

Within ten minutes, a fire in the heat stove was burning away the chill in his room. After holding his hands in front of the stove for a minute, he opened the box. As Felicity had said, there was a blouse and handkerchiefs next to three pairs of wool socks. She was remarkably well-informed about the contents. Had she peeked inside? He didn't like to think of it, for it reminded him of her delay in delivering his money to him. Surely, Mr. Tomlinson had packed his belongings for him and probably told her—at least he hoped so.

Laying the clothing on the bed, he found some of his old books. *David Copperfield* and *The Count of Monte Cristo* were on top. He didn't remember reading them, so these must be new purchases after he started working at the bookbindery. He stacked a dozen or so books on the writing table in his room. Best wait for his headaches to subside before digging into them.

Suspenders had fallen into a shoe at the bottom of the box. His fingers probed for holes in the intact soles of the scuffed brogans and found another item.

Papa's pipe. He inhaled the sweet, pungent aroma mixed with smoke. It still contained ashes from Papa's last smoke. The bank had taken everything of value to pay their debts. This was a treasure, indeed.

Closing his eyes, Luke held it to his cheek. It seemed the

last time he smelled that pipe smoke was a matter of weeks, not years.

He peeked inside the box once more. His breath shuddered. Nestled in the bottom was a large, sturdy black Bible. Luke picked it up reverently. Papa had read to them on Sunday evenings. He cradled it close to his chest, missing his parents more in that moment than he had since awakening in the hospital to a nightmare.

The pipe and Bible found a new home on his writing desk.

He owed Felicity his thanks for protecting these precious things. He'd tell her as soon as she arrived in the morning.

Moments after his head touched the pillow, he was asleep.

$\sim$

A splash. Frigid waters nearly stole Luke's breath. No time to pause. Kicking with stockinged feet, he took powerful strokes toward the area of that last head bob.

Shouts from the riverbanks. Splashes in the river fell like rain. Was it raining? Never mind that now. He must keep going.

There was no movement on top of the water when he reached the spot. Drawing in a deep breath, he dove deeper, hands reaching...

Luke thrashed against his tangled sheets.

Wake up. Push the nightmare away.

He rubbed his hands over his face and drew them back. His own sweat trickled across his palms.

This was his third nightmare of the kind since moving into Ash's home.

Raw grief for his parents tore at his soul. He hadn't been able to save them. Had finding the pipe and family Bible prompted the nightmare to return?

After lighting the lantern, he opened the Bible to the Gospel of Matthew and began to read.

◌

*C*old, steady rain accompanied Felicity to Julia's house to work the next morning. Her umbrella did little good because wind tossed the droplets onto her skirt and her cloak. She nearly ran the last quarter mile to push open the Mitchells' front door.

"'Tis drenched ye be." Luke, who stood in the hall outside the dining room, hurried to take her dripping umbrella and close the door. He set it, still opened, near the entrance. "May I help ye with that wet cloak?"

Mystified with the personal attention, she unhooked it and turned around. His hands brushed against her damp hair and then grazed her shoulders. She shivered as he held the dripping garment away from her. She spun around to look into his eyes.

He was close enough to kiss her.

Her heartbeat quickened. She had once been accustomed to such personal attentions from him. Now it flustered her.

Flushing, he stepped back. "You're cold. Little wonder. Please, warm yourself by the fire."

She hurried into the parlor. He was right to step away. Their courtship was a thing of the past. But, oh, how she longed for the kiss his eyes told her he'd wanted to give a moment ago.

No, that was wishful thinking. She must say something to break the spell that bound her—her love for Luke. "Where's Julia?" She held out her hands to the fire's warmth.

"Packing another box. She asks you to join her above stairs."

"I'll go straight away." Felicity turned on her heel.

"One moment." He held out his hand imploringly. "Please."

She looked up into his beloved brown eyes, the thick auburn hair sweeping across his forehead. He needed a haircut. "Yes?"

"I owe you me thanks." He tapped a loose fist against his

broad chest, broader now than before the war. "Pa's pipe and Bible were in the box. What treasures they are to me. Thank you for keeping it safe for me."

"It was my privilege." Her voice sounded faint. He hadn't waited to discover its treasures when she was here. It showed she was still on the fringes of his life. "I must go to Julia."

She was at the doorway when she recalled his appointment and turned back. "Dr. Watkins wants to see you tomorrow." Concern held her back from mentioning Oscar Miller's request to talk with him. Luke's former comrade could do more harm than good, she'd decided after praying over the matter. Someone must watch out for his best interests.

"He wants to know if me amnesia has abated." The animation left his face. "How I wish it had."

"It will, probably when you least expect it." She hated to see him browbeat himself for something he couldn't control. "By the way, I'll finish your overcoat tonight and bring it tomorrow."

"Many thanks for making the coat first. Let me know what I owe you."

"I will." She hurried up the stairs before she could answer what was in her heart to say.

All she wanted was for him to love her again. His desire for a kiss gave her hope. If the doctor recommended an honorable discharge, once it was finalized, she'd find little ways to help him remember her.

CHAPTER 13

$\mathcal{L}$uke was glad for the warmth of his new brown coat on the brisk walk to the hospital on Thursday. Felicity was working at the Mitchells' today. It would be strange to be at the hospital without her presence.

The upcoming appointment would disappoint the doctor, who'd rather send him back to the Twenty-first Mississippi than discharge. Perhaps the missing memories protected him from returning to Virginia, a blessing in disguise.

Nay, he'd rather have his memories than his freedom.

At least things were going well at the saddle shop. They had another order, this one from a farmer in Bovina. Ash had promised to wait for his return to cut the leather. Soon Luke wouldn't have his boss's expertise nearby, and he needed all the practice he could get—that is, if the army released him.

Upon arriving at the hospital, he first went to the nurses' room and then wished he had gone straight upstairs for the room's only occupant was Bessie Guthrie. Luke had witnessed enough of the interactions between the nurse and Felicity to sense the friction—for what cause, he had no notion. "Good morning, Miss Guthrie."

"Good morning, Luke." She set a tin cup on the table and arose. "This is a surprise. If you've come to see Felicity, she's not here."

"Nay." Suspicions heightened his senses. "Why did you think she's the reason for me visit?"

"She spent an inordinate amount of time taking care of you." Her mouth tightened. "Too much, if you ask me. We nurses aren't here to find a husband."

That seemed like a complaint rather than the root of her ire. Perhaps she was simply a difficult woman. "Dr. Watkins requested to see me today."

"Actually, he's in the first-floor ward. I'll tell him you're here on my way back to my patients. Help yourself to coffee if you've a mind to." She swept a hand at the coffeepot resting on a heat stove. "I'll bid you good day."

"Good day." He poured himself a cup of coffee and sat to wait. He considered Miss Guthrie's sometimes sour disposition. There'd been talk among her patients that she vowed to kill a Yankee herself before the hostilities ended in retribution for her fiancé who had died in battle.

He shook his head in unbelief, but, truly, he didn't know what to think about the nurse. Or the continued hostilities that changed gentle souls into embittered hearts.

Luke still felt lost about all that had gone before, but he'd best figure out what was happening now. He'd start studying the newspapers, even if reading worsened his headache.

He stood as footsteps approached.

"Luke, it's good to see you." Dr. Watkins entered the room and shook his hand. "We can talk in here. First, let me see your shrapnel wound." He pushed Luke's hair aside to probe the area.

Luke winced.

"Still painful, huh?"

"I'm careful when washing me hair. Other than that, I avoid

touching it." And he wished the doctor would leave it alone, too, else a blistering headache would accompany Luke's walk home.

"It's healing nicely." Dr. Watkins held an open hand toward the chair Luke had vacated. "Let's sit, shall we?"

"Did ye want some coffee?" Luke started for the stove.

"No, thanks. Had some an hour ago." He waited until Luke joined him at the table. "Now, what have you remembered?"

"Nothing." Luke curled his fingers around his tin cup. "Felicity sent a box from me old apartment this week. Papa's pipe and our family Bible were among its items inside. It stirred only memories of me childhood."

"So...things you already knew." Dr. Watkins watched him.

"Aye." He slumped against the back of the none-too-comfortable wooden chair. "'Tis a burden to me, losing five years of me life. I feel less a man."

"You want to remember."

"Aye. More than anything. It feels as if I've lost part of me soul." How could the man question it? "'Tis me main goal...to get those memories back."

"So you can return to the battlefield." Dr. Watkins crossed his arms.

It was a statement. An erroneous one. "It'd be tossing me life away to return without remembering me training or even the years leading up to the fighting."

"I don't need that on my conscience." He stood. "Let's cancel next week's appointment. I want to see you again in two weeks. Tell me what you remember at that time."

"Hopefully, me mind will be fully restored." He must have those memories back—else he'd never know the man he'd become. Yet, if that happened, Luke would most likely be on the next train back East. So how could he win in this impossible situation? Luke pushed back his chair and stood as Dr.

Watkins, always in a hurry, headed out the door. "Obliged for your care."

He might as well visit Oscar before he left. Ash shouldn't mind his absence lasting another quarter hour.

~

"What do you think is taking Luke so long?" Felicity scrubbed one of Luke's blouses over the washtub in the laundry room near the kitchen. Julia, having packed all she could send to Texas ahead of her, helped her.

"It hasn't been above an hour since he left." Julia rubbed lye soap on a mud stain on Ash's trousers. "What's bothering you?" She applied a brush to the stain. "You've been out of sorts."

She might as well tell her. "Luke still counts you and Ash as his friends. Not me. I feel shunned." On the outside again.

"That's the heart of what troubles you, isn't it?"

Felicity stopped scrubbing. "Seems as though he remembers everyone except the woman he once professed to love."

"He *did* love you. It was plain to all the man was completely smitten." She leaned forward. "Be patient. It will come to him again, you'll see."

"What if it doesn't?" She dipped the blouse in the rinse water and then looked up at Julia. "The doctor gave no guarantees."

"I'm praying all the important memories return. You must brace yourself for the possibility that there will be gaps."

Felicity turned away. She'd considered this and prayed daily she wasn't caught in those cracks. She felt unneeded as well as unloved. Worse, no new patients had been admitted to her ward since she agreed to spy.

Julia sighed. "In the meantime, he could use another friend. He doesn't have an overabundance of people he feels comfortable with at the moment."

"What about Savannah? Did he remember her when he saw her?" Felicity was certain he'd remember the beautiful, wealthy woman. She'd been around Willie, Ash, and Luke even more often than Julia in those early days.

"She hasn't been around to see him." Her brow wrinkled. "Come to think of it, I haven't seen her since Christmas Eve. She left the ball early, remember?"

"That's right. I was so distracted with worry for Luke, and then that messenger came, ending the ball." Felicity's stomach churned that she could have forgotten Savannah. She, Julia, and Ash had all spent as much time with her as they could while she grieved for Willie. "Perhaps the second Christmas was harder on her than the first."

"I will visit her tomorrow before going over to Mama's." Julia's eyes widened. "Say, I have an idea. There's a benefit concert next week for needy soldiers at Apollo Hall. Why don't we all go and invite Savannah? Eddie enjoys listening to the regimental bands that occasionally play around town. He and Mama would love it."

"And Luke always enjoyed band music and singing." Felicity's spirits lifted. "This is just the type of entertainment we all need to revive us from our doldrums."

"Would your aunt and uncle enjoy it?"

"I'll ask them." Felicity picked up one of Julia's dresses. How exciting. Her workload was too full to allow for many concerts. To attend one where Luke would be among the party made it even more of a treat.

It was just the kind of evening the two of them had often enjoyed as a couple. Perhaps the simple entertainment would jar a memory.

Then she thought of the doctor. But not too soon.

∾

"*Y*ou don't remember *anything* of our battles? Nothing?" Sitting on his cot, Oscar stared at him incredulously. He wore a Confederate uniform with a hole in the cuff.

"Nay." Seated beside the bed, Luke bit back his frustration. Did the man not realize such incredulity made him feel even worse about his predicament? "'Tis not from lack of trying."

"Being part of the Twenty-First Mississippi is something to be proud of, that's certain." He stared down at his bandage. "We did our share of fighting."

"Tell me about some of the battles." Such details could spark memories.

"Last summer, there was sharp fighting around Richmond. We pushed them Yankees away from our capital." Oscar glanced at Luke.

He was a Union spy now. Best play the part of supporting the South well. "We fought bravely, I'd wager."

"You'd win that bet." Oscar grinned. "We were at Malvern Hill. Lieutenant Colonel Brandon lost his leg at that one. A tragedy. Not sure he'll return to the fighting."

How could he? So far, nothing sounded familiar.

"We had a time of it at Sharpsburg. That's in Maryland. It was a wonder only three of ours were killed. Over fifty were wounded. Captain John Simms commanded us until near the end of that one. Colonel Humphreys arrived and took over then to cheer us along."

"I was in Vicksburg on furlough for that one." He sighed. "Or so I've been told."

"Don't be sorry you missed it." Shaking his head, Oscar stared out the window as if not seeing the sunshine breaking through the trees.

Luke waited. If he hadn't been at Sharpsburg, there was little advantage to hear the details.

Oscar's eyes brightened. "Here's something that might joggle your memory. We all joked about it often enough. The First Corps of the Army of Northern Virginia has had plenty of reorganizations. At the Battle of Fredericksburg, we were in Brigadier General William Barksdale's Brigade in McLaws's Division." Oscar paused. "Any of those names mean anything to you?"

"Nay. But go on. No one here will tell me what I've done." He was still irritated with Ash about that. He'd learned they often corresponded. Why hadn't he offered to let him read those letters? Surely, his friend knew *something* that would nudge those events sleeping in his mind.

"The battle at Fredericksburg, Virginia—that's where we were both injured."

Luke's attention sharpened. This was what he craved to learn. "What happened?" Oscar had told him weeks before the battle had been a Confederate victory.

"Fredericksburg is a river town. Our side had destroyed the bridges so the Union had to build pontoon bridges to cross the Rappahannock. Those were boats secured together in the river with a bridge deck laid across it. It took them a while, but they crossed it."

Luke rubbed throbbing temples, trying to massage away his worst headache since recovering from surgery.

"There are hills beside the town. That's where we waited for the Yankees."

Several patients in surrounding beds who hadn't been there when Luke was sat up in their beds, their gazes riveted on Oscar, who spoke as if unaware of anyone.

"When those Yankees charged the hill, we were ready for them with loaded muskets. We shot them. Then we shot them again after they fell while we waited for the next charge, sitting in that muddy fortification, sleet freezing our eyelashes together."

Nausea rumbled in Luke's stomach. This was something he'd never seen coming.

"Yankees charged again. And again. We shot them and reloaded. Some fellas got pretty close to our lines before falling." Oscar looked up at Luke, his face a mask of misery. "Takes courage to keep charging as your comrades drop beside you. Gotta admire that kind of bravery. Our position was so strong, I got to wishing they'd just stop coming. They couldn't win. Then a bullet ripped through my arm."

"Did I shoot at those who were already down?" Bile spread up his throat at the possibility. Had he grown that callous?

"You weren't close to me. Leastways, I don't recall seeing you in our battle lines. But shrapnel got a hold of you, so you fought that day." He scratched his head. "I reckon you really don't recall your training, because when the enemy charges, you'd best shoot or be killed."

"That's the truth of it." A soldier in a nearby bed spoke up.

"I reckon that training will come back to you when the army sends you back to the fighting." Oscar gave a decisive nod. "After a while, it's like those battle experiences have done more training than the drills."

If shooting fallen men was what he had done, Luke didn't want to remember. Sick at heart, he stood. "Thanks for telling me about the battle." He'd asked, but he could have gone to his deathbed a happier man for not knowing.

"It wasn't pretty, I'll give you that." Oscar studied him. "You ain't looking so good. All pale, like you'll fall where you stand. Should I call for the doctor?"

"Nay. Fresh air is all I require." And not to lose his breakfast in front of these folks. "'Tis happy I am that you're going home tomorrow. Good luck to you."

He stumbled out. Held tightly to the banister as he nearly tumbled down the stairs. Grabbed his coat from a hook by the door as he nearly ran outside.

Gulping chilly air in gasps, he put his hands on his knees. "Lord, did I shoot at fallen men?" The thought sickened him. He emptied his stomach behind a hedge of bushes.

What had he done?

Was his amnesia actually protecting him from some horrible event?

~

*L*uke barely managed to sit upright next to Ash as the buggy pulled up in front of the house. It was shameful enough that Ash had found him outside the hospital, incapacitated. Now Felicity and Julia ran outside to meet them, their faces slack with alarm.

"Let's get him inside." Felicity's calm nurse's voice shook.

"I found him on his knees outside the hospital." Ash limped around to Luke's side. "It's a good thing you suggested taking the buggy, Felicity. He'd been sick. Not sure what's wrong other than that. He hasn't talked."

Luke grimaced, embarrassed for her to know this.

Felicity touched his cheek in almost a caress. "He's in shock, or something very similar. Let's get him to bed."

He'd not argue with a short nap, but he was no longer an invalid. She and Ash both walked beside him as Luke climbed the stairs. Julia ran ahead to turn down the bed in his room.

Luke sat on the bed, bewildered at what Oscar told him. Was he such a monster?

"What did the doctor say, buddy?" Ash put his hand on Luke's shoulder.

"Come back in two weeks." He looked up at Ash. "I pray it isn't true."

"What's not true?" Felicity touched his forehead. "You're not feverish."

He glanced at her. Then his gaze dropped. "Oscar told me about the battle."

Felicity's blue eyes widened. "He told you his perspective of the event. He doesn't know what you saw or did."

"Aye." Hope glimmered as he looked up at her. "I'll hang onto that truth."

"Do you want us to bring you up a sandwich, or will you nap?"

"A nap, please." He looked at Ash. "A short one, if we can get hard at it afterward." He'd not be coddled.

"You bet." Ash clapped him on the back. "You've had a shock, but it's as Felicity said, Oscar's memories aren't your own."

Luke pressed cold fingers to his forehead.

"You have a headache." Felicity studied him with compassionate eyes.

"Aye. Me temples are pounding."

"I'll fetch your medicine and a cup of water." Julia rushed away and was back moments later.

She gave both to Felicity, who accepted them gratefully. "This should help."

Luke took the quinine from her and drained the cup. "It does when the pain is this bad. Obliged to all of you."

Felicity drew the curtains. "See you in a little while." She followed Ash and Julia from the room, closing the door behind her.

After removing his coat, Luke sank to his knees beside the bed. He didn't want a nap or a meal. He wanted to pray.

And that's how he spent the next hour, praying it wasn't true, that he hadn't so lost himself that he'd shoot fallen men, over and over.

CHAPTER 14

On Friday, Felicity finally received a new patient in her ward. Seventeen-year-old Victor Davis had arrived last evening from Louisiana. His broken arm had been set and was in a sling.

Bessie was already in the ward when Felicity got there. She ground her teeth. The woman had watched her since Luke left as if fearing she'd set her sights on another patient. Now was not the moment for questioning Victor. She greeted him, introduced herself, and then gave him a dipper of water.

She delivered meals to all the patients who could manage to feed themselves. Bessie left the room, presumably for another tray of meals for her patients.

This was the time. She could do this. She mustn't make a mistake. Ash counted on her.

Felicity carried Victor's bowl to him, her heart quivering. "I've brought you some arrowroot custard that should be easy on your stomach. Are you hungry?" He was still sitting with his back propped against the wall. That made feeding him a lot easier.

"Yes, miss, but..."—he looked down at his arm in a sling— "I'm not much good with my left hand yet. Reckon I'll learn."

"You'll do fine with practice. I'll help you today." She sat on the edge of his bed and spooned the first bite into his mouth. "And Dr. Watkins expects your arm to heal just fine."

"Glad to hear it." He took two more bites.

Felicity looked around. Bessie still wasn't back. "How were you injured?"

One question was all it took. The soldier talked for ten minutes about sharp fighting in an attack by three Yankee gunboats at Bayou Teche on the Confederate gunboat and fortifications. Since the Union already knew of its own attack, she listened with half an ear until Victor mentioned that General Kirby Smith had been given command of the Army of the Southwest.

That sounded like news the Union wanted to know. She'd walk to the Mitchells' that evening and tell Ash. Her midsection tightened at the possibility that she might see Luke.

He had gone directly to the shop after his nap yesterday, a good sign that he was feeling better. However, she hadn't learned what Oscar said to so upset him. She couldn't ask Oscar because his family had picked him up at dawn. Perhaps she'd learn the truth if Luke had opened up to Ash.

$\sim$

*L*uke was alone in the shop when Felicity poked her head inside. His cheeks heated to think that she'd witnessed how discombobulated he'd been the day before. "Good afternoon." He set aside the awl he'd been using and stood.

She greeted him rather self-consciously. "How are you today?"

"Fine." The sooner she forgot him in such a state, the better.

"'Tis sorry I am to have worried you all. I had a touch of a belly-ache." That much was true.

"I'm glad it was a passing malady." She smiled at him.

He hadn't said that. His heart was sick about what happened at Fredericksburg, what he might have done to Union soldiers he now wanted to protect.

"Is Ash here?"

He straightened, his senses on alert. This must have some-thing to do with spying, or she'd have asked after Julia. "Aye. He's in the house."

"I'll just go find him. Thank you." She hesitated at the door as if she wanted him to stop her.

"One moment."

She turned back eagerly. "Yes?"

"I don't want to pester you, but when will I have me first set of working clothes?" He couldn't ride with Ash until he shed his uniform.

"I have one blouse completed, and I'll start on a pair of trousers this evening. Perhaps on Monday? Is that soon enough?"

"Aye." She looked fully prepared to stay up all night sewing if he said otherwise. "Obliged to you."

Felicity nodded and turned away. Within moments, her light footsteps on the stone path leading to the house faded.

Would Ash mention that Luke was also to begin spying?

Perhaps this shared mission would help to build a friend-ship with Felicity.

~

Felicity spent another half hour feeding Victor on Saturday, the following day, at lunch. He told her of many skirmishes and fights, yet it was all old news.

Ash had been pleased with her information, saying it was

important when it first happened, as this seemed to be, because he didn't know it.

Julia had good news for her, too, about her visit to Savannah Adair, who had indeed been in the doldrums for weeks. Their mutual friend was excited to attend the upcoming concert. Julia's mama, Eddie, and Luke expressed interest as well. They'd all return to the Dodd residence for refreshments afterward. Felicity promised to invite Aunt Mae and Uncle Charles.

In the nurses' room, Felicity hummed as she gathered medicine for her patients who required it at noon. She'd best hurry because she'd have to serve lunch immediately afterward.

"He's too young for you." Bessie stalked over to the table.

"What are you talking about?" Bewildered by her coworker's belligerent tone, Felicity sighed inwardly.

"Your new patient, Victor Davis." Bessie crossed her arms. "Don't think I haven't noticed you spending extra time feeding him. Listening to his stories."

"I assure you, it's nothing of the kind." Felicity tried to keep her tone even. Showing her anger only fed Bessie's ire. "I'm well aware that he's three years younger than me."

"Just remember you have twelve patients, not one." Bessie extracted two pills from a brown bottle. "And here I thought you were getting better after Luke Shea left." She flounced out of the room.

Felicity ground her teeth. The woman was insufferable. She fumed as she checked the doctor's notes to ensure she had everything.

Then she stopped.

Perhaps she should be grateful to Bessie for letting her know how closely she was being watched.

Felicity would have to be careful not to arouse her suspicions further. Bessie hated Yankees. If she suspected Felicity of spying for the Union, she'd not hesitate to turn her over to

Confederate authorities. Felicity would be imprisoned and questioned at the least. She touched her throat.

Or worse, if they found proof of her guilt.

~

A week later, Luke still had not remembered anything new. Worse than that, he'd received one new set of clothes along with his coat—Mrs. Beltzer, Felicity's aunt, had even knitted him two sets of socks—but Ash hadn't taken him along for any message deliveries. He'd decided to wait until Luke was officially discharged, deeming it safer for everyone involved if the possibility of him returning to Virginia wasn't hanging over him.

But he couldn't go back. His very heart shriveled in his chest at the thought. He tried to calm himself by anticipating the pleasure of this evening's concert, the first social occasion where he'd wear his brown suit and a borrowed cream-colored vest from Ash.

Luke glanced into the hall. The couple sure were taking their time about dressing for the event at Appollo Hall. As he waited for Julia and Ash in the parlor after their early supper, he rubbed his eyes. The nightmares were nearly a nightly occurrence now. It weighed on him that he hadn't been able to save Papa and Mama. Those dreams weren't making it any easier.

Footsteps in the hall were a welcome reprieve from his oppressive worries.

"Are you ready?" Ash's blue jacket and trousers were of finer material than Luke's. The gray vest and white blouse were the perfect complement.

"Aye." He glanced at Julia's green dress. "And lovely the pair of you look for our evening's entertainment."

"Thank you. We have such few opportunities." Julia placed

her hand on her husband's arm. "We're quite looking forward to it."

"As I am." What would Felicity wear? Likely, one of her pretty dresses she wore to church. She looked as beautiful as a painting in them. No, he mustn't think of her that way. It was too dangerous for a man who didn't know his own actions.

"We'll ride in our buggy to Mama's. Silas, our—that is, *her* —driver will take us all to the concert."

His spirits brightened. "Felicity as well?"

"No, she's riding with the Beltzers." Julia smiled. "According to Felicity, her aunt is very excited about the evening. Savannah is pleased about it, as well."

"I remember her and Willie as the life of any party." He hadn't yet seen Savannah Adair at any functions since his injury. Seeing her without Willie would drive home his death. The grief of his passing had somehow become entwined with his sorrow about his parents. If only there was some word of comfort he could offer Savannah, but his own heart was empty too. The loss of his parents was too fresh not to sympathize with her.

"Shall we go?" Ash draped Julia's cloak over her shoulders.

"Let's." Julia radiated happiness as she smiled up at her husband.

Luke shrugged into his coat, an unaccountable loneliness stealing over him. Had Felicity once felt that way for him? He couldn't think about that now. It was another failure. The best he could do was try to remember who he was and make amends for his mistakes.

～

Felicity hurried toward their group waiting for them in the back of the crowded hall, where folks had worn their finery for the occasion, her eyes first on Luke, who seemed pensive. Feeling out of place, or did the cause run deeper? Pain lined his face, whether from his headaches, grief for his parents, or something else she'd try to discover later. No time to consider that now with the Adairs looking at her expectantly. "Savannah, how wonderful to see you again." Felicity hugged her friend. "I've missed you." They hadn't been able to find her after the Christmas ball ended a month before.

Savannah returned her hug almost convulsively. "And I have missed you." She stepped back, and Felicity, Aunt Mae, and Uncle Charles exchanged greetings with her parents, Eddie, Mrs. Dodd, the Mitchells, and Luke.

Felicity's glance gravitated to Luke, who looked especially handsome tonight in the brown suit that enhanced his eyes. How she longed for the right to stand by his side at such a gathering again. They both enjoyed music and had often attended concerts together in the old days. That idyllic time was so out of reach that it seemed a lifetime ago.

"Luke, we are so pleased to find you looking healthy." Mrs. Adair gave him a gracious smile. "We prayed for you upon learning of your plight."

"Much obliged for the prayers." He gave a crisp nod.

"You do remember me and my parents..." Savannah wagged a finger between her, Mr. Adair, and Mrs. Adair.

Of course, Luke remembered them. Felicity just managed not to roll her eyes. He remembered everyone he'd valued except her, Aunt Mae, and Uncle Charles.

"Aye. 'Tis only the people I met after me parents...died that gives me pause." His eyes softened. "Please allow me to extend me condolences. Willie was a great man and me dear friend I loved as a brother."

"Thank you, Luke." Savannah's looped blond braids brushed Luke's shoulder as she hugged him. "He often said the same of you."

Felicity caught a ragged breath. Losing Willie had been

difficult for all of them. Worse for Luke, perhaps, because he had done his mourning in Virginia, alone.

"It was your telegram that gave us the first news of his passing." Mr. Adair shook Luke's hand. "You've no memory of it, I'd wager, or that Ash brought it to us."

"Nay." Luke glanced at Ash. "I have no knowledge of these past five years, but I'm grateful to have lent a service to the family."

There was an awkward silence.

"Say, Eddie, have you done any fishing lately?" Uncle Charles's eyes twinkled at the eleven-year-old, who looked uncomfortable in his suit. He turned to Mr. Adair. "Ash and I took the boy and his friends fishing after picnicking beside the river a while back."

"I enjoy fishing myself." Mr. Adair looked at Eddie. "Perhaps our family can join your next picnic and fishing adventure."

"Soon as it warms up." Eddie grinned and looked at Ash and Luke.

"We'll try to plan it before we leave." Ash ruffled his hair.

"Oh, Ash." Mrs. Dodd ran a gloved hand over Eddie's hair now sticking straight up on the crown. "You know better than to bother his hair once I can manage to get it to stay down."

"Have you tried plaster?" Ash smothered his grin.

Mrs. Dodd's lips curved.

Felicity hid her smile behind a gloved hand, but she needn't have bothered. Luke's chuckle invited the other men to join in, lightening the melancholy that had descended over the group.

"We'd best take our seats." Mr. Adair offered his arm to his wife. They led the way toward a row near the front.

This might be the last concert Felicity attended with Luke, and she wanted to enjoy it at his side. He was turned from her and slightly ahead. She jostled in front of Julia and remained a pace behind as they strolled to their row. From there it was easy to sit beside him.

Before she could gauge if this situation was to his liking, the crowd stirred. Colonel Withers's Light Artillery Brass Band marched to the stage.

They opened with a heartfelt rendition of "I Wish I was in Dixie."

Felicity settled back to enjoy her first concert with Luke at her side in months. That it was probably her last she refused to consider. She gave herself up to the joy of his nearness, the music, and the company of family and friends.

～

*L*uke sat beside Felicity in the semi-darkness of the hall, secretly glad that she'd chosen the seat beside his. He breathed in the aroma of lilacs that always followed her.

He sneaked a peek at her lovely face, enthralled with the music. Those small yet quite capable hands rested on her lap. Had he held that hand that touched her cheek? They'd courted —how long, he wasn't certain—so it seemed that he must have known how it felt to clasp it. Or to tuck her hand over the crook of his arm while they strolled about Vicksburg.

Had they attended concerts as a couple? Plays? Picnics? Riverboat rides where they listened to the calliope music? Strolled to the Sky Parlor, a high hillside where folks congregated to view the Mississippi River? Had he kissed those pink lips, curved now in a smile of pure enjoyment in the songs?

Impossible to know unless he asked her...which he wasn't about to do. No need to give her false hopes that he'd court her again, should she entertain them.

He could not force himself on a woman who didn't deserve the likes of him.

When the concert ended, everyone stood. Conversations started all around them.

Felicity turned to him. "Did you enjoy the band?"

"Aye." Though truly, he'd been lost in thoughts of her throughout the concert. "And you?"

"Oh, yes." Her blue eyes shone with an intensity. "Did the songs make you think of...anything?"

"Nay." He didn't remember her, this beautiful woman who had no business throwing her life away on half a man. At least, he felt like half a man with so many missing years. He pushed back his shoulders. Seemed he couldn't escape the question. "Are ye coming back for the celebration at Mrs. Dodd's home?"

Disappointment shadowed those eyes. "Yes, we're coming."

He nodded and followed her into the aisle where the others waited.

Thirty minutes later, the ladies were seated in Mrs. Dodd's parlor, and Luke sipped tea across the room with the other men. He'd ridden back to the Dodds with Silas driving the family and Felicity following with her family. It was better that way. No misunderstandings that he accompanied her as her beau.

Felicity mustn't get the wrong idea about his intentions. He had none. How could an honorable man court a woman when he didn't know his past, especially one such as described by Oscar?

Yet he couldn't recall enjoying a concert so much. Was it due to the music, the company, the festive atmosphere, or the woman who'd sat beside him?

Luke was afraid to probe his heart for that answer.

*R*efreshments had been attractively displayed with a vase of purple pansies in the Dodds' dining room after the concert. It was a welcome sight to Felicity, who had spent many happy hours here with Julia before her marriage.

The women had selected from small ham sandwiches, cobbler made with canned peaches, oat tea cakes, lemon cookies, and pecans with coffee or tea and carried their plates to the parlor, where chairs were arranged before the fire. Felicity positioned herself so she could watch the door for Luke. When a quarter hour passed and the men didn't return to the parlor, she resigned herself to spending the rest of the evening apart from Luke. The euphoria she'd felt to enjoy a concert with him again stayed with her while joining in the chatter about the event and the people they'd seen.

"Felicity, when will Luke recover from his amnesia?" Savannah, who sat beside her, sipped her tea as she looked at her.

"No one knows." *Please, God, don't allow Luke to remember until after he's discharged from the army.* "The doctor advises us not to tell him of the past he no longer remembers."

"It does upset Luke, as we've seen." Julia set her empty plate on a side table. "We pray those memories are restored before we move to Texas."

"I wish you'd stay." Savannah's shoulders drooped.

"We can't. It's a requirement of his uncle's that he live there so he can inherit the ranch. Ash is excited about living in a place where he has so many fond memories. I am as well. I'll miss all of you." Julia's lips trembled. "But I'm happy Mama and Eddie are moving with us."

"It will be a few weeks yet." Mrs. Dodd covered Julia's hand with her own. "I've more packing to do. I must admit that Eddie can scarcely contain his excitement to learn how to ride like a cowboy."

"You must all visit once our home is built." Julia's glance included everyone.

"I'll come." Savannah looked at her mother, who nodded. "Once we send the Yankees back up North. Do you think they'll return Luke to his regiment?"

"He doesn't remember his soldier's training or any of the battles." Felicity fanned her suddenly warm face. "He can't return under those circumstances."

"I don't know." Savannah's brow wrinkled. "Willie had written that Luke was a good soldier and a crack shot during drills. We need all the men we can get." Looking at Julia, she raised her brows.

Julia's lips tightened. "One questions how good Luke will be if he can't remember how to fight."

Laughter erupted in the dining room. The men were having a good time. Thankfully, Luke was unaware that he was the topic of the women's conversation.

"What I'm saying is that it may not matter." Savannah sighed. "Some of the men in Willie's company write to me occasionally. Our men are brave but seem to be outnumbered."

"My dear, we all want the South to win as much as you do." Aunt Mae's voice was timid. "But I fear that would be throwing a man's life away in this case. I pray the doctor exercises caution in the matter."

Felicity's heart skipped a beat to hear her aunt express her own doubts.

"We all want what's best for Luke and our country." Mrs. Adair patted her daughter's hand.

Felicity wanted to scream. It had been difficult to let him go when he'd been trained, strong, and healthy, his mind sharp.

It would be torturous to watch him leave on a train in these circumstances.

But what if Dr. Watkins felt the same way as Savannah?

CHAPTER 15

On Monday morning, Julia poked her head into the laundry room where Felicity leaned against a tub of sudsy water on a table with her sleeves pushed up to the elbows amid piles of clothing on the ground. "Felicity, Ash wants to speak to you in the upstairs parlor."

Felicity had barely started the day's task. He'd never summoned her before. Julia always explained her daily jobs. This must have something to do with spying.

She glanced at four articles of clothing hanging on the lines strung from the ceiling with a sigh. The weather should soon be warm enough to hang clothes outside again. "I'll be right there."

"I'll see you up there."

Felicity finished a pair of trousers and hung them on the line. After wiping her soppy hands on a towel dangling from a hook, she hurried up the stairs. "Good morning, Ash." She entered the parlor, where he stood near the mantel.

Julia tatted lace before the low-burning fire on the hearth. "Please, make yourself comfortable."

Felicity sat next to her and gave Ash an inquiring look as he strode to the door and shut it.

"I just came back from a meeting with one of my spies, who gave me some disturbing news. A Union spy went missing up near Ripley, Mississippi. Possibly in Tennessee." Ash swiped sweat from his brow.

"One of ours?" Felicity's hands trembled.

"That I won't know until tomorrow. We have folks who ride that far." He clasped his hands together. "I don't even know if the spy is male or female."

Felicity gasped. "The Confederates may be holding a woman spy?"

"It wouldn't be the first time." His face turned grim.

A woman rider delivering secret messages? What courage that required. She shoved her hands into her apron pockets to hide their trembling. "What do you want me to do?"

"It occurred to me that a new patient coming in might brag about holding a spy. Hinting about how despicable spies are or something to that effect may spark a conversation. If they simply agree with you, it's unlikely they know anything helpful. Don't fret if no one knows anything." He ran his hands through his thick hair. "It's just that...after enduring capture myself, I'll do everything I can to get our spy back safely."

"Understood." Felicity didn't know specifics but had noticed that Ash employed a crutch for several months last year, and his limp continued to be more prominent than before the war began. "Bessie, the nurse who works in the ward with me, reprimands me when I spend too much time with one patient."

"Hmm." He rubbed his fingers over his mouth. "If she's that interested in your activities, you'd best watch yourself around her. Try to ask your questions when she's occupied elsewhere. Remember, you're a spy now. Our neighbors who support the South won't take kindly to that."

"True." A timely reminder. "Thank you, Ash."

"Well, ladies, I'll get back to the shop and Luke." He hurried away, leaving the door open.

"Surprising news."

Julia put a finger on her lips. "Indeed."

Standing, Felicity gave a nod. This secrecy was harder to maintain than she'd thought it would be. "Oh, yes...my cousin Petunia is looking for a job while her husband, Miles, is off fighting with the Confederacy. She asked if you need another maid, and I'm afraid I forgot to talk to you, with everything else going on. What do you say?"

Julia raised her eyebrows.

"I told her you didn't seem to." Felicity tilted her head, trying to convey without words that she didn't believe it to be a wise decision, though she hated to work against her cousin outright.

"Ash's mother hired a Confederate soldier's wife to replace her maid before leaving for Texas," she whispered. "It was a disastrous situation. We've learned our lesson."

"What of Jolene? Her husband serves at the foundry that supplies the Confederate army." Felicity spoke softly.

"She's been with the family since Ash was a child. They keep to themselves, though." She glanced at the open doorway. "Ash is monitoring the situation."

"I need to get back to my laundry, but what shall I tell Petunia?"

"Tell her we've everything we require in advance of our move to Texas." Julia put her tatting aside. "I'll help with that laundry."

Later, her hands elbow deep in the washtub, Felicity prayed for the missing spy and for God to send people in the path of Ash's spies who knew something about it. This war must end soon. The danger would continue until the hostilities stopped.

◊

here were four empty beds in Felicity's ward the next day and no new patients on either side, nor was anyone admitted that day. Dejected that she hadn't been able to help the missing spy, she arrived back at her aunt's home around four.

"Felicity's here!" Wilma ran to greet her at the door.

"Hello, Wilma." She bent to hug the sweet girl. "How are you this afternoon?"

"Mama says we can move here." Excitement radiated from her face. "We just have to tell Grandpa when he comes home from work."

"Where is everyone?" As Felicity hung her cloak on a hook, she wondered what Aunt Mae had to say about this turn of events. Her aunt tended to be lax where Petunia, her youngest daughter, was concerned. Perhaps it had something to do with her three other daughters living with their families in other states—the closest one near Nashville, Tennessee.

"Looking at the bedrooms. Come on." Wilma tugged at her hand.

"I'm coming." Felicity's footsteps dragged behind. She had felt the sting of her cousin's barbs since Petunia moved her family back to Vicksburg. Was the relative peace that had existed in the home to be shattered—not by the lively children, but by Petunia?

Releasing her, Wilma ran up the stairs and disappeared down the hall. Lifting her skirts, Felicity followed. To her surprise, Aunt Mae, Petunia, Little Miles, and Wilma were all in Felicity's bedroom.

Her full-sized bed was neatly made with a pink spread. Her hairbrush and bowl and pitcher were arranged beside the lantern on her dressing table. The doors to her oak wardrobe were closed. The only thing out of place was her nightgown draped across the pillow. Though she hadn't expected such perusal, at least the room was tidy.

"I'll take this one," Petunia declared without seeming to notice Felicity's arrival. "It used to be Rosemary's, and I wanted it when she got married, but you put Ginger in here instead, Mama. This room is big enough for me and Miles. The two empty ones across the hall will do nicely for the children."

"Dearest, this room is Felicity's." Tugging at her sleeves, Aunt Mae caught sight of Felicity. "Hello, dear. Wilma said you were home. We're having some excitement today."

"Yes, Mama told me Mrs. Mitchell won't hire me because she's moving to Texas." Petunia put her hands on her hips. "Since I haven't found any shops that are hiring, we're moving in here. With Mama and Papa."

"I see." She'd told her aunt of Julia's decision just last evening, knowing she often saw her daughter's family during the week while Felicity worked. "This has been my bedroom since I moved in with Aunt Mae." There were only four bedrooms on this floor. Two were already occupied.

"That's not a problem. There's a bedroom opposite the attic where our maid used to sleep. I believe the room is as she left it years ago." Petunia waved her hand. "That will do nicely for you, and I will be able to hear my children if they call for me in the night."

Why did a two-year-old need his own room? She looked at her aunt, whose eyes pleaded for Felicity's understanding. No, Aunt Mae wouldn't refuse her daughter's mandates.

So Felicity was to be relegated to the small attic bedroom that she'd only opened once—when her aunt gave her a tour of the home after she moved here from Bovina. No doubt, there were cobwebs and spiders rampant in the space. She tried not to shudder.

"I'll give it a good cleaning tomorrow." Aunt Mae patted her hand. "I'll air it out and wash the bedding while you're at work. You won't be put out at all, my dear."

Except to lose her comfortable bedroom.

Living with Petunia would be far worse than her working for Julia.

~

*L*uke started work before dawn on Thursday, hoping to make up for the hour he'd lose for his appointment with Dr. Watkins. This could be the day the doctor made his decision about recommending Luke be released to civilian life or returned to the army, and he was plenty nervous about the matter.

He hadn't remembered anything even after Oscar's battle descriptions. His nightmares about his parents' drownings came nearly nightly, serving to remind him of his failure to save them. He pushed those aside to assimilate new skills about saddle-making. Although Ash had complimented his surprising knack, there was much to learn, but after this current order, there were no others.

How was he supposed to learn his job without work to do?

Felicity had been at work for an hour, merely waving at him as she walked past the shop. He'd been avoiding her since the concert. If she had purposely sat beside him, he must make it clear to her that his main goals were to regain his memories and learn saddle-making skills. She'd eventually learn that he planned to deliver secret messages for the Union.

He could handle no more than that. Nor should he drag a wonderful woman like Felicity into his mire of the unknown.

The sun was fully up when Ash joined him. "We're going to make a side saddle when we finish this one." He fingered the stitches Luke had just finished. "This is good work. I'll deliver it to Mr. Carver tomorrow."

The customer from Bovina. "We've a new order, then?"

Ash shook his head. "We'll make it and display it until some woman is in need of it. Orders for side saddles don't come often, but you need to know how to make them."

That was wise. "Fair enough." He stood. "Care if I go to the doctor's now?"

"This is an opportune time." Ash folded his arms. "Want me to tag along?"

"Nay. I'll face the man's decision on me own." He buttoned his warm wool coat.

"We're all praying it's the right one."

Felicity was no doubt adding her prayers to Ash's and Julia's. "I will take all of those I can get." Taking a calming breath, he strode to the hospital.

~

*F*elicity had kept an eye out of the dining room window for the past hour, hoping that Luke would come to see her before going to the hospital. She was afraid for him. Afraid for herself. She bowed her head to whisper a quick prayer. *Please, God, move Dr. Watkins's heart to care more for his patient than the army's need of soldiers.*

Opening her eyes, her heart leapt at the sight of broad shoulders and a back that was ramrod straight. Luke's step was purposeful, determined, as he strode to meet his fate. Despite her fear, tears pricked her eyes in pride. He was a good man. A strong, faithful man.

And he had once been her beau.

The front door opened, allowing in a chilly breeze.

Felicity swiped at her cheeks and picked up her duster. Staying busy would help.

"Felicity?" Ash spoke hesitantly.

She turned. Ash and Julia stood arm in arm at the room's entrance.

"We want to pray for Luke. Care to join us?"

Felicity struggled for control. "Yes, please. I'd appreciate it."

～

*L*uke drummed his fingers against the table in the nurses' room. Thirty minutes before, one of the nurses, Mrs. Ellis, had scurried in and left with medicine after offering to locate the doctor for him.

Seeking a distraction, Luke wandered to the stove and poured himself a cup of coffee. It was weak, as if watered down. Not good.

He drank it, anyway. When the tin cup was empty, he pondered searching for the doctor himself. At heavy footsteps on the stairs, he stood. The doctor strode through the open door carrying a page filled with notes. About Luke's condition? He didn't have a chance to read anything before Dr. Watkins folded it.

"Luke, it's good to see you. Mrs. Ellis told me you were waiting." Dr. Watkins gave him a probing look. "Coffee any good?"

"Nay. Quenches the thirst, is all."

He chuckled. "I appreciate your honesty. Let's sit." He bypassed the coffeepot and laid the paper on the table in front of him as he sat.

Luke's heartbeat quickened as he complied. "I've recalled nothing of those lost five years."

"That frustrates you." Dr. Watkins studied him.

"Aye. I thought me memories would have surfaced by now." He swirled the grounds covering the bottom of his tin cup.

"Still troubled by headaches?"

"Aye." The one he had now worsened by the minute.

"What about Miss Danielson?"

Luke's gaze flew to the doctor's face. What was this? Why ask about Felicity? "Begging your pardon?"

"Do you remember that she was your girl?"

"Ye know about that?"

"She told me. You'd be likely to recall someone so important to you first." Dr. Watkins leaned closer. "Now...I want the truth. Do you remember courting Miss Danielson?"

"Nay." He rubbed his hands up and down his face. "I wish to do that very thing, for I'd not hurt such a fine woman for all the world."

Dr. Watkins surveyed him. "What of the battles you've been in? Fredericksburg, where you were injured?"

"Truly, I only have the word of folks such as yourself that such ever happened to me." He touched his head, where his wound was still tender. "Except for this scab and me headaches."

"What of your training? Firing a gun?"

Luke shook his head. "I know I hunted game with my pa. That's the extent of it. Ye cannot want these memories more than I do meself."

Dr. Watkins propped an elbow on the table and rested his chin on his fist. "I believe you." He sighed. "And I'm sorry this has happened to you, for those memories might not return. Some trauma could be blocking them. I don't know."

That wasn't what he wanted to hear.

"Or they could return in months."

Months? How long must his torment last?

"Each case seems to bring its own intricacies. And those headaches may continue for a time as well." The doctor sat upright. "I won't put this off. I'm going to recommend the army give you an honorable discharge. It may take a week or two for a response."

Luke sagged in his chair. At least a discharge was to be his, *if* the army agreed. "Will they heed your recommendation?"

"Quite likely." With a shrug, Dr. Watkins stood and extended his hand. "You won't need to return to the hospital unless your headaches worsen."

"Much obliged to you." Luke shook his hand.

"Thanks for proudly serving the South." With that, the doctor left with his notes.

Had he done that? Proudly served the South? Everything was so confusing.

Today's news was a mixture of good and bad. He could now concentrate on honing his skills at the shop and start delivering messages.

But he might never remember Felicity. That cut ran deep.

⁓

Felicity carried two dinner plates with servings of chicken croquettes, boiled potatoes, and biscuits with honey into the dining room where Luke, Ash, and Julia awaited lunch and set them in front of her employers. Jolene followed with two more plates.

Luke had returned half an hour before, saying he'd tell everyone his news at lunch.

Felicity's legs knocked together during Ash's blessing. Afterward, she fastened her gaze on Luke. "We're all very anxious to learn what the doctor said." That hardly described her agitation. She was surprised her voice didn't shake.

"Aye. Well, he believes I cannot remember and will recommend the army discharge me."

Relief so strong that it was akin to what she felt when learning Luke would physically recover from his wounds washed over her. God had answered her prayers. She wanted to dance and sing, and embrace Luke. She did none of these outwardly. But her heart did all of them.

"That's wonderful news." Ash's face relaxed. "You won't have to return to your regiment."

"You can concentrate on—" Julia stopped as Jolene entered with a coffeepot. "Jolene, Luke has just told us the army will—"

"Discharge him. Yes, I heard him all the way to the kitchen." She turned to Luke. "I'm sorry you won't be able to continue your duties, but I thank you for fighting for us."

Luke's eyes widened. "'Twas me pleasure, ma'am."

Jolene's response proved that her loyalties were to the South, something Felicity had wondered about. She was proud of him for giving the right answer.

The cook placed the pot on the buffet and then left the room.

"There's not much more to tell." Staring at his filled plate, Luke clutched his fork. "Except that Dr. Watkins worries that some trauma may be blocking me memories. They may not return." He raised miserable eyes to Felicity's face.

Every ounce of elation ebbed away. He was home for good once the army discharged him. That was wonderful news. Yet he might never remember loving her. Her heart felt as if it cracked open.

He'd changed. Gone was the laughing man who loved to tease her. Loved her, period. This new man he'd become might never love her.

She'd best learn to make her own way in this world.

Alone.

CHAPTER 16

elicity tried to push her conflicted feelings away for the sake of her patients the following day. She had one new patient. Zeb Tyndale had been shot in the foot. So far, the doctors hadn't removed it.

Bessie approached her midmorning. "I brought a corn muffin for my breakfast. I'll eat it with coffee for my break. When I come back, will you help me change sheets for three of my soldiers?"

"If you'll help with mine." Felicity chirped her response automatically. It only mattered for the men who needed help to a chair.

"All right." The dedicated nurse was gone in a twinkling.

Now was her chance to discover if Zeb knew anything to help Ash. She hurried to his side. "Mr. Tyndale, did you need anything?"

The curly-haired twenty-year-old stared at his bandages. "A new foot?"

She laughed softly at his attempt at humor. "May I ask what happened?"

"I was in a skirmish up in Tennessee. Collierville ain't but a few miles from the Mississippi line. The whole thing lasted about long enough to get shot."

Not much there. "I'm sorry about that. How'd the Yankees know where you were?" She glanced at the door. Bessie hadn't returned.

"There are spies everywhere, Miss Danielson." His brown eyes darkened. "Southern people like you and me passing on our secrets."

Someone exactly like her. Her breath caught in her throat. "That's terrible." She covered her mouth with her hand as if upset to learn *anyone* would betray them. "Did you ever meet one?"

"Nah. But one was captured up near Bolivar a few days ago. I hope they hang the feller. Spies have been no end of trouble to us."

And Felicity might possibly do the same. A cold feeling in her stomach began to spread. What she was doing was serious.

Bessie entered the ward.

"That does sound bad. Can I get you a dipper of water?"

"I'm parched—I ain't gonna lie." He pushed himself up against the wall.

"Let me fetch you a drink."

Bessie frowned as Felicity returned to Zeb's side with it.

She remained silent as he downed two dippers and then joined the other nurse. "Whose bed should we change first?"

Bessie glanced at Zeb and then back at her. "Will's."

Felicity's heart hammered against her ribs as they helped the man missing his left leg from the knee down.

She'd stop by to tell Ash the little she knew before going home. Besides, Petunia was moving in today. Felicity wasn't looking forward to going home.

∾

*L*uke walked with Ash toward the provost marshal's office after lunch. Now that Luke awaited his discharge, Ash seemed in as great a hurry as he was to show him what he did as a spy. About time.

They entered the small office to find four people ahead of them. One person was denied a pass. Luke glanced at Ash, who started explaining how to fashion a side saddle. It seemed an inopportune moment, but Luke tried to keep his mind on what Ash was saying until it was their turn.

"I'm Ash Mitchell, a saddler here in Vicksburg." He fished a folded paper from his pocket and held it up for the bored officer with a curled mustache to read. "I have to travel to purchase supplies for my shop occasionally. I hired this man, Luke Shea, last month. He'll purchase supplies for me at times and needs a pass."

The officer's dark gaze fastened on Luke. "Name?"

"Luke Shea." He straightened.

"Where do you work?

"At Mitchell's Saddle Shop. It's owned by Ashburn Mitchell here." He indicated Ash with a nod.

"What are your responsibilities there?"

"Cutting, stitching, punching—all the tasks involved in saddle-making." Luke felt Ash's gaze. "Also, purchasing supplies for the shop."

The officer sat back in his chair, eyeing Luke. "That's an acceptable reason for a pass." He scribbled on a form. "Keep this with you whenever you leave Vicksburg until your return."

"Obliged to you." Luke accepted the paper, thankful when the provost marshal's attention shifted to the short fellow waiting behind them.

They were outside before Ash spoke. "Casual."

It was a warning. Luke schooled his features, glad the score of soldiers outside the building couldn't see his fast-beating heart.

They were on Second North Street, Ash's street, when Luke spotted a cloaked figure ahead of them. "Felicity is coming to see Julia."

"Or me." He limped along at his side. "It's unusual for her to come on Fridays." Ash glanced at Luke. "Learn to watch for the unusual."

"Aye." He'd have to become more observant.

"Good job back there. For a minute, I feared he'd ask why we needed two people purchasing supplies."

"And I'd explain that you're moving to Texas." Luke kept his eyes on Felicity until she disappeared inside the two-story home that had become a sanctuary for him.

"Now you're thinking on your feet." Ash's face lightened. "Let's see what's brought Felicity here."

∼

Felicity straightened in her chair before the glowing hearth of the second-floor parlor when Ash entered with Luke and closed the door. "Ash, I hoped for a private word." She nodded at Luke. "Begging your pardon."

"It's all right. He can hear the news." Ash warmed his hands in front of the fire as Luke leaned on the mantel beside him and opposite of Felicity.

So Luke was joining their spy efforts. That was good. It would give him a new focus.

Glancing at Julia, who gave her an encouraging nod, Felicity told them what she'd learned.

"You say the spy was captured near Bolivar?" Ash studied Felicity's face from his stance in front of the fireplace.

"That's right. In Tennessee." Felicity sat beside Julia on the sofa. She glanced at the closed door. They didn't need Jolene to overhear—not that she ever came up here. Still, one couldn't be too careful. "Zeb Tyndale, my patient, certainly abhors spies. He hopes they hang the man."

"So it's a male spy. Two good bits of information." He turned to Luke. "Looks as though you and me will ride the train to Bolton tomorrow."

"I'm ready. This evening, if you prefer." Luke straightened.

"We've already missed today's train, and I've only one horse." His brow furrowed. "Think I'll see if I can buy a horse. I should teach you the back route, in case the trains aren't running."

"Aye. Teach me all you can." Luke's jaw set. "I remember everything from these present days. It's the past that's a problem."

"Fair enough. We'll get an early start tomorrow." Ash gave a decisive nod. "Well done, Felicity. Thank you."

Ash's praise fed Felicity's spirit. Luke didn't say anything but regarded her with a smile that might have held some surprise.

No more surprise than what she felt herself.

"Will you stay for supper?" Julia stood when Felicity did.

"Petunia is moving her family to Aunt Mae's today." No need to mention the loss of her warm bedroom. After all, she was a poor relation, not a daughter. Hopefully, Petunia wouldn't push her from the family circle, for she craved to belong to them—even more now that she no longer belonged with Luke. "It's likely to be chaotic. Aunt Mae will need me. I've tarried too long as it is."

Julia frowned. "Then how about tomorrow?"

"Just me? Or everyone?"

Julia's eyes widened. "How about just you this time? We'll host everyone on another occasion."

"Thank you." Felicity's glance lingered on Luke. "I'll pray for your safety tomorrow."

She was soon on her way, glad she'd been able to provide

information. And tomorrow she'd be able to learn what happened with Luke's first spy trip. It was an important bond they shared. Yet she dared not allow herself to hope it was enough to build what hadn't survived Luke's past.

~

*L*uke rubbed his hands together as if to warm them, but it was really to mask his trembling anticipation as he showed his pass to a soldier before mounting the train the next morning, the last day of January.

Ash chose a seat near the back, and Luke sat in the one opposite the aisle. Many folks in Vicksburg knew they were old buddies. It was important they not ignore one another in the city. Upon arriving in Bolton, Luke was to give Ash a five-minute head start on the forest trail leading to a tanner's homestead. Folks usually recognized Ash in Bolton and seemed to ignore him, or so Ash had surmised. This was Luke's first visit, and it was better in the long run if local citizens didn't connect them. It shouldn't be a problem to arrive at Jim Routledge's—the tanner's—home at the same time. Ash had warned Luke not to sit beside him on the return trip.

There was a lot to remember, including parts about delivering a message to a mill outside of Brownsville.

One other thing. He was supposed to keep a sharp eye on the folks traveling around him and the folks in town so he'd know if someone followed them.

No wonder Ash was a good spy. There were so many pieces to this spying mission that Luke had never considered. His head was already spinning from all he had to remember, making his head ache to a dull throb.

Had he needed these skills as a soldier? Reconnaissance, alert to any change, and the ability to sneak in and out of places without being noticed?

He sighed. There was no way to know unless his memories resurfaced.

Seven soldiers got on the train just before it pulled out of Vicksburg. Luke lowered his wide-brimmed hat over his eyes. He knew better than to look at them or call attention to himself in any way.

The other passengers were few. A farmer likely had sold some eggs, milk, or butter because he toted an empty crate. A gray-haired gentleman sporting a cane escorted a woman who was probably his wife. And five businessmen engaged in what appeared to be a conversation about the war. The engine was so loud that Luke heard only snatches of their conversation about a canal that the Union army was attempting to dig upriver of Vicksburg. They guffawed about the swamps and the swollen Mississippi River as a force of nature fighting for the South.

Luke settled back in his seat. The Northerners' determination to build a canal was nothing new. He'd learned of the digging in the newspapers he'd begun reading the past couple of weeks. Union General Grant had his eye on Vicksburg, but digging a canal to try to bypass the city was going to require months, in his opinion, if it was successful at all.

After the soldiers got off in Bovina, he relaxed. Julia had mentioned Felicity grew up here. A variety of brick or wood buildings near the depot where people lived and shopped showed it to be a nice place to grow up. Had one of the white clapboard houses belonged to her family? Did she have siblings? He knew only that she was an orphan, like himself. He suddenly longed to know more about her.

A handful of passengers joined them at stops along the way. Several cars held only freight.

Finally, they reached Bolton. Ash didn't even glance Luke's way before he disembarked. Luke followed at a sedate pace, making a great show of brushing soot off his hat while observing the path Ash took. Spotting a cigar shop, he stepped inside and purchased two cigars.

Five minutes later, Luke caught up with Ash a quarter mile into the forest.

"Good job." Speaking softly, Ash set off immediately. His limp didn't slow them much. "We could take the road, but Jim won't expect us on a Saturday. On the other hand, we've all learned to live off our wits, so our visit won't ruffle him." His glance darted in every direction.

"Aye." Luke followed his gaze. Besides maneuvering a muddy path, there was little to see beyond a carpet of brown leaves, barren trees, and bushes. Branches swayed in the wind. A desolate forest, to be sure. No sense of anyone being nearby. Not much place for someone to hide on the wintry day.

The path led out of the woods to a muddy, tree-lined road. A two-story stone house set apart by forests from neighboring properties came into view. A spacious corral with two mares, a filly, and a stallion grazing inside bordered a large barn and extended to the road. A rooster strutted among the hens, pecking at grain on the ground outside the open barn doors.

Ash lifted his hand to his side in a waiting motion. "This is the Routledge homestead." He peered at the well-kept grounds. "Don't see any strange horses tied to the fence. Let's head first to the barn where Jim tans the hides."

"Aye. I'm ready."

"That you are." Ash gave a crisp nod.

They crossed the street and the soft, spongy grass leading to the barn. They passed a full water trough beside the fence before stopping at the open door. Luke peered inside. Stalls for the horses were on one side with an opposite wall going halfway up running the length of the building. A stack of skins covered a table in the back of the building.

"Jim? You here?" Ash's gaze darted around the barn.

Silence except for the clucking of chickens outside.

"Reckon he's not tanning hides today." Ash strode to the house and knocked on the door.

A man in his fifties whose red hair was streaked with gray opened the door. "Ash, it's good to see you." Shaking his hand, he looked over Ash's shoulder. "And you've brought a guest."

"Hello, Jim. I brought the friend I was telling you about— Luke Shea." Ash turned to him. "Luke, I'd like you to meet James Routledge, the best tanner this side of Jackson."

"A pleasure, Mr. Routledge, sir." Luke shook his hand in a firm grip.

"Call me Jim, and you'll be Luke to me." He widened the door. "Come on in. The coffee's still hot. Warm yourselves by the fire if you need to."

Luke followed Ash straight to the hearth where a fire blazed.

"I see you're in civilian clothes, Luke. Did you get your discharge from the Confederate army?"

"Not yet. Dr. Watkins requested it."

"Ash swears to your Union loyalty." Jim set two steaming cups on the dining table outside the kitchen and gestured for them to sit. "I'd like to hear it from you."

"Me loyalty is to the Union even though I've learned I served in the Confederate army." Luke held the tanner's gaze. "Five years I've lost—and I pray me integrity is intact. I desire to see our country unified. This division tears at me very soul."

Jim studied him and then straddled his chair. "I believe you. Now what brings you two men here?"

One hurdle crossed. Jim trusted him. Luke sat as Ash explained what Felicity learned about the missing spy.

Jim drummed his fingers. "I've learned since you were here last that this Union spy isn't one of ours. He doesn't ride for us specifically, but let's get this information out today. I'd like to see him rescued sooner rather than later. Can you ride to Harv's, maybe introduce Luke to him?"

Luke recognized that as the name of the mill owner outside Brownsville whom Ash delivered information to weekly. It was a ride of sixteen miles to and from Bolton, all told.

"Planning on it, if we can borrow two horses," Ash said.

Jim gave him a scrap of paper and a pencil. "Use this to code the message."

Luke had also learned Ash never carried messages out of Vicksburg with the soldier guards and pickets on the watch for spies.

Ash began writing letters that made no sense to Luke. "I'd like to buy a horse for Luke, if you know anyone selling."

"I'll give you my mare Stardust, Luke, for spying for me. On top of the pay you'll make to do the runs as long as I'm a spymaster."

"'Tis a generous offer." One that made him uneasy. "Yet surely, I'll not earn so much by simply riding for you."

"Oh, you'll earn it, that's certain." His eyes dulled. "It's a dangerous job, for me as well."

Ash stiffened. "Is there a new threat?"

"You may as well know." Jim wrapped his hands around his tin cup. He was silent a moment. "One of my spies heard me mentioned as a Unionist and potential spy and warned me. I fear someone let my name slip."

This news was more than Luke had bargained for on his first spy trip. What if he inadvertently shared a secret with the wrong person and put Ash in danger?

"I've a good reputation among my neighbors. That may save me." Jim stared into the blaze in the hearth. "Or not. Maybe my name didn't make it to the Rebel army, as I have prayed. Regardless, I have white paint ready for my corral. If you see it, hightail it out of here and never return."

Ash went still. "You said once that you'd paint your fence white if you feared the Confederates were closing in on you."

"Exactly. Confederate soldiers in Jackson are the likeliest

bunch to come after me, with them being so close. I'll be right here, waiting for them." Jim's jaw tightened. "And you're not to try to rescue me either. I'll not have your imprisonments—or worse—on my conscience. It's got plenty enough on it already."

Jim feared he'd be captured. As Ash had been. Was that going to happen to Luke? Maybe Felicity?

Perhaps Luke deserved it.

Felicity didn't.

CHAPTER 17

$\mathcal{L}$uke rose to his feet. The immediate danger was to Jim. Ash had spoken so highly of him that Luke didn't want to see him in the hands of the Confederacy. "Come back to Vicksburg with us."

"No one will find you there. I've room for you in our home." Putting down his pencil, Ash stood. "I know Julia will agree."

"And put suspicion on all of you? More than you already face?" With a resigned shake of his head, Jim motioned for them to sit. "No, I'm a widower with no children to mourn me. If this is to be my fate, I'll meet it in my own home."

"Prison's not a place for you." There was a tremor in Ash's hands. "I know what it's like."

"And it nearly killed you." Jim spoke bluntly. "You'll soon be safe in Texas. Let's not jeopardize the safety of Julia and her family."

Ash's face tightened. Jim clearly knew him well, for he'd chosen an argument Ash couldn't refute.

Slow steps took Jim to the kitchen, as if he were exhausted. He returned with the coffeepot and refreshed their beverages before sitting. "I'll pay you fellows for February and March."

"I'm moving in March."

Jim waved his objection away. "Then leave whatever's left with Luke. I doubt there'll be any pay beyond that. If I manage to escape from prison, I'll make my way up to Nashville, where my sister lives, because I won't be able to return here."

"We'll help you leave today." Ash started to rise. "Pack some things while we ride to Harv's—"

"No. I'll fight as long as can." Jim rubbed his hands over his bearded face. "Ash, I'm content knowing that you and my other spies contributed to forts being captured and battles being waged."

Ash slumped back in his chair. Luke sympathized because he already liked the spymaster who had given so much to fighting for the Union.

"The next time you come, I'll likely have a new delivery route for you. With thousands of Union soldiers camped north of Vicksburg, I have folks working to set up new spies in Bovina or Edwards, railroad stops closer to you. If that comes about, I'll assign that one to you. We're avoiding you leaving directly from Vicksburg with coded messages."

That was one detail Ash had reiterated. No written messages inside Vicksburg.

"With over ten thousand Confederates defending Vicksburg, I agree with the wisdom of your decision." Ash frowned. "Should the route change, I'll have to find a place to buy shop supplies closer to home."

Their excuse to leave the city. Luke admired both spies' attention to every detail. His head reeled from all he'd learned.

"There's a tanner, Barney Williams, in Bovina so you can maintain your cover of buying shop supplies." Rising, Jim crossed to a roll-top desk near the hearth. He extracted several bills from a hidden drawer. Dividing it, he gave one stack to Ash and the other to Luke. "Barney's a staunch supporter of the South, so make certain you agree with everything he says."

"I'm grateful for the pay." Luke counted the bills. Fifty dollars for two months. "This is too much."

"Count it as combat pay." Jim sighed. "You'll earn every penny and more."

Like a soldier's salary? That made sense. "Thank you, then." This cash was in addition to his new horse. What a boon. He'd best save it for days ahead and live off the small salary the saddle shop provided because there'd been few orders.

"Happy to oblige." Jim sighed. "I'll keep that coming to you as long as I can."

Ash stood. "Should we take Stardust home today?"

"You'd best do that." Jim shook Ash's hand first and then Luke's. "Just to make certain you get her."

"Aye. Ye have me thanks."

"And you have mine." Jim put his hands on his hips. "I believe you were right about this man, Ash. Courage and loyalty are needed by the boatload, as you know."

Qualities the spymaster seemed to possess in abundance. He'd already earned Luke's admiration—and his prayers.

~

*L*ate Saturday morning, Dr. Watkins motioned for Felicity to join him in the hall. Her thoughts immediately flew to Luke's army discharge as she stepped outside her ward on the gray dismal day. Had it been denied?

"We can't save Zeb Tyndale's foot." Dr. Watkins frowned. "There are shattered bones in there. Dr. Barrington agrees with my assessment."

That the only two doctors in the hospital agreed on the diagnosis decided the matter. "Did you tell him?" Felicity was heartsick for the soldier who had provided information about the missing spy.

He shook his head. "I'll tell him and then attendants will

carry him down to our operating room." A room on the first floor had been set aside for this purpose to spare other patients. "Stay with him until they come."

"I will." She had looked for a chance to speak to Zeb privately to discover if he might know something else helpful to the Union army, but Bessie had stayed nearby all morning, almost as if she wanted to listen to Felicity's conversations. The poor man was going into surgery. He'd want to talk about family.

Felicity followed the doctor to Zeb's bedside. She pressed a hand against her stomach at the anguish on his face when the doctor delivered the verdict.

Dr. Watkins placed his hand on Zeb's shoulder. "Sorry that it's not better news, son." With that, he strode from the ward.

Zeb stared after him with dull eyes.

"I'm so sorry." Felicity sat on the chair the doctor vacated. "He tried to save it."

"It ain't your fault, Miss Danielson." Sweat beaded on his forehead. "Just never thought it'd happen to me. I might have stayed home and married my girl if I'd have known I'd lose my foot."

"Do you want me to write to her for you?"

"Nah." He looked away. "Don't know as Bethanne will have me now."

"Any woman worth her salt would be proud to welcome her wounded soldier home." Felicity tilted her chin.

"You act as though you know about it." Zeb clutched at his chest. "Did your beau get wounded?"

"He did." Felicity didn't usually talk about such things. The man needed hope. "He's still not himself, but I pray for him every day."

"Don't give up on him, Miss Danielson." He stirred restlessly. "Please, promise you won't. Soldiers see such hard things in battle. Their buddies right beside them getting killed...good men whose children will grow up without them. Please, Miss Danielson. Your beau deserves better than to be forgotten."

"Rest easy." She gripped his trembling hand. "I will never give up on him. And I believe, in my heart, that Bethanne will be waiting when you go home." She didn't know the woman, but this soldier, facing surgery, needed to cling to hope.

"Miss Danielson?" One of the male attendants, a muscular man in his thirties named Jeremiah, tapped her solder. "Dr. Watkins is ready for Mr. Tyndale's surgery."

"One moment." She leaned closer. "Shall I pray for you first?"

"I wish you would." Closing his eyes, he retained his hold of her hand.

She whispered a prayer for his surgery, his health, his family, and Bethanne before releasing him. "God hasn't abandoned you, Zeb, and He never will."

"That sounds like something my ma would say." Tears filled his eyes. "Thank you, Miss Danielson."

"He's ready." Felicity stepped out of the way.

Bessie hurried over as they carried him out. "Is he about to lose his foot?"

She nodded.

"It's a shame." Bessie gazed out the window at the bleak wintry morning. "I like to think that someone prayed for George before he passed." Her face hardened. "Best fetch lunch. Your patients are hungry."

Felicity was glad for an excuse to leave prying eyes, for she was certain those in adjoining beds had overheard her conversation with Zeb. She hurried out, needing a moment to calm herself.

She couldn't help wondering at Bessie, whose tender moments were few. Grief had made Bessie vindictive toward everyone from the North.

That made her the most dangerous person in the hospital for Felicity.

~

*L*uke was pleased with his new mare that he'd ride home later today while Ash took the train. Even so, after nearly eight miles of riding to Harvey's Mill, he could tell those summers where he'd ridden for miles with Ash and Willie were long past.

He memorized the surroundings—farms, homes, and forested areas. How frustrating that he could easily do this yet couldn't remember Felicity. They'd followed the main road until reaching a fork where they veered to the left. After that, they'd taken a lane that had a knotty magnolia that must predate the country's revolution against England.

Not too much to remember if Ash left him on his own.

Ash raised his hand in greeting to folks in their yards but didn't speak. Luke followed his lead.

"We're getting close." Ash spoke in low tones.

Luke's breathing quickened. This was it. Ash would do the initial talking and introduce Luke if all was well. Either way, Harv would get a good look at him and hopefully trust him for future deliveries.

They approached a homestead with a mill on the left. Faded black paint on a fencepost sign was still legible— *Harvey's Mill*. Though Ash wanted him to deliver the actual message, Luke had been warned not to give the note wrapped in a dollar in his hat to Harv's sons.

They rode into the deserted yard and dismounted. A door opened in the brick home some hundred feet distant. A red-haired girl of perhaps ten tossed a bucket of water near the well. She watched them curiously as she cranked the well and began to refill the bucket.

"Take your time," Ash whispered, barely moving his lips. "Harv's got a customer."

"Aye." Luke sauntered toward the mill. He slowly looped Stardust's reins to a hitching post outside the mill, next to a buckboard.

"Can't stall any longer without raising the girl's suspicions." Ash adjusted his hat, his arm blocking his face from her view.

"I'm ready." He followed Luke inside.

They met a gray-haired man dressed as a farmer exiting the building. Luke tipped his hat at him as the door closed with a snap.

A man with hair redder than Luke's and dressed in a blue plaid shirt stood beside a long table with built-up sides for holding the meal.

Ash stepped forward. "I need a five-pound sack of cornmeal."

"Have it ready for you in a minute." Harv's gaze darted toward Luke.

Wagon wheels squeaked outside as the earlier customer left. Luke relaxed slightly. "I thought I saw a blue jay on the way here." It was the code to let Harv know Jim sent him.

"You might have." Harv eyed him. "Seen one myself just yesterday."

That was the code that it was fine to make the delivery. Had he said, "Doubtful," they'd have purchased the cornmeal without delivering the message.

"Brought a friend with me today. Luke Shea." Ash spoke casually. "He's from Vicksburg. He will come by himself in a month or so."

"Fine by me. Happy to sell my grain to new customers. Luke, folks call me Harv." He began filling a burlap sack with a metal scoop.

"Harv, it's a pleasure."

"You leaving, Ash?"

"My wife and I are moving with her family to a ranch in Texas."

"Surprising." Not a muscle moved in Harv's face. "My best to you and your wife iffen I don't see you again."

Luke had to admire the man. Anyone watching or listening wouldn't know anything untoward was happening.

"My thanks for that, but we'll need more cornmeal before we go."

"Glad to hear it." Harv tied the sack closed.

Extracting a bill wrapped around the message from his hat, Luke stepped forward. "Thank you kindly." He extended it to the mill owner.

Harv's eyes darted at Ash, who nodded. "I hope to see you folks come back." They made the exchange.

Luke almost missed Harv's swift movement to drop the bill-wrapped note into his pocket.

Ash jerked his head toward the door. Within a minute, they were on the road again.

The knotty magnolia was in sight before Ash spoke. "Well done."

That's when it struck Luke what had just happened.

A former Confederate soldier was now a Union spy.

And *that* felt more right than anything he'd done since waking up in a Vicksburg hospital with five years lost to him.

~

*J*ulia had warned Felicity that the men couldn't talk about their day during supper because they all now knew that Jolene's excellent hearing allowed her to listen in on the conversations. While they sometimes closed the parlor door for privacy, the dining room remained open for every meal. To close it was to raise suspicion.

Knowing Luke's every expression so well, she could tell the

day had left him with mixed emotions. Had they learned that the poor spy had been killed in Tennessee?

"Has Petunia's family moved in?" Julia asked over apple cobbler made from dried fruit.

"Yesterday." Felicity's possessions had been moved to the attic room before she got home on Friday. Even now, her jaw clenched when she considered how her cousin had demanded the intrusion and her aunt had allowed it. "Petunia wanted to be out of her rented home before tomorrow, February first."

"Meals will be livelier with children around." Ash grinned.

"They are." Having the children there was the best part. "No complaints from me on that."

Luke's brow furrowed, as if he wanted to ask what she *would* complain about.

"Sounds lovely." Julia stood. "If you're all finished, let's move to the upstairs parlor where we have a cozy fire going."

They were soon seated in a semi-circle around the fire with Felicity in a chair beside Luke. The men took turns telling about the day. The delivery had gone without a hitch. Unfortunately, Ash's spymaster friend—whom he refused to name—was in danger of arrest.

"Can he not flee to us?" Julia fished her tatting from a basket in between her chair and Felicity's. "No one will find him here."

"He won't place you, your mama, and Eddie in danger." Ash tilted his head to one side as he looked at his wife. "I must agree with that caution."

"He has a sister in Tennessee." Luke shifted in his chair. "I wish he'd not wait."

"The two of you be careful." Lace threaded the finger Julia shook at them.

"We will. I've no desire to be recaptured." Ash pulled on his sleeve. "Or see Luke suffer such an indignity."

"Aye. We'll be careful, ladies." Luke looked at Felicity.

She couldn't tear her gaze from his. She'd do anything to end the war sooner and protect Luke. His set jaw showed his determination, yet the look in his eyes...it was as if he poured his very strength into her spirit.

Felicity tried to press her fear away, but it was too great. The sacrifices of spying rolled in on her full force. She didn't fear for herself.

It was Luke.

She didn't know what Ash had suffered, but she couldn't bear for Luke to be imprisoned. He was too loyal to betray anyone...and that dogged determination might cost him his life.

CHAPTER 18

*O*n Felicity's walk home from Julia's on Monday, February second, cannons from Confederate soldiers on the bluff blasted toward the river. Something inside her quivered. Her thoughts flew back to the two months the past summer when Vicksburg had been bombarded by the Union fleet. Another river battle?

People bolted inside homes and businesses.

Spotting a lone ship on the river taking fire, she picked up her skirts to run toward Aunt Mae's.

"Felicity!" Luke's voice.

She turned.

He nearly barreled into her, so fast was he running. Luke's muscular arm was around her shoulders in an instant. "Let's get you home." He urged her forward.

"Thank you." The ship didn't seem to be firing back, a blessing. Almost as big a blessing as being in Luke's arms again. She put her arm around his waist, convincing herself that he'd understand it was easier to run together this way.

Cannonballs splashed into the river below. Two found their mark as the couple neared Aunt Mae's home.

"It's up here. On the left." It saddened Felicity that he needed directions, because he'd once spent many evenings there with her, Aunt Mae, and Uncle Charles.

"Aye. Get inside. Methinks it's a one-sided fight, after all, but best be safe." He removed his arm and stepped back.

"Come inside."

"Nay. I've work to do, but please, allow me to see you safely into the house."

Disappointment waged war with gratitude that he'd dropped everything to protect her. Perhaps he did care for her. "Thank you, Luke. I'll see you Wednesday."

As she closed the door behind her, she wondered if Petunia's presence had something to do with his refusal. Her cousin had been miffed that Julia hadn't invited all of them to supper on Saturday. After church services ended on Sunday, Petunia had hinted how much she'd love to see Julia's childhood home for she'd learned that lunch was at Julia's mother's that day.

It humiliated Felicity that Julia's hints that they'd host them on another occasion were ignored. In the end, a meal intended for Mrs. Dodd, Eddie, Julia, Ash, Luke, and Felicity stretched to include Petunia, Wilma, Little Miles, Uncle Charles, and Aunt Mae. Gracious as always, Mrs. Dodd took the additions in stride, serving smaller portions. The children climbed over crates stacked in the hall in readiness for sending them to Texas in advance of the move. Felicity was grateful that Eddie played with the children, fashioning a small fort for all them to play in.

"Felicity, is that you? Are you all right, dear?" Aunt Mae came running from the kitchen. "I heard our cannons blasting away, and it was time for your arrival."

"That Union ship was trying to sneak past us." Petunia followed, carrying her sleepy boy. "Those Yankees thought they could pass without our soldiers seeing them in broad daylight. The nerve."

"Yes, dear." Aunt Mae patted Felicity's hand. "You must have been so frightened."

Felicity opened her mouth to say that Luke had accompanied her, but Petunia spoke first.

"She's a grown woman, Mama. No need to coddle her." She rolled her eyes.

"Quite right." Felicity didn't like the hard quality that had crept into her tone. She worked to soften it as she continued. "Please excuse me." She climbed three flights of stairs to her bedroom. It hadn't been as enjoyable to sew with Aunt Mae since Petunia had moved in.

Cannon blasts ebbed and then stopped within minutes. The day's scare had been over quickly. Luke's protective action, the feel of his arm around her, made the Union ship's escape all the sweeter.

If only he'd remember what she'd meant to him.

She made up a fire in the heat stove and then sank onto her bed, fully clothed. Luke hadn't received his official discharge. She'd not rest easy until it came. It was good that he'd thrown himself into his job and also the spying.

However, he'd shown no signs of renewing their relationship. Yet running to her rescue, the worry in his brown eyes, showed a concern she'd love to build upon.

Smoke from the stove seeped into the room as she recalled Zeb Tyndale's pleas that she give Luke the time he needed to heal. She'd do that.

Sliding off her bed onto her knees, she prayed for her beau —his memories and his safety in his spying tasks. She prayed longest for the spymaster who had reason to fear capture, that God would thwart efforts to harm him. Then she prayed the same for Luke, Ash, and, almost as an afterthought, herself.

~

uke woke up two days later recalling how right it had felt to hold Felicity close in the danger from cannonballs.

His first instinct had been to find Felicity and get her to safety. She'd been happy to see him and hadn't seemed to mind his arm around her shoulders.

Which had fit so perfectly.

Her arm around him made him feel secure. As though he belonged there.

How close had they been during their courtship? Had she fallen in love with him? Although she'd never said as much, she certainly seemed to care for him. Yet he'd been her patient. Some nurses formed a bond with their patients. Felicity was a good nurse.

That bond must linger for him to so fear for her safety. That's all he felt, surely.

After she was safely home, he'd stopped to watch shells fly toward the river. Some shots struck the ship and some missed. The Union steamer continued past the city. The artillery stopped once the ship floated from sight.

Had this been a common sight for him in these war years? Nothing swirled in his memory.

A knock on the door prompted him to throw back the covers. "Aye?"

"Breakfast in twenty minutes"—Ash's voice—"and then we'll saddle up."

"Be there in ten." Fine spy he was, thinking of Felicity when he should be readying himself to ride horseback to Bolton. This trip would teach him the back roads and forest trails to hide from Confederate troops in the area.

It was a long ride to Jim's, just under thirty miles, and they'd have to rest the horses on the way there and back. Julia had packed a lunch for them large enough to share with the tanner. Luke prayed the man was still at home. Both he and Ash were anxious to learn the latest about the captured spy. Ash met his spies around the city to protect his family, and none of them had passed on news about him. Ash did learn that the Union *Queen of the West,* the ship that had drawn Confederate fire the day before, had rammed the Confederates' *City of Vicksburg,* the engines of which were to be sent to Mobile, Alabama—something the Union would benefit from knowing.

Ash bypassed the town of Bolton via a forested trail. Before long, he dismounted. "Let's walk our mares from here."

An uneasy feeling crept over Luke and he scanned every direction. No signs of movement. Not even a breeze.

"You feel it too?" Ash's glance darted all around.

"Aye."

"Stay here with the horses. I'm going to scout ahead." Ash handed him Rosebud's reins. "No sound."

Luke nodded. Ash disappeared into bushes surrounding the trail. Luke marked his progress by the shaking of bushes until he was out of sight.

Funny. He didn't remember the same trail feeling this eerie on Saturday.

Stardust neighed.

"Quiet, girl," Luke whispered against the horse's ear.

The mare tossed her head.

Luke looked in every direction at barren trees with leaves beneath that would rustle should someone step on them. That gave him some reassurance.

Then the bush trail Ash had taken began to shake again. If caught, he had his Vicksburg pass and could simply explain he was out obtaining shop supplies.

Nothing could calm his quickened heartbeat as he waited.

A head appeared through the brush. Then a lanky form with a limp. Ash.

Luke had never been so happy to see his friend. Then he noticed his ashen face. "What did you see?"

"A white fence." Ash's voice shook. "The whole corral is painted white except for one section near the house. I think the soldiers must have interrupted him."

Luke's heartbeat thundered in his ears, so great was his fear for the spymaster, for themselves. "We'd best hightail it out of here." Luke mounted Stardust.

"We'll ride to Harv's. See if he knows anything about Jim." Ash swung his leg over the saddle and took off before his foot was inside the stirrup.

As Luke kept pace with him, his fear escalated with every gallop. Who had Jim and where'd they taken him?

A half hour later, Luke slowed and followed Ash into a copse of trees just out of sight of Harvey's Mill.

"We can see the mill from the other side of these trees. Let's wait until all customers are gone." Ash started to dismount.

"Wait. I'll go." Luke swung from the saddle and left his horse with Ash. He crept to the edge of the trees where bushes grew rampant. He crouched behind them to peer toward the mill. One wagon pulled away, leaving only a horse at the hitching post. Luke looked around but couldn't see Ash...only Stardust's head. That was good, for folks would consider it mighty strange for them to stop in the wooded thicket some hundred feet away.

Two minutes later, the customer left. Luke waited another minute before he returned to Ash. "Let's go."

Luck was with them. No one was on the road when they left the tree cover and rode to the mill. He groaned inwardly, for they hadn't taken the time to code their message for Harv.

He followed Ash at a casual pace inside and closed the door behind them.

"I'll take five pounds of meal." Ash stopped on the other side of the grain table where Harv stood.

"Got some today. May not have it later." Harv's gaze darted from Ash to Luke.

Uneasy with that answer, Luke deemed it best to say the code. "Thought I spotted a blue jay on the way here."

"Doubtful."

That was the code not to make the exchange. A cold chunk of ice seemed to spread in Luke's middle.

"We just came from a friend's homestead." Ash spoke casually while his gaze darted to the door. "He was painting his corral fence white when he must have been interrupted. Do you know what happened?"

Harv paled. He looked at the door. "Heard a group of folks went to Tennessee. One fellow wasn't keen on the trip. Friends of ours are looking into the matter."

So Jim had been captured and taken to Tennessee. "They need help?" Luke stepped forward.

"No." Harv's tone was firm. "Your friend was set on that."

"When did it happen?" Ash folded his arms

"Sunday. But he sent word to me Saturday evening." Harv strode to the window and peered in every direction. Long strides brought him back to the table. Reaching into his boot, he extracted a page. "Your new route. Memorize it and then destroy it before you get to Vicksburg." He gave it to Ash.

Luke peered over his shoulder. The trail began in Bovina and went up near Tiffentown.

"A tailor named Matthew Frost is your new contact." Harv's voice was barely audible. "He lives about a half mile from town."

"A half mile? Too close for comfort." Ash's eyes narrowed.

Luke agreed. Jim's home had been in the country, and they'd had to take care not to be seen.

"It's the best we could do on short notice." Harv's chin jutted, his jawline hardening. "Matthew's a short, heavyset fellow. Bushy gray eyebrows. Ask if he has any handkerchiefs for sale. If he agrees, he can talk and accept messages. If he says no, hightail it out of there."

"How about this Brownsville route?" A rush of adrenaline made Luke jittery.

Harv shook his head. "Too risky. No one's riding until our friend is found, but if you hear anything, come tell us."

Creaking wheels approached.

"Wait a week before returning for news." Picking up an empty burlap sack, Harv scooped cornmeal into it.

"Will do." Luke managed to yawn as a huskily built man opened the door.

"Morning, Carl. Be right with you." Harv added another scoop.

"What do you have your door closed for? It's pretty...for February." Carl eyed Ash and Luke.

"Oh, did it warm up? Keep it open, then." Harv gave the sack to Luke, who handed him a dollar minus a message. "Thanks, fellas." He turned to Carl. "Now, what can I get for you? Your family doing well?"

Luke toted the sack outside in front of Ash. Neither spoke as they rode the forested trail until reaching the other side of Bolton. Jim's homestead was likely to be watched for a few days. They went nowhere near it.

Ash stopped near a stream. Dismounted stiffly as if he'd aged twenty years since breakfast. "They've got him. If they have an inkling how many of us report to him..."

"Aye." Luke didn't know Jim as well as Ash did, but his heart was nearly broken, anyway. "I pray he's rescued before someone decides to grab a noose."

"He won't mention any of our names." Ash refilled his canteen while the horses drank their fill.

"'Tis certain he'd face death rather than betray a friend." Luke hoped the same could be said of himself, but had no proof of it. How that truth ate at him.

"Our mares need a rest. Let's eat our sandwiches here." Ash fished them from his saddlebag.

"Aye. Pretty spot." As if it mattered that the scent of pine and the soft blanket of needles from the trees lining the stream made this a pleasant location for a picnic. Jim was in trouble. Likely facing interrogations and prison at the very least. Perhaps hanging or the barrel of a musket at the worst. Luke shuddered. Such could happen to him. He'd already done enough to deserve it in the eyes of many Southerners.

Ash plopped down beside the trickling, clear waters. "This is as good a time as any to memorize our next route."

"Then we'll burn it." The soldiers guarding the roads to Vicksburg mustn't discover the map and ask questions. He and Ash didn't need to arouse suspicions.

There was already too much danger with their spymaster in Confederate hands.

CHAPTER 19

Felicity walked home from work the next day in a daze after learning of the spymaster's capture. Though she had never met the man, he had won Ash's friendship and Luke's respect. The possibilities of what the captured spy might be enduring set her pulse to racing.

Things were striking ever closer. First, Ash had been captured and imprisoned. Now, Ash's and Luke's spymaster—her own spymaster, too, she guessed—had been captured.

Was Luke next? Did such a fate also await her?

Her breath came in ragged hitches just considering it. Her own part seemed less risky because she didn't deliver messages. Still, she must be careful. She lived with Southern supporters—one of them the wife of a Confederate soldier.

Felicity must watch everything she said and did unless in her own attic bedroom. It was a difficult way to live. Added to that was Luke's amnesia. He'd maintained his distance since the shelling of the passing Union boat, which was the most painful cut of all.

With a sigh, she pushed open her aunt's front door. Voices led her to the parlor. "Good afternoon, everyone."

"You're home. I didn't realize it was so late." Aunt Mae placed a stack of books back into a crate on the floor. Several crates lay open or partially open across the parlor's rug. "Wilma has outgrown some of her dresses, and we're looking for old clothing from Rosemary, Ginger, Sage, or Petunia that can be reworked for the child."

Little Miles sat on the floor, lunging after marbles strewn across the rug. Wilma wrote on a slate at her mother's feet.

"You can do it, Felicity." Petunia looked up from a stack of musty dresses and underclothes. "You worked for a seamstress for years, right?"

"Two." She possessed the skills, but it would have been pleasant to be asked. As usual, her cousin merely assumed Felicity would leap at what she considered a privilege. Felicity squelched her resentment. After all, she was the poor relation. Thankfully, Aunt Mae had never made her feel that way. "I can work on a dress or two in the evening."

"You have plenty of time since Luke's no longer courting you." Petunia didn't even look up.

Felicity swallowed the sting left by the careless remark. It was true, after all. She crossed to the fireplace to warm herself.

"I think we've found everything we need. I'll ask Charles to take these crates back to the attic." Aunt Mae closed the lid on the box she'd been riffling through. "I'll start supper."

"Little Miles will need clothes soon. We can use the fabric from old dresses for that." Petunia glanced at Felicity.

"Of course, as long as you do not need the dresses."

"Rosemary's dresses are far too big for me." Petunia spread her hands over her slightly protruding stomach. "Be a dear and fetch the trunk with her clothes from the attic."

Felicity's lips tightened. Was this to be her life at Aunt Mae's now? Serving at her spoiled cousin's beck and call. Saving her money toward purchasing a seamstress shop with living quar-

RIVER OF PERIL

ters suddenly grew more appealing. Nearly all her wages from Julia were hidden in a worn cotton reticule at the bottom of her trunk. With any luck, she'd quickly replace her maid's position once the Mitchells left. Until then, she'd spend little. "I need to start a fire in my bedroom's stove, anyway." She left at a sedate pace, chagrined the children had been too busy to notice her arrival.

As she took her time building up the fire in her room's stove, she fought a wave of longing for her own siblings. None of them had been in a position to offer her a home. When Mama and Papa had passed, her oldest sister, Mabel, had been living in Kentucky and expecting her second baby. She and Matt now had a third child, and Felicity had only met the first one, Lacey.

Next in line was Jack, who lived in Louisiana with his sweet wife, Annabelle. She was the one of all Felicity's siblings and in-laws who wrote most often, and even those letters had grown sporadic. Jack's twin boys would soon turn three. He and Annabelle had since been blessed with Elizabeth, who wasn't quite a year old. Jack, who had worked as a tailor, was now a chaplain in the Confederate army. Though Annabelle's letters never stated it in so many words, Felicity figured that her brother hadn't wanted to fight.

Her brother Clarence had married his childhood sweetheart shortly after their parents' accident. He and Lilybeth had moved to Ohio, where he now worked for her uncle. Because of that job offer and her special fondness for her aunt, the newlyweds lived in a Cincinnati boarding house. Neither had been opposed to Felicity moving north with them. Unfortunately, she had no money to pay for a boarding room.

As far as she knew, Clarence hadn't enlisted for either side. Her last letter from him had come last spring, before the Union fleet's attack on the city.

None of her siblings had offered her a home in the intervening years, possibly because of her courtship with Luke.
Felicity had expected to be an engaged woman by now and was
certain her letters to them reflected those dreams.

More realistically, the war itself had halted any intentions to
welcome her into their homes. Some food items were scarce.
Another mouth to feed wasn't a decision to be made lightly.

So here she was, an orphan and possibly a burden to her
aunt and uncle. Petunia had hinted as much. It weighed on her.

Depression set in. There had been too much time to think
since moving upstairs.

Felicity had tarried long enough to make her point with
Petunia—that she preferred to be asked. Picking up a lantern,
she crossed the hall into the attic. She rubbed her arms at the
room's chill. Best make this quick. She'd been sent to fetch a
trunk. Hopefully, it was light.

Holding the lantern high, she looked for trunks.

An old cedar chest carved with angels that had been
painted white stood along the wall. Why, Mama had one just
like that. Perhaps Aunt Mae had a matching one as a child.

Her gaze remained riveted on it. Could this be Mama's
trunk, with her parents' possessions stored inside?

Felicity dropped to her knees before the trunk. Setting the
lantern on a nearby crate, she lifted the lid with trembling
hands. When she spotted Papa's Bible on the side, tears filled
her eyes. She cradled it against her heart. "Oh, Papa, I miss you
reading to us every Sunday evening."

Placing it carefully on the dusty floor, she reached for a
finely knit peach shawl that had been the perfect complement
for Mama's red hair and brown eyes, who had the same
coloring as Aunt Mae. Mama had worn it for every special
occasion.

Tears streaming down her face, Felicity kissed the soft wool.
"Oh, Mama, how I miss you."

Uncle Charles had said that everything had been sold to pay Papa's debts. Why hadn't Aunt Mae told her about this trunk of treasures?

She lifted stacks of books, clothes, dishes, and trinkets with little monetary value yet deeply valuable to her. Her siblings would want to know about this literal treasure chest.

Felicity repacked it, grateful beyond words that all hadn't been lost with their home.

Then she picked up Papa's dusty Bible from the floor. When she dusted off the leather cover, a page fell out.

Her heart turned cold as she picked it up.

The deed to her family's home in Bovina. The one that had been sold nearly four years ago.

It hadn't been sold, after all.

Why had Aunt Mae lied to her?

∼

*B*oth Luke and Ash were keeping themselves busy at the shop on Thursday, two days after they found the painted fence, when Ash put down the punch he'd be using to create holes in a saddle for decorative stitches. "I've got an errand this afternoon, and I want you to come with me."

"Aye." The look on Ash's face told him the errand had nothing to do with the shop. "What is it?"

"Let's talk in the house."

Ash strode toward his home without waiting for him, a sure sign he was agitated about something—or someone. Like Jim.

Luke followed, glad for an opportunity to see if Felicity had completed the laundry. She hadn't joined them at lunch because she was behind on the task.

Inside the home, Ash beckoned him to the parlor upstairs and closed the door. "I can barely focus on my job, I'm so worried for Jim."

Luke had spent a long time on his knees for Jim. He understood.

"I've a meeting with one of my spies this afternoon. You'll be taking over these meetings starting next month, unless you've changed your mind with the increased threats?" Ash raked his hands through his hair.

"Nay. I'm ready to do me duty." He'd rest easier once he received his army discharge. It was February fifth, just a week after Dr. Watkins requested it. He reminded himself patience was a virtue.

"This is a terrible time for us to move." Ash began to pace. "But we'll be here another four weeks or so. Surely, Jim will be rescued before then."

"What's today's meeting?" Luke prompted. He'd seldom seen his friend so agitated.

"It's with Nate Miller, a wharf worker who has lost his job. Thankfully, he's too old for the army, or we'd be hurting. He's a good man. He'll tell us what he knows without mincing words. Then he takes off just as quickly." Ash rubbed his hands together as he continued pacing. "We meet in the oak grove by City Hospital. He only shows if he's got something to say."

"I can respect such restraint." Not a man to waste time. Luke liked that.

"I can too." Ash stopped. "Other than Nate, all my spies quit after learning about Jim. It had already dwindled to three. They had grown skittish with all the soldiers in the city."

That made sense. There had been over twelve thousand Confederates who fought at Chickasaw Bayou above Vicksburg at the end of December. Soldiers outnumbered citizens twice over.

"One exception. I work with a blacksmith in Warrenton. Cal Jones is a family man, maybe forty. He's as steady as they come. He only comes to the shop when he's learned something important because he's a few miles downriver from us. He's got a pass to enter and do business in Vicksburg, but it's risky. He's got a wife and three sons to consider."

"Sounds like a good man."

"He is." Ash stopped pacing. "I'll introduce you to Nate. He knows I'm leaving soon. I'd considered having him ride with me before you were wounded."

"Don't like to think I took a man's job."

"No, you're the best choice. Nate's not an easy man to read, which is an excellent quality in a spy. He's also rumored to possess a temper. That's what made me hesitate in the first place."

That answer satisfied Luke. "Does Nate know Jim?"

"Actually, he used to report directly to Jim before it got too difficult to find excuses to leave the city several times a month." Ash shook his head. "Jim's effect was far-reaching."

"When should we go to the hospital?" Luke was anxious to learn how to go about this new task.

"Let's go."

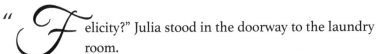

"Felicity?" Julia stood in the doorway to the laundry room.

"Yes?" She looked up from the shirt she scrubbed against the scrub board. "Sorry, I'm not quite finished. Maybe another hour."

"Leave it for the moment."

Felicity dropped the garment into the soapy water. Hours of tumultuous thoughts at this washtub had taken a toll. She was ready for a break.

"I have a sandwich and tea in the parlor." Julia took her arm and drew her down the hall and into the parlor, shutting the door behind them.

A cozy fire welcomed her. A plate was set on the table where Ash and Luke often played games with Eddie.

"I *am* hungry." Felicity sank onto a high-backed wood chair gratefully. "Thank you."

"My pleasure." Julia poured both of them a cup of tea. "I know something is bothering you. Are you worried about the spymaster?"

She sipped her tea thirstily. "Of course." With a pang, she realized she'd forgotten to pray for him that morning.

"Is it Luke's amnesia?"

"It breaks my heart that he doesn't remember me, but I must be prepared. He may never remember. I may have to make my way in this world without him." And perhaps without her aunt. How could Aunt Mae have betrayed her?

"He may fall in love with you without those memories ever resurfacing."

"I can't allow myself to dream of that, Julia. He's changed from the teasing man who kissed me goodbye at the train station at the beginning of the hostilities." She looked away lest her friend see the hurt.

"I understand that." Julia refreshed their tea. "There's something else bothering you."

Felicity bit into her ham sandwich. Should she tell Julia about the deed? It revealed a potential ugliness in her aunt that Felicity hated to probe until talking with her. There hadn't been a moment last evening when Petunia wasn't present to confront her aunt.

"Please. Won't you tell me?"

"Yes." Julia knew her well. "I found my mother's trunk in the attic yesterday." She mentioned her joy in holding her parents' possessions that she'd imagined were lost forever. Then she talked about finding the deed.

Julia gasped. "But...I thought your childhood home was sold long ago."

"That's what I was told." Her throat constricted as resentment welled up. "I turned sixteen just before moving in with Aunt Mae. Clarence was eighteen. Why, he and Lilybeth might have stayed in Mississippi had we all known about the house instead of going to Ohio. They could have moved into our childhood home after the wedding."

"You could have lived with them." Compassion shown from Julia's brown eyes.

"Exactly." Felicity didn't doubt it. "He was closest to me in age. Except for the normal spats between siblings, we always got along."

"Have you asked Mrs. Beltzer about it?"

Felicity shook her head. "My cousin is rather difficult. I'll wait until Petunia is at the shops or otherwise engaged to approach my aunt."

"That's wise." Julia frowned. "I'd offer for you to live with us if I could. As it is, Ash has already offered Luke a home. He'll stay here and watch the house for us until the conflict ends. Then we'll see what is to be done. How perfect it would be if—" She covered her mouth.

Felicity knew what she had planned to say. How perfect it would be if Luke remembered her and married her. They'd both have a home with each other.

Yes, that would have been perfect.

"Will you tell Luke?"

Felicity shook her head. "He's got enough on his mind."

"I can't think of a good reason for the Beltzers to lie about your home." Julia's brow furrowed. "And you've struggled so not to burden them."

Felicity pushed her half-eaten lunch aside. How different might her life have been had she known the truth? Her brother might live some ten miles away instead of hundreds.

If her aunt didn't have a good reason, Felicity feared she'd never trust her again.

~

$\mathcal{L}$uke stepped from behind an oak tree some three hundred feet from the hospital after a broad-shouldered, burly man stopped in front of Ash.

"I trusted you."

Luke halted mid-stride at the angry tone.

"What do you mean, Nate?" Ash cocked his head.

"You betrayed me." Nate Miller jerked his head toward Luke. "I've seen this soldier walking about town not a month hence."

"He's no longer a soldier. Please, listen to me." Ash held up his hand, palm facing Nate. "This is my friend and fellow spy, Luke Shea. He fought for the Confederacy until he was wounded. His amnesia prevents him from remembering being a soldier. He'll soon receive his discharge."

"That's a lot to swallow." Nate's brows lowered.

"'Tis true, nonetheless." Luke took one step forward and stopped. "I'm a Unionist. I wish to make up for that army service by spying for the North."

"Yet you do not recall being a soldier?" Nate rubbed his whiskered jaw. It sounded like sandpaper.

"Nay. None of it."

"Wonder what happened that's so bad you can't remember it?"

"Aye." His mind raced back to Oscar's description of the battle at Fredericksburg. He shuddered. "That's what robs me of sleep." That and nightmares about his parents' deaths.

"You know I'm leaving the city next month." Ash's gaze darted between his companions. "Luke will take over for me. You'll meet him here."

Nate eyed Luke and then turned to Ash. "You asked me to find out about our mutual friend."

Ash straightened.

"They first took him to Jackson. Several officers took turns shooting questions at him. Then they tossed him into prison with Union prisoners already held there."

Luke's stomach clenched. The man didn't betray them, he'd wager.

"So he's in Jackson."

"Not now." Nate shook his head. "My information is that the Rebs wanted to get him away from the area, where someone might know him...help him escape. He's been taken to Tennessee. Speculation is the area around Collierville."

"That's more than we knew before." Ash rubbed his hands together.

"I'm willing to help with the rescue." Nate placed his hands on his hips.

"We are too. Our mutual friend asked us not to be involved in the rescue. Too many strangers around an army camp make soldiers suspicious. Better to keep the numbers searching for him small. Our fellows have done this multiple times." Ash shrugged. "Hard to wait."

"Aye. Even for me, who knows him least." Both of Luke's companions seemed afraid for their friend, not themselves—a testament to the trust Jim had built with them.

"Come back Saturday. I'll be here if there's something to pass on." Nate took off for town before Luke could speak.

"Let's walk back by another road." Ash headed north.

Felicity would be gone before they returned to Ash's house. A pity, for she'd appreciate learning this news.

Luke waited to speak until they'd passed a row of houses. "Should we ride to the mill today?" He was filled with restlessness, wanting to help Jim.

"Too late. Can't get there before it closes."

"And we can't risk raising suspicions."

"Exactly." Ash gave him a side glance. "We'll leave early tomorrow."

Luke saw the wisdom of waiting. Yet he was anxious to prove to Nate Miller—and himself—that he was trustworthy.

CHAPTER 20

elicity walked home from the Dodds' on Sunday afternoon. Mrs. Dodd had invited her to join her, Eddie, Ash, Julia, and Luke for lunch after church. Instead of chatting in the parlor after the meal, Julia had suggested that her mama would benefit from help with packing. Mrs. Dodd had always relied on her daughter to absorb the bulk of her work, and that reliance didn't seem to have wavered with Julia's marriage.

The women had worked in Eddie's bedroom, beginning with toys and books. The men then toted completed boxes into the carriage and then took them to the wharf to arrange for transporting them across and down the river to avoid Union soldiers building the canal nearly opposite of Vicksburg, and on to the railroad farther into Louisiana.

So much packing had reminded Felicity that she'd soon lose touch with her dearest friend. Julia had always been a good friend, yet they'd grown even closer since she began working for the family. Felicity suspected she'd been invited to more family gatherings since Luke was in attendance to jar his memory.

Nothing had worked. Soon, Julia and Ash would be gone, and Felicity would seek another job, if anything could be found. Many businesses had closed, their owners having moved out of the city. Once the Mitchell family left for Texas, Felicity would only see Luke at church.

Those gloomy reflections weren't the only reasons Felicity had been happy to stay busy. The deed was uppermost on her mind. She dreaded confronting Aunt Mae. There had been no opportunity for an extended conversation with her aunt since Felicity found the legal document. Her imagination had taken flight, trying to create plausible explanations.

Why had she not been given her home as a place to live? Or to sell and share the proceeds with her siblings? This affected all of them. Her very soul longed to learn the truth.

She pushed open the gate of the black iron fence surrounding the familiar brick house and climbed a dozen stone steps. The door was unlocked as usual. She stepped inside the warm house. The children must be napping because a rare silence greeted her.

"Is that you, Felicity?" Aunt Mae called. "Your uncle and I are in the parlor."

After hanging her cloak, Felicity sat on a chair opposite Aunt Mae, who seemed quite happy to knit a blue blanket. Uncle Charles softly snored from his chair before the hearth. "Where's Petunia? And the children?"

"Spending the afternoon with Amelia Barnes." Aunt Mae didn't look up from her knitting. "They were quite close as children. Now they both are mothers. By the way, Petunia mentioned the dress Wilma wore to church is getting too tight. When will you have the first one done?"

"In a couple of days. It's the same amount of work as starting from scratch." Felicity fished the fabric from the sewing basket that nestled beside her chair with shaking hands. The moment was upon her. "Aunt Mae, something is troubling me."

"Plenty enough trouble to go around." She sighed. "What's bothering you?"

"I discovered Mama's old trunk in the attic." The unfinished pink dress lay untouched in her lap.

Aunt Mae slipped a stitch. "Oh, hadn't I mentioned it was there?"

"No, I was told that everything had been sold to pay Papa's debts."

"I can't imagine how you came by that impression." A scarlet flush crept up her neck. "It's been here since you and Clarence came to live with us. Perhaps he stored it there and forgot it."

Felicity blinked. "I had forgotten Clarence was here at first."

"For two months before his wedding that we were happy to provide." She gave a distracted nod. "He and Lilybeth were here another month before the job that her uncle was able to procure in Cincinnati was open. Clarence was quite pleased about his new job, and Lilybeth was happy to live near her favorite aunt."

She recalled that now. She'd passed those days in a fog. Details of the weeks immediately following the funerals were sketchy. Was this the frustration at missing pieces that Luke felt? No, his pain went much deeper. "I'm certain he would have told me if he'd left it there."

"My dear, I'm at a loss. Maribel and I were given identical trunks as little girls. Are you certain it wasn't my trunk you saw?"

Uncle Charles continued to snore with his head resting against the high-backed, cushioned chair. Was he still truly dozing or merely pretending so he didn't have to face the confrontation?

She lifted her chin. "I opened it."

Aunt Mae's knitting needles clicked together faster. "Now I remember. Your uncle was able to save a few mementos for you all. We would have presented it to you at your wedding or the end of the war, whichever came first."

Felicity flinched. The war would surely end before she became a wife. Why wait? Was her aunt being truthful? "I'll move it into my room, now that I've found it." Dare she confront her about the deed? She seemed to change her story with everything Felicity said. However, she did think some of it had a ring of truth. "I was thrilled to find Papa's Bible. I have such fond memories of sitting on the floor at his feet while he read to us children."

Aunt Mae's hand jerked. "That Bible belonged to his mother. It should not be handled overmuch."

"Agreed. Something fell out when I dusted it off." Anxious to discover the truth, Felicity forced herself to continue. "It was the deed to Mama and Papa's house."

"Oh, dear." Aunt Mae's gaze darted to her still-sleeping husband. "Well, you see...what happened was..." Her knitting fell to her lap. "The debts weren't as major as first suspected. One of the debtors canceled a loan a week or two after you and Clarence moved in with us. There was no need to sell the house, after all."

"Why didn't you tell us?" A chunk of ice formed in her stomach and crept toward her heart. "Clarence might have preferred to live there instead of moving to Ohio. Had she known, Mabel and Matt might have moved back from Kentucky. Either one of them would surely have offered me a home. Had they known." Felicity wouldn't have met Luke if that had happened, but she'd have been spared the pain of him forgetting her.

"Your uncle and I discussed the matter. Everyone had been told they were losing the home and already mourned its loss. We figured we could rent it to a deserving family to defray the expenses of supporting you and Clarence."

They'd rented it? A wave of dizziness passed over Felicity. She gripped the chair arms, all pretense of sewing forgotten.

"Once your courtship with Luke turned serious, we had thought to offer it to you at your wedding, but now that may not happen."

Offer what she and her siblings already owned? For her wedding that was as unlikely today as it had been the day Luke learned they'd courted in those forgotten years? Felicity covered her face with her hands.

"Our Southern soldiers aren't being paid on a timely basis, something that has also affected Petunia. Being the fine Southern woman that you are—volunteering at the hospital to care for our brave soldiers—it will no doubt comfort you to learn that the family of a Confederate soldier lives there now." Aunt Mae's face brightened. "And we were able to bless them considerably because she wrote to us last year of her hardships. She and her three children aren't paying rent, and that has helped them tremendously."

A wave of dizziness caused Felicity to fight nausea. A Confederate family lived in her family's home, free of rent, while she'd been made to feel—by her cousin—that she lived off her aunt's charity. It was an intolerable situation.

The front door opened with a bang. "Grandma! Grandpa! We're home." Wilma ran into the room and threw herself into her grandmother's arms. Little Miles climbed onto Grandpa's lap, who awoke when the boy jumped on him.

"Mama, we had the most marvelous day." Petunia took a moment to hang up their cloaks before entering the parlor. "She's invited us all to Sunday lunch next week." Her gaze fell on Felicity. "I'm sorry, Cousin. She didn't invite you to this first gathering of the families. We'll all be talking about old times."

"Not a problem." Felicity stood, heartsick that so much had been kept from her. "If you'll all excuse me, I think I'll retire for the night." It was before six. She didn't care.

If she had somewhere else to go, she'd pack a bag. Her closest friend besides Julia was Savannah Adair. The wealthy woman wouldn't understand Felicity's dilemma.

In the old days, Luke had been the first person she turned to in a crisis. He seemed to care for her as Julia's friend, but she'd not trouble him with this problem. He had too much to figure out already.

Emotionally drained, she climbed two flights of steps.

All those years, she'd worked hard to be less of a burden to Aunt Mae...

It hadn't been true. Her aunt and uncle had been well compensated beyond any expense Felicity had caused. At the very least, some of that rent should have been divided among her siblings. Small comfort that the overage could not be said to be going toward her room and board now that Aunt Mae had generously given for free what hadn't been hers in the first place.

Exhaustion overcame her. She was too tired to think about it.

But before closing her bedroom door, she dragged Mama's heavy trunk through it.

~

*L*uke was working alone in the shop the next morning when Felicity crept by the entrance without looking up. Her head was bent as if she was studying the stone walk. It was the slump of her shoulders that decided him. He raced after her and caught up with her halfway to the house.

"Felicity, ye forgot your warm cloak. 'Tis only the second week of February, and we'll suffer the winter's chill a bit longer."

She shivered. "I guess I forgot it. I left in a hurry before breakfast." Her beautiful blue eyes held a vague look, as if her thoughts were elsewhere.

"Come with me." He put his arm around her, pressing her cold dress against the warmth of his side. "We'll get you before the fire."

She cuddled against him, as if craving his warmth. Or did she long for something more? He couldn't embrace her, court her, as much as he wanted to—not until he knew himself. He was too lost to offer what he didn't have to give.

"Almost there." He propelled her along the path to the door. The poor girl was nearly delirious with cold. That was the only explanation for her burying her head against his chest as they walked. He opened the door. Relief filled him to find Ash and Julia descending the stairs.

"What's wrong with Felicity?" Julia ran down the last few steps to link arms with her.

"I only know she forgot her cloak and left without eating breakfast." Between them, they escorted Felicity into the parlor. Once she was seated before the hearth, Luke set to building up the fire that was mere embers.

"Ash, can you ask Jolene for some corn muffins and buttermilk? Bring them in here." Julia rubbed Felicity's hands between hers. "I want her to remain before the fire. Felicity, what happened?"

"So cold." She shivered.

The fire would take minutes to ignite sufficiently. Luke couldn't stand it. Bending down, he enfolded her in his arms.

Julia dropped her hand and stood back. "I'll fetch a blanket." She scurried from the room.

Felicity nestled against him, her face pressed against the drumming of his heart.

Was this how it had felt to hold her? This sense of coming home at long last?

Her body's shudders gradually relaxed.

Luke still didn't release her. Obviously, more than a missing cloak had upset her. He wanted to be the one to comfort her. There was something so right about her being in his arms.

Little wonder that he had courted her. This beautiful, intelligent, compassionate woman had once cared for him. What a wonder, to be sure. It wouldn't be difficult to fall in love—

Nay, that must not happen.

"I'm back with the blanket." Julia crossed to the chair.

Releasing Felicity, Luke stepped back. For a precious moment, he'd forgotten his amnesia. He must not do that again.

Julia draped a blue quilt over Felicity's lap. "Are you warmer, Felicity?" Her lips curled in a sly smile.

"Oh, yes, thank you, Julia. And Luke." Her cheeks flushed as she gazed up at him.

She was certainly pretty enough to turn a man's head. Had he loved her? To his shame, he didn't know. His face burned like fire.

"I have your breakfast." Ash strode into the room.

"Thank you." Accepting the plate and glass of buttermilk from him, Julia set it on a round side table beside Felicity. "Now, you must eat before telling us what happened."

Luke retreated to lean his elbow on the mantel, hardly knowing what to do. Had he given Felicity the wrong impression? Surely, she understood he was half of man until his memories were restored. It would be dishonorable to renew the courtship.

He must be very careful going forward.

∼

Felicity knew Luke so well that she was aware of his discomfort. He had merely meant to console her, but her whole heart had responded to his embrace. She must be strong for him, show him she knew he didn't love her. She sipped the buttermilk without looking up. "It's nothing that should keep the men from their work."

Julia frowned. "All right." She turned to her husband. "We may go to Mama's today as she requested."

"She has no cloak." Luke met Felicity's eyes briefly, and then looked away.

At least he cared enough to worry about her. It had been foolhardy to leave without it. She'd risen before the rest of the family. The sound of footsteps approaching the stairs had panicked her. She ran out the door, mindless of the morning's chill.

"I'll lend her one of mine." Julia clasped her hands together. "We'll drive the buggy by her house to pick up hers on the return trip."

The plan seemed to satisfy Luke. "There's work waiting for me."

"And me." Ash leaned to kiss Julia's cheek. "Fetch me if you need me."

The men strode from the room.

Felicity got up and closed the door. Her shameful news had nothing to do with spying, yet she didn't want Jolene to hear. She returned to her seat.

"Don't talk until you've eaten." Julia sank back in her seat.

Yesterday's lunch suddenly seemed a long time ago. She devoured both muffins.

"Luke seems mighty concerned about your well-being." Julia tapped her fingers together.

"He's a compassionate man. It's one of the qualities that drew me to him. But you saw him draw back from me." She shook her head. "He's careful not to give me the wrong impression."

"I think he's beginning to care for you again." Julia leaned forward.

Her cheeks burned hot as fire. "My heart can't dream of what may never be, don't you see that?"

"I don't believe I'm giving you false hope, but you know him best." Julia's mouth drooped. "Now, tell me what happened to put you in such a state."

Felicity told her about the confrontation. It was a relief to speak about it. "I prayed for guidance last night. I'll write to my sister and brothers, but there's little to be done about it with the war going on."

"I wish they would have told you from the beginning." Julia shook her head sadly. "To find out this way...why, it almost seems as if they never meant to return it at all." She covered her mouth. "I'm sorry. I shouldn't have said that."

"Why not? I've been thinking the same." Her throat constricted. "Aunt Mae is giving a family she barely knows the free use of my former home—something she's never given me."

"Outrageous." Julia clucked her tongue.

"Not that I'd consider tossing a family into the streets, especially while the conflict continues."

Julia sighed. "No, I'd feel the same. Will you stay with your aunt?"

"I've no choice. I don't have enough money to rent a seamstress shop, especially when so few can afford new clothes...not to mention the scarcity of fabric." She straightened her shoulders. "No, I'll just have to stay." Petunia might gloat over the rift between Felicity and her parents. She braced herself for it.

Julia's face brightened. "Why don't you come to Texas with us? I'm certain Ash will say the same."

Getting away from her aunt's home appealed to her. Yet... "I can't leave Luke even though he may never remember me. I've reconciled to that possibility." She was trying to, anyway. "If some trauma hinders his memories, Luke will need support." His best buddy, Ash, would be in Texas. "I can't leave him to face that alone. I love him too much. I'll help him face what he must and then fade from his life if he never loves me again."

"I didn't realize you loved him so sacrificially." Tears glistened in Julia's eyes. "Luke is a fortunate man."

"He doesn't feel blessed at the moment." Memories surfaced of seeing him every week at church, with each of them noticing one another without talking in those early days. It was her friendship with Julia that earned her invitations to picnics and riverboat rides where Luke was in attendance where they'd first really talked. "He helped me over the worst of my grief. We were friends before our courtship. Even if what he has suffered changes him once his memories return, I'm praying our friendship will survive." If he fell in love and married someone else, *then* she'd move to Texas. That might be far enough to leave behind the pain.

"The two of you had a special love." Julia swiped at her cheeks.

Tears burned the back of Felicity's eyes. She must not give in to her sorrow, or she'd cry for days.

"I remember how envious I was back then because I couldn't seem to find someone who really loved me."

"Until Ash. The two of you are perfect for one another." Felicity was grateful she'd been able to express her love for Luke aloud, but the time had come to be strong again. "This move to Texas is a great opportunity for your whole family. I know Eddie is excited."

"He is." Her face brightened. "Speaking of which, do you mind helping Mama and me today with her packing? Ash doesn't want to leave until his friend is rescued, but we must be prepared to leave shortly afterward. Maybe by the end of the month."

Everyone seemed to be abandoning her. One by one, she was losing those closest to her—her parents, Luke, Julia, and, seemingly, Aunt Mae and Uncle Charles.

Had God abandoned her too?

CHAPTER 21

Felicity spent Wednesday evening in her bedroom stitching together Wilma's dress, sitting first in the hard-backed chair near the window and then on her bed. She finished one sleeve about nine o'clock and decided to stop.

She'd read her papa's Bible before changing for the night. She opened the trunk to find that things had been moved. Had Wilma and Little Miles been in her room?

No, Mama's shawl was folded too neatly for a four-year-old to manage.

Aunt Mae searching for the deed?

Her fingers fairly flew to Papa's precious Bible. The deed was still there.

Uncle Charles had arrived home after Felicity. That left...Petunia.

Anger shot through her. She threw open her door and ran down to the parlor. Its only occupant was her cousin, writing a letter at the room's round table.

"Did you search my trunk?" Felicity crossed her arms.

"Good evening to you, too, Cousin." Petunia gave her a frosty look.

"Answer me."

Petunia lifted her chin. "As a matter of fact, I did. Quite harmless, really. I was searching for a thimble."

An excuse. "Which I keep in the sewing basket beside my bed."

"I'll know next time." Petunia sniffed. "There was nothing in it of value, anyway."

"You were looking for valuables?" At least her cousin hadn't found the only thing of monetary value—the deed.

"As if you'd have such things. You live off my parents' charity."

Petunia had said similar things before. Felicity wanted to laugh. She'd discovered they were well-compensated for inviting her to stay. Wait. Was it possible Petunia didn't know?

"You should be grateful to them for giving you a comfortable home."

"I've been grateful to live here." She held Petunia's gaze. "I don't search your room, and I'll thank you to respect my privacy as well."

She didn't wait for arguments or agreement as she flounced away.

~

On Thursday morning, Luke strode from the post office, a letter in his hand. It was impossible to wait until he got back to the saddle shop to learn the Confederacy's decision. It was February twelfth, three weeks since Dr. Watkins sent the request to release Luke from service.

Folks scurried past on the sidewalk on the sunny yet breezy morning. Not the privacy he might wish for in case it was bad news, yet it scarcely mattered. Leaning one shoulder against the building, he reached into his pocket for his knife.

Unfolding it, he slit through the wax seal before returning the knife to his pocket.

His hands trembled as he unfolded the page.

Relief flooded over him. They'd granted him an honorable discharge and thanked him for his service.

He didn't have to go back.

An answer to prayer and not only his own. Felicity, Ash, Julia, Mrs. Dodd, Eddie, and Mrs. Beltzer had all been praying for this discharge Luke held in his hands.

Felicity, Ash, and Julia deserved to hear the news first. He'd tell the others later.

Long strides took him to the saddle shop, where Ash pounded a piece of leather. "Follow me to the house." He grinned.

Ash's gaze fell to the letter in Luke's hand. "Right behind you." His eyes gleamed.

Julia was tatting lace in the parlor when he rushed in. "Where's Felicity?"

"Cleaning the upstairs parlor." She arose. "What's wrong?"

"Can you come upstairs with us? I want you all to hear this together." He didn't wait for her answer. His excitement mounted as he took the wide stairs two at a time and strode down the hall to the parlor. There she was, looking beautiful in her black skirt, white blouse, and a blue bib apron with ruffled edges protecting her clothes from dust. "Felicity, I have news."

She turned, gripping a feather duster. "What is it?"

Something in his face must have told her the answer. "You've received it? Your discharge?" She dropped the duster, her eyes riveted to his.

"Aye." His heart lit with joy at the sudden sparkle in those magnificent blue eyes. "There'll be no returning to the army."

"Oh, Luke." She clasped her hands together. "God answered our prayers." She looked as if she wanted to launch herself into his arms.

Then he realized he'd told her first. Because she had been his nurse? Footsteps and a rush of wind had him turning as Ash and Julia entered. "Felicity already guessed my news. The discharge came."

Ash whooped and strode across the room to shake his hand. "This is good news. Now you can concentrate on learning your new trade."

"Aye." Among other things...like spying, far more important while war raged on.

"I'm happy for you." Julia gave him a brief hug and then looked at Felicity.

Luke turned back to her. She stood in the same spot, a sheen of tears somehow not spilling over. He strode to her and held out his arms. She clasped him close to her—not like Julia's hug, but one that bespoke deep gratitude for his safety. If there was something more in the convulsive hug that ended too soon, he wasn't ready to acknowledge it.

⁓

*L*ater that day, Luke and Ash waited at the oak grove for Nate. Ash's tense expression indicated worry for Jim. If his captors knew all that Jim had been involved with since the war began, the Confederate soldiers would hang him from the nearest tree. Even a smattering of the whole truth was enough to get Jim killed.

"I'm glad your discharge papers finally arrived." Ash peered at the road as if willing Nate to come. He hadn't been here yesterday when they'd taken a chance on waiting for him.

"Aye." Its arrival had been like shedding a weight from his shoulders. "Something good amid the chaos."

"Very good. It was one of the matters I wanted to see resolved before I left. Not certain that will happen for everything. Letters from Texas have grown sporadic because mail delivery has been slowed. Grant's army cut off the railroad by digging a canal nearly across from Vicksburg. Uncle Clark's last letter stated he will wait for us in Monroe, Louisiana, starting March first."

Ash might leave earlier. Then Luke had best concentrate on honing his saddle-making skills and gleaning everything he could about this spy business. "Allow yourselves extra days. Remember you'll have to make your way into Louisiana to pick up the train in Delhi."

"Right. That canal is a headache for us." Ash turned toward the road.

"Aye." Anyone in Vicksburg could watch the Union army's movement across the river.

"He's here." Ash leaned a hand against a thick oak trunk.

"I'll make this quick." Nate started talking in low tones before he reached them. "Tell them to concentrate their search in Collierville. Our friend was there, alive, on Tuesday."

"Two days ago." Ash's legs wobbled and then straightened. "Anything else?"

"Nothing you don't already know." Nate took off toward the east side of the city without saying goodbye.

"Man of few words," Luke observed. "But the ones he speaks are potent."

"True," Ash replied softly. "Let's speak of other things until we get back."

So other pedestrians on the sidewalk wouldn't overhear. Noted.

They'd discovered Jim's location as of two days ago. Harv wasn't running spy secrets up the line yet knew how to pass on information about their spymaster. Indeed, it was the only information the veteran spy wanted to hear.

Every day mattered, but they couldn't safely go to Harv's this late in the afternoon. No doubt, they'd leave at first light tomorrow.

*a*fter Felicity finished her daily tasks on Thursday afternoon, she carried her basket to Julia in the upstairs parlor. "Will you store Papa's Bible in your home?" She extracted it from the basket. "I don't believe it's safe at my aunt's house."

Julia accepted it from her. "Surely, you don't believe your aunt would take this from you?"

Felicity sat on the sofa beside her. "No, she wouldn't." Since last night's confrontation with Petunia, Felicity hadn't seen her. "It's what's inside."

Julia opened it and extracted a thick page. "The deed?"

"Someone moved things around in my trunk yesterday. I confronted Petunia. She confessed...to searching for a thimble."

Julia scoffed.

"Exactly. She found nothing of value." She frowned. "I don't believe she knows about the deed."

"Hmm. She'd likely want you to live there instead."

That's what Felicity wanted too. Then again, Petunia might tell her doting mother she wanted to live there instead.

"She does seem awfully absorbed in her own affairs." Julia stowed the page inside the book's leather cover. "Since we're leaving in the next couple of weeks, I'll ask Luke to allow it to remain untouched in this room."

"Thank you."

"You were happy to learn Luke's news, I'm certain." Julia repositioned two angel statuettes on a set of built-in shelves behind a table in the back of the room and set the Bible there.

"Luke receiving his army discharge is an answered prayer." Felicity had praised God silently for the news. He'd held her close, however briefly, in celebration. She'd also cherish the knowledge she'd been the first person he told.

"It's a tremendous relief for Ash. Now we know that Luke

will watch over the house and continue to serve our customers. Er, that is, I suppose they will be Luke's customers for now." Julia joined her on the sofa near the fireplace. "We'll see what the war brings."

"What about Jolene?" And her own job as their maid.

"We'll leave money for Luke to provide household expenses and pay both you and Jolene to continue working at least until the beginning of June. We hope the saddle shop will be thriving by then." She raised her hands, palms up. "After that, I don't know. Jolene has been with the family a dozen years. We don't want to turn her out amid the war. This at least will give her three months to decide what she will do if Luke is unable to pay her. I think she will choose to stay on as cook for room and board."

If Felicity was a married woman like Jolene, she would work for room and board. These were difficult days for everyone.

"You rely on your job too."

"Yes." A wave of thankfulness washed over her to keep the job until June. But what then?

"Mama has set aside several of her ballgowns and a box of Papa's clothes to give you a start for your seamstress shop. With fabric being so scarce, folks will be grateful for remade clothes." Julia smiled. "I have some old clothing for you as well. Some of it is sadly out of fashion. I'll leave several rolls of lace as my and Ash's gift to you."

"That's so generous. Thank you." Felicity hugged her. She'd need the lace to support herself as soon as wartime scarcities eased and people were ordering new clothes again. "It makes my dream ever closer."

"Good. Mama wishes she hadn't already offered her home rent-free to her driver, Silas, her cook, Hester, and her daughter, Daisy, in exchange for watching over the place, or she would have allowed you to stay there for the war's duration." Julia's brow wrinkled. "She can't bring herself to tell them you'll live there, too, after everything is already settled."

"Understood. I'm touched that she even considered it." She didn't know what she'd have done living in the Dodds' stately home. Martha Dodd wasn't a wealthy woman, yet her husband and her father's family had left her a comfortable income, Felicity believed.

"Too late to change anything, I'm afraid." Julia brightened. "Silas did finally convince Hester to marry him. The wedding is tomorrow. Ash and I will attend with Mama. Eddie will be in school. He's going to miss his best buddies George and Tom. Those boys have been nearly inseparable."

"That will indeed be hard."

Julia's lips drooped. "The hardest part. George and Tom have already decided they'll be cowboys on our ranch when they turn sixteen."

Felicity understood how the boys felt. Saying goodbye to Julia would leave a huge pit in her life. She was her *only* support now that this rift happened with Aunt Mae.

"If you change your mind about remaining in Vicksburg, you must come to us in Texas. Ash says we'll build a big enough home for lots of children." Julia blushed.

Did she just... Felicity blinked. "Julia, do you mean to say..."

She nodded, her face radiant. "Yes, we're expecting a blessed event. I was going to wait until Ash's friend is found so we can truly celebrate. Mama knows, of course, but I can't keep the news from my best friend any longer. The baby will be born in late August."

"Oh, Julia." Felicity rose, and when her friend stood, hugged her. "This is the most marvelous news." Welcome news in the midst of turmoil. "What wonderful parents you will be. I'm thrilled for both of you."

She had squares of leftover white cotton fabric. She'd set

aside remaking clothes for Wilma to stitch some nightgowns and nappies for the baby.

Petunia wouldn't like it, but Felicity didn't care.

If not for Luke and her spying for the Union, Felicity would stash everything she owned into her mama's trunk and leave with them.

~

*D*espite a continuing steady rain that had started an hour before and soaked them to the skin, Luke and Ash took their time dismounting outside Harv's mill at midmorning the next day. It was Friday, February thirteenth. Luke's mama had once been a mite suspicious about the unlucky day. He and Papa had always laughed away any bad luck. Today, Luke was too nervous for the spymaster to make light of the suspicion.

Not that he'd laughed too much since awakening in the hospital almost two months before. His sense of humor seemed as rusty as his memories.

A buckboard outside the mill alerted them to a customer inside. Still, it appeared stranger for Ash and Luke to fiddle with their saddlebags in the rain than it would to go inside.

Ash raised his eyebrows at Luke, who tossed his head at the door.

They strode inside, where Harv was filling a twenty-pound sack with cornmeal.

"Be right with you fellas." Harv didn't look up from his task. "Warm yourselves by the fire."

"Obliged to you." Luke spoke as if they were casual acquaintances. He crossed to the heat stove with Ash, extending his hands to the delicious warmth.

The customer, a scrawny, bearded man who looked as

though he never got enough to eat, glanced over. "You fellas must have come a far piece, being soaked to the skin."

"Not too far. Cold for February." Luke turned to the stove, hoping that satisfied the man's curiosity.

His headaches had never gone away. The weather combined with his worries had escalated the current one into a throbbing pain.

"That'll be seven dollars, Joe." Harv tied the second sack with a piece of burlap.

Money exchanged hands. Joe didn't seem in a big hurry to leave.

"You need to borrow a length of India rubber cloth?" Harv put his hands on his hips.

"Nah, I brought some."

"Let me help you outside with these." Harv slung a sack over his back as if it weighed one pound rather than twenty. "Be right back, fellas."

Joe gave Ash and Luke a long look and then followed Harv outside.

"I don't mind waiting a bit beside this fire," Luke told Ash. Though he'd be colder when he went back outside.

"Agreed. I'm sure the rain's not doing your head any favors."

"Nor your leg." Ash's limp always worsened after long rides.

The sound of wheels splashing in the mud wasn't as loud as rain pounding the roof.

Luke shook droplets from his wide-brimmed hat. The ride back wasn't going to be any more enjoyable than the one here.

Harv stepped inside, swiping raindrops off his face. "Thanks for waiting. So what can I get you?" Harv's hearty tone likely carried to the yard.

"I'll take five pounds of meal." Ash raised his voice as Harv shut the door.

"Tell me quick. Joe's a curious one." Long strides took the

miller to the grain table where he grabbed a sack and began scooping meal into it.

Luke gave the message to search for Jim in Collierville.

The door opened. Joe stood there.

Had he heard Luke's whispered message? Unlikely, with the rain striking the roof.

"I left my team under the shelter of trees." Joe closed the door. "Don't mind if I sit a spell, do you, Harv? The road's gonna be a muddy mess when this lets up."

That meant Luke and Ash would have to ride in it or get caught alleviating the curiosity of a stranger. Not a difficult choice.

"That'll be a dollar." Harv handed the sack to Ash, who paid him.

"Much obliged." Ash placed the sack inside his coat.

Luke tipped his hat to Harv and followed Ash outside.

Ash stored the food inside his saddlebag. After he mounted, the horses picked their way through the mud.

They were back under the relative shelter of the forest trail outside Bolton before Ash spoke. "At least you got to state our message."

"Aye." They would have spoken longer, without doubt, but Ash was right. The important details had been relayed.

That had been too close for comfort.

~

The following Monday, Luke and Ash made their trip on the new route to Fox, a little town near Tiffentown. A new patient of Felicity's on Saturday had provided Confederate plans, details especially important with the Union army still digging a canal in Louisiana.

For this first run, they both rode their horses rather than the train to Bovina, where they were to pick up the route about ten miles from Vicksburg. Luke was especially watchful for a place to rent a horse outside the small town of Bovina in case he needed to ride a train for a future delivery. Otherwise, Stardust, Luke's gift from Jim, would have no trouble doing the whole trip. The tailor's house was only eleven miles from Bovina.

The new route was forested part of the way. They passed a few farms and two churches with small cemeteries. Had he ever been here before?

They veered onto a wooded trail that led to a muddy road. The map had shown a two-story home set among a copse of trees on one side. It was the last house in a row of sporadically spaced houses.

"Methinks we found it." Luke spoke softly when he spotted a brick house with a wraparound porch. He and Ash hadn't spoken since they left Bovina, and his throat was still scratchy from the dousing they'd taken on the ride to Harv's three days before.

"I believe you're right."

"Remember, I'll speak." This was his route. He was the leader on this one.

Ash nodded.

They dismounted outside the home. A small painted sign read, *Matthew Frost, Tailor*. Yes, this was the place.

Adrenaline rushed through Luke. He knocked.

A short, portly man with bushy gray eyebrows opened the door. The family must live on the second floor with the tailor shop on the main floor.

"Come in. Name's Matthew Frost." He extended his hand as they entered a wide hall that had likely once held a rack or two for coats and shirts. In the current scarcity, there was only a cupboard with one filled shelf. A large oval mirror hung on the wall beside it and an empty table on the opposite wall. An open door on the left showed tables of fabric, a coat hung in a cupboard, and spools of thread nestled on a sewing machine. "I've not had the pleasure."

"Luke Shea, and this is Ash Mitchell, me boss and friend." He shook the man's callused hand and stepped back for Ash to do the same.

"Good to meet you folks." Matthew closed the door. "What can I do for you?"

"Have you any handkerchiefs for sale?" It was the code to let the tailor know they were spies sent by Jim.

Matthew straightened his shoulders. "I can spare a couple."

"One will be enough." Good. They could talk. "We didn't code our message this time."

"Tell me quickly. I'm expecting a customer, Frank, within the half hour who hates Yankees." He grinned. "A sentiment he believes we share in common."

"The Confederates plan actions to delay operations at Yazoo Pass." Luke spoke softly. "The Union generals will want to know which particular area is to be targeted so they can deploy their troops."

"Good to know," Matthew whispered. "For longer messages, code them for me in a message. Otherwise, I can recall short ones. The less we write down, the better."

"Agreed." Luke exchanged a satisfied look with Ash. Word of mouth was safer.

"One moment." Matthew turned to the nearly empty cupboard in the hall. A short stack of handkerchiefs was stored between two cotton blouses. He gave one to Luke. "That will be one dollar."

Luke gave him a bill. He was stuffing the handkerchief into his pocket when the outside door opened.

"Frank, you came at a good time. These folks are just leaving." Matthew opened the door wider and ushered them outside while Frank watched from the hall. "Remember me if you need your trousers or coat altered."

"I will." Luke spoke to a closed door. He took it as a hint to skedaddle, which they did.

He didn't speak until they were back on the forested trail. "Let's find a place to bury a pencil and some paper."

"Exactly what I was thinking." Ash clapped him on the shoulder. "You did fine."

"I was trained by the best." The praise fed his spirit. He was helping the Union.

What had he done to aid the Confederacy?

The not knowing tortured him as much as his headaches and nightmares.

CHAPTER 22

Felicity had a new patient in his mid-twenties, Abe Pruitt, for her hospital shift on Tuesday. A musket ball had been removed from his leg before his arrival. The wound wasn't healing properly and required cleaning twice daily.

The brown-haired man slept through breakfast. She brought him some mulled buttermilk with spoon biscuits midmorning to hold him over until lunch. He sat up with his back against the wall to eat and could feed himself. Bessie was out of the ward, so Felicity scooted a chair over to her new patient's bedside.

"Mr. Pruitt, I will clean your wound and change your bandage after you eat all your breakfast."

"Fine by me, Miss Danielson." He shoved a biscuit into his mouth. "Haven't had spoon biscuits for months. Mighty tasty."

"Good." She smiled. "Your chart says you're from Tennessee."

"I'm camped there. I'm from Georgia."

Not helpful. Bessie wasn't back yet. She decided to press further. "Where is your regiment camped?"

"Up near a little place called Collierville. You probably ain't heard of it." He grimaced at the buttermilk but took a long swallow, anyway.

Her heart skittered. "I guess it's big enough for things to happen there—what with your leg wound."

"I got this in a skirmish. This ain't nothing. But"—he lowered his voice—"we've had some excitement lately."

"Oh?" Felicity picked at a loose thread on her apron as if only mildly interested. Inside, she quaked.

"We caught us a spy." Abe gave a decisive nod.

It had to be the spymaster. Felicity pressed her hands into her lap to hide their trembling. "A spy? You mean someone against us Southerners?"

"They're out there." His brows drew together. "You wouldn't think it, a nice girl like you taking care of soldiers so they can get back on the battlefield...but it happens."

"This is so exciting." She leaned closer. "What happened to the spy?"

"He's been jailed. Getting bread and water because he ain't giving us the names of folks who work with him." He plopped the last biscuit into his mouth. "I'd wager that Yankee spy would give up his boots for a breakfast like this one, though."

"What will happen to him?"

"He's a Southerner, just like you and me. I say, hanging is too good for him." His eyes narrowed. "A bullet through the heart will be faster—if that Yank's got a heart."

Felicity's skin tingled at the vengeance in Abe's voice. "Have you seen him, then?"

"No, he's in a little house in another camp. He's lucky I ain't laid eyes on him." Abe clenched his fist. "Southern spies are worse than Northern varmints because they've turned on their neighbors."

"Felicity, you're supposed to be changing beds." Bessie had

her hands on her hips. "Not passing the time of day with patients."

The hair stiffened on the back of Felicity's neck. Had Bessie heard anything to arouse her suspicions? "I have to change Mr. Pruitt's bandage first." She pressed her hands against shaky legs as she stood. "Then I'll help with you with yours." That might mollify her fellow nurse.

"Be quick about it." Bessie turned with a flounce of her black skirt.

"She your superior?" Abe gestured after the nurse stalking away.

"No. We work together." Felicity gathered his empty plate and glass.

"You wouldn't know it."

Felicity silently agreed. Bessie was easier to get along with when she thought she was in charge. "I'll take these to the kitchen and then grab the bandages."

"Thank you, miss." He lounged against the wall. "I ain't going nowhere."

Felicity must get this information to Ash and Luke as soon as she could. That meant sneaking out after making the beds and before lunch. She took a ten- or fifteen-minute break on mornings when they weren't busy. Walking to and from Ash's house would take twenty minutes.

Bessie would be fit to be tied when she discovered Felicity missing.

She'd work on a good excuse later.

~

*M*idmorning, movement at the door caused Luke to look up from the skin he was measuring to cut. Felicity was here? She was supposed to be at the hospital.

Ash was inside the house, preparing for his move. "Felicity? You're here on a Tuesday?" Rising, he hurried to her side.

"Quick. I have to get back to the hospital. Is Ash around?" Her breath came in gasps, as if she'd sprinted to the saddle shop.

"In the house." He clasped her icy hands in his. "You can tell me, and I'll relay your message."

"Good. Please, shut the door."

This was spy information, then. His senses alert for any sound out of place, he released her hands and closed the door against the cold weather and prying eyes. "Now, what is this about?"

Felicity whispered what she'd learned from her newest patient.

Luke gave a low whistle. "This will help those searching to hone in on his location. Thank you, Felicity."

"I've been gone too long. I must get back." She turned to the door.

"Want me to drive you in the buggy?"

Felicity shook her head. "It will take longer to hitch up the horse. Just please, pass that along. We can still save him."

"Aye. Be careful."

A hurried pace took her back toward the hospital.

Luke strode to the house and found Ash in the master bedroom, its contents in disarray. "Ash, Felicity brought news."

Dropping a stack of shirts, Ash strode toward him. "Where is she?"

"Gone back to the hospital. 'Tis a good thing she came." Closing the door, Luke told Ash what she had discovered.

"We've got to pass this along. Today." Ash raked his hands through his hair.

"Why don't we go separate ways today?" That way, they could cover more ground. "I'll take the new route."

"And I'll go to Harv's. Good idea." Ash reached for the door-knob and stopped. "You ready for this?"

"Aye. 'Tis time for me to do more than tag along."

*A*t the hospital, Felicity hung her cloak on a wall hook and then raced upstairs to her ward. She met Bessie's furious stare as soon as she stepped into the room.

Bessie stalked over. "Where have you been?" She hissed in her ear.

Felicity answered as calmly as she could. "I stepped outside for a few minutes." That much was true.

Bessie narrowed her eyes. "Why?"

She tried to hide that her breath came in gasps after her fast-paced walk back. "I took a quick walk on my break."

"Next time, tell me first." Bessie snapped at her. "Dr. Watkins wanted to ask you about Abe's wound."

Felicity's stomach knotted. That was unfortunate. He must not become suspicious of her too. "I'll seek him out immediately."

"And then see to Pete Flanigan."

A patient who'd been with her a month. "What about him?"

"He wants to send a letter home."

His right hand was useless at the moment due to a shrapnel wound. "I have time to write it before lunch."

It was a good thing they were both busy. Else Bessie would have asked more questions about where she went, that much was certain.

*L*uke rummaged through his clothes for something requiring alteration. The two sets Felicity made him were perfect. His Confederate gray trousers were too loose—even with Jolene's good cooking, his appetite hadn't fully returned—but he had no plans to don them again. Ever.

The shirt he'd worn during that last battle needed mending. He'd take that to the tailor's. One of Matthew's customers had witnessed Luke purchasing a handkerchief yesterday. He couldn't return the next day for another. The torn blouse was a better excuse.

Ash, with a longer ride, had left a quarter of an hour ago, waiting only for Julia to make them both a sandwich.

Luke patted his coat pocket where his pass to leave the city nestled. The message about the captured spy hadn't been written. He'd hidden paper and pencil along his route—he wouldn't use it today. Matthew could remember the details.

He stuffed his shirt into his saddlebag with his lunch and a canteen of water. Had he forgotten anything? No matter. He had the important things.

Confederate pickets outside Vicksburg checked his pass. Luke was on the road to Bolton before he remembered he didn't bring money to purchase skins for the saddle shop, his ostensible reason for taking the trips. He'd have to return by a different route, a wooded trail Ash had shown him to avoid the soldiers guarding the city.

Forgetting such an important piece trampled on his self-confidence. He'd never be the spy Ash had become. Luke prayed he'd forgotten nothing else.

At least it was a sunny day, warm for February. He'd been in bed with a cold for two days following last week's rainy ride. No such problems today.

From Bolton, he followed the forested road, passing the

area where he'd hidden writing utensils. It cheered him that he recognized the thick line of pines hiding the precious objects.

Matthew's home beside a copse of trees loomed into view around noon. A saddled horse nibbled on grass outside the home. Luke secured Stardust's reins beside the water trough. Tilting his hat masked his survey of the surroundings for strangers. Matthew's was the last in a row of homes. A child played with a cup and ball in a yard four houses down. Otherwise, Luke spotted no one. Neighbors were likely eating lunch.

As he knocked on the door, garment in hand, Luke didn't fool himself—the boy wasn't the only one watching him.

The door opened. "Luke." Matthew's hearty tone belied the warning look on his face. "I see you've brought me some work to do. I'm with a customer. Would you care to wait?" He gave a slight shake of his head.

"I don't mind returning at a more convenient time." Luke hadn't even mentioned the code. This must be a *very* bad time to call. "Much obliged." He spun on his heel.

"No need to make the poor fellow come back tomorrow." A portly man with a brown beard entered the hall without a coat. "Ah, it's you. Thought I recognized your Irish accent from yesterday. Matthew, it must be mighty important for him to return so soon."

Luke's heart skipped a beat. The tailor had described his customer as someone who hated Yankees. Undoubtedly, he despised Union spies even more.

"Frank, I didn't get a chance to introduce you yesterday." Matthew swiped at his sweaty brow. "This here's Luke Shea, a new customer. Luke, this is my neighbor and childhood buddy, Frank Yates."

"A pleasure, Mr. Yates." Luke shook his hand. "Is there a place to sit and wait?"

"Of course." Matthew pointed to a small parlor with a desk,

four high-backed wooden chairs, and a heat stove. "I'm measuring Frank's altered coat."

"You can take care of him first. I'll wait." Mr. Yates studied Luke. "Where did you say you were from?"

"A few miles south of here in Vicksburg. I'm a saddler."

"Getting much business these days?"

"Nay." His sigh was real. They'd been making saddles even without orders so Luke could hone his skills. "Some folks have barely enough for food, much less saddles."

"It's the fault of them Yankees." Mr. Yates pounded his fist onto a hall table.

Best agree, as Matthew had said he did. "Aye. They forced this conflict upon us. We didn't want it." That was a comment he'd overhead on Vicksburg streets. Luke had no idea if it was true or not...thanks to those missing years.

"You've got the right of it, my boy." Mr. Yates wagged a finger at him. "All our troubles can be laid on the Yankees. Why didn't you fight for the Confederacy? The South needs young men like you."

Luke's glance darted at Matthew. Did the tailor know he was a former Confederate? Would that truth frighten him? "I did." Hopefully, the sadness in his voice would be interpreted as sorrow that he was a soldier no longer. "Took shrapnel in me head at Fredericksburg. I've been discharged."

Matthew's eyes widened.

"Proud of you, my boy." Mr. Yates shook his hand. "What a pity your wound will keep you from the fight."

"Aye." Though he'd joined another fight—one fought by spies.

"Matthew..." Mr. Yates clamped a hand on the tailor's shoulder. "You must see to him first. I'll wait in the parlor."

"Well, if you're certain."

"I insist."

After he went into the parlor, Matthew and Luke entered a cluttered workroom with several tables and a sewing machine.

Matthew closed the door. "Now, then. Let's see what you've got for me." He glanced at the closed door. "Tell me quickly," he whispered.

Luke whispered where the spymaster could be found and then raised his voice. "There's a tear here, at the neck. Can it be repaired?"

"Let's see." He put on his spectacles and inspected the torn fabric. "Were you really a Confederate soldier?" he whispered.

"Aye. Me head wound gave me amnesia." Luke spoke quickly. Had he destroyed the tailor's confidence in him? "You can trust me."

Matthew's eyes narrowed. "Don't betray me."

"We be in this together." He lifted his chin.

The doorknob jiggled. Matthew's glance flickered past Luke toward the door.

Luke stiffened. Had his last comment been overheard? He glanced over his shoulder. Frank stood in the doorway.

"You're in luck," Matthew said quickly. "I can repair this shirt next week. Oh, Frank, come on in. We're just finishing."

"Good to hear you can help one of our heroes." Frank strode toward them.

"Obliged to you for waiting, sir." Luke gave him a nod. The other man's friendly manner was still in place, so maybe he hadn't heard the whispered conversation. "Thank you, Matthew. I will return next week."

"That's fine, then." Matthew rubbed his hands together. "Frank, let's see if that coat fits."

Heart pounding like a sewing machine needle, Luke was riding away within a minute.

He hadn't planned to tell his fellow spies about his army service. Had he allayed Matthew's fears?

~

Felicity took her time walking home from her hospital shift on Tuesday, confident that news of the spy's location was speeding its way toward those searching for him. She was grateful her second new patient in four days had vital information, especially about the imprisoned spy. How she longed to give Luke a Confederate secret or two for his new route. He'd talked to her today, at least long enough to get the information.

Truthfully, he seemed to fear being too close to her. That day he'd held her, shivering, in his arms...he'd acted as if he'd overstepped his bounds.

No, she didn't misinterpret his distance. If he never recovered from his amnesia, this was what their relationship was to be.

Part of her dreamed that he'd fall in love with her without knowing their past. Yet her greatest dream was seeing joy light his face when he one day remembered her.

When Julia and Ash moved away, she'd probably only see him when cleaning his home. Aunt Mae hadn't expressed a desire to invite him for Sunday lunch or Saturday supper, as she'd often done in the past.

Spying would soon be the only thing that bound her and Luke. That and church. The two households often sat together during services. Perhaps that would continue.

It was nearly dark when Felicity entered her aunt's home.

"Felicity?" Petunia stepped into the hall. "Where have you been?"

"I work at the hospital on Tuesdays." She removed her cloak without looking at her cousin. Felicity was getting rather impatient with her rude behavior.

"You're nearly ninety minutes later than normal."

She gave her head a shake. "Why does it matter?"

"You haven't finished Wilma's next dress. She needs it for Sunday." Petunia put her hands on her hips. "We're invited to a birthday party at my friend Amelia Barnes's house. That is, *my* family is."

The dress was cut and ready to sew, but Julia's gifts came first. "I'm sorry. It won't be done by then."

"What? You're such an ungrateful creature—"

"What's this?" Aunt Mae rushed down the hall from the kitchen, dish towel in hand. "There can't be trouble between two cousins, such gracious ladies that you are."

"Mama, Wilma's dress won't be ready for the party." Petunia rounded on her mother. "You know how we long to make a good impression on Amelia's guests."

Why did Petunia care so much about this old friendship? Then Felicity realized where she'd heard the Barnes name. Amelia's father-in-law owned a cotton plantation near Bovina, putting her in a wealthier social class.

"Oh, that is unfortunate." Aunt Mae raised a pleading gaze to Felicity. "Do you think you could finish if you work an extra hour or two a day on it?"

At one time, such a request from her aunt would have been enough to persuade her to either change her plans or stay up late to accommodate her. Felicity, still hurt from the secrets kept from her and her siblings, wasn't inclined to do it. "I've other sewing that comes first. My regrets."

"You'll upset poor little Wilma when she learns her beautiful dress won't be done." Petunia tilted her head with narrowed eyes.

Petunia would make a fuss of it to her daughter. It was a low blow. The little girl had done nothing to deserve such treatment. Felicity's lips tightened. "I'll see what I can do."

"There now. That will make everything better, right, Petunia?" Aunt Mae patted her daughter's shoulder.

"I'll make myself a sandwich and eat in my room so I can

get started." Clearly, her aunt's concerns were for her daughter. With a flounce of her skirt, Felicity swept toward the kitchen.

"Oh, no need for that," Aunt Mae called after her. "You can begin after supper."

Felicity sliced off two pieces of bread, heat coursing through her. How she wished there was someplace for her to get away from her troubles.

In the old days, she used to run to Luke for comfort and sound advice. He'd always listened and eventually had her laughing.

He was no longer her fortress.

Soon Julia would be gone and she'd truly be alone, like a rudderless ship caught by a current on the mighty Mississippi.

CHAPTER 23

*L*uke told Ash about Matthew's customer, Frank Yates, that evening after supper. They sat in the upstairs parlor with Julia, who had set aside her tatting for sewing.

"I wish you hadn't told them you were in the Confederate army." Ash shifted in his seat. "Matthew needs to trust you."

"Aye. I regretted it immediately." Luke tapped his foot. "Me intent was to satisfy Mr. Yates that I support the South."

"It can't be helped." He sighed. "I've got bad news. Activity in our area continues to escalate for both armies. Mostly skirmishes, but there's been migration to the west. Long waits for the train in Delhi have been reported. Some families have waited three or more days for empty seats."

Luke had interrupted Ash packing a trunk that morning. "So you'll be leaving sooner rather than later."

"Mama's anxious, especially with..." Blushing, Julia looked at Ash.

"We have good news as well." Ash clasped his wife's hand. "We're expecting a blessed event at the end of summer."

Joy for his friends pushed back Luke's worries. "Good news,

indeed." He stood and extended his hand to Ash, who shook it. "Now you've another reason to get to Texas quickly."

"True." Ash's forehead wrinkled. "You've taken to making saddles as I suspected you would. I just want to know Jim's been rescued before..."

"Let's wait until Monday. That's the twenty-third. We should be at the ranch at the beginning of March." Julia patted her husband's arm. "We'll try to wait for news of Jim, yet we must not jeopardize our family's safety."

"Aye." Luke gave a firm nod. That was paramount. "I will send word if you all leave before you know."

"If he's found alive, write that the missing tool has been found. If they hanged him..." Ash swallowed. "Write that the tool is damaged beyond repair. If he can't be found, write that the tool has vanished."

"Agreed." Luke's stomach lurched. He prayed he would be able to fill his best friend's shoes.

~

Felicity learned the Mitchells' planned departure date the next day, Wednesday. Julia told her as she hung up her cloak. It made her even angrier that Petunia had forced her to put aside her own plans to sew baby gifts. "How can I best help you get ready to go?"

"I knew you'd offer." Julia hugged her. "Let's launder the sheets to the closed-off bedrooms and store them. It will be easy enough to make the beds whenever guests come."

Doubtful that guests would ever come. Luke shied away from old acquaintances he didn't remember. "Let's work on one bedroom at a time. You mustn't overdo. If you start feeling poorly, you must stop."

"I will. I can't be sick for the trip." Julia touched her stomach. "I've been queasy in the mornings."

"My sister was too. It got better when she rested."

"Mama said the same." Julia smiled. "I don't mind the queasiness."

Were Felicity married to Luke and expecting, she was certain she wouldn't mind either.

Best not dwell on what couldn't be.

They finished Daphne's old bedroom—Ash's youngest sister—by the end of the day. Luke had avoided direct conversations with Felicity at the noon meal, further depressing her spirits.

On Thursday, Felicity laundered the family's clothes while Julia, having worked to exhaustion the previous day, rested until lunch. Sorrow filled Felicity's heart at the imminent parting. She helped Jolene serve chicken pie with the realization that this was her last meal with the Mitchells during a work day.

"How do you feel, Julia?" Felicity seated herself opposite Luke, who met her glance briefly.

"Much better for resting, thank you." Julia unfolded her napkin. "I don't know what I'd have done without you to help me all these weeks."

"It was my pleasure." Warmth spread through her at the confirmation that she'd aided her friend. She met Luke's glance. Was that pride in his eyes? Who could know, when he looked away so quickly?

Ash asked the blessing, adding a prayer for their upcoming trip and the loved ones they were leaving in Vicksburg.

"I neglected to tell you that Mama will be at home for any friends who want to call Sunday after church." Julia poked at her meal as if uncertain whether to eat. "We'll have light refreshments all afternoon. Will you mention the invitation to the Beltzers? Of course, your cousin and her children are also welcome."

"They are invited to a party." Felicity was halfway finished with Wilma's dress. "Although, I'm certain they will stop in either before or after. I will tell my aunt."

"Thank you." Julia ate a bite and grimaced. "Luke, we do hope both you and Felicity will remain at the party all afternoon."

Felicity's gaze flew to Luke's startled glance. The way Julia had worded the request, it almost seemed they were a couple again.

"I can only speak for meself that I will stay." Luke studied the chicken pie on his plate as if it were about to run away.

Felicity kept trying to tell herself not to dream of a future for them, yet his rejection stung. "I will be happy to stay. I'll come early on Monday to see you off. What time will you leave?"

"I've arranged for a boat to take us across the river at dawn." Ash's brow furrowed. "A rented carriage will meet us on the other side to take us as far as Delhi."

"We'll take one trunk for traveling." Julia put down her fork. "It all seems so final."

"Not having second thoughts, are you, my dear?" Ash tugged on his collar.

"Not at all." She smiled at him. "It's just difficult to leave with so much uncertainty."

For a moment, Felicity almost wished she were going with them. Then she looked at Luke's worried face. She'd not abandon him. Someone who knew him well must be there when his memories flooded back. She'd not desert him when he most needed her.

~

*N*ate hadn't met Luke and Ash at the oak grove on Thursday, so they returned to the meeting spot on a dreary yet mild Friday—Ash's last opportunity to see his best spy. They had just arrived when Luke spotted Nate striding up the steep road toward them.

"Nate, I hope you have news." With a jerk of his head, Ash beckoned the spy closer.

"Good news." Nate folded his arms. "Our friend has been rescued. They're taking him halfway to his sister's home in case he's pursued."

"Praise God." Ash looked heavenward.

"Aye. We've longed to hear it." Luke silently sent up a prayer of gratitude.

"It's a relief for all of us." Nate rocked back on his heels.

"Thank you for bringing good news for our last meeting." Ash extended his hand. "I'm leaving Vicksburg on Monday. Luke will continue on from here."

"I'm sorry to see you go." Nate shook Ash's hand.

"If you're ever in need of a job, come to my ranch in Texas."

"I'll remember that. I'd follow you now if I didn't feel needed here. Godspeed." Nate's face relaxed.

"Thank you, my friend." Ash clapped him on the back. "My prayers are with you."

"Never been a praying man." Nate pushed his hat back. "But I've had cause to be glad that you are. I'd welcome your prayers." He turned to Luke. "See you next Thursday."

With a final wave, he turned and left by a different road.

Luke's legs felt a bit wobbly as they set out, so great was his relief that Jim was safe. "Matthew doesn't want me to return until next week, but I'll ride up to Harv's tomorrow."

"I'll go with you to say goodbye." Ash's limp was more noticeable. Perhaps his relief made him unsteady, something Luke shared.

He'd earned Nate's trust somehow. Hopefully, he hadn't destroyed Matthew's trust with his blunder about being a Confederate soldier.

~

*F*elicity had written to her siblings about finding the deed to their childhood home and the gist of her subsequent conversations with Aunt Mae but hadn't heard back from anyone. That didn't surprise her because of the sporadic mail service around the country, depending on battle locations. Though she was curious about their reactions, there was plenty to keep her busy leading up to Julia's departure.

Wilma wore the dress that Felicity remade for her to church, holding the pink folds wide so she could look at them. The little girl's joy in the dress eased Felicity's ruffled feelings about being forced to make it so quickly.

Her aunt, uncle, and cousins left immediately for their party, to Felicity's relief. She strolled in the sunny, mild weather to Mrs. Dodd's home carrying a basket filled with gifts for Julia's baby.

Other than Luke, who was helping Ash arrange seating for guests, Felicity was the first guest to arrive. Julia and her mother exclaimed over the three nightgowns and six nappies and gave Felicity hugs in thanks for the gifts. Soon so many guests arrived that the room filled with the low hum of chatter and exclamations of joy upon learning that Julia and Ash would be blessed with their first child at the end of summer.

Felicity helped Hester and Daisy replenish trays of food and wash dishes because for every family that tearfully left, another one arrived. Felicity carried around cups of tea, taking over as hostess so Mrs. Dodd and Julia could talk with their guests without worrying about such duties.

Savannah sought Felicity out before she left. "Even though I haven't seen her much lately, I'm going to miss Julia." Her mouth drooped.

"I understand." How would she cope herself, without being able to confide her sorrow over Luke?

"I plan to visit them in Texas." She sighed. "*When* depends on this war."

After Savannah left, Felicity wondered if living at the Texas ranch wasn't also in her future. For now, she must concentrate on discovering secrets vital to the Union.

~

*R*apid-fire shelling from across the river mid afternoon during the party drew everyone's attention westward. Luke rushed to the street with Ash and other men. Were they under attack? No shells seemed to falling on the city.

Those digging the canal had lopped occasional shots toward Vicksburg, as if to remind citizens of their presence—an unnecessary act since they could see movement across the river from the bluff—but today's shelling seemed different.

Luke touched the shrapnel wound on his head. The scar was proof that he'd seen such activity before. One would think cannon fire, once experienced, would be indelibly imprinted on one's mind.

"What are them Yankees doing now?" One gentleman peered toward the river.

"Hard telling. Folks are headed to vantage points to watch." Another stranger pointed to the courthouse hill and the Sky Parlor. "Want to go?"

The general consensus was to watch from the courthouse. The men left except for Ash and Luke.

"Is this an attack?" Luke was at a loss how to protect Felicity and the others.

As suddenly as it had begun, the shelling ended.

"I don't think so. There'd be more concentrated fire aimed at us." Ash peered toward the river. "Wait. Today is February twenty-second."

"Washington's birthday. A celebration?" That was the best possible reason because it was impossible for Ash's family to leave during an attack.

"Possibly. They've done similar demonstrations in the past. Let's rejoin the guests." Ash gave a nod to the door. "The women are watching from the window. We'll keep an eye on the situation. If nothing further happens, our trip will begin in the morning."

In the Mitchells' absence, if—when—an attack came on the city, he'd figure out how to protect Felicity. His gut told him that day wasn't far off.

~

elicity rode in Mrs. Dodd's carriage in a misty dawn to the wharves the next morning with the family. They had picked her up at her aunt's home, and she'd go to Julia's—now Luke's—home to clean after her friends left. Her heart was heavy at this goodbye. She'd been good friends with Julia for nearly four years, and they'd grown even closer with Felicity working as her maid. She'd miss her friend.

Indeed, since Luke's injury, Julia had become as beloved as a sister—even dearer, because it had been months since Mabel's last correspondence.

However, she was glad for their sake that the trip was to begin today. After a constant string of changed plans and routes and transportation, Ash, Julia, Mrs. Dodd, and Eddie were finally leaving for Texas—by carriage, of all things.

Luke rode with Ash on the driver's seat. This would be a difficult parting for him as well.

"You must write to me every week." Julia swiped at her cheeks inside the dark carriage.

"I will." Sitting beside her, Felicity squeezed her arm. "And

I'll want to hear all about the ranch, Ash's family, and how everyone is settling in."

"Uncle Clark says there's plenty of room to ride a horse." Eddie jumped up and down in his seat, making the carriage sway.

"That sounds like fun." Felicity thought back to her childhood. "I used to ride horseback with my brothers every week in the summer. I haven't ridden for years. I hope to find an opportunity to do so again."

"I'm certain you can do whatever you set your mind to doing." Mrs. Dodd spoke with conviction. "You're a remarkable, talented woman. I've always been glad of your friendship with Julia. I do hope you'll stay in touch with us."

"Thank you. I will." Felicity was surprised to hear such praise, especially with Petunia's negative comments so prevalent in her head. "I promise."

"You must come to us in Texas if you need a place to stay." Julia gave her a watery smile. "My baby will want another 'aunt,' I'm certain."

"I'll remember." After the war, maybe. Traveling difficulties effectively closed the door on Felicity traveling to them as a woman alone during the hostilities.

The carriage stopped.

"We're here." Eddie pumped his fist. "Our adventure begins." Opening the door, he jumped to the grassy City Landing.

"Indeed." Mrs. Dodd laughed. "It will be an adventure, to be sure."

Luke helped the ladies from the carriage while Ash talked to the captain.

Felicity was the last from the carriage. She tucked her hand into Luke's firm clasp and stepped down.

"I will walk you back to your aunt's home." Holding her gaze, Luke released her hand.

"I work at Julia's—your house—today." That flustered her. She was now a maid in Luke's household.

"Then I will escort you there."

The sun hadn't yet risen, and a fog hung low over the river. Wharf workers were standing around. Some of them stared at her. No doubt, Luke had noticed them when driving here.

This wasn't a safe environment for a woman alone in the predawn darkness.

Something cold within her began to thaw at his protective attitude.

Whether he ever loved her again or not, he cared enough for her to protect her.

It was a start.

~

"Godspeed." Luke waved at Ash and his family as the ferry left the wharf just after six o'clock.

"Goodbye." A tear wound its way down Felicity's cheek as she waved.

A chorus of goodbyes and reminders to write wafted over from the boat. Fog soon shrouded their features.

"'Tis difficult to say goodbye to such good friends." Luke fished in his coat pocket for his new handkerchief and pressed it into her hand.

"Harder than I ever expected." Felicity swiped at her cheeks.

The ferry's landing was about a half mile downstream, which would place them on a road toward Monroe. Luke and Ash had studied alternate routes late into the night in case something happened.

"Be ye ready to stroll back?" A tear glistening on Felicity's cheek wrenched at his heart. How he longed to shield her from pain.

Nodding, she picked up her skirts and turned.

Luke glanced at several rough-looking men regarding them. His spy, Nate Miller, who was a former wharf worker, wasn't among them. "Let's get back."

They maintained a brisk pace until they reached Washington Street, where many shops and businesses were located. A misty sun peeked over the horizon, soon to melt the fog away. Citizens were beginning to stir about the streets. Soldiers headed to restaurants for breakfast.

His stomach growled. There'd been no time for a meal this morning. "Have ye eaten breakfast?"

"No." She gave him an incredulous look. "I hoped Jolene might have something for me to nibble on."

"Let's eat breakfast at that little restaurant on Walnut." It was a splurge, but he'd saved nearly all his money except for the clothes she'd made him. They both needed cheering up.

Her face turned crimson. "I—it wouldn't be seemly..."

Of course. A man didn't usually escort a girl to breakfast unless she was a woman of the evening. Heat spread up his face. How could he have so forgotten the proprieties? "Ye have the right of it. I'm sorry. I meant no insult."

"I know." She walked silently at his side to the next street corner. "Lunch or supper at that restaurant would be welcome."

A hard knot formed in the pit of his stomach. He was too broken inside. "I merely meant to cheer the pair of us."

"I see." She studied the sidewalk. "It was a nice thought."

He'd hurt her. Best steer the conversation to safer topics. "You're aware that your job as me maid is secure until the beginning of June."

"Yes. Julia told me she left money for my and Jolene's salaries. Quite generous." She didn't look up from her perusal of the sidewalk. "I will look for another job in May."

"I will try to keep you on longer." He had two side saddles and two other saddles ready to sell. If those sold, it would provide for Felicity to stay on through the summer. Then what?

"Thank you. I will appreciate any extra weeks." They turned onto Luke's street. "My dream is to buy a seamstress shop with an apartment on the second floor."

"A worthy dream." No doubt, she'd achieve it. She was a determined, capable woman.

"I won't be beholden to you forever."

He frowned at her choice of words and her brittle tone. Odd. It was almost as if she was letting him go.

But...he didn't want that. He wanted her to part of his life. Craved her friendship. Desired to court her someday.

Yet if his memories remained dormant and she gave up hope, he might not have a choice.

CHAPTER 24

"*Y*ou look tired, dear. Petunia is putting the children down for a late nap. They've been quite fractious today." Aunt Mae's footsteps creaked against the stairs as she descended the afternoon of Julia's departure. "You've a letter waiting from Jack's wife." She gestured to the hall table. "It was delivered by a gentleman, a stranger to me. Curious. We always walk to the post office for our mail."

"I'm glad to hear from Annabelle, whether a stranger picked it up accidentally at the post office or not."

Felicity's spy instincts kicked in. That delivery sounded like what a letter carrier was paid to do—transport secret missives without going through the postal service. Of course, it could have something to do with the sporadic mail service across the Mississippi River, especially with the Union army digging in full view of Vicksburg's citizens this winter, but she doubted it.

Her own letters to her siblings had been mailed less than two weeks before. Felicity hadn't known Jack's current location. He moved with the Confederate army in his position as chaplain, so she'd sent her letter about the deed to Annabelle.

"One wonders how she, the twins, and sweet little Elizabeth

are managing with Jack away." Aunt Mae twisted an embroidered handkerchief.

"I'll read it in my room and let you know any news." She could scarcely read it aloud when it might contain Jack's response to her aunt's deceit.

"Of course, dear." Her shoulders hunched.

Felicity swept past her and up the stairs to her cold bedroom, clutching the envelope. A fire could be lit in the stove after reading her letter. She broke the seal and unfolded the page from Annabelle. Turning it to catch sunrays from the window, she sat on the room's only chair.

Wednesday, January 21, 1863

Dearest Felicity,

I have hesitated to write you this news, for it will come as a shock. I must ask you first and foremost to keep silent about this matter, or at least be very selective whom you tell.

Jack isn't a chaplain in the Confederate army as you believed. Oh, he did begin as a chaplain but deserted to the Union army at the first opportunity. He became a private with a Michigan regiment. Our neighbors will consider him a traitor, should they discover it. Perhaps you do as well. Jack didn't think so. It's my fervent prayer that your love for your brother will keep you silent on this matter. He was a protective big brother to you always. Perhaps you will respond the same way in his hour of need.

I received a letter from one of Jack's comrades by private carrier (the same way I sent this note to you) informing me that he went missing during a battle in December of last year. He may have been shot and captured. Or worse. Yet my heart screams at me that my children's father yet lives.

No! Jack was missing? Her dear brother, whom she imagined to be safe while serving as a chaplain. It couldn't be true. The letter had been written before Felicity even discovered the deed. Tears blurred her vision. She swiped her eyes with her sleeve, too frantic to search for a handkerchief, and read on.

I've spared you the details because I don't know how you will receive this news. I covet your prayers for Jack. Please use every discretion if you speak of this. Your aunt and uncle will be displeased to learn of his change of alliance and may consider him a traitor, as will others in Vicksburg. I request you keep this from them to protect their future relationship, for this war must end eventually.

We shall emerge from this conflict as a family—all of us—if my fervent prayers are answered.

John and James are only three, and Elizabeth is nearly eighteen months. They are growing like those proverbial weeds, blissfully unaware that their mama bears this burden alone, now shared with Jack's dear sister. Since Clarence lives in Ohio, his loyalties may be for the North. Mabel's definitely aren't.

Felicity agreed with that assessment of Mabel's loyalties. She was also unsure about Clarence, who hadn't enlisted to her knowledge. Yet it was a comfort that Annabelle had decided to trust Felicity.

Dearest Jack, her strong, serious brother in the prime of his life at twenty-five. His faith had been strong even as a boy. It hadn't been difficult to picture him as a chaplain, praying for men before they headed into battle.

She fell to her knees. "Dear God, if Jack is still alive, help us to find him. Bring him safely home to raise the sweet little ones who call him 'Papa.' Bring him back to Annabelle, a warrior in her own right. Protect my brother and bring him back to us."

Heaviness settled over her limbs—indeed, her whole body. Felicity couldn't tell Aunt Mae or Uncle Charles. If Julia could have waited one more day to leave, she and Ash could have added Jack to their prayers...and been a shoulder to lean on.

That left Luke. He'd never met Jack, who had married Annabelle and moved to Louisiana a year before Felicity met him.

Luke had enough to deal with. She never knew the past details that were going to trigger a setback for him, affect him adversely.

No, it was best to tell no one.

~

*A*fter a nearly sleepless night, Felicity dragged herself to the hospital in the drizzle and fog the next morning before dawn. She read the doctor's notes with blurry eyes.

Having a new soldier on her side of the ward shook her back to her task of spying. What a comfort that Jack supported the Union as she and Luke did. It suddenly became more important to discover those secrets for her brother's sake as well as for her beau. Both now suffered for their Northern allegiance.

The new patient, Reginald Foster, had come in yesterday from the area of Greenwood, Mississippi, with a fever. Dr. Watkins noted that quinine lowered his fever but didn't keep it away.

Felicity prepared the dose and carried the medicine along with a fresh water bucket into the dimly lit ward. Bessie wasn't here yet. If Mr. Foster was awake, Felicity could talk to him before the other nurse arrived.

She lit two lanterns. Leaving one on the table beside the door, she carried the other down the aisle, looking for anyone in distress. Everyone was sleeping except a man so tall his feet hung from the end of the bed. Since she didn't recognize the soldier with a thatch of blond hair, this must be her new patient.

"Mr. Foster?" Speaking softly, she bent closer.

"Yes, Reginald Foster is my name. Who are you?"

She set down the lamp. "I'm Felicity Danielson, your nurse." His face was flushed, his forehead hot to her touch. "I'd say it's time for another dose of quinine."

"Yes, miss." He pushed himself up. "The night attendant gave me some before midnight, I reckon."

"Let me fetch the bucket." She'd left it on the table. She hurried back with it to give him first the pill and then a dipper of water.

After drinking, he gave her back the dipper. "Thank you."

"Where are you from?"

The patient in the next bed stirred. Felicity glanced at the door. A man headed toward the privy. No sign of Bessie.

"Georgia, but I came here from Greenwood."

"Since a fever sent you to us, I'd wager not much is happening there." She strove for a casual tone.

"You'd lose that bet."

Her heartbeat sped. "Oh?"

"General Loring is having us construct a fort where the Tallahatchie and Yalobusha Rivers meet to form the Yazoo. We'll have artillery batteries there. Some of the fellas were digging earthworks. I was helping to build up the cotton bales for protection when my fever got worse."

"A fort? How exciting." Movement at the door caught Felicity's eye. Bessie was here and turning up the lanterns to brighten the ward.

"It's called Fort Pemberton for our commander, Lieutenant General John Pemberton." His broad chest thrust out with pride.

"What an honor for the general." She looked up and met Bessie's curious gaze.

"Felicity, the men are asking for their breakfast." Bessie crossed her arms.

"Well, we'd best get to it, then. I gave Mr. Foster his medicine. He was the only one awake when I arrived."

"Others are up now," she snapped.

Felicity bit back a retort. It had never made anything better in the past.

She'd learned about the new fort, ensuring a conversation with Luke.

~

"*D*on't think about sneaking out like you did the other day." Bessie stood at the entrance to the nurses' room a half hour later, glaring at Felicity.

She actually *had* considered leaving at her lunch break to tell Luke the news. The hard look in Bessie's eyes changed her mind. "Of course not. We have a full ward."

"At first, I imagined you only worked here to find a husband, but you don't spend extra time with every patient." Her brow furrowed.

"Only the ones that need it. There's not enough time in the day, right?" Felicity consulted the doctor's notes for her four patients requiring medicine before breakfast. She had everything gathered.

"One wonders why you spend an inordinate amount of time with your new patients." Bessie put her hands on her hips.

The hair lifted at the back of Felicity's neck. "I like to introduce myself...discover their aches and pains so I can help them." She took two steps toward the door.

Bessie didn't budge. Her eyes narrowed. "You wouldn't be spying on our brave men, now, would you?"

Her hands holding the pills began to sweat. "Why ask such an outrageous question? I'm as loyal as anyone here." To the North. Felicity tried to sound indignant when all she wanted was to bolt. But Bessie blocked the door.

"Maybe I should start getting here a little earlier...so I can keep my eye on you." Bessie crossed her arms.

It was a threat. Bessie would make a formidable enemy. "Suit yourself. I'm certain you'll be disappointed because the men usually sleep until the sun rises or we turn up the lamps." One more step brought Felicity within a foot of the stormy-eyed woman. "Johnny was writhing in pain when I left to fetch his morphine. If you'll excuse me?" Inwardly quaking, Felicity held her gaze.

Bessie stepped out of the room. "I'm watching you."

Silently, Felicity followed her up the stairs. She should have moved away from Reginald as soon as she spotted Bessie. However, she didn't regret having information to share with Luke.

~

*W*hen footsteps approached the saddle shop the afternoon after Ash left, Luke looked up from fashioning a stirrup, hoping for a customer interested in one of his extra saddles. The day was mild enough to keep the door open, encouraging folks to enter, as a lieutenant had done yesterday. The tall officer had ordered a saddle to be done Saturday. The ones already completed weren't big enough for the portly customer.

Felicity peeked her head inside. "Good afternoon, Luke. Are you busy?"

He stood. "Just working on an order. Come in. I didn't expect you today."

"Good." She closed the door behind her. "I see you've kept Ash's tradition of keeping the door open."

"'Tis a pleasant day. An open door invites folks to come inside. I'll close it in the cold weather, unlike Ash." It was good to see her. Something about her grounded him. Made him want to see her more often.

"A sound plan." She smiled, holding his gaze.

Wanting to respond to the longing in her eyes, he forced himself to look away. Of all the memories he'd lost, losing her hurt most.

"Sorry to interrupt your work." Her voice had lost its vibrancy. She told him about a new fort the Confederate soldiers were constructing.

"'Tis a good thing you came today with this news." That the Southerners were building up defenses near Greenwood was significant. He hadn't returned to the tailor's house because he felt Matthew had warned him to stay away for a while. "I will pass it on tomorrow. Thank you."

"Of course. It's my job." She turned for the door.

"Felicity?" He stepped toward her. "Be ye upset about something?"

Her hand rested on the doorknob as she paused. "One of the nurses has noticed that I spend extra time with new patients. She warned me that she's watching me."

Luke studied her tense face. How could she still be so beautiful when worry plagued her? "Then don't question the next patient to arrive. Put her off the trail."

She looked up, those beautiful eyes the color of a summer sky filled with hope. "If you can wait, Bessie might simmer down in a couple of weeks."

"Then let's give her at least three weeks." Luke touched her cloaked sleeve. "If the problem with Bessie continues, I'd ask that you stop altogether. Never could I condone putting you in danger." The shadows in her eyes remained. "But there's something else concerning you, right?"

Her brows pulled in as she pinched her bottom lip.

"Felicity? You can tell me."

"Thank you. Perhaps I will. Sometime." She gazed up at him.

This time, there was no mistaking it. She wanted him to kiss her.

Oh, how he wanted to. This blasted amnesia erected a barrier he must not cross.

His hand slid from her arm as he stepped back. "Nay, tis me who is grateful for brave women like you who support the Union."

Sorrow filled those beautiful eyes at his rejection. "And I for brave men like you." A rush of cool air chilled him after she left.

Sadness filled him. There could be no feelings between a man with no memories and a woman who knew them all. Perhaps she finally understood.

~

*H*ead aching, Luke dragged himself from bed the next morning. Continuing nightmares about his parents' drownings kept the grief fresh. No time to dwell on that. There was a trip to the tailor's to accomplish, his first mission since Ash left. He made certain he had money to pay for mending his torn blouse as well as buying another skin for the saddle shop. He'd avoided looking at Felicity, who was in the kitchen, when he'd picked up his sandwich for the trip. The poor girl had been so forlorn yesterday. She'd hinted at additional worries on top of Bessie's suspicions, and he'd prayed for both situations last night. He must guard against giving her the impression he'd court her again. There must be something bad hiding in his memory, as Nate Miller had observed...something his mind shielded him from knowing.

Such was exactly what he needed to know before moving on with his future.

Around ten o'clock, he passed the tanner's house in Bolton where he'd buy a pigskin on the return trip. Concerns about revealing his service in the Confederate army escalated with each mile. Matthew had seemed to feel betrayed. Jim, the spymaster, must have hidden Luke's past from the tanner as well, an intolerable dilemma. Perhaps he could clear up the misunderstanding between himself and Matthew today.

He didn't follow the road to the tanner's. Instead, he chose a forested trail paralleling the road for the last half mile. There were no buggies, wagons, or horses at Matthew's house, so Luke doubled back to take the road.

Luke allowed Stardust a long drink before looping her reins to the hitching post. His knock was answered immediately.

"Mr. Shea, come in." Matthew lowered his brows as Luke entered. "I've mended your blouse."

"Obliged to you." The spy seemed more reserved than formerly. "Do you have any handkerchiefs?"

"Perhaps we should step into my workroom first." He opened one arm wide toward the room cluttered with stacked fabrics. Once inside, he closed the door behind them. "I'd like to hear a little more about you serving as a soldier."

"Aye, I wanted to explain that very thing." Speaking softly, Luke explained that his reasons for enlisting were to aid a friend despite his Unionist sympathies. He told of his head wound that left him with amnesia, a condition that still tormented him. "None of this do I recall. It's what I've been told. To me, it feels like 1857, and that I buried me parents months ago rather than years ago."

Matthew gave a low whistle. "That's some story. Six lost years?"

"Five. Me injury happened in December. The worst of it is, I can't recall courting Felicity Danielson."

"I'll wager she's fit to be tied."

The sadness in her eyes told a different story. "More hurt than angry."

Matthew sighed. "Doubt you'd make up a tale like that one. I planned to tell you not to return..."

Luke tensed. Harv had asked him to stay away for a month because of the scrutiny everyone faced. Luke didn't have anyone else to pass secrets to—he knew no one else on the chain.

"But the story about your girl convinced me. Your sorrow is real. I can always tell when a man's lying to me. You told the truth." Matthew straightened. "Now, tell me the news quickly, then you can pay me and be on your way."

Everything was accomplished within two minutes.

"Shall I return next week?" Luke rolled up his mended shirt to fit in his saddlebag.

"Once weekly only. I've got mighty curious neighbors." He scratched his chin. "In fact, it might raise fewer eyebrows if you bring your girl with you sometimes."

His eyes widened. "Felicity isn't me girl. We're not courting."

Matthew wagged his finger. "That's another change you should consider."

Luke's thoughts were still chaotic when he stopped in Bolton to purchase a skin from Barney Williams, a very vocal Confederate tanner. Barney didn't tell him anything new. Luke soon rode off on Stardust.

Now that Ash was gone, Luke could take turns riding first Rosebud and then Stardust to keep them both rested. Or he could bring Felicity along on one of them.

No. He'd not consider it. Matthew's suggestion to bring Felicity along on his spy missions was outrageous. Risky. Downright dangerous. She was already being watched by her fellow nurse. Felicity would be guilty of far greater transgressions if she started riding with him. He refused to ask it of her.

He wouldn't tell her, either, for the strong woman might insist on joining him.

CHAPTER 25

*F*elicity sat with her aunt's family at church on Sunday, the spot they'd saved for Luke vacant. She craned her neck looking for him during the first hymn and finally spotted him on the last row. He gave her a smiling nod but made no move to join her.

Aunt Mae hadn't mentioned inviting him to lunch, as she had done so often in the old days. Felicity wouldn't see him today unless she gave him some broad hints. She tried to make her way to him before he left. Old Mr. Marley *would* pick this day to block their pew with one of his marathon conversations. The mild-mannered, lonely widower talked until Aunt Mae invited him to lunch.

By then, Luke was gone.

Felicity trailed behind her aunt's family on the walk home. Luke was avoiding her. He'd known she wanted him to kiss her —those expressive eyes she knew so well had given him away.

Yet he'd chosen not to.

Of course not. He didn't remember the strolls, the picnics, the gatherings after church, the suppers at her aunts, the parties, the balls where they'd danced the evening away.

He didn't remember the first time they'd professed their love for one another followed by their first kiss that nearly made her swoon with happiness.

No, Luke didn't remember any of that.

Sudden clarity brought a dull ache to her heart—it didn't appear as if he'd fall in love with her without those memories. Her simple self wasn't enough to make him love her again.

After lunch at her aunt's, the day stretched long before her. A strange restlessness filled her when she considered Jack's whereabouts. She'd told her aunt only that while Annabelle missed Jack terribly, the children were healthy and happy. Men went missing every day in this war. That didn't mean Jack had died. It certainly meant he was in trouble. Felicity didn't know details, so there seemed little she could do for Jack beyond praying.

Yet prayer was a powerful thing because of the one who listened and answered. She'd once believed that, anyway…and reckoned she still did, though her brother's troubles seemed one more sign God had abandoned her. He'd taken everyone she'd ever leaned on away—that was certain.

Felicity must find something to occupy her. The hospital. She donned her drab brown dress and went to work after telling her aunt her intentions. The nurses had the patients' care well in hand on her ward, so she spent several hours writing letters for soldiers in another ward. With paper growing scarce, she confined each letter to one page. At least she'd brightened someone's day, something she couldn't seem to do for Luke.

A new patient was admitted on Tuesday afternoon to an empty bed on Bessie's side. The other nurse glared at Felicity while Dr. Watkins examined him.

Felicity, who had avoided her coworker as much as possible since she'd delivered her warning, picked up an empty bucket and headed to the water barrel on the first floor. Bessie was waiting at the bottom of the stairs when she returned from the kitchen.

"I thought you were working with the doctor for your new soldier." Felicity didn't like the steely look in the nurse's eyes.

"Don't even think about talking to my patient." Bessie crossed her arms.

"My beds are all full. I don't have time to do more than introduce myself." Felicity strove for a mild response. Since Bessie's warning last week, it seemed every time Felicity looked up, she discovered her fellow nurse observing her. She'd made certain there was nothing to see.

"Don't bother. I've already told Dr. Watkins you're likely a spy." Her eyes narrowed.

Felicity felt the blood drain from her face. Was she going to prison? "Wh-what are you talking about?" She set the heavy, dripping bucket down.

"I learned you came in on Sunday. Spent the day in another ward." She raised her brows. "Not that you told me."

"I had nothing to do and came to help." Felicity's heart nearly burst with fright. "It's as simple as that. I wrote a few letters."

"Looking to find out all you could about our soldiers by writing letters to their girls, am I right?"

Felicity gasped. "No, that's not true." In this, at least, Bessie maligned her. Julia had been gone over a week. It hadn't taken that long to discover how much of her free time had been spent with her friend's family. "I wanted to be of some good to someone. The nurses didn't require assistance."

"Seems to me that you're only here to get information." Bessie tilted her head. "You'll be in prison once I can prove it."

So she had nothing beyond her suspicions. In the right environment, however, suspicions were enough to turn the tide against a spy. "There's nothing to prove." She picked up her bucket. "If you'll excuse me, I've patients to tend to." She climbed the stairs, stopping outside her ward.

What did Dr. Watkins think of Bessie's suspicions? Water sloshed from the bucket in her trembling hand. It was a good thing Felicity hadn't done any active spying since Bessie's initial warning—nor would she, for the time being. The best thing she could do now was to bring water to her soldiers.

And wait for Dr. Watkins to speak to her about the accusations.

~

*F*elicity didn't have an occasion to speak to Dr. Watkins the rest of the day. Part of her rejoiced that he hadn't sought her out to either relieve her of her duties or have her arrested. The other part accepted that his procrastination was likely only delaying the inevitable.

Prison.

She spent the evening alternately praying for deliverance and sewing Wilma's last dress in her attic bedroom. She was trying to do a good thing for the Union, be of service to her country. Why wasn't God on her side? She needed His blessing. He'd already snatched the ones who supported her spiritually and emotionally. How much more would He take from her?

She was beginning to feel like Job, the Biblical character who had suffered such significant losses. At least, God hadn't taken his wife from him.

Luke, who had once been a stalwart support no matter the obstacle, was too busy convincing her that he didn't intend to court her to notice how she suffered.

Yet he ought to be warned, in case something happened.

The next morning, she stopped into the saddle shop before entering Luke's house. "Good morning, Luke."

"Top of the morning to you, Felicity." He stood. "Do you have news for me?"

Of course, in his eyes, that was the only reason she'd have for interrupting his work. "I won't take too much of your time." She shut the door.

"What is it?" He strode to her side.

"Bessie told Dr. Watkins that I'm a spy."

"Nay." His face blanched. "Do you fear arrest?"

"I do...if he believes her." Her heart thudded at the possibility. Aunt Mae and Uncle Charles proudly supported the Confederacy. Should even the suspicion reach their ears, it would destroy what was left of their tenuous relationship. When Petunia learned of it, Felicity would be turned out from the home. She might do that, anyway, should she learn that Jack was a Union soldier.

"Dr. Watkins said nothing to you of the matter?" He rubbed his knuckles over his chin.

"Nothing." The familiar gesture distracted Felicity. Luke rubbed his chin when deep in thought. Good to know that his mannerisms hadn't changed.

"Perhaps he doesn't believe her. I'd surmise she's a difficult person, one who looks to find fault."

"True." She studied the dusty floorboards. "All she cares about is getting the soldiers healed and back on the battlefield. She hates Yankees more than most because her fiancé died in battle."

"Without doubt, Dr. Watkins noticed the same drive burning in her." Lifting his chin, he gazed into her eyes. "Go on as normal, as if nothing worries you. My hunch is Dr. Watkins would have called for the soldiers immediately had he believed her."

Those brown eyes seemed to pour strength into her. This comforting, strong man was the Luke she knew. She swayed toward him.

His gaze dropped to her lips.

She gasped. Was he growing to care for her again? Hardly daring to breathe, she took a step closer.

Luke gave a shake of his head and then stepped back. "You have my prayers."

No, she'd misread the depth of his emotion, which had been rooted in concern, not love. It was as if an icy blast swept through the shop. Another rejection. "Thank you."

An awkward silence descended on them.

"A farmer bought three saddles yesterday, including one of the side saddles." Luke ambled back to his bench.

"Good news."

"Yes, he's moving his family to North Carolina, where his wife's family lives. Soldiers have stolen all his chickens and one of his cows. He's afraid they'll return for the horses. He was leaving at first light this morning, so he was grateful for the saddles."

Felicity followed his glance to a side saddle. It brought back memories of riding with her brothers as a child—innocent, carefree days before the war had snatched Jack to be numbered among the missing and had caused Luke to lose his memories.

"Good enough reason to continue making saddles without orders, as Ash advised." He ruffled his auburn hair. "It helped that stranger yesterday. And a lieutenant ordered the saddle I'm making now."

"I'm glad." He needed the money because Ash was no longer here to pay him a salary. It was March fourth. Julia and Ash had been gone ten days. "I've had no word from Julia. Do you think they've arrived at the ranch?"

"Ash figured tomorrow was the soonest they'd reach their new home. Early next week is likelier."

She nodded. As much as she wanted to remain, she had a job to do...and so did Luke. "Shall I clean the upstairs rooms today?"

"Whatever you think." He waved a hand. "You know your tasks better than me."

"All right. I'll get to it." She turned to go.

"Felicity?"

She paused with her hand on the doorknob.

"Ye can come to me anytime, should ye need me help."

She nodded. There was a time, long past, when he wouldn't have needed to say it.

～

*L*uke prayed for Felicity's safety, then tried to concentrate on the saddle's stitches. Between his lingering mild headaches and being new to the craft, he was too slow for his liking.

Worry for Felicity pushed to the forefront. Bessie seemed determined to cause trouble for her.

Even if Dr. Watkins didn't believe Bessie, she could poison the patients against Felicity. Even a hint that someone was a spy was enough to set off tempers in the current environment.

He bowed his head again to pray for her safety, that any darts aimed for her fell on him. She had a family who loved her. He had no one. If someone was to be captured, imprisoned, or hung, it should fall on him. Not his sweet Felicity.

The unspoken description, buried in his head, jerked him to his senses.

She wasn't his sweet Felicity any longer.

How he regretted the loss.

～

*F*elicity cleaned the upstairs rooms and then ate lunch with Jolene in the kitchen. The two of them were becoming friends, though Felicity chose her words carefully around her. Jolene didn't talk much about the war and never maligned the Northerners as so many of their neighbors were prone to do, but Felicity reminded herself constantly that her husband, Joseph Hutchins, worked at a foundry supplying artillery and weaponry to the Confederates. There was no question about his loyalties being with the South.

"You don't mind eating with me?" Jolene replenished her cup of tea.

Felicity looked up from her chicken stew. Truly, it was difficult to think of anything except her potential arrest and her deteriorating relationship with Luke. "I'm grateful for the company." She had hoped to eat lunch with him alone three days a week. That hadn't happened. Luke had slipped into the habit of eating at the shop in order to accomplish more tasks. At least, it was kind of him to make it appear that way. To Felicity, it stung.

"Mr. Ash used to eat in the shop during busy seasons." Jolene stirred a lump of sugar into her tea. "Be grateful for every saddle sale, for it extends our jobs. I've discussed the matter with Joe. Things being as tough as they are, he's agreeable for me to work for room and board if it comes to that."

"That's not an option for me."

Jolene sighed. "Reckon it wouldn't be seemly—especially since he used to court you."

Felicity's eyes widened. "I didn't realize you knew of our former courtship."

"If you keep your mouth shut, you learn a lot of things." Jolene took a bite of her stew without looking up.

Did Jolene know she was a spy? Felicity set down her spoon. "Such as…"

"Such as the reason Mr. Ash took so many trips to buy leather for his shop only to return with one skin." Jolene gave her a direct look. "Now Mr. Luke does the same. Don't take no book learning to figure out both of them are Union spies."

"Why, that's preposterous." A wave of dizziness washed over her. First Bessie, now Jolene. Both she *and* Luke were going to prison.

"No, it ain't. Mr. Ash and Miss Julia often forgot to close their doors. I finally told them that sound carries down the hall so Joe wouldn't find out the same way I did."

It was difficult to breathe. "If you suspected this, why haven't you told the authorities?"

"If I *was* going to, I'd have done it before Mrs. Mitchell, Miss Caroline, and Miss Daphne moved to Texas last year." Jolene leaned closer. "If you ask me, Mrs. Mitchell—that is, Mrs. Louise Mitchell—knew more than she let on."

So Ash's mother had figured out her son was a Union spy. Was that the reason she moved her daughters to Texas last April? "I would never have suspected Ash of spying."

"Not many folks would." Jolene turned her attention to her meal.

Felicity sat back in amazement. Did Jolene know Felicity was a spy? Best not ask. "Can I ask you something?"

"Can't promise to answer." She continued eating.

"Jolene, are you a Unionist?"

"That's a hard one." She put down her spoon. "I ain't against the South. Mississippi's been my home all my life. That doesn't blind me to what's going on. Some things have to change around here. Folks can't continue to live in bondage, generation after generation. It's plain wrong."

"Agreed." Felicity hadn't intended to voice an opinion, merely to listen. Her own strong convictions got in the way.

"I ain't against the North neither. Seems grown people ought to be able to figure out how to get along with one another without folks dying." Sighing, she pushed her nearly empty bowl away. "I'm plumb tired of going to the shops and seeing empty shelves...of seeing men lose their jobs because the ships aren't coming into the wharves. Mostly, I'm tired of reading names of our city's dead and wounded posted in our newspapers."

"I can't argue with anything you've said." Felicity studied her agitated expression. "I've never heard you talk like this before, Jolene. I wish I'd known."

"Nobody asked." She almost snapped the words. "I can't tell Joe, though, because he's Southern through and through. If he finds out what Mr. Luke is doing..."

"I'll make certain Luke knows his business actions appear suspicious." Felicity closed her eyes in gratitude. "You're a true friend to this family. Thank you."

"Been with them since my first husband died. I ain't about to do nothing to hurt them." She stood. "If you're done eating, will you fetch Mr. Luke's dishes for me?"

"Yes." After rising, Felicity pushed her chair against the table. "And God bless you, Jolene."

"It's good to say what you've been thinking sometimes." Her face relaxed.

Felicity hurried to the shop. She couldn't wait to tell Luke what she'd learned.

CHAPTER 26

"You're fooling me." Luke couldn't believe his ears. Jolene knew about his and Ash's spying and had never let on.

"No. She told me at lunch." Felicity shook her head as if in wonder. "Do be careful around Joe. He doesn't know anything."

Good to know. "I rarely see the fellow. He's not around much." Just the same, he'd be more careful around both of them.

"Also, she and her husband are willing for her to remain as cook for room and board when the money Ash left runs out."

Jolene's devotion and long service to the family deserved some loyalty in return. "That was some conversation."

"Aye." She laughed lightly.

He laughed aloud at her attempt at an Irish brogue. "Not bad."

A knock on the door silenced their laughter. He strode to open it. "Dr. Watkins? I didn't expect a doctor's visit. Come in."

The doctor removed his hat as he entered. "Miss Danielson?" His gaze darted between her and Luke. "Have the two of you renewed your courtship? I heard laughter."

"No." Her cheeks turned scarlet.

"Nay." Luke's own face heated. "She was attempting to emulate me Irish accent."

"Ah." The doctor set down his hat. "I actually have questions for both of you."

Did the man suspect Felicity, after all? Luke's heart hammered against his chest. "If you're wondering about me amnesia, there's been no change."

"You've recalled nothing new?" Dr. Watkins raised his brows.

"Nothing. Not even that recent short cannon fire stimulated any memories." He sighed. "Ye cannot be more disappointed than I am."

"I'm sorry. I thought by now…well, you may yet recover some memories." The doctor clapped him on the shoulder. "Try seeking out folks who knew you—such as Miss Danielson or men who worked with you—and have conversations about events you attended together. See if that stirs anything."

Luke shied away from what Felicity might reveal, but there were not many folks around he could ask.

Dr. Watkins turned to Felicity. "May I have a word with you outside?"

Luke wanted to follow them. Perhaps the doctor would have included him had he not been so insistent their relationship hadn't resumed.

~

Felicity, praying silently for the right words, stopped halfway between the shop and the house. "What is it, Dr. Watkins?"

"I don't like to take time away from my duties to deal with such unsavory matters." His Adam's apple bobbed up and down. "I believe Miss Guthrie spoke to you about your habit of spending what she calls an 'inordinate amount of time' with new patients. Am I correct?"

"She mentioned it. I don't understand her concerns because I talk with all my patients." A breeze cooled her suddenly hot face.

"That's the way I see it—that you are simply taking care of your patients." His lips pursed. "She feels that you are doing something untoward with the information you learn."

Tears blinded her. This was it. She was going to prison for spying—a disgrace to her aunt who, while profiting from housing her, had given her a home.

"I'm sorry to repeat the accusation, my dear. I knew that would hurt your feelings. You care for the men in your ward. I saw it most distinctly with Luke Shea—of course, he was your former beau and quite a different situation. Yet your compassionate nature shines through with everyone, a quality that makes you a splendid nurse."

"Th-thank you, sir." She fished a handkerchief from her apron pocket to swipe her cheeks. "It's impossible not to care about them."

"You're one of our best volunteers. I don't want to lose you." His tone grew firm.

"I don't want to go." Hope stirred that prison wasn't in her immediate future.

"Good. Do you want to work in a different ward? Perhaps with Mrs. Ellis?"

Mrs. Ellis was an excellent, capable nurse. She'd learn much from her, but changing wards would only convince Bessie she was right about Felicity's motives. "No, Doctor. I don't want Bessie to worry about what I'm doing—which is simply my job." Part of which used to be spying. She'd find another way to aid the Union.

"That's wise. I don't mind telling you Miss Guthrie is of the mindset to damage your reputation outside the hospital, so you must be careful."

Felicity's skin tingled. He'd hinted at prison, what she most feared.

"She's got a bee up her bonnet, to be sure." His brow furrowed and then cleared. "The only way to placate her is to keep you away from new patients. From now on, all those who arrive on your work days will go to her side of the ward."

"That should ease her concerns." Felicity took a shuddering breath, grateful beyond words that Dr. Watkins was championing her.

"You must stay away from them." He wagged a finger. "Else she may do your reputation some harm, something I'm trying to avoid. Agreed?"

"Agreed."

"I'll tell her we've talked. I don't want the problems between you to affect your jobs. The needs of our soldiers are paramount." His eyes narrowed. "Understood?"

"Yes, sir. That won't happen."

"Then I will see you on Friday. I must return to the hospital." He spun on his heel, his stride as rapid as if he rushed to surgery.

Luke opened the door as the doctor disappeared around the corner. "Want to tell me about it?"

Tears stung the back of her eyes. He'd often spoken that same phrase to her. Nodding, she joined him inside to share the best news—that Dr. Watkins trusted her and she wasn't going to prison.

And yet it ate at her that Bessie was right...about everything. Felicity didn't deserve grace from her employer. She had betrayed them all in the fight to restore unity to her country.

∼

*F*elicity arrived at her aunt's home in the late afternoon. Aunt Mae hurried down the hall from the kitchen. "My dear, you look as though you've had a difficult day. You didn't go to the hospital after all, did you?"

"No." She couldn't explain Bessie's suspicions and how Dr. Watkins was now watching the pair of them. The depth of her betrayal to her own kin suddenly descended on her. Would Aunt Mae forgive her someday? It was unlikely Petunia or her uncle, who worked to supply munitions for the Confederacy, ever would.

They must not discover her secret, not even after the war ended. That conviction came to Felicity in sudden clarity.

"Is Petunia here?"

"She and the children are in the yard picking china balls." Aunt Mae rubbed the back of her neck. "You and I haven't had any time to speak about your childhood home."

"I haven't wanted to discuss it in front of Petunia."

"That's wise. She's quite jealous of you. Come, warm yourself by the fire." Aunt Mae drew her into the parlor toward a low-burning fire.

"Jealous of me?" Felicity nearly toppled onto her armchair, so great was her surprise.

"Yes, dear." Her aunt selected a chair facing her. "Luke is here in Vicksburg while Miles is still fighting in Virginia, hundreds of miles away. You can see Luke every day if you choose, while it's been months since Petunia saw Miles."

She gasped. "She does realize Luke doesn't remember me?"

Aunt Mae nodded.

"He won't court me now because the last five years are gone." She understood why a man of integrity had to deal with his past first, hard as it was to accept. "I love him as much as ever, but he doesn't even remember loving me. It's an intolerable situation."

"I know, dear. I see how worn you are from that appalling dilemma, but it doesn't matter to my daughter. All she can think about is that Luke is here and Miles is not."

That actually made sense. She recalled her jealousy over Ash staying home. Witnessing Julia falling in love with him had made Felicity miss Luke all the more. "I think I understand."

"Good. Petunia can be..." Aunt Mae's forehead furrowed. "Difficult. She's also jealous of my love for you."

Felicity's eyes widened.

"Oh, I love her as much as ever, make no mistake. Yet I have grown to love you as one of my daughters. This rift between us has torn my very heart out." Splotches of red marred her face. "I'm very sorry we kept the deed a secret from you."

"Thank you for saying so." Tears pricked the back of Felicity's eyes. None of her siblings had responded about this link to their childhood home. Either they had more pressing matters to contend with as the war raged around the country or their responses hadn't reached Felicity yet.

"We truly didn't mean to keep it forever. It was our way of providing for you. Your brother also."

"Clarence?"

"Yes, we paid for their passage to Cincinnati and also two months' lodging at a boarding house. Six months later, they asked for help again. Clarence was working, but Lilybeth had incurred doctor bills after her miscarriage."

"A miscarriage?" Felicity's heart leaped to her throat. "No one told me."

"That was Lilybeth's request, my dear, and we honored it. She can't bear to speak of it even now." Aunt Mae's head went down. "Charles convinced me you should know these things now because you were so angry about the deed."

"It felt like a betrayal." But hadn't Felicity betrayed them too? After all, she was a Union spy living under the roof of Confederate supporters.

"I realize that now. There's more. Charles feels you should know everything."

"I agree with Uncle Charles." What else had been hidden from her? "Please, tell me all."

"The deaths of your parents hit you the hardest." Aunt Mae twisted her handkerchief. "Your grief traumatized you."

"I remember little about it." She had passed those early weeks in a daze.

"Mabel didn't have room for you in her small Kentucky home. Jack wanted you to move to Louisiana with them, but Annabelle was having a difficult pregnancy. She spent most of her days in bed. In fact, the doctor advised her not to travel. We convinced Jack you were better off with us. All our girls had married and moved away. We could take care of you."

Felicity hadn't known Annabelle had difficulty carrying the twins. Had she been so lost in her grief as that? "What about Clarence?"

"He was willing to delay his marriage to Lilybeth for your sake yet was excited to move to Ohio and start afresh." She hesitated. "We all, including Jack and Mabel, convinced him not to wait and possibly miss the job opportunity."

"I wanted to go with Clarence and Lilybeth."

"So you recall that much." She nodded. "They were not much older than you, Lilybeth but seventeen. In the end, it was decided you'd be better off here where we could care for you."

"*Who* decided?" Felicity didn't remember the discussions about her future.

"Jack. He was quite worried about you."

That calmed Felicity more than anything else she'd learned. Her siblings had been unable to take her, not unwilling. She'd actually been closest to Jack, who had been the one to help her out of childhood scrapes and watched over her. Jack, who was now missing, and she couldn't tell her aunt. Had Annabelle learned anything more? How could she safely find out?

"Just so you know, we've also sent money to Mabel now and again. We've tried to stand in place of your parents."

Both Clarence and Mabel had benefited. That was a relief. "I wish you had told me a year or so after. It would have been a delightful surprise instead of…"

"Betrayal." Aunt Mae flinched. "I wish we had. After you and Luke fell in love, Charles and I intended to tell you at your wedding."

The words had a ring of truth. All of it did.

"Whatever you and your siblings decide is fine with us." She wrung her hands. "I hardly feel good about turning that poor mother and her children out into the cold without a roof over their heads…"

"They can continue living there. For now." It comforted her to be consulted. "I may move there someday. I'll be in Vicksburg for as long as Luke needs me. That is, if you'll have me."

"We will have you, indeed." Tears slid down Aunt Mae's cheeks as she stood, holding out her arms.

Felicity hugged her, some of the hurt thawing with the revelations.

The back door slammed. Running footsteps foretold Wilma and Little Miles were in search of their grandma.

"Felicity!" Wilma threw herself into her cousin's waiting arms. "Want to make chinaberry soap with us?"

"Chinaberry soap?" She'd never heard of such a thing. She gave her aunt an inquiring look.

"Millie Westover gave me a recipe using china balls. The fruit makes a decent soap." Aunt Mae picked up Little Miles. "Since soap has become so scarce, we're making our own. If it makes more than we need, we'll sell it."

"Fascinating." Felicity raised an eyebrow.

"I've been boiling batches of wood ashes to make lye all day. That makes a strong alkali." Aunt Mae tilted her head.

Petunia passed by the parlor's open door, her children's cloaks in her hands.

Felicity noticed the worn-down look on her cousin's face for the first time. How had she overlooked it before?

"I can't miss the fun." Felicity extended her hand to Wilma, who immediately tucked her little hand inside.

Her heart had been cleansed of some of its hurt by learning the truth. However, her own secrets about spying for the Union and Jack's Union service, were Aunt Mae to discover them, would do more harm than good.

~

A splash. Frigid waters nearly stole Luke's breath. No time to pause. Kicking with stockinged feet, he took powerful strokes toward the area of that last head bob.

Shouts from the riverbanks. Splashes in the river fell like rain. Was it raining? Never mind that now. He must keep going.

There was no movement on top of the water when he reached the spot. Drawing in a deep breath, he dove deeper, hands reaching...

Luke tossed from side to side, struggling to awaken. To release the grip of the nightmare.

Throwing back the blankets, he sat up. As usual, sweat trickled down his forehead and over his shrapnel scar.

Still dark outside. How long had he slept this time? He lit the lantern and carried it to the writing table where Papa's pocket watch lay. Nearly four.

He splashed cold water from the pitcher on his face. Might as well start working. There wouldn't be any more sleep tonight.

As the nearly nightly experience had taught him.

~

*B*essie was reading the doctor's notes in the nurses' room on Friday when Felicity arrived at a quarter before six.

"Good morning, Bessie." Although her fellow nurse had stirred up trouble for her with Dr. Watkins, Felicity was determined to treat her cordially. "You're here early."

She looked up from scrutinizing the page. "To keep my eye on you." Her tone had lost none of its belligerence.

"If you feel it's necessary, I don't mind." Felicity faced her squarely. "Dr. Watkins warned me he doesn't want tensions between us to affect our patients."

"You'd best heed his warning." Bessie lifted her chin.

"His warning was for both of us." She barely prevented herself from snapping the words. So much for her determination to be pleasant. "The needs of those soldiers are more important than our own."

Bessie raised her brows. "You finally said something I can agree with. Nothing matters more than getting our men healthy so we can send them back to their regiments. The South needs every man it can get to whoop up on those Yankees."

"We must end this conflict sooner rather than later." Felicity chose her words carefully. "Too many have died already."

"More of them Yankees will die." Bessie put her hands on her hips. "And we'll all be the better for it."

Felicity tamped down her anger. She was being tested. "We'll all rejoice at the war's ending."

"Especially the South." Bessie studied her.

"Indeed." It was what Bessie wanted to hear. Perhaps her agreement would mollify the nurse for a few days. In the meantime, Felicity must control her words and deeds carefully.

❧

*I*n the middle of March, Luke received his first civilian saddle order since Ash left. The customer was loathe to pay half the price up front, as Ash had advised him to insist upon. The Vicksburg man finally agreed if he could pick it up on the twentieth. Five days pushed Luke, especially since he worked at a slower pace than Ash. However, he could not reject any paying job.

As she passed by the shop on her way to the house, Felicity's shoulders were hunched, as if she had the weight of the world bearing down on them. She wore only a light shawl over her black skirt and white blouse today. Little wonder, for it was a sunny morning with a promise of spring in the air.

"Top of the morning, Felicity. Can you spare a minute?" He hadn't sat with her and her aunt's family at church since Ash left and had bolted out every week when the service ended to meander around town, listening to street conversations. It had borne fruit for spying but not for his relationship with Felicity. He'd wager she needed to talk.

"Good morning." She came inside. "What is it?"

"Tell me what troubles ye. Please, sit." He shut the door. She perched on the bench, and he crossed to sit on the other end. Her unhappiness did strange things to his heart. "Is it Bessie?"

"Bessie's still a thorn in my side." Her brow furrowed. "But there's something else, and I hope you can help me. I don't know where else to turn."

"Anything in me power, I will do." Luke glanced at the leather, measured but uncut for his rush order. He could work late in the evenings.

Her blue eyes widened. "That means a great deal to me." She looked away. "It's about my brother. Everyone thinks he's a chaplain in the Confederate army. He deserted to become a Union soldier."

She went on to tell him that her sister-in-law had written—

by private carrier—that he'd gone missing during a battle. Felicity knew no specifics and wanted to learn if he'd been found.

"Me heart bleeds for ye." She looked so worried, he longed to comfort her. "What is it ye ask of me?"

"I want to send a letter by a carrier to the village of Rosedale, Louisiana. My brother made his living as the black-smith there, and that's where his wife and children live." She clasped her hands together. "Do you know anyone who can deliver letters privately? Perhaps wait for a response?"

Nate might be able to find a Union letter carrier. He'd ask him on Thursday. "Give me a few days. Let me find out for you."

"Thank you." She stood. "I'd best get to work."

"Thanks for trusting me." More than he trusted himself.

She turned at the door. "That has never wavered." Then she was gone.

He shook his head. She believed in him more than he believed in himself.

~

*T*wo weeks later, Felicity was on the sidewalk leaving for home when Luke strode up from the opposite direction.

"Headed home, I see." Luke unlocked his shop. "Have a minute to talk?"

"Of course." *Always for you.* She followed him inside.

He shut the door behind them. "It took a while for a friend to locate a Union letter carrier," he whispered.

"I knew you would." She flung her arms around his neck. "Thank you."

His arms went around her waist for one precious moment, and then he stepped back. "It's not all good news."

Her arms fell to her sides, though she could not be sorry for the comfort of his embrace, however brief.

Luke's face reddened. "Turns out, this one is skittish. The fewer who know of his Union ties, the better. He will deliver your letter and bring a response back from his next trip to that area, but that may not happen for three weeks. Perhaps longer."

"Three weeks?" She'd expected a quicker response.

"'Tis disappointing, to be sure." He studied her face. "And he'll only deal with my contact."

"I won't mind that." It was safer. "But his concern feels like a warning to me."

"I had the same thought."

"I believe I'll send a carefully worded letter through regular mail and hope Annabelle understands the meaning." The canal that Union General Grant's army had been digging was reportedly ended. Talk was that Grant abandoning the canal plan meant Vicksburg could expect an attack. Folks were already digging cave shelters as they had last summer.

"A better plan, indeed." Luke gave a crisp nod.

She'd write it here and mail it the same day so no one at home would stumble across it. Surely, Jack had been found by now. Annabelle's letter had been dated in mid-January, and it was March thirtieth. Felicity ached to hear good news of her brother.

~

Felicity received a letter from Julia on the first day of April. She tore it open as soon as she arrived home from her job at Luke's.

"Julia finally wrote you." Aunt Mae hurried in from the kitchen, wiping floured hands on her apron. "Oh, I see you found it."

Felicity scanned the letter. "They arrived at the ranch on March eighteenth, ten days later than planned."

"Thank the Lord, they are safe." Aunt Mae put her hand to her throat.

"They had delays at nearly every turn. Seems everyone was on the road with them. It was difficult to find both food and lodging."

"Oh, my. The situation is growing more difficult every week. It's good they made it to the ranch."

Petunia descended the stairs. "More soldiers and strangers in the city these days than neighbors. I fear we'll come under fire again. It's no wonder people are having caves dug for shelter from shelling."

"Your papa promised to have one dug." Aunt Mae looked from Petunia to Felicity. "He hasn't hired anyone yet."

Last summer's Union navy attack had shown them the ugly side, the fearful side, of war. With the Union army already in the vicinity, the coming attack would no doubt be even more dreadful.

Continuing her reading, Felicity barely hid a gasp. Julia had written that Ash had been recognized by a Confederate soldier and detained for a week. A search of every scrap of luggage revealed nothing, and they were finally released.

For the past three weeks, Felicity had stayed away from new patients as required by Dr. Watkins, so she didn't have any direct information from the battlefields. Bessie still watched her every move but didn't snap at her constantly. They had drifted toward a shaky truce that Felicity hoped would remain.

Luke had mentioned he had passed on information he'd heard by simply strolling the streets. She'd try that if she didn't learn anything at the hospital.

CHAPTER 27

*L*uke could scarcely believe Ash had been recognized, detained, and searched. Ash's missions had taken him on some of the same routes Luke traveled. Was he becoming recognizable too?

He was riding in a drizzling rain to Harv's one last time to tell him that while Ash was safely at his ranch, he'd been recognized. Luke no longer felt safe traveling the route Ash had taken so often. From now on, his spy missions would focus on delivering to the tailor's.

Luke skirted Jim's property in a drizzling rain in Bolton after noon the next day on the way to Harv's mill. Spring foliage hid him from view. He hunkered down behind the bushes. Three Confederate soldiers strode toward Jim's house. Smoke billowed from the chimney.

Had an officer taken over Jim's homestead as his headquarters? It was a common occurrence. It could also mean other soldiers were in the vicinity. Best get away from here. He'd wanted to tell Ash about the state of Jim's home because the two were almost like family. He regretted it now. Either a low-ranking officer had taken over Jim's property with few soldiers as guards, or those fellows were deserters.

Luke didn't desire to meet them under any circumstance.

Staying low, Luke led Stardust by the reins off the path deeper into the forest. The scent of apple, peach, and pear trees blooming warned that he neared a farm. His senses on high alert to the slightest movement, he increased his pace once the homestead was behind him.

After he'd put two miles between him and Jim's homestead, he picked his way back to the main trail. He mounted Stardust and cantered toward Harv's. No horses were waiting outside the mill. Luke strode inside and asked for five pounds of meal.

"I've got that much." Harv jerked his head toward the open windows. "Any news of Ash?"

"Aye." Luke whispered that he'd been detained as a possible spy. "Someone recognized him. This had best be my last run here."

"Situation's getting hotter. As long as you keep information going to the tailor's, that will be fine."

"Rode by our friend's homestead on the way. Saw soldiers."

Harv's scoop paused in midair. "You're joking."

"Nay."

"That's just happened. Good thing he's safe at his sister's home." His brow furrowed. "I'll find out who's there. Doubt we can do anything about it."

Luke doubted it too. He paid the man. "Obliged to you. For everything."

"Same to you." Harv shook Luke's hand. "Return by a different route."

"Sound advice." Luke left with a mixture of relief and regret. He might not see Harv again, because the danger had at least severed another connection with a good man of like conscience.

~

*B*y listening to soldiers talking on the streets, Felicity had been able to discover troop movements to pass on to Luke twice that month. She'd been happy to be contributing again without Bessie's knowledge or interference. Yet the days were exhausting. To make matters worse, she hadn't heard any news from Annabelle by Thursday, April sixteenth.

After the children were tucked in bed, Felicity sat around the kitchen table with Aunt Mae, Uncle Charles, and Petunia.

"It's been so long since I've drank a real cup of coffee." Petunia stared at light-brown liquid in her cup.

"I know, my dear." Uncle Charles patted her arm. "There's none to be had in the stores."

"I've done my best to make it from other foods." Aunt Mae tilted her chin. "Parched potatoes didn't taste good as a beverage. Amanda Cosgrove told me to try burned meal."

Uncle Charles shuddered. "Not to my taste in the slightest."

"Roasted acorns weren't too bad." Felicity agreed with her uncle about the meal. That had been her least favorite. "Okra seeds work well."

"Who'd have thought we'd be happy to drink okra coffee before the hostilities started?" Aunt Mae sighed.

"None of us." Petunia's mouth drooped. "There's a ball tonight at Major William Watts's home. If Miles were on furlough, we would have been invited to the dance."

Felicity was sorry for her. She knew what it was to fear for the safety of the man you loved more than your own life.

A sudden roar of guns shook the floor. They all sprang to their feet.

"Are we under attack?" Uncle Charles ran outside to their porch, Felicity and the others at his heels.

"There are ships on the river." Felicity pointed.

"Six Yankee steamers." Uncle Charles put his hands on his hips. "We're well defended by thousands of brave soldiers. We'll get them."

The hiss of shells lopped toward the city. One struck a brick building.

Wails came from the second floor.

"I'll see to the children." Petunia raced up the stairs.

"I'll help." Aunt Mae picked up her skirts and followed.

Shells whistled toward the ships from the bluffs.

Uncle Charles cheered. "We're returning fire. That'll show them."

"Should we go to our cave shelter?" Petunia joined them on the porch. Little Miles had his face buried in her shoulder.

Their shelter had been completed for two weeks. Felicity had been as relieved as Aunt Mae.

"Not yet." He looked over his shoulder. "Take those children to the kitchen."

Petunia rushed inside, closing the door behind her.

The barrage from the bluffs continued. Incoming shells rooted Felicity to the porch with fear. It brought back memories from last summer that she'd sought to bury.

Running footsteps drew her eyes toward the streetlamp-illuminated lane. Luke?

⁓

"Felicity? Be ye unharmed?" He bolted up the steps to her side, his gaze raking her precious form for wounds. That the attack came in darkness made it all the more fearful.

"We're fine."

She clasped his hand. Tight. "I had to make certain." He sandwiched her hands between his.

"The streets aren't safe, my boy. Buildings have been struck." Uncle Charles glanced at their clasped hands. "Let's all wait inside until this is over."

The bombing continued. Cheers from the bluff snatched Luke's attention to the river. A boat was sinking.

"They got one." Uncle Charles pumped his fists. "Come on, boys. Show 'em 'what for.' Sink another ship."

Luke pretended to study the burning ship, saddened by Mr. Beltzer's obvious delight. He didn't want to see *anyone* hurt.

"Come inside." Felicity tugged on his hand.

"I believe that's wise." Luke retained hold of her while keeping the door open for her uncle. He'd feared for her, rushed to see if she was unhurt. He was falling in love with her. He couldn't speak of it but couldn't deny it either.

The shelling might be slowing as the surviving Union ships floated out of sight.

His heart had taken a beating, too, for it now belonged to Felicity...and he couldn't give it to her.

$\approx$

"I asked you weeks ago to bring your girl with you." Matthew ushered Luke into his workroom on Monday, May fourth, and closed the door. "I wish you'd listened. No bachelor visits his tailor weekly—not unless his mother or his girl is the driving force behind his need for new clothing. My neighbors have begun to ask me what the tall red-haired man buys that he must come so often."

Luke's heart sank. "I'm loathe to put Felicity in danger."

"But you don't mind adding risks for the pair of us. Everyone's suspicious in these troubled times. Even my poor wife has been hounded with questions." He spread his hands with a jerk. "Questions could have been avoided by bringing her, ostensibly to select fabric and such. You've placed me in the pickle barrel—I don't mind telling you. Perhaps we should end this arrangement."

Luke's heart raced. This mustn't happen. Matthew was his only contact for smuggling Confederate secrets North now that he'd cut ties with Harv. "Nay. Please don't do that. The situation is escalating. Grant crossed the Mississippi River with two corps of his army beginning April thirtieth at Bruinsburg." Nate had come to the shop yesterday, something he'd never done, to pass on the information. The Union army was several miles downriver from Vicksburg. Danger was escalating for everyone in the state. "In response, Vicksburg's commander, General John Pemberton, has requested reinforcements be sent to defend Jackson. Soldiers from General Beauregard's and General Bragg's armies are said to have been ordered to Mississippi." The state's capital city already had a Confederate force, though not nearly large enough to fend off the twenty-five thousand Union soldiers that had already crossed.

Matthew whistled. "Battles are coming. Soldiers from both sides will soon fill the countryside. It won't be pretty."

Luke could see no way to avoid the coming bloodshed. He didn't have to recall his months of soldiering to realize lots of men died when large armies fought.

"Such details are too important not to send to the Union officials." He pinched his lips together. "Even so, I must consider my wife's safety. Bring Felicity next time or don't come."

"I will ask her." He had no choice. She'd agree, especially since her only spy information of late had stemmed from over-hearing conversations as she strolled about town. His soul filled with dread to put her at further risk. At least it would only be one ride weekly. Matthew didn't want him coming more often. "I won't come next week without her. Expect us on Monday or Wednesday."

"Thank you. One visit with your girl may suffice." Matthew

handed him a handkerchief, for which Luke paid him a dollar. "Bring her next time. It's for the best."

Luke mounted Rosebud with a heavy heart. It was better for everyone except Felicity. How could he ask it of her?

~

*T*hree weeks after the sinking of the Union ship, Felicity looked up from her washtub at a grave-faced Luke. "Will ye join me in the parlor?"

"All right." Was this about the recent troop movements? The Union army was attacking different areas, burning towns, and wreaking havoc on citizens in Mississippi. Were they marching to Vicksburg? She dropped a blouse into the soapy water. It splashed her apron. "I'll come immediately."

Nodding, Luke left.

She paused only long enough to swap her wet apron for a dry white apron, tying the back as she scurried after him. Luke had never asked to see her during the day. Their friendship was growing, but he had avoided touching her since the night of the shelling when he'd sweetly run to her rescue, held her in his arms, and refused to release her hand. Unfortunately, he'd turned cold before he left that night. He still shut down any romantic gestures before they had a chance to blossom.

Felicity stepped into the parlor. "What did you want to talk about?"

Luke turned from the window. "Please close the door."

A young lady might imagine a young bachelor had romantic intentions at such a request. Not when it was delivered in such a serious tone. How she missed his laughter, his teasing, his love. She closed the door and joined him at the window. "What is it?"

"I need your help. I'm hesitant to put you at risk."

"I've always wanted to do more." Hope fluttered that she'd be of greater service to the Union. "I'll do it, whatever it is."

"A bit dangerous to say so." He chuckled, despite the worry lines marring his forehead.

She laughed with him. "You know what I mean. Now tell me."

He explained that his spy contact, a tailor, refused to see him unless she came on his next mission to quiet his neighbors' gossiping tongues.

"Will we ride horseback?" Riding together again would be a bittersweet nostalgia.

"Aye. Do you know how to ride? I never thought to ask."

"We rode together when we courted." She tamped back her sudden sadness. That he rushed to her side when the Union hurled perilous shells at Vicksburg from the river last month had given her hope he might learn to love her without regaining his memories. What about her made him love her back then? If only she could unlock the mystery. "Will you mind my using the side saddle on display in your shop?"

"Now I'm glad we made two of them. Aye, use it."

"Anything special I need to know?"

His brown eyes darkened with worry for her. It fed her spirit. How she craved his love, yet his friendship was a precious gift.

"Be ready for anything. Now that the Union army has crossed the river, more troops are on their way to Jackson. Soldiers from both sides are coming at us." He rubbed his chin, his eyes smoky with concern. "We must do our part to inform Union officials of the Confederate army's location. Matthew chose the worst possible month to insist on you accompanying me."

Her breath hitched in her throat. "I want to help. Are there any other obstacles in my way?"

"Ye don't have a pass to leave the city. There's not a good

enough reason for you to ride along as my employee. The provost marshal would likely refuse a request for a pass, anyway, what with all the activity around the city. We'll take the back roads and avoid the Confederate pickets."

"All right. I trust you." It would be an adventure. And a day spent in Luke's company. "I'll go."

CHAPTER 28

The next few days, Luke roamed through the city at every opportunity, listening to conversations on the streets. Citizens moved their belongings into cave shelters. Mrs. Beltzer had strongly encouraged him to shelter with them last night as he helped tote two beds, tables, and chairs to their recently dug shelter. Two bedrooms with an open common area felt more like a home with furniture. Figuring it would be awkward to be in such close quarters with Felicity, he didn't decline or accept but promised to relay the invitation to Jolene and Joe.

No one doubted the Union army was headed to Vicksburg. Speculation was when they'd arrive. Three days? Four? The attack seemed imminent.

Union soldiers had cut telegraph wires, hurting Confederate General Pemberton's communications with his other generals. The Southern commanding general was now in Vicksburg. Luke heard enough to believe Jackson was to be targeted before Vicksburg. A battle had been fought at Port Gibson, Mississippi, on the first of May, a Union victory. Confederate Brigadier General John Bowen had retreated.

Luke met with Nate in the oak grove on Tuesday. Cal, his other spy, had quit a month before, finding it too difficult to get into the city without arousing the guards' suspicions.

Nate minced no words. "This thing is heating up. The Union army is making its way to Vicksburg. Superior forces with more coming. I suspect the South won't have half their numbers when the battle starts. It's what we've worked for, but it ain't going to be pretty. I told you last week that General Bowen's retreat from Port Gibson cleared a path for Grant to move inland. Bowen is said to be camped on Clear Creek near Bovina."

Luke gulped. His route to Matthew's took him by Bovina. He'd have to study the maps for a different route "How many soldiers?"

"About eight thousand were engaged in the battle. Besides that, Pemberton has troops scattered from Warrenton to Bovina."

That meant they couldn't ride south and skirt Bovina that way.

"What's wrong?" Nate studied him.

"I was supposed to ride past Bovina tomorrow with Felicity." He could give no more details to protect Matthew's anonymity.

"Troop location is more important than ever. Find a way." He put his hands on his hips. "I didn't want to work with a former Confederate, but you've proven me wrong. You've done a good job. Ash was right about you."

"Obliged to you." Nate's praise fed something in his soul. Perhaps a man suffering amnesia *had* made a difference. "Your information has been invaluable."

"It hasn't always been easy to obtain." He glanced toward a group of soldiers striding toward the center of town, muskets resting on their soldiers. "I won't keep our meetings once the battle starts. The Union army will be here, anyway, doing their own reconnaissance."

"True. I'll be here Thursday as normal." Luke held out his hand. "Thanks for allowing me to join this venture. A worthy one, to be sure."

"That it is." Nate shook his hand. "Be careful tomorrow."

With that, he took off in the same direction as the soldiers. Luke didn't doubt Nate would try to overhear their conversation, the same as he had done for weeks.

Confederate soldiers camped near Bovina. Not good news for their safety.

Unsure when Felicity's shift ended, he settled to wait for her to leave the hospital across the street. She needed to make an informed decision.

~

*F*elicity readily consented to stroll with Luke toward a less populated area of the city. Her surprise at seeing him on the walk outside the hospital quickly turned to concern at the worry lines creasing his forehead.

He invited conversations about her patients until they passed the last house. Then he told her about Confederate troops camped along the route he'd planned to take.

"I will study the maps for an alternate route this evening. We'll leave after you get to my home tomorrow." Shadows crossed his face. "Be ye willing."

"I'm willing." They might be unable to avoid the soldiers. Though her stomach quaked with fear, she'd go. Luke must not face the danger alone. "I'll wear my riding costume and bring a dress to change into when we return." She and Aunt Mae had become close again. Should she tell her about her ride with Luke? No, for no one would believe she'd ride for pleasure with so many soldiers in the vicinity. She'd leave before her aunt arose, as she did the days she volunteered at the hospital.

"We'll plan to return by midafternoon so no one will wonder where ye are."

"That's best." She didn't want to worry Aunt Mae and Uncle Charles.

Male voices on the road ahead carried to them, but Felicity couldn't understand the words. Confederate pickets? Or it might be one of the camps for the thousands of soldiers in their city. She didn't want to meet them in either case.

Luke jerked his head. They turned back, increasing their pace until they reached a row of houses.

Would they run into soldiers tomorrow? The possibility sent icy chills through her veins.

No matter. Her country needed her. More importantly, Luke needed her. She'd go.

~

*L*uke studied Ash's maps in his bedroom that night. He rarely saw Jolene's husband, Joe, the strong Confederate supporter living in his house. Still, he didn't take any chances that the foundry worker would discover his spy mission. This might be his last trip to Matthew's. Today was May twelfth. With so much happening east and south of Vicksburg, Grant could have his army attack before another week passed.

Tomorrow's ride would be the most challenging one yet. The best and easiest road from Vicksburg to the small town of Fox took them across Clear Creek where Bowen's men were camped. True, the creek was several miles long—eight thousand men took up considerable space, he reckoned. Yet was that area more than a mile or two?

Luke had never needed to remember his army experience

more than now. He prayed fervently for its return until his head throbbed from the effort.

Nothing from those lost years, even after all these weeks.

He picked up the map. They'd head northeast of the road crossing Clear Creek and then south to the tailor's.

He rubbed his throbbing temples and then blew out the candle. Best take candles for the trip. It grew dark early on wooded trails.

If it wasn't so vital to get the troop locations to Union officials, he wouldn't risk Felicity's safety.

~

A splash. Frigid waters nearly stole Luke's breath. No time to pause. Kicking with stockinged feet, he took powerful strokes toward the area of that last head bob.

Shouts from the riverbanks. Splashes in the river fell like rain. Was it raining? Never mind that now. He must keep going.

There was no movement on top of the water when he reached the spot. Drawing in a deep breath, he dove deeper, hands reaching ever wider...

Movement. Luke grabbed a thrashing arm and took them both to the surface. Darkness hid the man's face.

Luke shot from his bed. Sweat poured down his brow.

This nightmare had been different. This time, he'd found someone in the water.

Not his papa. Or his mama. Who, then? A mere dream? Someone from his past?

He'd rescued Willie from the muddy Mississippi waters when they'd been but boys. This hadn't seemed to be Willie.

It would soon be dawn. Might as well prepare for the day.

He dropped to his knees to pray for a successful mission. And safety, especially Felicity's.

~

elicity ran down her aunt's stairs at half-past five, comforted to find Luke waiting at the fence. Escalating numbers of troops in the city ensured some of them were always out and about, as they were this morning. Luke's solid presence at her side gave her a sense of protection she didn't often feel.

"Ready for this?" He spoke softly as they took off at a quick pace.

"I am." Felicity had prayed for their safety.

Joe Hutchins, Jolene's husband, approached them, presumably en route to his job at the foundry.

"Top of the morning to you, Joe. Just escorting Felicity to the house." Luke's tone was friendly, his face shadowed in the streetlamp's dim light.

Felicity gave him a nod. She barely knew the man.

"Morning." He gave them a suspicious look before continuing on his way to the foundry.

This wasn't a promising start. Felicity wore her riding costume without a shawl in the warm yet threatening weather, so Joe couldn't have missed that she intended to ride horseback, not work as a maid. Best mention it to Jolene so she could figure out an explanation.

After storing her things, Felicity hurried to the kitchen. "Jolene, I'm riding with Luke today."

"He's out saddling the horses." Jolene glanced at her navy blue riding habit. "Do you think that's wise with so many soldiers surrounding us?"

"Likely not. But it's important we go." She told Jolene about seeing Joe.

Jolene frowned. "My Joe can be an inquisitive one. Don't worry. If he brings it up, I'll soothe his suspicions somehow. Maybe hint the two of you are courting again."

SANDRA MERVILLE HART

"That might help." How she wished it was true.

"Be careful." Jolene gave her two sacks of food and two bottles of water.

"Thank you." Felicity hugged her. "Pray for us."

"I will. Now go on with you. Luke's waiting."

Her heart might have fluttered at the comment on a day less fraught with danger.

~

*L*uke set off to the northeast on the newly memorized trail. More troops in Vicksburg added to the challenge of leaving the city undetected. As he picked his way through the forest footpaths, eyes darting in every direction, he was grateful for the trails unknown except to locals.

Felicity rode silently on Rosebud behind him. He'd warned her not to speak until the city was well behind them.

The trail crossed a trickling stream thirty minutes after leaving the city.

"Can we stop a moment?" Felicity swiped at her forehead with her wrist, left bare by elbow-length sleeves.

Luke looked in every direction of the wooded trail. Nothing but squirrels, chipmunks, and rabbits. "Aye. Let's get a drink and refresh our water." He dismounted and reached for her.

She placed her hands on his shoulders, looking into his eyes.

He lifted her to the ground. "Ye weigh no more than a child."

She blushed. "Thank you."

He realized his hands were still on her waist and snatched them away. They were on a risky mission. He must remain alert.

She drank from her canteen while he bent to splash his face. "Tepid." She dumped the contents. "I'll get more."

The stream's cold water refreshed him. "We cannot tarry long. We're going a roundabout direction that will take longer."

They were on their way within five minutes, both horses having drank their fill. A large gray cloud would soon hide the sun. He opened his pa's old pocket watch. Half-past seven. With any luck, they'd be at Matthew's in two hours, even with giving his horses a rest.

Up ahead was the main road. They'd ride parallel to it until reaching farms and plantations. The least number of people who saw them on this day, the better.

$\sim$

*I*t was midmorning when they stopped in front of a two-story brick home. To Felicity, the line of houses in the country town seemed the perfect setting to raise a family. Except for the copse of trees on one side and the absence of the railroad, the place reminded her of homes in Bovina.

She was grateful for Luke's strong arms to lift her down. She'd quickly caught his urgency to arrive at their destination and stopped asking for breaks. As a result, the lower half of her body was sore. A three-hour ride after two years of respite hadn't been a good decision. She shifted her focus from the return journey looming ahead. The tailor inside was her purpose for coming.

"Be ye ready?" Luke whispered.

Sore muscles and all. "Aye." She grinned at him.

His eyes lit with appreciation. Good. She'd encouraged him, as she meant to do.

Taking her hand, he walked beside her up the steps.

She wondered at him holding her hand and then remembered that they pretended she was his girl.

Luke excelled at the pretense. That proud look in his dark

eyes bespoke deep affection. He released her to knock on the door.

It opened immediately. A gray-haired man not much taller than Felicity surveyed them. "Luke, so good to see you." He shook Luke's hand. "And you've brought your girl along. Come inside."

She stepped into a small foyer with an empty table. Blouses and one coat hung on a rod between two mounted hooks with a nearly barren cupboard and mirror on the opposite wall. The room to the left was as cluttered as this one was clean.

"I'm Matthew Frost, the tailor here in Fox." His friendly voice eased a bit of her nervousness. He closed the door behind them.

"This is Felicity Danielson, me g-girl."

Felicity's face heated at Luke's hesitation to claim her. "It's a pleasure."

"The pleasure is mine." He raised his eyebrows with a glance at the open window. "Oh, you want to select fabric for your beau's coat? I have a few for your selection." He ushered them into the workroom.

Felicity stiffened. The tailor's raised voice must be for someone else's benefit.

"Have you any handkerchiefs for sale?" Luke spoke in a low tone.

He must be aware that something wasn't as it seemed.

"One or two only." Mr. Frost pointed to a short stack of wool fabrics. "My dear, there are your selections. Take your time. My next appointment isn't for another thirty minutes."

So they should hurry because they wanted to be long gone by then. Felicity exchanged a worried glance with Luke before crossing to a cluttered table.

"Tell me quickly." The tailor's whisper carried to Felicity.

Luke explained the location of Confederate troops.

"Some are camped at Clear Creek, you say?" He tilted his head.

"Right. We came the long way."

"Head north when you leave. There's a road on the left that will save you considerable time."

"The soldiers aren't this far north?"

"Not yet." Mr. Frost leaned closer. "There was a battle at Raymond yesterday. Confederate Brigadier General John Gregg's men fought, but the Union's Major General James McPherson's army outnumbered them three to one. It was a Union victory."

Felicity listened unashamedly. Raymond was south of Bolton and west of the capital city. The Union army was marching toward Jackson, their capital. Hopefully, the city surrendered quickly.

"Do ye believe Jackson will fall?" Luke folded his arms, an intent expression on his face.

"Almost certainly. Grant's men outnumber them."

The tailor's tone wasn't as exuberant as Felicity expected. Nor did she rejoice that her state's capital would be conquered. She knew folks who had fled to Jackson last summer.

"Vicksburg's turn edges closer. It might prevent my return next week."

"That may be for the best. You've done your work well. This thing is escalating all around us." The tailor rubbed his hands over his face. "None of us will escape what's coming."

Felicity agreed. They all wanted the Union to win, but they'd suffer with everyone. "How about this blue wool?" She held it up.

"An excellent choice, my dear." His hearty tone had returned. "Here's that handkerchief you requested." He gave a folded cotton square to Luke, who gave him a dollar. "Give me about two weeks before you return for your fitting."

"Aye. Thank you."

"Yes, thank you, Mr. Frost." Felicity stepped forward, sensing the tailor wanted them gone.

"My pleasure, as always." He leaned closer. "Be careful out there. Godspeed," he whispered.

Luke shook his hand and ushered her to the horses. "Act pleased about the fabric you selected," he whispered.

They were still acting a part. She gave a slight nod.

As they rode away, she described the coat they hadn't actually ordered or paid for in glowing tones in case people were listening through the windows, opened wide because of the May heat.

Important information had been passed, yet the trail home was dangerous with Confederate soldiers near.

CHAPTER 29

*L*uke glanced up at the darkening sky, hoping the storm that threatened would pass by without dumping rain on them. The breeze that the clouds had stirred up cooled his skin.

The forested road Matthew had suggested was wide enough for him to ride beside Felicity. She said that she recognized it, having ridden there as a girl with her brothers. They'd passed only two riders and one wagon. Either the local folks were too leery of Confederate soldiers south of here, fearing to be caught in a skirmish, or this was a generally lonely road.

Uneasiness set into the pit of his stomach. Why had he listened to Matthew? The route they'd taken that morning had only added an hour to the journey.

He halted beside a bridge. "I have an uneasy feeling." He didn't see anything or hear anything. Come to think of it, even the birds were silent in the branches of mature elm, hickory, and oak trees lining this part of the lane. Bushes and small trees filled out the spaces between the trees.

"Me too." She pulled up on Rosebud's reins. "Let's turn back and take the other route."

"What do you want to do that for?" A stranger's voice.

Tensing, Luke reached for a musket that wasn't there. He'd taken Ash's lead and traveled without one. How he regretted that decision.

Bushes shook. Six armed soldiers wearing Confederate gray stepped out and blocked the road in front of them. "What are you folks doing here?" One man with a brown beard that reached his chest stepped forward. No stripes on his sleeve. Likely Confederate pickets, guarding the thirty-foot bridge.

"We're out for a ride, me and me girl." *Stay calm.*

"That right?" The spokesman looked at Felicity.

"As you see." She swept an elegant hand toward Luke. "We Southern women certainly are grateful to our brave soldiers for protecting us."

"Our pleasure, miss." He tipped his hat at her.

"We need men to serve with us." A gruff-looking, burly soldier looked up at Luke.

"I served in the Twenty-first Mississippi. I was discharged after a shrapnel wound." He touched the scar.

"I got worse scars playing in the schoolyard." The burly man glared at Luke.

Felicity bristled. "His injury was serious, I assure you."

"What do you know about it?" He shifted his attention to Felicity.

Luke touched her bare arm. He didn't want the soldiers focusing on her. She was too beautiful for them not to notice her. "As much as a girl knows about her beau. She spent hours at me side at the hospital."

Felicity lifted her chin. "He has amnesia."

The men laughed derisively.

"Where are you from?" The bearded man leader eyed Luke.

Luke hesitated. If they managed to get away, he didn't want them to come looking for him. At least, Felicity had thrown them off with her flattery. They didn't suspect them of spying.

Yet.

"I thought you were lying. That settles the matter. Fellas, we've got another recruit." He stepped forward. "And the captain will get a new mount out of the deal."

This was intolerable. He couldn't be a soldier again. He didn't remember his skills. Nor could he leave Felicity to find her way home amongst the Confederates. "Felicity, run!"

She turned Rosebud's head back the way they came and kicked her heel. Luke was right behind her.

"Hey! Stop!" A shot fired.

Air rushed by Luke's ear. "Faster, Felicity!"

She leaned toward her mare's mane as another shot rang out.

"Let's get our horses," someone shouted from behind them.

They must be cavalry. "They're coming after us." Wind from his horse's speed sent Luke's hat flying. "Turn left at the main road. Then we'll hide in the forest."

Pounding hooves behind them. One horse? Maybe only one soldier's horse had been near. The thought gave him hope. He could outrun one man, or, if not, square off in a fair fight if the fellow didn't shoot him first.

"Felicity, head into the forest and meet me by the main road."

"No, I won't leave you." Her face was filled with fear, indecision in her eyes.

"Ye must. Someone's gaining on us." He pointed at a break in the trees to the left.

She slowed to take it. "Come back to me." Dust clouds followed her as she disappeared into the foliage.

He must kick up dust so the men who followed them might not notice she'd veered from the path. "Faster, Stardust." He urged on his horse.

Pounding hooves behind told him a single rider still gained on him. He looked over his shoulder. A gray-haired horseback rider approached through the dust clouds behind him. Who was this whiskered man, clothed like a farmer? None of the soldiers had appeared over thirty.

"Hide!" Luke shouted back to the stranger. "Soldiers are shooting at me." He didn't say which side. The warning should be enough.

But it wasn't. The whiskered man gained on him.

Luke yelled again. "Hide in the woods." The rider was right in the line of fire, squarely between the pursuing soldiers and Luke.

The man's old mare, with the speed of a stallion, pulled up beside Luke. "I heard what those cavalry men said to you. I'm on your side. I'll ride with you a ways." He matched Luke's speed toward the main road.

"They're shooting at me, man." Luke looked incredulously at the stranger. "Save yerself."

"Those soldiers had hidden their horse in a thicket a hundred yards from the bridge."

Good to know. They were maybe two minutes ahead of the cavalry soldiers.

"I'll help you first." Eyes the color of the Mississippi River glanced at him as they continued galloping toward the road. "Then we'll find Felicity."

How did this stranger know Felicity? Right—he'd called her by name in front of the soldiers. This farmer had heard the conversation. Luke hadn't seen him hiding in the woods as well as the soldiers.

Some spy he'd turned out to be. He'd put his girl in danger and then lost her.

His girl?

He must continue his play-acting, but to him, it was real. He'd die saving her if need be. He loved her, and she was alone somewhere in these woods crawling with soldiers.

He must find her. But where was she? He and the stranger

slowed their horses. Faint sounds of clopping hooves picking their way in the distance gave him hope. The main road was still ahead of them. "That might be Felicity." He manuevered Stardust between two bushes and entered the woods still at a near trot.

The stranger was right behind him, "Could be. Name's Michael, by the way."

"Call me Luke." First names were fine with him. It made the situation safer for both of them if someone in authority questioned them. "That old horse of yours kept up fairly well." Several yards into the woods, Luke urged his horse to walk.

"Old Nell may not look like much"—Michael chuckled softly—"but she's a tough old gal. Been with me a long time." He spoke casually, as if they weren't being hunted by cavalry. "You and I have a mutual friend."

"Who's that?" The spymaster, Jim?

"Ash Mitchell."

Ash? Luke's head jerked around toward Michael. He seemed like more than someone who tilled the land. This man might well be a spy.

Multiple horses running on the lane quickened his heartbeat. He looked over his shoulder. Hooves pounded the road he and Michael just left. He couldn't make out the movement of the cavalry riders through the trees, so they couldn't see him, either, hidden as they were by the forest. They rode hard and fast toward the main road. Luke would avoid that route once he found Felicity, but that might not be enough. The soldiers wanted both him and his horse.

There was a break in the trees ahead. A creek? Or was he back at the river? Glancing over his shoulder again, he continued riding. No sign of the the soldiers. Distant hoofbeats showed the soldiers were still pursuing them, probably on the main road by now.

They'd lost them. Luke could breathe easier.

Soft sounds of water trickling over rocks up ahead indicated that they'd reached a creek. A snake slithered into the water.

Stardust stopped and reared, catching Luke by surprise. He fell into the water with a splash.

Everything went black.

~

elicity had been riding Rosebud in the woods for a quarter hour, constantly watching for Luke. There'd been no sign of him or the cavalry. The woods weren't familiar, but the road had been vaguely so. She and her brothers had come this way once.

Never had she imagined she'd one day flee from Confederate soldiers here. During a war.

Alone. Abandoned.

Snatches of gray sky shown here and there under a canopy of leaves. "Where are you, God? It's just You and me. Alone, as always. That seems to be my lot in life." Bitterness tasted like bile on her tongue as she whispered the prayer. "Everyone has deserted me. I prayed for Luke to remember me. I prayed for Jack to be found, but there's been no mail from anyone for a month because of the war. Oh, and I asked You for safety today. Luke's probably been captured, and I'll have to find my way back." She'd never spoken to her Maker in such bitterness of soul, but, once started, she couldn't seem to halt the complaints. "If You could help me find him, I'd appreciate it."

Her legs were numb from the long ride on the side saddle. Moving slowly, she clumsily shifted her sore right leg from around the pommel. With her left foot in the stirrup, she swung her leg over and slid the last couple of feet to the ground.

Felicity waited for her legs to bear her weight again, looking in every direction. If the soldiers found her at this moment, she couldn't mount quickly enough to flee. Her heartbeat sped at the possibility.

Did they find Luke? His sacrifice had surely made her safer. Had it cost him his horse and his freedom?

The soldiers had been so focused on new recruits that they hadn't considered she and Luke had been spying. A very good thing.

She tucked wisps of hair under her hat. Her fingers stilled as they touched a hole in the brim. From a bullet? She'd heard a whistling rush of wind by her ear on their mad flight. Had the men tried to *kill* her?

Fear fought with anger, and anger won the battle. Why, the nerve of them. She ought to slap their faces.

Then fear set in. They must avoid those soldiers at all costs, who were so intent on stealing their horses that they'd kill to get them.

Where was Luke? She scanned every direction. The only movement was a squirrel circling a tree.

Luke had asked her to wait by the main road. First, she must find it.

Picking up Rosebud's reins, she began walking.

~

*L*uke shivered as he crept through the darkness near the Rappahannock River in December's frigid air. General Burnside's Union army that he longed to be serving was across the river from Fredericksburg, where General Lee's army of nearly eighty thousand waited. The Union had greater numbers, but Luke, a mere private, didn't know how much greater.

Union engineers had begun to build a pontoon bridge to cross the Rappahannock. Southerners had been successful in harassing them. Luke had been among those who'd hidden in buildings and shot at the engineers to slow their work. It had long been Luke's practice to shoot over the Union soldiers' heads—in this case, into the river. They weren't his enemies, though he must pretend they were.

Colonel Humphreys had tasked him with delivering a message to Lieutenant Colonel Fiser. Luke had often volunteered for the dangerous task in the past. Tonight, the fog cast an eerie gloom over the grassy terrain by the river as he crept along.

"Halt!" A shout came across the water.

Luke froze. A man stood on the partially completed bridge. He'd seen Luke.

He raised his rifle.

Luke raised his and fired off a round, intending to nick the Union soldier's sleeve in warning. Papa had once bragged he could shoot a gnat's wing at fifty feet. He needed that very same accuracy now.

A yell and a splash. Shots fired from both sides.

What had he done? The man would drown.

Dim light from town buildings was just enough to see a head bob above the surface. The wounded man would drown without help. Dropping his musket, Luke untied his shoes and kicked them off. Running on the unyielding ground to the bank, he plunged into the river.

A splash. Frigid waters nearly stole Luke's breath. No time to pause. Kicking with stocking feet, he took powerful strokes in the inky blackness toward the area of that last head bob.

Shouts from the riverbanks. Splashes in the river fell like rain. Bullets. Couldn't the Northerners see he was trying to save a life? Never mind that now. He must keep going.

There was no movement on top of the water when he reached the spot. Drawing in a deep breath, he dove deeper into the current, hands reaching ever wider until he felt a kick, thank the Lord.

Luke grabbed a thrashing arm and took them both to the surface. Darkness hid the man's face. "Speak to me, man!"

He coughed, spewing river water.

Best get him to shore. Luke turned the struggling man onto his back. "Don't fight. I'm trying to save your life."

The soldier stopped resisting. Bullets ceased to rain down on them.

Strong strokes didn't take them far, hampered by two men's weight. "Kick your feet, if you can," Luke said.

He kicked.

It helped considerably, and they quickly reached the shore.

"Who's there?" Pat Straham's voice, one of his comrades from the Twenty-first Mississippi.

"Luke Shea." His teeth chattered, and strong arms from every direction pulled them both out. "Got a wounded soldier here. Get him to the hospital."

"You're going too. The Rappahannock is freezing. You'll catch your death." Pat raised him to his feet. "What made you jump in?"

"To save a man's life." It was his shot that put him in the water. The others started shooting afterward. He hooked his hand under the dripping man's arm. "Can ye stand?"

"With help." The Union soldier's teeth chattered. Southern accent. A Mississippian?

Luke put an arm around his right side. Pat supported the left and got him to his feet.

"Where're you hit?" Luke searched the man's blue coat for dark patches.

"Arm. Near where you lifted me. It burns like fire." Violent shivers shook him.

Shame burned Luke's face. He managed not to apologize for shooting. His comrades wouldn't understand.

"Let's get you both to the hospital." Pat retained his hold on the man's left arm. "Then it will likely be Libby Prison for him."

It was all his fault. But Pat was right. They'd both be sick if they didn't get warm. Luke's clothes began to freeze on him. The difficult walk along the road toward a hospital set up in one of the town's buildings seemed to take an hour but was likelier a quarter of that. Pat left them in front of a heat stove on the first floor of an abandoned home. One other man stretched out on a blanket on the other side of a round table and chairs. Not many had been injured yet in the short exchanges of gunfire.

"You sound Southern." Luke shrugged off his coat that crackled with ice crystals. Then he eased the coat sleeve off the soldier's left arm, the one that wasn't bloodied.

"Originally from Mississippi." He winced when the right sleeve came off. "I live in Louisiana now with my wife and three children. Thanks for saving my life. The shock of being hit and the frigid water nearly did me in."

Alarm bells went off. Luke studied the tall man's curly hair and blue eyes. "Was that...Bovina, Mississippi?"

"That's right." His gaze sharpened. "Jack Danielson. Wait, you said you're Luke Shea."

"Aye." He could barely speak. They stared at one another.

Jack. Felicity's beloved brother. He'd shot him.

And now he'd be sent to a Confederate prison.

A chill shuddered through his body. Two doctors entered and took them into different rooms.

All Luke's fault. Would Felicity ever forgive him? How could she? How could he forgive himself?

This was a nightmare from which he'd never awaken.

~

"*L*uke." Michael shifted him out of the knee-deep creek. "You're not in battle. We're here in Mississippi."

He blinked, coming to himself slowly. "I shot Felicity's brother. She'll never forgive me." Now he knew what his mind had shielded him from remembering. It all tumbled back.

"Did you kill him?" Michael lifted him with surprising strength the rest of the way from cold water to sit against a sturdy trunk.

"Nay. It turned out to be minor, but we both suffered from a dousing in the frigid Rappahanock." Heat rose up his neck, enveloped his face. "He was to go to prison after he recovered."

"Tell Felicity everything. It will hurt. Not knowing is worse, don't you agree?"

He did. She only knew he was missing. "I remember it all. Our courtship. How leaving her to go to war tore out me heart. The drills. The battles. The camps. Losing me best buddy, Willie, to typhoid and then getting it meself." He shook his head. "I remember it all."

"It's a lot to take in. Lots of tragedies in the war." Michael knelt beside him. "Don't try to remember any more than has already surfaced. Allow it to come to you as it chooses."

Memories swirled relentlessly.

"Luke, focus on today. The soldiers are after us." He spoke in no-nonsense tones. "Felicity is in danger. We must find her. And you'll tell her about Jack at your first opportunity."

"Aye." He emptied water from his boots and put them back on, fearing he'd remembered Felicity only to lose her again. But first, to find her.

Luke mounted Stardust. "Let's find Felicity." How he'd wronged her, impossible to repair.

Shielding her from the soldiers came first. Would he get there in time?

CHAPTER 30

Felicity eventually found a road. Impossible to know if it was *the* road. She never wanted to see the soldiers looking for them again, especially without Luke. Had he been captured? He was a strong man but outnumbered. *Lord, please watch over him.* She found a log several yards into the forest to wait where she could peer through the leaves at the lonely lane but was hopefully hidden from the enemy searching for them.

Rosebud nibbled on leaves and weeds. Felicity extracted a bag of oats from her saddlebag for the mare. She'd wait until Luke came to eat lunch. She had to believe he'd come for her.

The neighing of a horse urged her to her feet. She peered to the right. Someone was coming. A soldier?

The clip-clopping hooves of at least two horses scared her. Luke was alone, so it wasn't him coming for her. Where to hide? She grasped Rosebud's reins to shelter behind an oak tree. Then she prayed for deliverance for both Luke and herself.

The riders were moving closer. She closed her eyes, afraid to see. Her legs trembled as if unable to support her. If she tried to get away on Rosebud now, she'd be spotted.

"Felicity?"

She'd recognized that Irish brogue anywhere. "Luke, I'm here." She stepped from behind the tree. A gray-haired farmer accompanied him.

Luke dismounted. "Felicity, be ye unharmed?"

"I'm fine, now that you're here." She looked at his pale face, his wet clothes. "What happened?"

The farmer nudged his mount several feet away.

Shadows darkened his eyes. "I fell off Stardust, into the creek. I...I remember everything."

She gasped. "Even me?" But something was wrong.

"Especially you...and Jack." He stepped closer.

"Jack? Did you know him?" Dread quickly replaced joy. "Is he..."

"Nay. He is alive, as far as I know."

Relief flooded her soul. Her brother was alive.

"But I...shot him."

She backed away from him. "*You* shot Jack?" She covered her face with her hands. "No, it can't be."

"There's more." Misery stared back at her. "The shot sent him into the river. I dove in and rescued him."

"Rescued him after you shot him." Her brittle tone surprised her.

He paled even more. "Aye. When he recovered, he was to go to Confederate prison. Possibly Libby Prison."

She shook her head. "This is too much." More than she'd dreamed. *Luke* had shot Jack. Worse, he was responsible for sending him to prison. Her beloved, kind, strong brother.

"Aye." He looked away.

"Ahem." Someone cleared their throat.

The stranger. She'd forgotten him.

Luke didn't meet her eyes. "Felicity, this is Michael. He knows Ash."

"A pleasure." She peeked up into the most extraordinary

eyes she'd ever seen. There was something in his expression, a kind of deep strength. This was no ordinary man.

"The pleasure is mine." Michael glanced over his shoulder. "We must hurry from the area. We're not out of danger yet."

The soldiers. Focus on the current danger. Felicity mounted without aid. She couldn't bear Luke's touch right now. She needed time to think.

"True." Luke mounted as well. "Let's ride parallel to the road."

"Agreed. Come on, Nell. Our day's not done." Michael nudged his horse forward.

The stranger knew Ash. Curious. Felicity followed Luke's lead, too heartsick to focus on the news.

~

They had been riding silently toward the main road for less than five minutes when Luke spotted a clearing yards ahead. Was it the road they sought? It had to be close. Luke's senses were on high alert in the forest, a feeling he'd often experienced before battles and skirmishes. That alone was enough to warn him that something was wrong. Worse, an angry Felicity was with him. Worse still, he was unarmed. Ash had believed they looked less threatening to Confederate pickets if they didn't carry weapons, a decision Luke had supported.

Until now.

A horse neighed to their left. The burly soldier from earlier urged his horse from around a tree. "We meet again."

Five other riders suddenly blocked the northern path in front to them with rifles in hand.

Luke's blood turned to ice. They'd been lying in wait.

"My comrades and me have been wondering what you all

were doing out here." The leader stopped several yards away. "We figure you're up to no good."

"Nay. 'Tis a beautiful May day for a ride with my girl."

The soldier's eyes narrowed. "But it isn't that simple, is it? You're spying on us. Admit it."

Not him, specifically, but the experienced soldier was too close to the truth. Would they hang him and Felicity or take them to their captain? Neither was good. "Get to the road, Felicity! Head south."

She must have been ready for anything because Rosebud took a sharp turn right, bushes swaying as they disappeared.

"Go, Luke!" Michael shouted. "I'm right behind you."

With one glance at the wide-eyed soldier, Luke followed Felicity to the road. She went south.

Shots rang out and then hoofbeats thundered behind him. Michael wasn't the only one following this time.

"Come back here, you fool! It'll be the worse for you now."

Luke looked over his shoulder. Dust clouds behind Michael showed the outlines of six riders in pursuit. However, their tired horses couldn't maintain this pace.

Michael gained on him until they rode side by side. "I have an idea. Follow me!"

His instincts prompted him to trust the man. "Aye. Take the lead."

Michael whispered in Nell's ear. The mare shot ahead, easily passing Felicity's mount.

A glance behind. Dust hid the soldiers from view, a good sign they'd lost momentum.

He and Michael might save Felicity yet.

Michael turned to a lane on the right. Felicity and then Luke followed until Michael stopped. "My wagon's hidden in a thicket a quarter mile up this road. There's too much trouble coming from the Union army to worry overmuch with you. Leave your mounts on the road for them. Doubt they'll look for you long after they get what they want. Follow that trail." He pointed to a dirt path not wide enough for a horse. "I'll ride ahead and get Nell hitched up. Hurry." Without waiting for agreement, he left.

Luke hated to give up his horses. Good mounts, both, which was why the cavalrymen wanted them. Yet when he weighed that against Felicity's safety, it didn't compare.

Luke dismounted and then reached up for Felicity. She was already down. Of course, she didn't want him to touch her. He couldn't blame her. "They're too close. It's the only way."

"All right. We'll give them the horses. Not the saddlebags."

"Aye." Those held his money, candles, matches, and their food. He grabbed them.

The sound of running horses spurred them to the wooded path. When the cavalry halted on the side road, Luke and Felicity squatted behind some bushes, able to make out forms moving through the leaves.

They hadn't come far enough. Should the men look for them, they'd be captured. Luke's very spirit uttered a silent prayer.

"Here's their horses." The burly man.

"Not the old man's." A stranger.

"That old nag? We got the best ones right here." Another voice.

"That old nag outran us for a time," the first speaker pointed out.

"What about them spies? They can't be too far." An angry voice.

"They might not be spies." A calmer voice. "We don't know they are."

Silence.

"We've wasted too much time already." The burly man spoke with authority. "The captain said to get him a horse after his was shot out from under him. We got him two. Let's get back."

They took off the way they came, Stardust and Rosebud in tow.

"Let's get to the wagon." Luke trotted over the dirt path with Felicity close behind, thankful that the horses were all they'd lost.

~

"*What* do you mean?" Felicity nearly choked on the last bite of her sandwich thirty minutes later. The sky was as overcast as her spirits. She could scarcely believe so much had happened already today and it was barely three o'clock. Luke rode beside Michael on the bench seat along the bumpy lane while she sat in the back of Michael's wagon with sacks of grain, turnips, and potatoes. "Can't you drive us to Vicksburg?"

"Not safe. Soldiers are scattered in some places and concentrated in others." Michael munched on the sandwich they'd shared with him as he drove a lonely stretch beside a field of corn. "Train will get you home quicker than I can, anyway. The Union army has destroyed miles of tracks. You'll have to get on in Smith."

It was the stop past Bovina on the way to Jackson. And the best option, though Felicity couldn't stop thinking about Jack. Luke had shot him. She wasn't looking forward to spending any more time alone with him than necessary.

"The depot at Smith is about a half mile ahead on this road." Michael stopped the wagon. "It's better if you walk to the station from here. Should they change their minds, those cavalrymen will be asking questions about the three of us together."

"Thanks for everything." Luke shook his hand and then jumped down. "We'll not tarry."

"Don't forget the saddlebags." Felicity pointed to the bags behind the seat as she climbed out unassisted.

"I'd leave them. It'll look mighty strange for you to walk up with saddlebags and no horses." Michael gave her a piercing look.

"Aye." Sighing, Luke removed the money and then put them back in the wagon bed. "What can I give you for the ride?"

"Get safely back to Vicksburg." Michael tipped his hat to Felicity. "That will satisfy any debt you owe." A moment later, he started the wagon back the way they came.

"Sorry about your horses, " Felicity said, turning from Luke. Despite her anger, she knew the loss of the horses, saddles, and bags hurt him financially. Then she gasped. Where was Michael's wagon?

Luke followed her gaze. "How did Michael disappear so quickly?"

Felicity gave her head a little shake. The bend was at least one hundred feet away, and there weren't even any dustclouds.

He faced her, expression grim. "We didn't get to finish talking about Jack."

"There's nothing more to say." Felicity stalked in silence a bit ahead of Luke.

"It was dark." His tone pleaded for understanding. "I couldn't see his face."

Anger shot through her. "As if that justifies it."

"He raised his rifle first."

She quickened her pace. They passed a row of clapboard houses. "It's war. I know that. But I don't know..."

"If ye can forgive. 'Twas my fear from the first." His voice cracked. "Let's just get ye safely home." The depot and tracks loomed ahead. A train whistle in the distance heralded its coming. "I'll purchase our tickets."

Twenty minutes later, Felicity tried not to quake at finding the first car filled with Confederate soldiers. Thankfully, none of them were the cavalry who'd stolen their horses. The second one had four empty seats in back. Gray-clad men sat in the rest.

The very reason Michael hadn't driven them to Vicksburg was to avoid Southern soldiers. This train was filled with them.

She avoided meeting Luke's eyes.

Few of them spoke to each other at all. Their faces were still masks while turmoil filled their eyes. They glanced at Felicity as she strolled toward the empty seats and then looked away.

Maybe this was the best plan, after all. No one raised an eyebrow about civilians on the train. Thoughts of the potential battle must consume them.

She sat and smoothed the folds of her dust-covered riding costume over her lap.

Her riding costume. A sign that she'd been riding horseback and was now a train passenger. She nearly groaned aloud. Folks were suspicious of everything now. That would surely be noticed by the Vicksburg guards.

The whistle blew. Luke took the seat opposite the aisle, staring out the window.

Black smoke and the smell of coal brought childhood memories of living in sight of the train tracks. When they stopped in Bovina, Felicity looked past soldiers milling about the town to her childhood home. A school-aged boy and two younger girls, perhaps five and three, played in the dirt outside the house for which she held the deed. This had to be the family to whom Aunt Mae had given free rent.

Surprising, the comfort the sight of the children brought to her. One of them likely slept in the room she'd shared with her sister. No amount of money would entice her to cast them from the house during the war's upheaval.

At the shrill blast of the train's whistle, the children jumped up and ran toward the tracks. They waved as the train set in motion.

Soldiers in their car waved. Smiling, the children returned the greeting.

After they passed, Felicity studied the soldiers' faces. All of them on the right side were on their feet, pressed against the windows, their eyes hungry...for the sight of children playing... or town life...or a slight sense of normalcy in the midst of war.

Whatever prompted it, Felicity was glad she'd seen it, for the soldiers' joy to see the children reminded her that more bound the opposing sides than separated them.

~

*L*uke checked his pocket watch. Half past five. Felicity should have been home by now. Her aunt was probably already worried. Hopefully, she'd never learn how close her niece had come to being captured by the side she supported. Nor Luke's role in Jack's capture. Felicity certainly blamed him, deservedly so.

Other concerns pressed in. The closer they got to Vicksburg, the more worried Luke became. Felicity didn't have a pass, nor had he bought supplies for the saddle shop. Worse, Felicity wore a riding dress. If the soldiers were looking for reasons to detain them, any of those would arouse suspicion.

With Confederates three feet away, Luke didn't voice his fears. In fact, he'd followed Felicity's lead and remained silent the entire trip.

They stopped at the Vicksburg depot. Standing, he waited while the soldiers filed off, then he followed them in front of Felicity.

All too soon, it was their turn to disembark. Luke helped Felicity down the steep steps.

A captain hurried over to them. "Pass?"

"Aye." Luke gave it to him. "This is me girl, Felicity Danielson."

The soldier tipped his hat at her before reading the pass. "Luke Shea. You're the new saddler?"

He nodded at the unexpected question.

"Why aren't you a soldier? You're the right age."

"I served nineteen months before being wounded." He lifted his hat to show the scar. "It gave me amnesia. I was unable to remember me training, me skills, or being a soldier. The army gave me an honorable discharge."

"Still have your musket?"

"And me uniform as well." What was this about? The lack of questions about saddle supplies or Felicity mystified him. "And me discharge." He added that in case the provost marshal was checking such things.

"Never mind about the discharge. We need every man who can hold a rifle in the fight. The Yankees may have us outnumbered, but we got them beat with our courage."

Luke's jaw slackened. "What be ye saying?"

"Go home and get your weapon. Pack your knapsack and haversack. Fill your canteen and report back here tomorrow morning." He clapped Luke on the shoulder. "You'll defend your city and your girl."

"What of me amnesia?" He'd keep quiet about his healing.

Frowning, the man squinted at him. "We'll put you in the earthworks closest to the city."

The man gave him no choice. Could this day get any worse? Yet agreeing might keep the officer's attention from Felicity. "Whom shall I report to?"

"I'm Captain James Whitehurst." He shook Luke's hand. "Meet me here at six o'clock tomorrow. I'm off to search for more recruits."

Luke met Felicity's shocked gaze. Yes, this was a nightmare —and he couldn't awaken.

CHAPTER 31

"You can't go." Felicity had thought her biggest fear was Jack dying in Confederate prison as she hurried toward Luke's home at his side. Luke supported the Union, and now that army captain was forcing him back into the Confederate ranks. "Why didn't you refuse?"

He glanced around them. "He ignored me discharge. I figured if I didn't fuss about it, he'd not ask to see your pass." He spoke in whispered tones. "It could have been worse."

"How?" She didn't want to be reasonable. Luke would again be in the line of fire. "You can hide from them." But where? Not at Aunt Mae's. Even if she could convince her uncle he shouldn't fight, Petunia would never stand for it.

His brows lowered as he looked at her steadily. "I'll not shirk me orders."

A sense of disaster washed over her. She'd heard the details about the Union's superior forces. So had Luke.

"I'll be fine." But his voice wavered. "You want to change out of your riding dress, I wager, before going to your aunt's. She'll be worried if you miss supper."

"She will." She was still angry with him, but Aunt Mae and

Uncle Charles would want to say goodbye. "Can you come with me?"

"Aye." He took a quick breath. "But I must not tarry."

"I'll pray for you." It was the best she could offer in her current emotional state. If something happened to Jack... She didn't want to think about it. She couldn't tell Aunt Mae about Jack, but she'd write another coded letter to Annabelle, who hadn't answered the first one.

They'd miraculously escaped capture. What a close call they'd had.

But more danger was coming. The Union army was still making its way to Vicksburg.

And Luke would be defending it.

~

Cannon fire from the east awoke Felicity at dawn on Sunday, May seventeenth. Jackson, their capital, had fallen the day after those cavalry soldiers had chased them. Luke had reported for duty last week, as ordered. She hadn't seen him since he said goodbye to them all together on Wednesday. Talk spread among the neighbors that their soldiers were digging more fortifications in preparation for battle. No fighting yet around Vicksburg.

"Shall we move into the shelter?" Aunt Mae stared out the kitchen window as she and Felicity washed the breakfast dishes. The atmosphere felt too unsettled to attend services that morning.

"Let's gather the dried and canned fruits and vegetables. I'll help store them inside before I go." As long as the cannon blasts remained distant, Felicity would volunteer at the hospital after the food was moved to the shelter.

An hour later, she was free to go the hospital. It was a good thing, because ambulances were arriving, one after another, from a battle taking place at the railroad bridge on the Big Black River. Dr. Watkins entrusted her with cleaning and bandaging minor wounds.

They had received so many casualties from Saturday's Union victory at Champion Hill that Bessie didn't gripe at Felicity receiving new patients. That the Union army approached her city and Luke was somewhere close by, preparing for a battle he didn't want to fight, caused her legs to shake as she listened to soldiers recount burning the bridge and three steamboats to slow the Yankees' pursuit of them.

The bleating of sheep drew her eyes to the open window where Bessie stood staring out with a horrified look as Felicity finished bandaging a soldier's arm in the ward's aisle. Curious, Felicity walked to the hall window, which had a better view of the streets. The sight of bedraggled Southern soldiers entering the city made her gasp. These defeated men had obviously taken part in one of the recent battles, possibly at Big Black River, so dejected did they look.

It wasn't an orderly entry into the city. Mules, caissons, wagons, horses, cows, and sheep flooded the streets. Some women offered dippers from water buckets outside their homes. Felicity fully expected that Aunt Mae and Petunia were doing the same.

The Union army had won all recent battles in Mississippi on their path to Vicksburg. If only her city would surrender outright to avoid the carnage...

~

*L*uke struggled to awaken from the nightmare that held him in its grip. Not the one that had haunted him nearly nightly for months, but the reality of returning to the Confederate army. He was justly punished for hurting

Felicity. His subconscious had known how his shooting her beloved brother would destroy her.

It had also destroyed their relationship.

Just as soon as he'd remembered all her sweet qualities that had drawn her to him in the first place, it was over. Her teasing, her laughter, her faith, her kindness, her compassion.

And her strength.

Truly, he had fallen in love with her twice.

As he dug fortifications about two miles outside the city he loved with other soldiers sweating as profusely as him, a rumbling in the ground foretold of distant cannon blasts. Grant's army would be victorious in the current battle and would be here all too soon.

He'd been placed with Major General John Forney's Mississippi troops overlooking Jackson Road, which led into the city. The division occupied the center, but Luke was near the back, as the captain had promised. It could have been worse.

Some fellows around him bragged that Vicksburg could not be taken. That they were ready to fight the Yankees and send them in retreat. Others worked quietly, as Luke did.

This was the kind of talk he remembered from pre-battle jitters when with the Twenty-First Mississippi. He'd feel a sight more comfortable were he facing the fight with comrades he knew.

But nothing could change the fact that he wore the uniform he'd vowed never to don again, defending the side he didn't support.

~

This, Luke remembered. Hunkered down behind the relative safety of the fortifications he'd helped to strengthen. Staring across a field at an enemy that wasn't an enemy. Sweaty palms clutching his musket in anticipation of a battle. Aye, those memories were embedded as deep as his fear.

Not being in the front lines, his orders were to remain ready to fight. Hopefully, the Union charge would not reach this far, for that meant lots of bloodshed and hand-to-hand combat.

The sun's position told him it was about two in the afternoon. His kepi barely shielded his face from the blistering sun as he kept a keen eye on the eastern tree line, filled with woods and thickets. It wouldn't be easy for Union soldiers to cross. The advantage of land was with the South because the Northerners would have to tread uphill toward its fortifications and rows of cannons. The Southern army, with Lieutenant General John Pemberton in command, encircled Vicksburg in a six-mile front to defend it.

Yet the very spy information that he'd passed on showed that the Union army commanded by Major General Ulysses Grant possessed superior numbers—if they'd all arrived in Vicksburg.

And then they came, shoulder to shoulder, cheering as they charged.

Southerners opened continuous fire from behind the protection of logs. Sections of Northern soldiers fell. Gray smoke crept down the hill they were charging up. Shouts and groans mixed with the blast of bugles and drumbeats giving orders.

Amidst the chaos of battle, Luke clutched his musket and watched for hours as the Union troops were repulsed only to rally and charge again.

Part of him wanted Grant's army to win this battle on the first day and minimize casualties, but the setting sun confirmed it wouldn't happen yet.

The other part wanted the Union army to flee and thus limit the suffering of Vicksburg's citizens...and Felicity.

God, keep her safe.

~

*L*uke hadn't been involved in Grant's first attack on Tuesday, May nineteenth, that had resulted in worse losses for the Union than the Confederacy on heavily fortified hills.

The assault that started three days later around six in the morning was another story. Luke had barely finished his breakfast of bacon and pea bread—a hard cracker made from ground field peas that he had to soak in water from his canteen to eat—before the Union sent artillery flying into Confederate lines.

Well over a hundred cannons must be involved in the attack. Luke hunkered against the dirt wall of his trench. Logs running along the top of the trenches splintered and cracked from artillery hits.

"They've unseated one of our cannons." Jed, a Mississippi soldier on Luke's right, clutched the barrel of his musket, blue eyes shadowed with worry in his dirt-smeared face.

It was hardly surprising with the hiss of cannonballs and shrapnel exploding overhead or on impact. Luke's gut clenched as he passed on the message to Zach, the fellow on his left. The noise was such that one couldn't hear a comrade's words from six feet distant.

"They're letting us know they mean business." Zach, a father of two, peered at the sky. "Be ready to fight." He conveyed the warning to the soldier beside him.

The hair stiffened on Luke's neck. He only shot at another soldier when it was a matter of kill or be killed. Even then, Luke aimed to take out their shooting arm, not their life.

When the cannon fire halted, Luke braced for a Union charge, but the whistle of mortar shells came from the direction of the river. "Are they attacking us from the Mississippi?"

Zach's eyes narrowed. "Union ironclads are shelling the city."

Luke's heart skittered. Felicity. "We've got to help them." He put his hands on the ground above his shoulders to heft himself out.

A strong arm pulled him back. "We got all we can handle right in front of us." Zach turned him back to his assigned position. "The citizens hide in cave shelters. They're safer than us."

Luke tried to calm himself. Always before, he had run to Felicity's assistance whenever she was in danger. He couldn't go to her now. *Lord, keep Felicity safe. Protect her.*

"Them Yanks are getting ready to charge our position." As he stared toward the Union line, Jed's brow furrowed.

Luke's head jerked around. Three lines, each at least fifty paces from the next, began charging, shouting as they came.

"Wait until the first line is within easy firing range to shoot," shouted an officer. "Then let 'em have it."

Luke raised his musket. The Union soldiers drew closer. The wait was torturous. Then hundreds of muskets opened fire on the charging soldiers and many fell. Luke shot over their heads. Then the artillery fired into the Union ranks, taking down many others in the no-man's land between the opposing armies. Some lay groaning. Shouting for help.

Still others advanced to make it to the front of the Confederate line. Some leaped into the trenches and began hand-to-hand fighting, while others continued toward Luke's position. Now it was kill or be killed. They all shot and loaded as quickly as possible.

One blue-coated soldier made it to Luke's fortification. Dropping into the trench between Luke and Zach, the Union private jabbed his bayonet at Luke.

He swung the barrel of his musket into the barrel of the soldier's rifle. The force sent the Union private's weapon against the mud embankment, where it crashed to the ground.

"Halt!" His heartbeat hammering against his ribs, Luke aimed at the man's shoulder.

Zach leveled his musket at the man's chest. "You don't want to do this."

The Union soldier gulped and raised hands that trembled. He looked younger than Luke.

"Good choice." Zach whistled. "Why, lookee here, Luke. We got us a prisoner."

Luke's breath hitched. He'd been involved in capturing another prisoner. Somebody's son. Someone's brother. Just like Jack.

But at least he hadn't compromised his convictions by killing the man. He could hold his head up about that much.

~

*F*elicity cowered away from the cave's entrance. She and her family had moved into their dugout as soon as the shelling started from the Union navy. Confederate soldiers fired off cannons from the bluffs toward the river, striking some boats and sinking others. Mortar blasts from the Union fleet seemed to fall in every direction. The ground shook from the impact of another cannonball.

This nightmare had been going on for hours, and having been in the city for part of last year's attack, she knew the attack could last all night, too...for days on end.

The Union navy wasn't the only force attacking. Shelling from the battlefield surrounding the city also rumbled the earth beneath her feet.

And Luke was out there. She might not have forgiven him —just how did one forgive someone for shooting their brother and then sending them to military prison?—but she wanted him to live.

A whistling noise overhead ended in a crash of bricks. That one struck a building. A home? Had a neighbor been hurt?

Impossible to know without leaving the relative safety of the shelter.

Wilma whimpered behind her.

She turned toward Petunia's family laying on a quilt covering the dirt floor, with Aunt Mae knitting furiously by lantern light in a rocking chair beside her husband.

Wilma buried her face against her mama's shoulder. Little Miles began to cry at Petunia's other side.

To her shame, Felicity's fear had made her forget her family. She rose from her spindle-backed chair. "Can I help?"

"Will you?" Fear fought with exhaustion in Petunia's eyes. "Can you comfort Wilma?"

"Of course." Felicity knelt beside the frightened girl. Gathering her close, she rocked her back and forth. "Do the big noises frighten you?"

Wilma nodded without looking up.

"They scare me too. Why don't we pray together for God to watch over all the people we love to keep them safe?" Felicity spoke in soothing tones, feeling calmer to be called upon to be strong for a loved one.

"Can God hear over all that noise?" Wilma raised huge eyes to her.

Felicity's heart broke. There was a time when she'd wondered if God heard her own prayers. "You want to know a secret?" she whispered.

"What?" Wilma leaned closer.

"God can hear the smallest whisper. In fact, you don't even have to speak your prayer aloud because God can hear what your heart is saying." Felicity brushed wisps of hair behind Wilma's ear.

"Good." Wilma relaxed against her. "Because sometimes I'm too afraid to talk."

Felicity's breath caught. "Me too." Especially with Luke out there fighting a fierce battle. *Lord, protect him.*

~

*L*uke was exhausted. His heart wept for the men who lay unmoving. Zach had taken their prisoner to join the others captured that day. Luke prayed the fellow would soon be exchanged, along with Jack. He'd been responsible for both men's capture, yet he'd been fighting for his life in each case. Would that make a difference to Felicity?

Unlikely. He couldn't blame her for her inability to forgive him. Could he forgive himself?

He stared out over the field where Union soldiers lay in no man's land between the two armies, calling for help. Calling out for their mothers. Crying out to God. The desperation stimulated Luke's own prayers that they'd live. He'd heard similar cries after other battles when combat stalled for the night. It wrenched at his soul.

The Union hadn't charged again after that last retreat. The battle seemed to have ended for the day. It had been hard fought on both sides. Grant's army wasn't able to defeat Confederate General Pemberton's army. Either they'd attack again tomorrow or starve them out.

Felicity's safety was paramount. He prayed for her throughout the long night. Luke nodded off a few times. Fear of Grant's plans awoke him again and again.

There were no charges the next day, yet the Union army kept artillery fire coming at them. A siege began—just what he didn't want, for it would affect the town too. Union cannons continued the attack. Union soldiers trained their rifles on Confederate trenches. If someone stood above the embankments, they were shot, sometimes fatally.

Taller than most of his comrades, Luke had to remind himself over and over not to stand to his full height.

Yet mortar fire from the Mississippi River worried him more, for that fire was striking the city.

~

Felicity pinned on her hat at the shelter's entrance, preparing to help at the main hospital or one of the military tent hospitals that were going up all over the city.

"Must you go to the hospital again, dear?" From a rocking chair outside her shelter bedroom, Aunt Mae set aside her knitting. Two lanterns provided enough light in the dank cave for her to make socks. "I worry about you."

"I'll walk with her." Uncle Charles looked up from a game of cards that he played on a round table across the ten-foot living area. Petunia was napping with the children in the bedroom the three of them shared with Felicity.

"Truly, Aunt Mae, I must do something to ease the suffering." She couldn't help Luke. Was he hurt? Her anger didn't prevent her from praying for his safety. "Else this confinement will drive me crazy."

"Wait until the shelling slows, then."

Felicity's promise to do so cost an hour of waiting. At last, she found Dr. Watkins on the first hospital ward. "Where can I do the most good?"

"Most of the newly injured are going to the battlefield tent hospitals and those in the city." Creases lined his forehead. His eyes were bloodshot. "Can you go to one of them? Your experience is desperately needed."

"Of course."

She chose the closest one, a walk of five minutes. Two women and a child were among the wounded. Felicity was able to remove the pebble-sized shrapnel in the little girl's leg, and her mother took her home. A cannonball had struck a cotton bale that the other woman had hidden behind, showering her with wads of cotton and dirt. Felicity set one of the new volunteers to soothe her and clean her scratches while Felicity bandaged a deep cut in a soldier's shoulder.

Another soldier begged her to remove a musketball from his bearded face. "It burns like fire." Blue eyes pleaded with her.

Felicity probed his cheek with gentle fingers. The bullet lay just under the skin. If she didn't try, how long before a surgeon could aid him? "Looks like the musketball shaved the area." She strove to lighten his fears with her teasing.

"There's a blessing in disguise." He gave a weak laugh. "If you'd pretend it's just a big old splinter and remove it, I'd be obliged to you." He handed her a knife from his belt.

Accepting it, she drew a shaky breath. She'd extracted plenty of splinters, some of the them quite thick. "I've nothing to dull the pain."

"Miss, I doubt you could hurt me worse." He lay back on the ground and closed his eyes.

Felicity poured water over the knife. While wiping it on her apron, she uttered a quick prayer. "Please stay still."

The soldier kept his eyes closed. "Go as quick as you can."

Felicity touched the knife's tip. Sharp. That was good. "I'm starting now."

Beyond tensing his muscles, he didn't move as she worked. In less than ten minutes, she held the metal in her palm. "It's out."

He blew out his breath. "Thank you, miss. The burning nearly stopped."

She patted his shoulder and then concentrated on bandaging his face. Hopefully, she'd not be called upon to do that again, but what a blessing to have relieved his pain.

After dark, many back-breaking hours of work later, Uncle Charles stuck his head in the tent. "Felicity, I've been searching every tent for you this past hour. Your aunt is worried sick."

Ships had been shelling the city every day and night. Tonight was no exception. "All right." Felicity straightened her stiff back and joined him at the tent flap. "I can leave." She nodded to the wounded men lounging on the grass nearby. "I'll check on you all again tomorrow."

Stepping outside, she kept an eye out for mortar shells. Her legs and back ached as she trudged back to the shelter beside her uncle.

~

*L*uke was grateful for the coolness of night. The stars twinkled above the haze left in the path of hundreds of cannonballs. One would think Grant's army would have run out of ammunition by now, so often did they fire at the Southerners. A regimental band played "Dixie" somewhere to his left to try to keep their spirits up, a difficult task when one didn't have sufficient food, water, or sleep. They'd been on half rations since the first of June. Just three days, and Luke was already starving.

The siege had been going on for two weeks, yet the incessant musketry and artillery continued with deafening regularity. He had his memories intact, and he'd never endured anything of the kind.

He was tasked that night with shoveling dirt to enlarge their fortification. Others filled sandbags or wrestled logs into positions to provide more protection.

He prayed that Felicity and her family were safe. *Forgive me, Lord, for shooting Jack and being the cause of his troubles.*

Help me forgive myself.

~

"*T*hey're back again." Uncle Charles huffed, squatting to peer out the three-foot cave entrance. It was a sweltering mid-June afternoon, made hotter by the mortar flying overhead.

"Soldiers are getting our water again today?" Aunt Mae scurried to join him. "How many men so far?"

"Better than forty filled their canteens." Straightening, he folded his arms. "That's just today, and it's not even three o'clock. I'm going to put a lock on our well."

"Oh, but must you?" Aunt Mae twisted her apron. "The brave men protecting our city have earned a cold drink of water."

Felicity set aside the little apron she was sewing for Wilma, as torn over the matter as her aunt. A canteen of water didn't seem too much to give, but when one multiplied it by dozens of soldiers stealing into their city daily to help themselves to local wells and fruit trees, it put struggling families in a bind.

"I don't mind aiding our soldiers, but I must take care of my family. There are too many. Why, they'll drink our well dry." He shook his head. "No, my mind's made up. I'll fashion a lock for it from supplies in the house."

Aunt Mae sighed. "Let these few have their fill first."

"Very well."

Uncle Charles left for the house as soon as the men were gone.

"He's protecting us." Felicity put her arm around her aunt. It was a quality she appreciated. Luke possessed it in spades.

"I know." She smoothed her crumpled apron. "It's not just the water—it's the food."

The food she and her aunt had so carefully prepared was in shorter supply. Only three pieces of jerky remained. Aunt Mae gave everyone one bite of jerky a day. Little Miles sucked on his because he couldn't chew it yet. "Why don't we make a cup of beef broth for each person with the jerky? That would be delicious."

Her eyes brightened. "It would, indeed. I'll use less to make it last longer and add a can of vegetables with it."

"That sounds lovely." Most of the canned vegetables were

gone. Aunt Mae was also rationing the dried apples and peaches. They cooked outside the shelter when the Union navy gave their artillery a rest. Corn muffins or vegetable soup flavored with pork fat had became quite a treat. Scrambled eggs had been good while they lasted.

Felicity had been sheltering in her family's cave for over three weeks, terrified whenever a shell fell nearby. The Union navy continued to send a barrage of mortar shells on the city that shook the ground. Everyone not in shelters fled to them when shelling started.

The worst were the shells that exploded in the air, sending shrapnel in every direction. When she stood near the cave's entrance, the whoosh of the cannons warned her that a projectile was on its way.

The children became fractious with the enforced stay in their cave. Uncle Charles told them every story he knew and then made up some of his own. He read to them from the Bible every evening.

There were short periods of silence during which Uncle Charles escorted her to the hospital when shelling slackened and fetched her home again when the situation grew worse.

Today had been a bad day for shelling, or she'd be caring for the wounded who needed her. But she wasn't safe in the tents or the homes that were now teeming with wounded—not with shells striking houses, businesses, and cobblestone streets. Signs of destruction were everywhere. She prayed for everyone's safety, especially Luke's. Though her worry nudged at her heart to cool her anger against him, she ignored it. She could want him to survive without forgetting what he'd done to her brother.

After supper and the Bible reading, Felicity resumed work on Wilma's apron. She passed the time by sewing clothing for each person by candlelight. It broke the monotony and gave her time to reflect. She'd supported the Union as a spy, having no notion of the danger she'd face because of her decision. She'd done hard things...and learned she could be trusted in hard times.

It also gave her time to think about Jack. Luke had said it was dark and that her brother had aimed his rifle at him. Did she truly wish Jack had shot Luke instead? She shuddered at what had been a possibility.

Jack hadn't been badly hurt, but Luke had somehow rescued him from drowning. He'd done all he could. She didn't want him to simply stand there and allow a Union soldier to shoot him.

Her reaction hadn't been thought through well, coming in the midst of a dangerous encounter with the enemy.

She stared out into the darkness lit by a cannonball exploding on impact. "Come back to me, Luke."

≈

*R*ations were low. Dangerously so on the last Friday in June. Luke was starving like every man around him. They were all on quarter rations now. He'd eaten mule meat whenever it was offered without asking questions in the last ten days. A man faint with hunger couldn't afford to confirm that the army was killing its mules to feed its soldiers. As sick of the pea bread as he'd become, he'd give all his pay for a supply of it on this sweltering day.

What he wouldn't trade for a fishing pole and the freedom to fish. Men had crawled out of the trenches, risking death at the sight of a single squirrel in the woods behind their lines. There used to be an abundance of food sources around Vicksburg—deer, small game, bears, berries, and nuts.

There weren't many small animals left in the woods. He hadn't seen a rabbit for many days. It appeared that both armies and citizens of the besieged city had pretty much wiped out every animal in the vicinity, including mules not claimed by the officers.

Going without water was worse. He received a cup a day for a while. That eventually stopped. Sitting in the hot sun day after day with only sips of water and a couple of crackers a day was wearing all of them down. The men were ready to surrender.

Neither Zach nor Jed talked much these days. Luke didn't either. He didn't possess the energy to swat a fly.

Starvation and thirst was like a slow death. Luke longed for the cool cave shelters in the city. And Felicity.

The Union had continued to dig fortifications. Only a few feet separated the two sides. Dangerously close. That distance could be breached within seconds.

Meanwhile, the Union army continued to blast cannons at them and shoot anyone who raised his head to look across the battlefield.

Luke prayed that General Pemberton would surrender before they all died of starvation.

~

On Thursday, July second, there were murmurings in the trenches that Pemberton intended to surrender. Luke prayed fervently that it was so. He, Zach, Jed, and others around him were too weak to fight a battle. Added to that, they were all low on ammunition. Still, the shelling continued.

The next day, amidst flying bullets, a brave rider emerged from the Southern side unfurling a white flag. Soon all guns went silent for the first time since May twenty-fifth.

Silence—after weeks of musketry and the roar of cannons —was eerie. Unnatural. But welcome.

Word quickly spread that the two opposing generals, Pemberton and Grant, planned a meeting to discuss surrender.

Zach also told Luke that some soldiers near the back of the lines had been sneaking into Vicksburg for water or fruit from the trees. If they surrendered, then surely, General Grant would feed them. Luke's mouth moistened in anticipation.

For the hundredth time, he wondered how Felicity and her family fared. Were they starving too?

That evening, Luke sneaked into the city. He had to know if Felicity survived, if she could forgive him.

Folks moved about near their shelters. Noticing his gray uniform, they asked what had happened. He uttered a single word...*surrender*. His voice sounded groggy from lack of water. A few of the women railed at him for his lack of courage.

Luke was glad his father instilled such a great respect for women because he was able to hold his tongue and not describe the terror, the starvation, the thirst. Dirty and disheveled as he was, he went directly to the Beltzers' shelter, where Felicity and her aunt stirred something in a kettle over a small fire outside the opening. Her dress was smudged. A straw hat tied with a blue ribbon nearly hid her blond hair. He drank in the sight of her, certain he'd never seen her looking so lovely.

As if feeling his gaze, she turned to look at him. The spoon in her hand clattered to the ground.

Mrs. Beltzer screamed and threw up her arms.

Mr. Beltzer burst from the shelter, followed by Petunia and her children.

"Luke!" Felicity ran to him and threw herself into his arms, holding on as if she'd never let go—a hopeful sign that her anger had cooled.

"Felicity..." His tongue was so parched, he could barely talk.

"He needs water," said Mr. Beltzer.

Felicity rushed inside and brought out a water bucket.

Luke drank two dippers before stopping. Tepid water had never tasted like nectar before. The drink revived him as nothing else had since the siege began.

He looked into Felicity's concerned blue eyes. She had smudges on her face, and the hem of her skirt was brown with dust. She'd never looked more beautiful. "Rumor is that General Pemberton is surrendering. I don't know when. Soon."

"Don't go back, son." Mr. Beltzer patted his shoulder. "Stay here and rest tonight. No need for you to take part in the surrender. You were honorably discharged. That captain just asked you for this one battle. It's over."

"Aye. 'Tis over." If such a staunch supporter of the South felt that way, he'd stay here. He'd be taking an oath of allegiance to the North at the earliest opportunity, anyway. "Felicity, may I have a moment?"

"Always." She snuggled against his arm as they walked to the veranda.

The moment was upon them. He turned to look at her, drinking in her lovely face that he'd never thought to see smiling at him again. "Can ye forgive me for hurting Jack?"

"I do." She caressed his face, covered by six weeks' growth of beard. "Truly, I don't know what else you could have done and lived to tell about it."

He searched her eyes. She meant it. His pulse calmed, steadied as her forgiveness flooded his senses. "That's what I've wanted to hear." He grinned ruefully. "I've got something to say, but let me go home and clean weeks of grime away first."

Her eyes widened. Then she smiled. "Don't be long."

~

*A*n hour later, Felicity had bathed inside the house in cold water—no time to wait for it to heat—and was back outside looking out for her beau. Petunia, once she understood that Felicity was filling the bathtub, had insisted on bathing first. Aunt Mae put her foot down, relieving Felicity of the necessity. Now Petunia was taking her turn.

Felicity didn't care. She simply watched for Luke.

And there he was. Clean-shaven. A blue plaid cotton shirt in place of the uniform jacket. He walked right up to her. He smelled of shaving soap. Heavenly.

"Felicity, may I have a moment?"

Her heart beat a staccato rhythm as she stood before Luke on the veranda. Twilight brushed his dear face. She memorized the loving sparkle in his eyes. The moment she'd prayed for had arrived.

He caressed her cheek. "I fell in love with you again this spring."

"You did?" The pain of his rejection lingered still. "Yet you pushed me away. You even ate in your shop to avoid me."

"I feared what remembering me past would reveal. What it did reveal." He leaned forward and brushed her lips with his own. "Sorry. I couldn't wait."

She giggled. "I think you'd best finish whatever you have to say before you steal another."

"I apologize for what I did to Jack. We'll find him some-how." He sandwiched her hands between his.

"We will," she whispered. "I love you. Your loyalty and integrity are what drew me to you from the beginning."

"Do you still see those qualities in me?" His forehead wrinkled.

"Every time I look at you." Her heart lightened to see his sorrow recede like a tide.

"Felicity, me heart." He closed his eyes. Then he knelt on one knee. "I have a question for you."

"I know." She laughed softly. "I'm waiting to hear it."

"Felicity Danielson, will ye make me the happiest of men and marry me?"

Never had she loved the musical quality inherent in his Irish brogue more. "Luke Shea, I will marry ye and be happy to do so."

He leaped to his feet. "Ye will?"

"Aye." Tears of joy fell from the corners of her eyes as she looked up at her future husband. The look of love for her was in his eyes again.

A laugh of pure joy burst from him. Then he enfolded her in his arms and kissed her. He drank in every feature of her face and kissed her again, taking his time. He'd never kissed her like this before—this hunger, this joy, this need for her all mingled together. Felicity returned his kiss, reveling in the knowledge that the future held more such kisses.

The explosion of a dozen cannons couldn't shake the ground more than his kiss. This was the embrace she'd waited months to receive. Her arms slid around his neck as she returned his kiss.

"Ahem." Uncle Charles cleared his throat.

Felicity stepped back. Heat rushed to her face as she took in her smiling family lining the veranda.

Luke put his arm around her. "She said yes."

Aunt Mae burst into tears and ran to hug Felicity. That made Wilma and Little Miles cry. Felicity bent to comfort them and assure them that Grandma was happy.

"There's one more formality." Luke raised his voice to be heard above the bedlam. "And I want you all to witness it."

The children stopped crying.

Mystified, Felicity straightened.

Luke drew a white handkerchief from his pocket. "Felicity, will ye do me the honor of wearing me mother's ring? Ye'll have another ring on our wedding day."

"Yes, I will." She was touched as she accepted the handkerchief. He had so little left from his parents. Every item was precious. She opened it carefully. Everyone leaned close. She gasped to find a silver band with a single pearl. "It's lovely."

"I hoped you'd think so." Taking it from her, he put it on the ring finger of her left hand and raised it to his lips. "It fits."

"It does, indeed." She smiled at him and then showed it to Aunt Mae, who exclaimed over it.

Luke looked back at Felicity. "As soon as we can, we'll be married."

She nodded. "Not a big wedding. Just the minister, ourselves, and our family." She nodded. "I love you, Luke Shea. You came back to me."

"I always will, as long as I have breath." He sealed the promise with a kiss.

Did you enjoy this book? We hope so!
Would you take a quick minute to leave a review where you purchased the book?
It doesn't have to be long. Just a sentence or two telling what you liked about the story!

Receive a FREE ebook and get updates when new Wild Heart books release: https://wildheartbooks.org/newsletter

ABOUT THE AUTHOR

Sandra Merville Hart, award-winning and Amazon bestselling author of inspirational historical romances, loves to discover little-known yet fascinating facts from American history to include in her stories. Her desire is to transport her readers back in time. She is also a blogger, speaker, and conference teacher. Connect with Sandra on her blog, https://sandramervillehart.wordpress.com/.

ACKNOWLEDGMENTS

I've learned much through the editing talents of Erin Taylor Young and Denise Weimer. Misty Beller is such a blessing, as is the whole team at Wild Heart Books, who have been both professional and gracious to me. I look forward to working with them on the next book in this series.

Historical novels require much careful study to add authenticity. Months of Civil War research continues as I write the book. My research trip to Vicksburg reaped many benefits. The battlefield has been beautifully preserved to mimic conditions, as much as possible, during the 1863 battle and siege of Vicksburg.

My husband and I toured the battlefield at Vicksburg Military Battlefield with Michael Logue, author and licensed battlefield guide. We exchanged many texts before our meeting, enabling Michael to tailor the tour to my needs. I was near the beginning of my research. That Michael's family history is entrenched in the area—his ancestors owned land on the battlefield!—was extremely beneficial. Michael also sent me an original map of the city—and what beautiful details it provided for the story. Thank you, Michael.

I'd also like to thank Kyle Kitagawa, one of the rangers at Vicksburg Military Battlefield who spent time further explaining what happened in specific areas of the battlefield. He was extremely helpful. Thanks to him and the whole staff.

Thanks to family and friends for their continued support,

especially my husband, who is on this whirlwind journey with me.

Thank you, Lord, for giving me the story.

AUTHOR'S NOTE

I learned that Vicksburg didn't celebrate our country's Independence Day for one hundred years. What tragedy did this city's citizens suffer that made this a difficult day a century later? I knew there had been a long siege before Vicksburg surrendered on July 4, 1863. A desire to learn what happened inspired books four, five, and six in this series.

It may be surprising that there were Union supporters in the Southern city. A few found the courage to aid the North by spying—and it did require courage as well as the ability to keep secrets and to think quickly. This fictional story portrays dangers faced by Union spies living in the South rather than being based off a specific spy's experiences.

The main characters are fictional. The struggle Vicksburg's citizens faced isn't. A few historical figures who lived in Vicksburg grace the novel's pages. Union General Ulysses S. Grant and Confederate Lieutenant General John Pemberton commanded the opposing armies at Vicksburg. Luke, our fictional hero, was placed in Major General John Forney's Division, which occupied the center in sight of Jackson Road, which led into the city. Other historical military leaders are mentioned throughout the story.

For the most part, Vicksburg citizens read the writing on the wall. They knew that the Union army would try to capture their city for its strategic location on the Mississippi River. They could see the Union army digging a canal across the river during the winter. When that mission was abandoned, Grant's army invaded Mississippi. As the Union defeated city after city, citizens knew their turn was coming. Many left. Others literally dug in by building cave shelters. They toted beds, rugs, tables, and chairs to their shelters. They took canned and dried fruit and vegetables with them in preparation for a long battle or siege, for most didn't intend to surrender.

They couldn't have imagined how bad things would get. Yet the soldiers taking refuge in the fortifications struggled even more than the citizens.

Surrender came as a relief to a majority of the Southern soldiers. Some openly wept when learning they'd been forced to surrender not only the army but also the city.

Tides of Healing, book six, will take the characters we love into the turmoil of surrender and living in an occupied city.

After all my research, I'm convinced that most of the spying never made it into the history books. Spies kept their activities hidden to protect themselves and their loved ones. Of course, Northern spies received praise after the war ended. Southern spies received scorn.

I hope you enjoyed this story set in Vicksburg from December 19, 1862 to July 3, 1863. There is much more to tell. Book six will continue to highlight the city's history. I invite you to read the whole series.

Sandra Merville Hart

If you love historical romance, check out the other Wild Heart books!

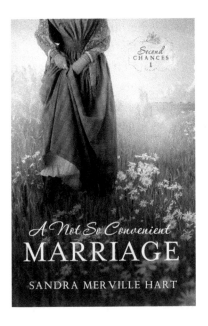

A Not So Convenient Marriage by Sandra Merville Hart

A spinster teacher...a grieving widower...a marriage of convenience and a second chance with the man she's always loved.

When Samuel Walker proposes a marriage of convenience to Rose Hatfield so soon after the death of his wife, she knows he doesn't love her. *She's* loved *him* since their school days. Those long-suppressed feelings spring to life as she marries him. She must sell her childhood home, quit her teaching job, and move to a new city.

Marrying Rose is harder than Samuel expected, especially with the shadow of his deceased wife everywhere in his life. And he has two young children to consider. Peter and Emma need a mother's love, but they also need to hold close the memories of their real mother as they grieve her loss.

Life as Samuel's wife is nothing like Rose hoped, and even the townspeople, who loved his first wife, make Rose feel like an outsider. The work of the farm draws the two of them closer, giving hope that they might one day become a happy family. Until the dream shatters, and the life Rose craves tumbles down around them. Only God can put these pieces back together, but the outcome may not look anything like she planned.

~

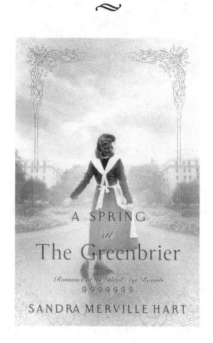

A Spring at the Greenbrier by Sandra Merville Hart

They have so much in common...yet love is not allowed between the wealthy and the staff.

Marilla will sacrifice anything for her family, so when her sister's doctor suggests daily sulphur spring baths, an amenity her family could never afford, Marilla takes a job at The Greenbrier resort bathhouse in order to give her sister the care she needs. When her sister befriends another girl staying at the resort with a similar health condition, Marilla finds herself crossing paths with the girl's handsome, charming, older brother. And despite their growing attraction to each other, anything more than friendship with Wes must remain a dream. After all, resort staff cannot court guests and Marilla will not risk her sister's health for her own happiness.

Wealthy resort guest, Wes Bakersfield, has dreams for a future and plans to make his family's business his own. And while he finds himself drawn to Marilla, despite their differing social classes, he can't help but wonder if she's really interested in him—or in his wealth.

Can the couple find the trust to help their love succeed, or will their differences pull them apart?

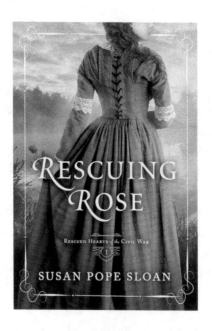

Rescuing Rose by Susan Pope Sloan

His army destroyed her livelihood. She represents the people he scorns. How can they reconcile their differences when the whole country is at war?

When the Union Army marches into Roswell, Georgia, and burns down the cotton mill where Rose Carrigan worked, not only is her livelihood destroyed but she's also taken prisoner and shipped northward with the other workers. Only the unlikely kindness of one of her guards makes the trip bearable.

Union Captain Noah Griffin hates the part of his job that requires him to destroy the lives of innocent civilians, but at least he's able to protect these women he's been ordered to transport to Louisville, Kentucky. Especially the one whose quick wit and kindness draw him.

While they're forced to wait in Marietta, two fugitives arrive to complicate matters between Rose and Noah. As Rose heads north and Noah returns to the battlefront, they each face fears and prejudices. With survival so tenuous, only faith can help them find love in the midst of so much tragedy.

Printed in the USA
CPSIA information can be obtained
at www.ICGtesting.com
LVHW010246090924
790178LV00009B/79

9 781942 265986